Playing With Bonbon Fire

A SOUTHERN CHOCOLATE SHOP MYSTERY

Dorothy St. James

NEW YORK

Copyright © 2018 by Dorothy McFalls

All rights reserved.

Published in the United States by Crooked Lane Books, an imprint of The Quick Brown Fox & Company LLC.

Crooked Lane Books and its logo are trademarks of The Quick Brown Fox & Company LLC.

Library of Congress Catalog-in-Publication data available upon request.
ISBN (paperback): 978-1-68331-730-2
ISBN (hardcover): 978-1-68331-468-4
ISBN (ePub): 978-1-68331-469-1
ISBN (ePDF): 978-1-68331-470-7

Cover illustration by Rob Fiore
Book design by Jennifer Canzone

Printed in the United States.

www.crookedlanebooks.com

Crooked Lane Books
34 West 27th St., 10th Floor
New York, NY 10001

Hardcover Edition: March 2018
Paperback Edition: August 2018

10 9 8 7 6 5 4 3 2 1

For Jim.
(I think I might love you
more than chocolate.)

Chapter 1

"This can't be right." I frowned at the sagging chocolate lumps. Oily cheddar cheese mixed with bits of pretzel leaked out of what were supposed to be perfectly formed chocolate bonbons.

"Penn, did you follow Mabel's recipe?" Bertie Bays asked. She was my temporary partner and the only one with any cooking ability. She stood beside me in the back kitchen of the Chocolate Box, her dark, time-worn hands clasped behind her back. "Why do they smell"—she wrinkled her nose—"like scorched wet dog?"

"I don't know," I wailed. "I did everything the recipe said. I'm sure I did."

"They don't look right." Bertie walked away.

"Thanks for pointing that out. I hadn't noticed." Was she going to leave me to figure this out alone?

"They should be coated in the chocolate. And round. They definitely should be round." She took her apron from a peg behind the kitchen door and slipped it on over her head.

"I've seen bonbons before," I said rather defensively.

She sighed. "We'll have to start again. There's no saving this batch."

This wasn't the first time I'd ruined one of Mabel's

chocolate recipes. I'd spent months working with the group of islanders who'd each been taught one of the Chocolate Box's signature candies. When I worked with someone knowledgeable, the recipe worked. But whenever I tried my hand at crafting any of the chocolate recipes myself, it came out wrong.

It made me feel wrong, like I didn't belong here.

Mabel Maybank, the maternal grandmother I'd barely gotten to know before she died, had entrusted me with the Chocolate Box in her will. She was the one who'd spent years teaching her recipes to the group of eccentric islanders so they could in turn teach me after her death. The shop had been in Mabel's family for three generations. The building that housed it as well as a surf shop and two apartments upstairs had survived hurricanes, floods, and economic downturns.

But would it survive me?

Mabel should have given the shop to someone who had more than a marketing degree. She should have found a master chocolatier who possessed the instinct and skill for making truffles and bonbons and candies that lived up to her legacy of crafting symphonies of flavors. I had no right to be here.

Bertie put a steadying hand on my shoulder. "You're trying too hard, child."

"How can that be? I manage to ruin every recipe I attempt. Clearly, I'm not trying hard enough."

She shook her head so vigorously it almost knocked the bright pink flowered bandana from her hair. The older woman had impeccable fashion sense, choosing tailored suits and dresses that flattered her curvy frame. That is, except when she came to work at the Chocolate Box. I don't know what happened to her mind when she picked out her work clothes. I suppose she dressed for comfort. Old jeans. Cheap white sneakers. And graphic tees. Today's pale pink tee featured a large camellia bloom with the words "Camellia Beach" in curlicue text sprawling across her chest.

She straightened the neon pink flowered bandana on her head to hold back her short salt-and-pepper hair.

I wondered if I should dress more like her, in sensible clothes. I glanced at my reflection in the metal mixing bowl. While the tailored cream suit with pencil skirt and matching heels looked great on my tall, boxy frame and was perfect for working in an office, did it constrain my cooking? Was my wardrobe the problem?

Bertie should know what clothes worked best for the kitchen. She'd been Mabel's partner in the shop for decades. When Mabel had willed the shop to me, I'd tried for days to convince Bertie to take it. After all, she already knew how to turn Mabel's rare Amar cacao beans into a dark chocolate candy that thrilled the senses. Most of her truffles came close to matching Mabel's masterpieces. People drove in from the nearby City of Charleston just to buy Bertie's sea salt chocolate caramels.

But she hadn't wanted the shop. She often talked about retiring and moving to a posh retirement community in Florida. I didn't know what I'd do if she ever decided to actually leave. And yet I couldn't depend on Bertie's talent in the kitchen forever.

"I'm afraid no matter how hard I try, I'll never learn how to make a proper chocolate candy."

"Be patient with yourself. It'll come." She made a wide gesture that took in the entire shop. "Whether you believe it or not, this is where you belong."

Oh, how I wished that were true. I'd searched my entire life for a place of my own, a place I could call home. Could Camellia Beach really be that place?

My gaze traveled back to the charred chocolate blobs. "But . . . but . . . I can't even . . ."

"Now don't get yourself worked up. We have too much that

needs to get done today. We don't have time for you to panic and start running around like a wet hen." It seemed as if Bertie had spent most of the past five months warning me not to panic.

But how could I *not* panic? I'd promised Congressman Trey Ezell that I'd provide him with several dozen of Mabel's sweet and savory bonbons for the booth he'd rented on the pier during tonight's first concert in Camellia Beach's inaugural Summer Solstice Beach Music Festival. The congressman had recently become one of the shop's biggest supporters.

Without a healthy infusion of cash, the Chocolate Box would have closed shortly after I inherited the shop. Although I had a trust fund from my father's side of the family, Grandmother Cristobel had set it up in such a way that it was nearly impossible to access the money. I had to submit requests to the trustees of the fund. Those trustees answered to Cristobel, who didn't have a high opinion of my financial acumen. In the past, most of my requests for a withdrawal had been denied. Because of that, I hated asking them for the money that was actually mine. It made me feel like a beggar. But the shop meant so much to me that I'd swallowed my pride and submitted a request to the trustees shortly after taking ownership of the Chocolate Box. While I waited for an answer, the bills continued to pile up.

Congressman Ezell had come to my rescue. He'd assisted me in securing a small business loan that allowed me to pay the bills while I got the shop up and running again. And now that he'd decided to run for U.S. Senate, he'd turned to the Chocolate Box to provide snacks for his events and to also serve as an example of the successful local businesses his campaign supported.

He deserved better than unappetizing lumps of chocolate and cheese.

And, as if keeping Ezell happy wasn't enough, I also had work to do for the beach music festival, which I'd been spearheading to attract visitors to the island and boost sales at local businesses. Planning demanded hours of my time. I'd even agreed to pick up the festival's headliner from the airport later that day. There weren't enough hours in the day for me drive to the airport and make (and hopefully not ruin) yet another batch of bonbons. The copper bell hanging over the shop's front door chimed, a reminder that we also had a shop to run.

"Customer," Bertie sang out. Her brown eyes sparkled with a zest for life. "You handle the front counter, and I'll see if we have enough ingredients to make another batch of savory bonbons for the congressman."

"Thank you, thank you." I wiped my hands on a damp cloth and hurried out of the kitchen.

Running away—that's what I did best. Only I was trying not to run anymore. After fleeing from a bad breakup in Madison, Wisconsin, I'd stayed in Camellia Beach to manage Mabel's shop. I'd even stayed to make friends with the same residents I'd once accused of murder. But really, was it such a crime to run from these horrid chocolate creations? I hoped Bertie would clean up all evidence of their existence before I returned.

The front of the Chocolate Box was divided into two sections. One side was devoted to glass display cases where a wide variety of chocolate truffles and bonbon were offered for sale. The other side of the shop served as an informal café. Half a dozen round tables and metal chairs, two sofas, and a counter with a self-serve coffeemaker created a cozy, air-conditioned place for locals and tourists alike to grab a quick breakfast or relax after a long day at the beach.

The time between the breakfast rush and the afternoon crowd was usually slow, but tourists occasionally stopped by to buy edible souvenirs. I plastered on my best saleswoman smile and paused to compose myself at the doorway before heading out into the front of the shop.

"Hello? Am I in the right place?" a man called out. "This can't be the right place. What's that awful smell? Burnt cheese?"

I recognized that voice. Any woman in the world would recognize that voice. My heart skipped a couple of beats as I jogged through the doorway.

"Bixby?" What in the world was he doing here? His plane wasn't supposed to arrive until this afternoon. He shouldn't be in the state yet, much less in my shop.

"Bixby?" I'd expected larger-than-life. I'd expected screaming crowds. What I found standing just a few steps inside the doorway of the Chocolate Box was an ordinary guy dressed in ordinary jeans and a plain gray T-shirt.

The last time I'd seen him, he'd been wearing heavy stage makeup, tight leather pants, a designer label ripped shirt, and my half sister on his arm. His dark brown eyes had looked sharp, almost vicious.

Though his features resembled the famous singer's, it couldn't be him. His brown eyes were relaxed and happy. His face was too cleanly shaven. And what self-respecting rock star would wear new white sneakers? They were the cheap kind that Bertie liked to buy from a discount chain store.

"*Bixby?*" I whispered.

He leaned toward me and whispered back, "*Yeah?*"

His soulful eyes met mine.

I chuckled. "You're not Bixby Lewis."

That's right. *The* Bixby Lewis, winner of six Grammy Awards and pop star sensation, had agreed to perform at Camellia Beach's dinky concert festival. He was flying in from California to spend an extended weekend on this little spit of sand on the coast of South Carolina as a favor to my half sister.

Tina had dated him, and they'd parted on good terms. Unlike me, Tina was an expert at leaving men *and* leaving them happy.

6

"I'm hurt." He clutched his chest. "You really don't recognize me?"

"Of course I recognize you. But . . . but you're not supposed to be here. Not yet." Unless I'd gotten his flight information wrong. Had I left a megastar like Bixby stranded at the airport? "Tell me you weren't waiting for me to pick you up."

"Tina told me you'd say that when you saw me." He laughed and then swept me up in his arms and spun me around. Even my legs came off the floor, which totally surprised me. I was at least half a foot taller than him. "It's good to see a familiar face."

"I . . . I . . ." I stammered, not sure what I was trying to say. His spinning me around must have spun my brain clean out of my head.

He laughed again. "Do you always sputter like that? Or is it something you do just for me?"

He set me down and planted a huge kiss on my lips.

When he released me, I staggered back a step. Had that really just happened? Had one of most eligible bachelors in the country just kissed me?

"Did . . . did I forget to pick you up at the airport?" I stammered, apparently unable to stop myself.

He kissed me again, a quick peck on the lips. "Stop worrying and stop with all that freaking sputtering. I took an earlier flight and rented a car."

"You . . . you . . ." I bit down on my tongue. Hard. That seemed to fix the stuttering problem. "You took an earlier flight? Why?" And why had he just kissed me . . . *twice*?

"Changing up my schedule keeps the crazies on their toes."

"Crazies?" I asked. "What do you mean, crazies?"

Before he could answer, the front of the shop exploded.

Chapter 2

Bixby grabbed my shoulders and tossed me to the ground. He then landed on top of me, using his body to shelter mine as glass shattered all around us.

In the ringing silence I peeked out from under Bixby's arm, expecting to see all kinds of wreck and ruin. Thankfully, only the plate glass window we'd been standing next to had been shattered. Everything else in the shop looked fine.

"What in tarnation is going on out here?" Bertie demanded as she sprinted into the room.

I wiggled out from under Bixby and jumped to my feet. He scrambled to his feet as well. "Sorry," he said.

I was too busy trying to figure out what had happened to ask him what he had to be sorry about. Had a bomb gone off?

No, not a bomb. Among the shattered glass cubes scattered on the floor all around us was a fist-sized rock.

"Someone must have tossed that through the window," Bertie said, pointing at the jagged chunk of granite.

I shook my head in disbelief. "It sounded like an explosion."

"That's because we were standing too close to the window when it shattered," Bixby said, as if these kinds of things happened to him every day.

A sheet of college-lined notebook paper had been fastened to the rock with several pink rubber bands. I picked it up, removed the rubber bands, and unfolded the paper until it lay flat on the nearest display case.

With Bertie and Bixby leaning over my shoulder, I read the note. Someone had written in big looping script, "I will see you burn."

"Ah, just as I thought." Bixby reached around me and plucked the paper from the counter. "That's for me," he said as he crumpled it.

"Someone is trying to kill you?" I squeaked.

"I get these all the time. Rabid fans who believe they're in love with me. It's never anything to worry about. I'll pay for the glass."

"Nothing to worry about? Nothing to worry about?" How could he say that? I was already worried. "Are you sure you're the target? As you've already said, no one should know you arrived into town early."

He shrugged. "It's not like anyone would be after *you*."

"That's not true," Bertie was quick to come to my defense. "Penn has plenty of enemies."

"You do?" Bixby's thick black brows shot up into his shaggy hairline.

"Even though Grandmother Cristobel pretends I don't exist, I'm still part of the rich and powerful Penn Empire."

My father, who was in college at the time, had foolishly gotten a fortune teller pregnant with me. Since coming to Camellia Beach, I'd come to the conclusion that the fortune teller—a woman I'd never met—was probably Mabel's eldest daughter. She'd run away from home decades ago, never to be seen again by any of her family. After giving birth to me, she'd followed that pattern by handing me over to my college-aged father and had disappeared from his life as well.

Try as I might, I'd been unable to find Mabel's missing daughter, Carolina. Not that anyone in my family had lifted a finger to help me. My existence remained an embarrassment that they'd rather deny than accept.

"While my father's family does everything in their power to keep me away from any kind of money or privilege, there have always been people in my life plotting to use me to get their hands on my family's fortune," I said.

"And, honey, that's just the tip of the iceberg," Bertie added. "She's—"

"He doesn't need a full accounting of my troubles," I said, not wanting to put voice to the thought that the shop and my place in Camellia Beach could suddenly be jerked away from me. Was it possible? Would someone from my *mother's* side of the family threaten to burn the shop to the ground?

Mabel's children had vowed to do everything in their power to overturn the will in order to get control of the Chocolate Box, including this building as well as its supply of rare cacao beans. Led by her oldest son, the formidable lawyer Edward Maybank, her children had contested the will. The proceedings were still making their way through the courts.

Her children were determined to defeat me. Not that they wanted to run their mother's shop. They had no interest in her handcrafted chocolates. They were only interested in the land underneath the shop. While Camellia Beach is a shabby little town, it's a shabby little town perched on the Atlantic Ocean in sunny South Carolina, less than an hour's drive from the historic City of Charleston and three hours from the ultra-touristy Myrtle Beach. Pressure to replace its time-weathered buildings with something polished and expensive had been building for years.

One of my uncles had already tried to use violence to get me out of the picture in order to hurry the sale of the property. So the thought that one of Mabel's greedy children had tossed the rock through the window in an attempt to scare me into packing my bags and going home shouldn't have surprised me.

The joke was on them, though. I didn't have a home to go back to. My father's side of the family made sure I'd never feel at home in any of the Penn mansions. My half sister Tina was the only member of my family who treated me with kindness.

If not for her, Bixby Lewis wouldn't be standing in my shop right now.

"If this rock was aimed at you, we need to report it," I said to him. "Even if it's just a threat from an overzealous fan, we have to keep you safe."

"Penn's right. I hate to say it, but we need to tell Hank Byrd," Bertie agreed.

"Not him." Just the thought of talking with Camellia Beach's police chief made me groan. According to Byrd, crime hadn't existed in his quaint beach town until I'd moved in.

While he didn't suspect me of breaking any laws, he blamed me for bringing criminals into town with me. The arrival of Bixby Lewis and his crazy stalker fan would only add fuel to that ridiculous theory of his.

Even so, Bertie was right. I needed to make that call.

"No!" Bixby grabbed my wrist and pulled the cell phone out of my hand before I had the chance to punch in the numbers. "Don't tell anyone. The publicity will only cause more crazies to crawl out of their hidey holes to make trouble. Trust me on this one. I deal with this almost every day."

"Son, someone tosses rocks through your window on a daily basis? That would burn my biscuits," Bertie drawled in her lovely, deep Southern voice.

I introduced Bixby to Bertie and explained how he was a singing star of mega proportions.

"I know who he is," Bertie fussed. "I might be old, but there's nothing wrong with my hearing. I listen to the radio. I love your 'Honey Got a Hold on Me' tune. Listen to it while folding my laundry." She tossed back her head and belted out the refrain, which included a description of the singer going back to his girl-friend's house and making the walls tremble. It sounded quite naughty coming from someone well over seventy years old.

Bixby's cheeks turned beet red as he politely thanked her for enjoying his work.

I giggled. I often giggled inappropriately when I got nervous.

He smiled kindly in my direction before saying, "Don't worry about the window. I'll replace it. In the meantime, I'd rather focus on celebrating great beach music than wasting time talking with the police."

"But—" I started to protest.

"I'm fine, Penn." He put his hand on my shoulder in the same way Bertie had earlier to calm me down. With him, though, the gesture had the opposite effect. My insides fluttered wildly. "Sweetheart, you don't have to worry. I promise nothing bad is going to happen."

Chapter 3

"Something bad is going to happen unless you get yourself over to the pier right now. And I mean right now." Althea sounded desperate.

Althea Bays, Bertie's only child, owned a crystal shop smack dab in the middle of Camellia Beach's blink-and-you'll-miss-it downtown. And she was a nut. I mean, what sane person believes in ghosts, crystal powers, and the ability to see into the future? Despite her nuttiness (I tried to ignore that flaw in her personality), Althea was fast becoming my dearest friend on the island.

"Why do I need to be there? What's going on?" I asked as I shifted my cell phone from one ear to the other. I hadn't planned to visit the beachfront pier until after the chocolate shop's closing at five that afternoon.

For the past two days, crews had been setting up the sound stage on the two-story pavilion that capped the end of the pier. On the long boardwalk that led out to the pavilion, businesses were busy erecting display booths and outdoor seating areas.

Althea had volunteered to take the lead in organizing that part of the setup for the festival. Since I hadn't heard from her in a while, I'd assumed everything had been going smoothly.

Apparently, I was wrong.

"Just . . . just get down here. *Please*." Althea sounded even more desperate.

It was nearly two o'clock in the afternoon. I'd just finished getting Bixby settled in the beach house we'd rented for him to use during his weeklong stay on Camellia. It was one of the newer, monstrously large homes on the beach. I thought it was plain ugly. But it was modern, and everyone on the planning committee had urged me to rent it for our superstar since that was the kind of housing he'd be used to having.

Now that I was back at the shop, Bertie needed me to work the front counter. I also needed to meet with the man from the window-repair shop while Bertie worked her magic in the kitchen whipping up a new batch of savory bonbons for Congressman Ezell.

"I'm sorry, Althea. I have my hands full here."

The phone went silent save for the background sound of waves crashing against the sandy shore.

"Althea? Did you hear me?" I asked. "It's going to be several hours before—"

"*They're going to kill each other*," she whispered.

"What? Who? What's going on?"

"Lawd-a-mighty, he's already started to cream his corn," she drawled with a trembling voice.

"Who's doing *what*?" Even after living five months on this very coastal Southern island, I didn't understand much of the colorful language most folks spoke around here. "Why in blazes does anyone at the pier have corn?" I never did get an answer to that question. Althea had hung up.

I explained the situation to Bertie, who seemed to think creamed corn was a terribly serious matter. She nearly pushed me out the door, telling me that she could handle things at the shop. Apparently I needed to stop some guy's corn from getting creamed.

My arms pumping, my long legs stretching, I hurried down Main Street toward the ocean. At the end of the road sat a large wooden pier. Initially constructed in the early 1900s, it'd been rebuilt four times in the years that followed. The pier had been destroyed by two fires, one hurricane, and one bankruptcy. From what I'd seen from historical photos, this latest pier and pavilion, constructed in the mid-eighties, was much smaller than previous structures.

Back in the 1930s and all the way into the 1950s, every Saturday throughout the summer the pier would host evening concerts. The concerts attracted huge crowds and big-name bands. The swinging sounds of beach music would fill the air as residents and tourists shagged the night away. Occasionally, upwards of ten thousand people would turn up.

I shuddered at the thought. If ten thousand people showed up at the pier that stood here today, I wasn't sure what we'd do. The pavilion could hold a few hundred, tops. We'd made plans to guide any overflow crowds to the surrounding beach, where they could still listen and dance on the sand. But I doubted the beach was wide enough to hold ten thousand people.

As I rushed toward the mysterious corn disaster waiting for me on the pier, residents called out happy greetings and expressed excitement at their upcoming opportunity to go shagging under the stars. I noticed the first sign of trouble as I climbed the stairs that led to the pier. A crowd had gathered. I recognized many in the crowd as the white-haired brigade who used the Pink Pelican Inn—an outdated concrete block motel located next door to the pier on the beach—as a retirement home.

"It's Penn," a ninety-year-old woman clad in nothing more than a broad-brimmed straw hat and tiny rainbow-colored string bikini announced with a sigh of relief when she spotted me.

Many pairs of wise eyes turned in my direction. The crowd

stepped out of the way, like the parting of the waters, as I approached.

"She'll know what to do," a man in a seersucker suit and hunched back said with a nod of approval.

Their blind confidence unnerved me. What could I do that Althea, who'd lived on this island her entire life, hadn't already tried? I didn't even understand what was going on.

But since Mabel had given her stamp of approval by entrusting me with her shop, many of the residents expected me to be as much a leader as Mabel had been. I drew a deep breath and said a little prayer, hoping I wouldn't disappoint anyone today.

"Where's the corn?" I demanded. I hadn't seen anyone with corn, creamed or otherwise.

"Corn? Do you really think now is a proper time to be asking about vegetables?" Althea cried, her voice strained from the effort it took to physically hold apart two men who both towered over her. She was dressed in a blue batik sundress. Her wrists and ankles were covered in crystal bangles. Around her neck, she wore three brass mandalas that clanked together as she struggled to keep the men from throwing punches.

I recognized the bigger of the two troublemakers. The hulking figure windmilling his arms was Bubba Crowley, president of the Camellia Beach business association.

"You were the one who told me there was corn involved," I said to Althea before focusing on the trouble she was literally in the middle of. "Bubba, stop that. You nearly hit Althea in the face just now."

"Boy, your mama would never forgive you if you hit a woman, even if it were an accident," the hunched man in the seersucker suit shouted.

The mention of the formidable Mrs. Gretchen Crowley, a former state senator, had the same effect as throwing a pail of cold water over two fighting dogs. Bubba's arms, the size of logs, dropped to his sides. His wide shoulders drooped as he stepped back from Althea's staying hand.

His opponent, who in contrast was a much smaller man, took advantage of the situation. He swore vividly as he lunged forward, knocking my petite friend to the ground.

I grabbed hold of Althea's arm just as her knees hit the boardwalk. With a tug, I pulled her back to her feet.

"I don't care what this disagreement is about," I said as calmly as I could with my heart pumping an angry mile a minute. I jumped in front of the small, aggressive man, putting myself in Althea's place. I had at least a foot of height on him. And he didn't look as if he'd seen the inside of a gym in years. "There will be no fighting at my music festival. None. Zip. Zero."

He slammed a fist into his hand. "You can't talk to me like this. Don't you know who I am?"

I didn't. "It doesn't matter who you are. Anyone who doesn't behave will be banned from performing at the festival. Do you understand me? This applies to you too, Bubba," I said to the silent giant behind me.

Bubba grunted. His foe didn't take the warning nearly as well. "You wouldn't dare ban me, missy. You wouldn't have a festival without me. I *am* the festival."

The threat meant nothing, especially since I really didn't have a clue who he was. My lips eased into a confident smile. "I have Bixby Lewis. I don't need anyone else."

He leaned in uncomfortably close to my face as if trying to intimidate me. The movement made his blond comb-over slip, revealing a shiny bald spot. "We have a contract. You kick me out, you'll still have to pay me and my band."

"Fine. But I don't want to kick you out. I just want you to behave." I drew a long breath, hoping it would calm me. "No fighting at the pier. Or anywhere on the island."

"Fine. But get this through your thick head, Bubba, The

Embers are dead! D-E-A-D dead!" the man shouted before shoving his way through the crowd and down the steps leading away from the pier.

As soon as he was gone, I whirled around to Bubba. He was a prominent island leader. He'd been the one who suggested the town host a beach music festival. He'd been the one who walked around Camellia Beach with a goofy grin plastered on his face for the past several months as we worked long and hard to pull all the details together. He shouldn't be picking fights or scowling like he was now.

"Tell me the truth, Bubba. What's going on here?" I demanded.

Thanks to him and his connections in the music industry, the festival was already a success. While the popular rock idol Bixby Lewis was attracting the younger crowd who, like me, knew nothing about beach music, bands from beach music's second golden age were gathering to please the older crowd. Music lovers were coming in from miles around to visit the beach and listen to the "oldies but goodies."

Almost all the beach rentals were booked. And the motel was full. Business owners were thrilled.

Even Bubba had been thrilled. The concert festival wasn't just good for business; it had also given him the perfect reason to bring back his band, The Embers, which hadn't played for more than forty years. All of this was quite a coup for any small town.

So why was he acting stupid and getting into a fight?

"It's nothing," Bubba said and started to walk away.

"Wait. Wait. It's got to be something, and a whole bunch of somethings," I called after him. "Talk to me."

His long, lumbering stride remained steady as if he hadn't heard a word I'd said. We all watched him follow the same route the other man had taken.

"Thanks for your help," Althea said in the stunned silence. "I wouldn't have called, but I didn't know what else to do."

The skirt of her silky dress had ripped in the fall, and she'd skinned her knee. Her hair, usually a mass of black curls kept in check with a headband or silk scarf, stood up at all angles completely unfettered.

"I still don't understand what's happening." I dug around in my pocket for a clean napkin she could press on her bleeding knee. "I assume the argument wasn't over corn. Am I right?"

"Corn?" She wrinkled her perky little nose. "Why do you keep asking about corn?"

"Because you told me on the phone that someone's corn was about to get creamed."

The crowd, still gathered around us as if we were actors in a show, howled with laughter.

"Honey," the ninety-year-old bikini babe said with a refined Southern drawl, "that's just an expression. It means someone is about to get all bloodied up."

"You'd think I'd remember you weren't raised speaking proper English," Althea said. "That flat accent of yours should remind us that you're from off every time you talk."

"Far off," someone in the crowd said as everyone nodded.

"But she's kin," another said to more nods.

"Mabel's kin."

"Even if she does talk funny."

"I don't talk funny. People from the Midwest don't have accents. You guys are the ones with the nearly indecipherable accent, not me."

"Hmm . . ." Althea said as she laughed. "You don't talk like us, not one itty little bit. That means you have the accent."

"People around here talk how God intended man to sound," the bikini babe added.

"That's the truth." Althea hooked her arm with mine. When we'd first met, I'd bristled every time she tried to touch me.

I was raised without a mother and by a family who'd treated me like an unwanted pet. Most of the hugs I got were from people who wanted to use me to get close to my family's power and fortune. Over time, I'd built barriers. A friendly touch was an assault against my fortress of protection.

While I still flinched when Althea pulled me snug to her side, my muscles didn't seize up as they would have done just a few months ago. It was progress.

"What's going on with Bubba?" I asked. "And who in the world is that other guy? *Should* I have known him?"

She led the way down the pier toward the pavilion jutting out over the water. "That other guy is Stan Frasier."

"Who?"

"Stan Frasier. Lead singer of Ocean Waves?"

"Again, who?"

"Don't let Stan hear you say that or he really will pack up his bags and leave in a snit."

She directed us to a bench near the pavilion. The warm sun beat down on our backs, but the gentle sea breeze kept the heat from feeling unbearable. The breeze carried with it the sound of children's laughter from the sandy beach below. In the bluish-green water, a line of surfers sitting on their long, waxy boards bobbed silently, waiting for the next big wave.

"Ocean Waves had one big hit back in the seventies, 'Love on the Waves.'"

"You don't mean 'Love on the *Way*'? Ugh . . . some of the girls played that song over and over when I was in high school. They were trying to be retro, wearing bell-bottoms and knit pantsuits while listening to that annoying old song."

"That's the song. It is actually 'Love on the Waves.' Lots of people never got the title right. That's Stan's song. It won him a Grammy."

"Oh, good for him. So what does that have to do with Bubba?"

She bit her pearly bottom lip. "This goes back to before I was born, so I don't know all the details. Back in the late sixties and early seventies, Stan Frasier was the lead singer for Bubba's group, The Embers. For some reason, he abruptly quit and started his own band, Ocean Waves. Growing up, I heard time and again people saying that Stan had gotten too big for his britches and had started thinking he was wasting his talent with The Embers."

"That's right." Arthur Jenkins, the man with the hunched back, hobbled up to where we were sitting. "Even as a child, Stan felt he was too good for this town. Had big eyes, that one."

"If he thinks Camellia Beach is too small a town, why did he agree to play at the festival?" I asked.

"A boy like that can't turn down gigs," Arthur said with a cough.

"But he got his big break, right? He had his hit song," I pointed out.

"Just one song," Althea said. "After that, Ocean Waves never made another splash in the music business. What I've heard is that they play bars up and down the coast and sometimes are invited to play at county fairs. People around here often wonder how he makes enough money from those gigs to even buy food."

"I heard that boy is getting money from somewhere else," Arthur said. "But he spends it on expensive cars."

"If he desperately needs money, that would explain why he got so huffy about getting paid whether or not his band played," I said.

"I would think so," Althea agreed.

"So why is Bubba upset?" I asked.

"Because Stan is as stubborn as an ass," Arthur grumbled, which didn't explain anything. I looked to Althea.

She shrugged. "Bubba had scheduled The Embers and Ocean Waves to sing on different days so there wouldn't be a conflict. He'd done it because he wanted The Embers to come back together and sing."

"And Stan won't sing with them?" I'd been so wrapped up in overseeing the advertising and securing of corporate sponsors, I hadn't paid that much attention to what was happening on the musical end of things. After all, organizing the talent was Bubba's responsibility.

"He was supposed to," Althea said. "But as often happens with reunions, apparently old war wounds have reopened."

"If Stan doesn't sing . . ." I started to say.

"The Embers won't be able to perform," Althea finished for me.

And that would put a big gaping hole in our festival's big finale. The Embers were scheduled to perform on Sunday night, the festival's last day.

"I need to fix this." I jumped up from the bench and hurried down the pier.

"Where are you going? What are you going to do?" Althea called after me.

"I'm going to get Bubba a lead singer."

Chapter 4

"I can't believe you did this." Bubba Crowley's toothy grin took up most of his face. He swayed to the Beach Boys crooning over the sound system. "You really did this."

We were both gathered at the base of the stage Thursday night, the first night of the festival. We'd scheduled Bixby Lewis to sing on opening night to ensure the music festival started with as much fanfare and press coverage as possible.

But tonight's headliner performance wasn't what had Bubba excited.

Late in the day, I'd talked with Bixby about The Embers, about how their music had shaped a generation of music lovers on the island, and how they'd suddenly found themselves without a lead singer. Surprisingly, Bixby had agreed right away to step in and fill the role of lead singer for the band. Without asking to talk with the band members first, without asking to listen to their music to judge the quality of their songs, he'd agreed. The way he was acting, I got the impression he already knew their music. But when I asked him about it, he claimed he'd never heard of them.

"Beach music is beach music," he told me. "It's all fabulous!"

The Beach Boys were fabulous. I wasn't sure about Bubba's

band, which involved a group of guys who hadn't picked up an instrument for over forty years.

But the news of Bixby filling in for Stan had so thrilled Bubba that he'd started smiling and even dancing again. It pleased me to see him like this. I wished my feet knew the quick swinging movements of the Carolina shag as Bubba urged me to partner with him.

Chuckling, I held up my hands. "Let me practice in private first. Otherwise I might swing you right off the pier and into the ocean."

Tiki torches lined the length of the pier and continued around the pavilion and soundstage where we were standing. Their bright orange flames flickered in the hot ocean breeze while a summer thunderstorm rumbled in the distance. A large wave crashed on the shore just as a streak of lightning lit up the night sky.

"I'm just glad Bixby agreed," I said, eyeing the distant clouds with concern. "Underneath all the bad-boy press he gets, I think he's actually a nice guy."

That had to be the reason he'd agreed to sing with The Embers. It was because he was a nice guy, right?

I sincerely hoped so. In my experience, people with "nice guy" facades were always angling to get something they didn't deserve. But that couldn't be the case here. It was my half sister's charm that had convinced Bixby to come to Camellia Beach, not the beach music.

"Nice guy?" Bubba crowed. "That's an understatement if I've ever heard one. That boy ain't just nice, he's magnificent! Have you seen the crowd on the beach waiting to hear him sing? It's been ages since I've seen this many people show up for anything at Camellia. You did this. I can't thank you enough, Penn!"

He twirled me around in time with the music and then

pulled me into a tight bear hug that stole my breath. I quickly wiggled out of it. "Yes . . . um . . ."

His mentioning the crowd reminded me of the threatening letter that had crashed into the shop on the back of a rock.

Bubba was right about one thing: no one had predicted the size of tonight's crowd. Thanks to Bixby's fame, the pavilion tickets had sold out weeks ago. A standing-room-only crowd formed a human wall on the beach surrounding the pier. Further away, the less rabid fans had set up beach blankets and lawn chairs.

We didn't have enough security for a pack of people this size. I shivered as I watched even more fans arrive. Someone, either on the beach or in the pavilion, had threatened to kill Bixby, or more precisely, to set him on fire.

The pier and pavilion were both constructed of wood. They had already burned twice. Once by arson.

Did the security team know to watch out for fire starters? Althea was overseeing security. I called her on my cell phone, but the call went to voicemail. As I was leaving a message, I noticed a shiny bald head weaving its way through the crowd toward Bubba and me.

I smiled.

"Congressman!" I called out, waving my hands in the air. I had hoped to get a chance to speak with him tonight. Bertie had promised to deliver the savory bonbons, and I wanted to check in with him to find out if he was satisfied with our work.

"Good evening, Penn. What a turnout. You're certainly an asset to the community." Congressman Trey Ezell, who was a few inches taller than me, flashed his VIP badge to a security officer to come join us behind the cordoned off area set up off to one side of the stage.

He smiled, causing his teeth to sparkle in the flickering torchlight. He wore his signature dark gray suit with a red power tie. A crisp white handkerchief with lace edging peeked out from his suit coat's pocket. Although he was nearly twenty years older than my thirty-seven, he was quite a handsome man with his crisp features and square jaw. And after all he'd done to help out with the shop, I considered him a good friend.

A young boy who looked about ten or eleven years old followed the congressman into the VIP area. The dark-haired boy, dressed like a mortician in a tailored black suit and red tie, was grinning so hard his cheeks had turned ruddy red. While the congressman shook Bubba's and my hands, the boy swayed to the music being played over the sound system until the congressman used his elbow to give the boy a nudge. Still grinning, the boy straightened and looked all the adults in the eyes.

"I'd like y'all to meet my nephew, Tom Ezell," the congressman said. Tom parroted his uncle, extending his hand to greet Bubba and me with the same polished grace as his uncle. "Tom has been helping out with my campaign." The congressman lovingly put his hand on his nephew's head. "Since I don't have any sons of my own, Tom here is going to follow me into the family business of politics. He's got quite the aptitude for it."

I supposed that explained why a preteen would be wearing a suit and tie to a rock concert.

"Did Bertie deliver the bonbons to your booth?" I asked Ezell.

The congressman nodded happily. "She delivered them a few hours ago." He held up a prettily packaged cellophane bag. "She also included an extra for taste-testing."

"And?" I asked nervously. "What's the verdict?"

"Penn, you have Mabel's gift in the kitchen."

"That's Bertie's gift," I tried to explain.

"The chocolates are amazing. Almost as good as your grandmother's. The apple didn't fall far from her tree with you. Camellia Beach is lucky to have you. Speaking of which, how are things going with you and your shop? Did the loans come through?"

"They did. They did. Thank you." We chatted a bit about the financial process while his nephew silently watched the crowd, his eyes growing wider and wider.

"Are you a Bixby Lewis fan?" Bubba asked Tom, trying to keep the poor boy from being too bored with all this talk about bank loans and collateral.

"Oh, yes indeed, sir," Tom answered. "I still can't believe he'd come here."

Bubba leaned forward and stage-whispered into the boy's ear, "Penn is a good friend of his."

"Really?" Tom gasped as he looked at me with new eyes.

Before I had a chance to answer, someone from behind grabbed me around the waist.

I whirled around, ready to defend myself. Through the years I'd taken several self-defense courses in hopes of bolstering my self-confidence. After all, anyone who'd spent their childhood being reminded of how they were an unwanted burden would need help with their self-confidence.

Thanks to the thick crowds and this morning's threatening letter, my entire body was on high alert. I swung like I wasn't going to let anyone take advantage of me ever again.

The man who'd snuck up behind me ducked.

Thank goodness he ducked.

"Bixby! What are you . . . ? You're not . . . you're supposed to be getting ready for the show."

Gracious me, had I almost socked our superstar in the nose seconds before he was supposed to go onstage?

He grinned but held up his hands as if preparing to ward off any errant fists that might fly his way again. "You're a live wire, aren't you?"

"I'm sorry," I said quickly. "I . . . I . . ." I had no excuse. I should have reacted with better care.

Bixby looked like the superstar I'd met several years earlier backstage at his concert. He was dressed in black leather pants that outlined his toned legs and a black T-shirt. His stage makeup darkened his eyes in a way that made him look tough. Dangerous almost.

This was the Bixby Lewis the fans expected and adored.

Bubba took Bixby's hand and started shaking it as if he were operating a water pump. "I can't thank you enough for agreeing to sing with The Embers on Sunday. We haven't had the chance to perform for nearly half a decade. And we couldn't do it now without you."

"Glad to do it," Bixby said as his arm kept pumping up and down, up and down. "Um . . . can I have my hand back now?"

"Oh! Sorry. I'm just so excited."

"That's okay. I'm actually looking forward to performing with your group. I have a—"

"Bixby Lewis, is it? It's an honor to meet you. I'm Trey Ezell, local representative to the state house and currently running a vigorous campaign for the U.S. Senate," Congressman Ezell cut in to say. "Thank you for agreeing to perform this weekend. You're helping to put our little town on the map."

"I . . . um . . . glad to do it," Bixby said. "I'm looking forward to getting back to my roots. Growing up, my parents played all the classic beach music tracks. The swaying rhythm has seeped deep into my bones. I've long dreamed of making a beach music album."

"Well, you couldn't have found a better place than Camellia Beach to find inspiration. There's a wealth of talent here. You could throw a stone and hit someone with amazing musical ability."

"That's what I've heard," Bixby said politely. "Bubba—"

"As I've said," the congressman continued, "I'm running for U.S. Senate. Here's a campaign favor Penn helped me put together. I'd like you to have it." He held up the chocolate-filled cellophane bag tied with red, white, and blue ribbons with an attached "Ezell: Your Next Senator" pamphlet. He thrust it into Bixby's hands. "The savory bonbons filled with cheese and pretzels are mind-blowing. Read the brochure and let me know what you think."

"Um . . . sure. Thank you," he said. "Now, Bubba—"

"Bixby"—this time it was Bubba who interrupted him—"you need to meet your biggest fan." Bubba smiled down at Tom, who was shaking like a leaf. "Tom Ezell is the congressman's nephew."

"My biggest fan?" Bixby extended his hand to the boy. "That's quite an accomplishment, Tom."

Tom's cheeks turned bright red. "I love all of your songs, sir."

"We're all friends here. Call me Bixby."

"Bixby?" Tom tried it out and looked to his uncle for confirmation that he hadn't blundered.

Ezell nodded encouragingly.

So did Bixby.

"Bixby?" Tom said, looking to his uncle again. "May I ask you a question?"

"Ask away," Bixby said.

"I have a friend who wants a music career. Do you have any advice for him, sir?"

"Advice?" Bixby pursed his lips for a moment. "Tell your friend to learn to read music and to always keep an eye out for the next big hit. All you need to break into this business is to find that one good song, the song everyone is going to be humming after hearing it."

"One good song," Tom repeated. "Thank you, sir."

Bixby winked at the boy before turning back to Bubba. "I need to talk with you about The Embers. I was looking over the songbook you sent to my beach house this afternoon. Tucked in with the scores was a piece of paper with a roughly handwritten song called 'Camellia Nights.' It completely blew me away. I love the 'three times three, he took her out to sea' refrain."

"Really? 'Camellia Nights'? You like that one?" Bubba sounded stunned. "I wrote it."

"You wrote it?" Bixby asked, impressed.

"Well . . ." Bubba scratched his stubbly chin. "I wrote the music. Stan wrote the lyrics."

"The song Stan wrote?" Ezell asked, sounding slightly desperate to be part of the conversation even though, like me, he didn't have a musical background.

"You've heard of it?" Bubba asked.

"I kind of remember Stan talking about putting together a new song right before he moved away to form Ocean Waves. It must have been that one." Ezell crinkled his brows as if trying to remember the details.

"It's brilliant," Bixby said. "I want to get my hands on the full score. I want to sing it. Heck, even if the rest of the song is only half as good as what's on the worksheet I found in the songbook, I want to buy it. How did it not become a chart buster?"

"We never had a chance to perform it, not even during a practice session." Bubba sounded bitter about it. "Stan quit the group and The Embers broke up."

"Really? No one has ever heard this song? Ever? Then we'll just have to add it to your set list for this week's performance."

"No. That's not going to happen." It wasn't Bubba who'd objected but Stan Frasier. The aging singer had worked his way through the crowd by flashing the VIP badge hanging from a lanyard around his neck. Like Bixby, he was dressed in black leather pants and a black T-shirt. Unlike Bixby, however, he looked washed out and tired. I felt sorry for him. He'd spent years chasing the kind of fame Bixby had attained. He'd traveled from place to place with nowhere permanent to call home. That lifestyle had clearly taken a toll on him. Deep lines crisscrossed his face. He looked years older than Bubba or Trey, who were his contemporaries. Perhaps it was the years of disappointments that had caused him to sour. Perhaps those same disappointments were driving him now to try to block The Embers from finding their way back into the spotlight.

"You don't have a say in what The Embers do," Bubba growled. "Not anymore."

Bixby took a step back as if worried another fist might go flying in his direction.

"It's *my* song. You can't sing it," Stan said.

"You're forgetting that it's half my song too," Bubba countered. "And Bixby doesn't just want to sing it with the band. He wants to buy it. Just think what 'Camellia Nights' could do for this town if we put it in the hands of a superstar like Bixby."

Stan's entire face turned red. "Half or whole, it doesn't matter. I'm not giving permission for you to sing or sell that song . . . or any of my songs. To anyone." He poked Bubba in the chest with his stubby finger. "Pack it up, loser. If The Embers sing again it'll be over my dead body."

Stan stormed off before anyone could react.

"Well, then, he's just going to have to die, because The Embers are coming back," Bubba sneered.

"Please, Bubba," I said. "Don't make any trouble." *Especially not in front of Ezell's nephew.* "I'll talk to Stan. I'll do what I can to make it all work out. We have time. You don't perform until Sunday."

Bixby, clearly uncomfortable with the argument his interest in the song had caused, glanced nervously at his smartwatch and cursed. "I have a concert waiting."

He disappeared through the curtain that led to the make-shift backstage area. Two burly security guards stood watch at the curtain's opening to keep out unauthorized entrants. I prayed the security team we had in place would be enough to keep Bixby safe.

"Don't worry your pretty head, Penn," Bubba said when he noticed my scowl. "Everything will work out for the best."

The torches' glow created a dance of light and deep shadow on Bubba's face as he moved to the beat of the music. The effect made his grin appear too happy, grotesque even. Sure, he was generally a jovial fellow, laughing easily. So I couldn't understand until later—much later—why his maniacal smile made me feel so queasy.

Chapter 5

Bixby Lewis's performance on the pier that night didn't disappoint. He jumped onto the stage and sang his megahits as well as a few oldies from the golden age of beach music, which made the local crowd go wild with excitement.

In his trademark black leather pants and black T-shirt, he looked every inch the sexy bad boy any woman would dream of taming. I had to cover my ears for most of the concert. The squeals of delight from the crowd were deafening. He crooned one of his more popular songs that featured a driving backbeat. The audience who came to shag screamed with even more delight. Despite the jam-packed floor, everyone started to dance the Carolina shag as if their feet had been doing those steps their entire lives.

Before singing his last song of the set, Bixby announced that he'd return sometime during the weekend to perform with one of the local bands. The crowd went wild again, cheering louder than ever.

I was impressed. Bixby wasn't just a talented singer; he also knew the secret to marketing and how to create a buzz. By keeping the details of when he'd sing and which band he planned to perform with a surprise, he would boost ticket sales for every night of the festival.

33

After the applause died down, Bixby stepped off the stage and signed autographs and chatted with his fans for nearly an hour. With a nod in our direction, he left the pier accompanied by several burly security guards.

Not long after that, the bulk of the crowd shuffled down the pier's steps, either to walk the beach or to head back to wherever they were staying—a hotel, a rented beach house, or their own comfortable home.

As the vendors were busy shutting down their booths, I walked the length of the pier, helping the staff pick up trash that had been left behind and chatting with our sponsors, making sure everyone was happy. I noticed Congressman Ezell's booth was empty. The box of bonbons we'd delivered sat on a chair behind a table. The lid was still taped tightly closed. My first thought was that he needed to get those into a fridge for the night.

My second thought was to wonder why he'd insisted we get him the bonbons for tonight if he wasn't going to give them away. Certainly it wasn't because he was worried that Bixby's crowd wouldn't vote. Most of the ticket-holders were, like me, well into their thirties. This venue should be *his* voting public. Besides, the pretzels in the bonbons stayed fresh for only a day or two. So why hadn't he handed out the pamphlets and chocolates?

Was it because he had stayed with Tom in the VIP area for most of the concert? Young Tom had certainly enjoyed himself, singing along with Bixby as loudly as any of the other fans while swaying to the beat of the music.

I planned to ask Ezell about it the next time I saw him. Nicely, of course.

During the concert, clouds had marched across the moon-less sky, making the island's old abandoned lighthouse that sat on the far horizon appear even bleaker. Thunder still rumbled. Its deep voice had grown louder. We'd get the storm before morning.

One thing that surprised me about living on the beach was how aware I'd become of the weather. Out here, on the edge of the continent, slight changes in the wind and humidity seemed amplified. I leaned against the pier's railing and could feel the approaching storm's breath brushing my cheeks.

As I watched the white foam shining faintly in the breaching waves, a deep red light down the beach caught my eye. I squinted. Was that a bonfire? The red glow shimmered and danced.

Someone must be enjoying a post-concert party, I thought absently as I watched the flame grow brighter. Shades of yellows swirled with the reds.

Bonfires. Fires.

"I will see you burn," the threatening note had read.

I gripped the pier's railing tighter and tighter.

The yellows and reds swirled as if trying to reach out toward the approaching storm.

A security guard ambled by. I grabbed his arm and demanded, "Did Bixby make it safely home?"

"I don't know, ma'am."

"Get on the radio and find out." I didn't know what I'd do if something happened to Bixby. All of the sudden, I had trouble catching my breath.

"What's going on?" Althea asked as she came up beside me.

"I'm . . . I'm not sure." I pointed at the flames, which were now licking the black night sky. I couldn't keep the words from Bixby's note from dancing in my head. *I will see you burn.* "It's probably nothing. But it could be one of Bixby's crazy fans looking to make trouble."

Unfortunately, Police Chief Hank Byrd happened to be nearby and overheard me. "I knew it." He yanked up his ill-fitting pants so they covered his oversized belly. "I knew you'd bring lawbreakers to our town with this filthy music festival of yours."

"It's not my—" I started to say, but then stopped myself. Chief Byrd would believe whatever he wanted to believe. Nothing I said would change his mind.

"We need to go check out the bonfire . . . just in case," I said to Althea. "I'm sure it's nothing."

In the pit of my stomach, I knew that was a lie.

* * *

Even though it was a warm night on the beach, Althea shivered as she jogged to keep up with my long-legged stride. I pumped my arms as I hurried toward the bonfire.

She shivered again. "Can't you feel that?"

"Feel what?" I started to jog.

"The spirits are strong tonight."

"Spirits? You mean what you've been drinking is strong?"

She clucked her tongue. "No, Penn. Spirits, ghosts, fairies even. They're rising. Can't you feel it? Can't you *see* it?"

"Please." I didn't even slow my stride. She believed in nonsense and knew I didn't. Our friendship worked mainly because she'd agreed not to discuss her crazy around me.

"You don't have to be afraid of the supernatural." She jogged alongside me. "It might be the summer solstice creating ripples, although I don't remember . . . Oh! Surely you saw that. A Confederate soldier just marched by."

"Oh, come on, Althea. I think you need to get your eyes checked. The only light I'm seeing is that bonfire."

As we passed people—real live, breathing people—walking along the beach, no one claimed the bonfire. Even I knew this was unusual. Groups of friends, usually men, would build the fires and stand around watching the kindling burn out while downing beers. So why would someone go to that much trouble to build a full-fledged fire and then abandon it?

"Oh, no," Althea whispered, pointing, as we approached the dancing flames.

A pair of leather-clad legs jutted out from underneath the burning woodpile.

Next to a bare foot, I spotted one of the Chocolate Box's cellophane-wrapped bonbons tied with red, white, and blue ribbons. That's when I remembered Congressman Ezell had only given away one of the bonbon packages.

"Bixby," I cried just as my knees lost all will to stand.

Chapter 6

I lay awake all Thursday night dreading the call I'd have to make in the morning. A famous singer had been murdered. I couldn't let my half sister find out about his death from television news.

The sun rose. I looked at my phone. Surely I was too busy for this. First, I had to walk Stella, my silky Papillon dog. Then I had to open the Chocolate Box. I didn't have time to make a lengthy phone call.

The shop had been open for less than ten minutes when Bertie stopped me from handing a man who'd ordered the double espresso a cup of plain decaf. "Go back upstairs and get some sleep, child. You're no help to me here."

Instead of heading upstairs—I wouldn't find sleep until I made this call—I stepped out the shop's back door. A brick patio overlooked the wide grassy salt marsh and tidal river that separated the mainland from the small island town.

Cell phone in hand, I slumped into one of the purple lawn chairs. "It's an hour earlier in Chicago than here in Camellia Beach. If I call right now—eight o'clock her time—I might wake her up," I said to myself instead of dialing.

While the police hadn't yet confirmed who we'd found in the bonfire, it was only a matter of time. Given the possibility that the victim was a superstar like Bixby Lewis, the coroner had probably worked through the night to identify what was left of the body.

It was Bixby. I was sure of it. And soon the world would know they'd lost a great performer. I needed to make this call.

So, after drawing a deep breath . . . and then another deep breath . . . and just one more deep breath for good measure, I dialed.

"Hello?" I barely recognized the scratchy, sleepy voice answering the call as belonging to my half sister.

"Tina, it's Penn," I said.

"Penn? What time is it?" she asked.

"A little after nine." The rustling of sheets and a clank answered me.

"You're an hour ahead of me," she said finally. "You know I love to talk to you, but why are you calling so early?" When I didn't answer right away, her voice sharpened. "Did something happen with Bixby? You do know I sent him there hoping something would happen."

"H-h-h-happen?" I squeaked.

"Ah . . ." Sheets shifted around on her end of the line again. "It's just as I'd hoped. The two of you *did* hook up."

"No! Goodness, no, that's not what happened. He . . ." I drew another fortifying breath. "Bixby is dead. Someone murdered him."

Silence answered me.

"Are you still there?" I whispered.

"I'll be on the next plane out," came her terse reply.

"No. No, don't come. There's a murderer on the loose." And Grandmother Cristobel would flay me alive if anything happened to any of her precious grandchildren because of me. "Tina, please. You don't need to come here."

But Tina had already disconnected the call.

I leaned forward, my elbows on my knees and my head cradled in my hands. My trembling fingers rubbed my suddenly throbbing temples.

Not much on this earth scared me more than Grandmother Cristobel. I'd rather face down a murderer than try to explain the trouble I'd gotten myself into (again) to my own disapproving kin.

"Are you okay?"

I jerked my head up and found my upstairs neighbor, Harley Dalton, crouched beside my chair. Water clung to his slightly curly blondish-brown hair like salty gems. His damp board shorts clung to his hips, tracing every muscular plane. Not five feet away, a longboard leaned against the shop's back wall.

"Peachy," I said. "You?"

This past winter, Harley and I had grown close. Almost too close. He was Mabel's lawyer and neighbor. Now that I was living in Mabel's apartment with Bertie, he was *my* neighbor. He was also my lawyer. And yet, when the days had grown longer and the weather hotter, Harley had begun keeping his distance.

This distance between us had started shortly after I'd returned from spending about a month back in Madison, Wisconsin. I'd used my time in the Midwest working to settle matters with my ex, the Cheese King, and to pack up and move out of the cute bungalow I'd shared with Granny Mae, who wasn't really my grandmother. With everything I owned stuffed into every inch of my Fiat, I'd driven back to Camellia Beach to begin my new life here.

After my return and much to my dismay, Harley had stopped dropping by our apartment for one of Bertie's delicious breakfasts. He'd stopped coming into the Chocolate Box for a morning coffee or hot chocolate. He'd simply stopped coming around at all. What I'd thought might bloom into a beautiful romance between us had apparently died on the vine.

I'd expected to at least see him at the previous night's

40

concert. It had seemed as if every resident of Camellia Beach had purchased a ticket.

I hadn't expected to see him *now*. What a time for him to show up. I'd barely combed my hair. Lack of sleep had left dark smudges under my eyes. I felt about as huggable as the prickly pear cacti that grew in the nearby dunes.

His deep green eyes searched mine for a moment. "You're angry with me," he finally said, then started to move away from where I was sitting.

"There was a murder last night." I didn't know why I told him that. It wasn't as if I expected to get any comfort from him. "At my concert."

He swore under his breath. "I hadn't heard. I turned in early last night and have been surfing since dawn." He pulled a hand through his hair. "How could this happen . . . again?"

I shook my head. "Despite what you or anyone else thinks, it's not my fault."

"Of course it's not your fault, Penn. I wasn't suggesting—"

"Tell that to Chief Byrd. He already believes I'm the fount of all evil on this island. I was the one who found him, you know. I found Bixby." It was my turn to swear. "I should have provided him with more security. I should have—"

Harley clasped my hands tightly between his rough palms. "Don't play those what-if games with yourself. It'll only make you crazy."

He crouched directly in front of my chair. It should have made me feel trapped, but with Harley, nearness always felt safe.

"I'm sorry that it happened, Penn," he whispered. "I know how much of yourself you've been putting into planning the festival."

How would he know that? He hadn't been around. At all.

I didn't get a chance to ask him because he continued talking, using his reasonable, calm lawyer voice that sometimes made me want to scream. "I also know how you take personal responsibility for everything that could possibly happen. Unless you killed Bixby yourself, it's not your fault."

"A man was murdered." Ugly tears sprang to my eyes. "A man I'd invited to come here to this death trap of a town. Of course it's my fault."

"Someone was murdered? When? Last night?" It was a voice I'd never expected to hear again. My head whipped toward the back door, where what had to be one of Althea's ghosts was emerging. I was glad I was already sitting. If I hadn't been, my butt would have hit the ground.

"*Bixby!*" I shrieked.

Chapter 7

It couldn't be Bixby.

He'd burned up in that bonfire.

But hadn't Althea mentioned just yesterday some nonsense about how the island's spirits and ghosts were growing more active as the summer solstice approached?

No. No. No.

I didn't believe in ghosts or magic. They were cons, tricks used to deceive and swindle. Even so, I freed my hands from Harley's comforting grasp and stumbled out of the lawn chair. I backed away from the specter until I was nearly falling into the marsh's deep pluff mud. "S-stay away."

"What?" He held up his hands.

Harley bravely put himself between me and the dead guy. "What's going on, Penn?"

"Yeah, Penn," Bixby demanded, "what's going on? Bertie screamed when I entered the shop, and not in a happy fan shriek. It took me forever to get her to tell me where I could find you. And you're acting really weird, too. What did I do?"

"You're . . . you're dead," I stammered. "That's what you did. You died."

He rolled his deep brown eyes. "Now why would I be dead?"

"Because I saw your dead body in a bonfire last night."

He shrugged. "It wasn't me."

"But the dead guy had your chocolates. You know, the ones Congressman Ezell gave you last night?"

"Chocolates? What are you talking about? I don't remember getting anything from . . . Wait. Who did you say gave me chocolates? I hope this congressman was a congress*woman*. I mean, I like all my fans, but it's the women I want giving me presents."

I blinked.

My pricy leather low-heeled ankle-wrapped pink pumps sloshed through pluff mud as I took a step backward and then braved a step toward him. I blinked again and then peered around Harley to take a closer look. Again, I was struck by his appearance. Bixby was dressed like a—well, to be honest, he was dressed like a slob. His worn jeans hung low on his hips. His plain gray T-shirt looked as if it had been beaten against a rock and then driven over by a fleet of cars. If I'd passed him on the street, I wouldn't have given him a second look. This was the same superstar who'd captured everyone's attention last night? This was the megastar who had lovesick women sending him letters threatening to burn him alive?

"Are you sure there aren't two of you running around?" I asked, then waved the question away. "Never mind."

I was so thrilled to see that our star hadn't died a horrible death because of me that I pushed Harley aside and ran to Bixby like I was one of his silly fans and tossed my arms around his middle. "You *are* alive!"

"And suddenly even more alive than ever." He planted a kiss on my lips that made the world feel as if up was down and down was up. He then framed my face in his hands and looked at me as if he'd never seen me before. "How in the world did I overlook you that first time we met?"

"You were dating my sister at the time, remember?"

"Still, a guy has eyes. I should have—"

44

"Someone was killed in that fire last night," Harley's deep voice reminded us.

With a jerk, I dropped my arms that had been tightly wrapped around Bixby's waist and tripped over my feet in my haste to step away from him.

Harley knew only too well the bad track record I had with men. And here I was, falling into the arms of a handsome man just because he gave me some attention, with Harley standing witness to it all.

My cheeks burned as if they'd been kissed by the summer sun. Bixby, obviously not understanding the reason for my discomfort, tossed his arm over my shoulder and pulled me close to his side. "So, Penn, you thought that because I got a letter from one of my crazies, the dead guy had to be me?"

"*And* there was the bag of chocolate at the man's feet. The congressman didn't hand out the other bags we'd made for him. So I figured the bonbons we found had to be the same ones he'd given you."

Bixby shook his head. "Honestly, people are always giving me things. I can't keep track of who gives me what. But I can tell you that gifts of food always end up in the nearest trash bin."

Harley was looking from me to Bixby and back to me again. His lips twisted into an odd sort of frown.

I wasn't sure why the sight of his disapproval made me squirm. It really wasn't any of his business who I kissed. Even so, I stumbled over introductions and ended up sounding like a squeaky teenager.

I cleared my throat while the two men squared off as they shook hands. Harley, who was my height—which meant he was about six inches taller than Bixby—seemed to win whatever testosterone-fueled contest they were playing.

"Now that the matter of my premature death has been cleared up," Bixby said as he turned back to me, "I was hoping you could help me get in touch with Bubba. I need to talk to him some more about his music. In addition to 'Camellia Nights,' there are some other real gems in the band's songbook. I tried calling the number he gave me, but it keeps sending me to his voicemail."

"That's odd," Harley said. "Bubba lives with that phone of his glued to his hip."

"You don't think Bubba was the one in the . . . ?" I didn't want to finish that thought. Luckily, I didn't have to.

Detective Frank Gibbons from the Charleston County Sheriff's Office stepped through the back door of the Chocolate Box to join us on the patio. "Police Chief Byrd tells me you've been causing trouble for him again." Gibbons, a large man, wore his size like a pro. His gray suit fit his pear shape as if it had been cut specifically for his body.

He stayed near the building where some shade could be found on this humid summer morning. He dug a white handkerchief from his pocket and wiped his brow as he gazed at the clear blue sky. "Going to be a scorcher today."

"Humidity's not going to help matters. Last night's storm only made the air wetter," Harley said, following the local custom of thoroughly discussing the weather before ever getting down to business. It was a custom that drove me batty, especially now, when I needed to know what Gibbons knew about last night's murder and why he was looking for me.

"Good day for—" the detective started to say in that leisurely Southern drawl that never went anywhere quickly.

"I didn't see you at the crime scene last night," I blurted, rudely cutting him off. But honestly I didn't have the patience to wait for him to dissect the weather conditions before getting around to telling me what was going on.

He shrugged his broad shoulders. "Had dinner at my wife's sister's house. Connie would've divorced me if I'd left early. And after thirty years of living with the same woman, I'm kind of used to going home to her scowling face." He pulled his pocket-sized notebook from somewhere in his suit coat's interior, and after jotting something down on a page, he turned to squint at Bixby.

The superstar who'd handled a death threat without even a tremor of nerves suddenly looked as if he wanted to escape. Gibbons didn't give him the chance. "Aren't you that Bixby fellow my granddaughters are all gaga over?"

"Bixby Lewis, sir." He sounded unusually subdued, nervous almost. "Were they at last night's concert?"

He nodded, but didn't look pleased about it. "I suppose they'll kill me if I don't ask for an autograph." He then turned to me. "Since you and Althea were the ones who found the victim, Penn, I'll need to talk with you."

"Has the coroner been able to identify the body?" I asked.

He nodded again.

"It's not me," Bixby spread his arms as if showing off his not-scorched-to-death body to the detective.

"No, it's not." His gaze flicked in the superstar's direction. "The victim was Stan Frasier."

Chapter 8

"Stan is dead?" I asked, my voice slow and measured.

Not Bubba. *Thank goodness.*

"Did you know him?" Detective Gibbons asked.

"Not well. Just met him yesterday." *Unpleasant guy.*

I didn't say more. All of the sudden I felt uncomfortable speaking ill of the dead. It must have come from hanging around Althea too much. Her crazy must have started rubbing off on me. Because, really, it wasn't as if the dead cared what I said about them.

Gibbons nodded.

"He was in town with his group, Ocean Waves," I added.

"That guy?" Bixby's expressive brown eyes grew wide, capturing everyone's attention and reminding us all why he was the big star with hordes of screaming fans. "You don't mean the guy who was giving Bubba a hard time?"

I grimaced. "That's him."

His death was going to leave a hole in our festival's schedule. But that wasn't what had my teeth clamping down so hard it made my jaw hurt. No, it was something else entirely that had me fearing I'd crack a tooth.

Last night Bubba had threatened to kill Stan.

Had he carried through on his threat?

"What do you know?" Detective Gibbons leaned toward me. "What aren't you telling me?"

"Nothing. Really, nothing," I answered quickly. Too quickly.

His brows furrowed. "Need I remind you what happened the last time you held back important information? If not for your friend Harley's quick thinking, you probably wouldn't be standing here today."

And the Chocolate Box would have met the wrecking ball. But that wasn't a tale that needed to be repeated today.

Today, I needed to focus on Stan's murder and on whether or not the president of Camellia Beach's business association had actually carried through with his threat to kill his former bandmate.

*　*　*

The chocolate. That *stupid* bag of chocolate bonbons. It was a piece of the crime scene that made absolutely no sense to me. How had Stan gotten his hands on the chocolates the congressman had given to Bixby?

I'd told Detective Gibbons about seeing the bag of chocolates, which I was sure had made its way into evidence. He'd nodded and written it down in his little notebook but didn't seem nearly as interested in what it might mean as I was. Instead, he spent most of his time questioning me about who I'd seen the previous night on the beach and if I knew anyone who had a beef with the cranky singer.

In the end, I told him about the altercation between Bubba and Stan on the pier where they'd nearly come to blows but stopped short of telling him how Bubba had threatened to kill Stan. Gibbons was good at his job. He'd find out about it soon enough. He didn't need me doing everything for him.

"Hello? Penn? Do I need to do everything for you?" Bertie

scolded in her gruff but never unkind manner less than an hour later.

"What?" I asked, startled.

She pointed at the trays of truffles I'd been restocking for the front counter. "You usually do a better job with that."

I shook my head with dismay. The coconut truffles had been mixed in with the sea salt chocolate caramels, which had been mixed in with the raspberry bonbons. Apparently, I'd been putting truffles and caramels and bonbons randomly on the trays. They weren't even lined up in neat rows.

"Sorry about that." I pulled off my gloves and popped a caramel in my mouth. Once I finished savoring Bertie's chewy specialty, I added, "My mind is wandering all over the place."

"Clearly." She slipped on a pair of gloves and started fixing the tray. Her hands moved with a grace and confidence I prayed I'd one day possess. "Is it the shock of finding a body? You do realize anyone who lives on the beach long enough eventually finds one? A body, I mean. Though the poor souls usually wash up onto shore from the ocean; they don't usually find themselves at the bottom of a . . ." She shook her head. "It's understandable that your nerves would be keeping you from being able to think straight."

"It's not that. Well, not *just* that." I followed Bertie as she carried the tray back to its display case in the front of the shop. "*It's Bubba,*" I whispered. I didn't want the few customers who were enjoying their morning coffees and pastries to overhear. Although the shop mainly sold chocolate truffles, bonbons, and gourmet chocolate bars, we served the breakfast crowd chocolate croissants and assorted pastries that we had delivered in daily from a bakery in nearby Charleston. "Last night. He said he was going to kill Stan."

Bertie slammed the tray of chocolates into place and spun

around to glare at me. "Child, that was talk. Stupid talk. He didn't mean it."

"You already know that he threatened Stan?"

"He said it in front of half the town. Of course I know about it. He didn't mean it."

"How do I know that? He sounded . . . I don't know . . . pretty darned determined." And he hadn't said it in front of half the town. We were standing in the VIP area. I tried to remember who else had been in the area and close enough to overhear him. "He sounded furious. How do I know he didn't follow through with the threat?"

She shook her head again and walked away.

When I followed, she whirled around to stop me. Her already stern face hardened with anger. "You know it's true because I told you it's true."

I trusted Bertie, honestly I did. But how could she be so sure? I would have pushed her to explain herself if she hadn't looked so scary just then and if a new customer hadn't chosen that moment to walk up to the counter.

As I filled the lady's order, I kept glancing toward the narrow hallway that led to the kitchen at the back of the shop, where I presumed Bertie had gone. Why was Bertie so upset by my mentioning Bubba? She and the business association president hardly ever spoke to one another.

I thanked the customer for her business and had just about worked up the courage to go talk to Bertie when the customer, who had the stamp of a tourist complete with camera hanging around her neck, decided she wanted to stay and collect some local gossip.

She hugged her bag of chocolates to her chest and asked in a hushed but excited voice, "Did you hear about what happened last night?"

I decided to play it stupid. "The concert was amazing, wasn't it?"

"Not the concert," she said and then whispered, "*The murder.*"

"Yes. It was quite a shock."

"I heard the police already have a prime suspect, a former band member. What was his name? Bud?"

"Bubba?" *Please say no, not Bubba.*

Much to my chagrin, she nodded vigorously. "That's him. Everyone is saying he's guilty as sin."

"Not everyone," I grumbled.

"What's that?" she asked.

"I said I hope you'll be able to enjoy your visit to Camellia Beach despite last night's tragedy."

With her eyes sparkling with excitement, she nodded vigorously again and promised she would.

Good gracious, I knew that news travels fast in small towns, but the speed at which this tidbit had made its rounds had to have set a record. I'd talked with Detective Gibbons less than an hour ago. And I hadn't even told him about how Bubba had threatened to kill Stan.

Camellia Beach had an odd way about it. Sometimes the residents would circle the wagons and refuse to talk with anyone who wasn't born on the island. Other times, like now, the residents were as gossipy as a women's church group.

I hoped Bertie could shed some light on what she thought was going on and why she was so certain Bubba hadn't carried through on his threat. I started to make my way to the back of the shop again to search for Bertie when the bell above the door rang.

Congressman Ezell entered with his young nephew following along.

"Penn!" he called out. Both Trey and Tom were dressed in

similar light tan suits and red power ties. Ezell's pants were creased to knife points. The two of them made their way around the café portion of the shop, greeting everyone and shaking hands. "I need to talk with you," the elder Ezell said to me as they finally made their way over to the counter.

"Do you need more bonbons?" I asked, even though I knew he hadn't yet handed out the ones we'd made for him yesterday.

"No, but maybe I'll order some more after tonight's concert." With his back to the voting public, his smile faded.

"Be sure to keep them in a refrigerator. They will melt," I warned.

"I will. I will." He then ordered a chocolate croissant and hot chocolate.

"Did you enjoy last night?" I asked Tom as I filled the order.

The young man nodded vigorously. "I did indeed, Miss Penn. Bixby Lewis is an amazing entertainer. I'd love to be just like him."

"Do you fancy yourself a future rock star?" I asked as I put the order on a tray and handed it over the counter to the congressman.

"Of course he doesn't," Ezell said. "He's going to be a politician, following in the footsteps of his ancestors. Did you know that there was an Ezell at the Continental Congress?"

"That's impressive," I said.

Ezell nodded proudly as he handed the boy the tray. "Tom, please go sit over there." He nodded toward a small table near the front of the shop. "I need to talk with Penn for a moment."

"Yes, sir."

Ezell smiled as he watched the child sit down at the table he'd indicated. "He's a good kid. Now, Penn, I need to talk with you about—" He glanced around and lowered his voice. "Is there somewhere we can go that's private?"

"Not really. As you can see, I'm working the front while

Bertie is . . . Well, I'm not sure where Bertie is or even if she's still in the shop."

"I just talked with her outside. She was getting into her car," Ezell said.

"She was? Did she say where she was going?"

"Seemed rude to ask. She did look mighty upset. But then again, after last night, we all are." He looked around as if trying to figure out what to do. "Are you sure you can't step away from the counter for just a little while?"

"No, I can't. What's this about anyhow?"

"I could watch things here for you," Althea offered. I hadn't even noticed she'd come in. Dressed in a pale green silk maxi dress that perfectly complimented her dark complexion, she tilted her head toward me and nodded encouragingly, as if she really wanted me to have this private time alone with the congressman.

"Don't you have a shop of your own to run?" She owned a store on Main Street that sold "magical crystals" to unsuspecting tourists. Well, the added quotes might not be exactly fair of me. Althea actually believed in her crystals' powers and felt as if her shop provided a needed service to the community.

"I hire high school seniors to work in the summer. It gives them a chance to learn about the powers of crystals while they earn money for college expenses, and it gives me a chance to enjoy my summers at the beach. But with everything that happened"—her brows furrowed as she searched for the right word—"yesterday, I thought you might need some extra help around here."

She was right. With Bertie gone, I could use the help. I thanked Althea before leaving her in charge.

"And while we're gone, please keep an eye on young Tom over there." I grabbed my purse from underneath the counter. "We won't be long."

"I need to take Stella for her midmorning walk anyhow," I explained as I led the way to the back door that opened out onto the marsh.

Ezell seemed pleased. He attempted to hook his arm with mine as we climbed the back staircase to the building's upstairs apartments. When we reached the apartment, Stella ran to the door to greet me but stopped short at the sight of a stranger. Her huge ears, which were much larger than her head, trembled as she yipped nonstop at the congressman. When she moved, it looked as if clouds of silky fur were floating across the room. It was a stunning example of beauty in motion. Her fur nearly reached the floor. Though she was a mostly white pup, her head and ears were black and tan. She had a dark brown spot at the base of her tail and another on her back.

My ex-boyfriend, the Cheese King, had given me Stella. He'd mistakenly thought every girl with a huge trust fund needed a small dog to carry around in her Gucci purse. He should have asked whether or not I had access to that trust fund or if I even owned a Gucci purse. The answer to both questions would have been a resounding no. Plus, I hadn't wanted a dog.

When I'd first met Stella, she had bitten my nose. Since then, she had bitten noses, toes, and fingers. She was a menace. And even though I didn't want her, I didn't dare give her to a shelter or rescue organization. Dogs with a history of biting didn't have a good chance at finding a new home.

"Stella has an odd charm that grows on you . . . eventually," I told Ezell, who was eyeing my little beast with dislike. I didn't take offense. Most people looked at her that way.

I managed to block Stella's path to her latest foe. His slacks looked expensive. With the costly repairs I'd been making to the shop, I couldn't afford to buy him a new pair of pants.

I tossed my little dog a handful of bacon Bertie had fried that morning just for this purpose. While growling—after all, she was still unhappy at the sight of our intruder—she gobbled up her favorite treats.

I quickly snapped a leash to her collar before she finished the last piece.

With Congressman Ezell following along, Stella led the way down an informal path that skirted the edge of the marsh at the back of the island. It was low tide. Shiny black fiddler crabs were out of their holes. Most were scurrying around the pluff mud, doing whatever it was fiddler crabs did in the summer. A few were standing still with one large claw held up as if volunteering for an important task.

"You found the body," the congressman said as we walked.

I nodded.

"That must have been horrible. Are you okay?"

I shrugged.

"What did you see?" He sounded concerned.

"Mainly the bonfire," I answered. Did he really think I wanted to talk about last night? To relive the traumatic moment?

I stopped abruptly, which made Stella start to bark again. I turned toward him. "Last night you gave Bixby one of the bags of bonbons the Chocolate Box had made for you. Did you hand any of the others out?"

He seemed surprised by the question. "I . . . um . . . I . . . no. I'm sorry, Penn. I know how hard you worked on them. Bixby's fans aren't exactly the voting crowd I want to court."

"What do you mean? Last night's crowd seemed fine to me."

Ezell gave me a patronizing smile. "I'm sure they're fine. It's just that Bixby's fan base includes too many young kids. And kids run by and snatch up the chocolate without bothering to read the literature. Why should they? They're not even old enough to vote."

"Really? I'd thought the crowd was a good mix, and mainly made up of thirty-somethings."

"Trust me. I have more experience with these things. I do plan to start handing out the bags tonight. An older, more thoughtful crowd will come to hear . . ." He shook his head. "Oh, dear me. I'm so sorry. The Ocean Waves are scheduled to play tonight's concert, aren't they?"

Good gravy, they were. That was just one more reason why I needed to find Bubba. He had connections with the local music scene I didn't have. I hoped he'd be able to find a last-minute replacement to fill tonight's slot. Why wasn't he answering his phone?

I had too much work that needed to be done today. I didn't have time to chitchat with the congressman. "What exactly did you need to talk to me about in private?" I asked.

He looked suddenly uncomfortable. He tugged at his tie. "I . . . Look, this murder, it's not good for the town. It's not good for my campaign. I need to know if you saw anything at the bonfire—no matter how small," he quickly added, "that might embarrass the town even further. Being in marketing, I'm sure you understand the need to stay one step ahead of the press. We can't have any more surprises, not during the peak of tourist season. And not a few weeks before the primary election."

I shook my head. "The only thing I saw was the bag of chocolate bonbons you'd given to Bixby."

"Why do you think Stan had them?" He walked away and then came back, which made Stella bark. "I don't understand any of this. Why would someone kill Stan? We grew up together, you know."

I hadn't known.

"We were close, like this." He held his palms against each other, pressing them together until there was no sunlight coming between them. "We were tight like that for as long I can remember. I just can't imagine how anyone could hurt . . ."

His face twisted with grief.

I tentatively touched his arm. "I'm sorry. I hadn't realized the two of you were friends."

"The best of friends." He stared at the sky while blinking heavily. "After he left to search for fame on a bigger stage, there were some in this town who resented Stan for reaching beyond what many of us could even imagine. Some of his friends even vowed to never to speak to him again. But I understood what Stan was trying to do. With this run for the U.S. Senate, I'm doing it, too."

"So you think someone killed Stan because they were jealous of his success?" That didn't sound right. Stan had only experienced a fleeting success. From the sounds of things, he was taking any paying gig he could find.

"I don't know, Penn." He furrowed his slightly graying brows. "You said you found that bag of chocolate at the bonfire. You don't think Bixby might have something to do with Stan's death?"

"Bixby? I hadn't considered that he might be somehow involved." I couldn't picture the superstar killing anyone, especially not like that. At the same time, I couldn't blame the congressman for trying to find answers, especially if Stan had been his friend.

"Detective Gibbons is good at his job." Heck, he'd already focused in on Bubba as a main suspect. "I'm sure he'll make an arrest soon. And then we'll all have our answers to what happened last night."

I prayed the answers the detective would uncover with his investigation wouldn't prove that Bubba had carried through on his threat to kill Stan.

"I'm sure justice will win in the end, Congressman," I said.

"Thank you. And please, Penn, call me Trey." He tried out a smile.

Stella didn't give me the chance to respond. She decided at

that moment to chase after a marsh rat. Barking like a maniac, she pulled on the leash.

"Stella!" I tossed her a bacon treat. She ignored the treat. The marsh rat stood bravely just beyond the reach of Stella's leash and stared at her with its black beady eyes, taunting her.

I ended up picking up my little dog and carrying her, still barking, back toward the apartment.

"I need to take her home," I shouted over the noise. "I'll let you know what we plan to do about tonight's concert." Hopefully, we wouldn't have to cancel.

"Sure, Penn. Thank you, again. And please let me know if there's anything I can do to help save the town's festival."

Chapter 9

When I returned to the shop, Bertie was still gone. The kitchen was empty. I found Althea working the front counter. Tom had joined her and was helping fill orders. Ezell was working the room again, talking with prospective voters.

"There you are, Penn," Althea said. "The phone has been ringing off the hook." She handed me a stack of messages. Many were requests for refunds on tickets for tonight's concert. Some were even seeking refunds for concerts that were scheduled later in the week.

Oh, no. I didn't have time for this. But I couldn't ignore it, either. I'd learned from my experience working in marketing that hiding from the customer only made bad press worse. I needed to return all those calls, and I also needed to contact the local news outlets and start putting out assurances that, despite last night's tragedy, the Summer Solstice Beach Music Festival would still happen. Security would be tightened. And we were going to do everything in our power to keep everyone attending safe and happy.

I took a moment to thank Tom for his help at the counter. I packed him a small bag of milk chocolate truffles as a thank-you gift before wishing him and his uncle good luck at the pier that night.

After they left, I started to say to Althea, "I hate to ask this—"

"Then don't." Smiling, she plucked the messages out of my hands. "What do you want me to tell them?"

We discussed a plan of action for handling the public: offer assurances, give them free chocolate (if necessary), and if all else failed return the ticket money.

Returning the money had to be our last choice, since the profit margin on the concert was already on the thin side. Most of the money from the advance ticket sales had already been spent on setup costs and housing for the band members.

Once Althea and I had decided what needed to be done, I made some quick calls to the local newspaper, the *Camellia Current*, and the local television news stations. I talked with the reporters at each news outlet about the festival and where things stood. I promised to email formal statements and any adjustments to the schedule by early afternoon.

It was already close to eleven o'clock, which meant I needed to get moving.

"Before you run off again, you need to tell me. How'd it go?" Althea asked, her eyebrows doing a funny little dance.

"What do you mean?" I grabbed my purse from where I'd stashed it under the counter.

"With Trey." She sang his name, making it sound as if it had two syllables.

"He wanted to talk about last night's murder. Stan was his friend."

"Really?" Her eyes grew large. "How awful for him. But why did he come here to talk to you and not to the police?"

"Are you suggesting he's interested in me?"

"Maybe." She started to tick off items on her fingers. "He went out of his way to help you secure a business loan. He places large orders at your shop. And he's always using the Chocolate

Box as an example of a successful small business in his speeches around town."

"He's doing what any politician should do: help the little guy. And I've just taken over the Chocolate Box, so his mentioning it as a successful business has nothing to do with me and everything to do with your mother and Mabel."

"He never mentioned the shop or even stuck his head through those doors until you arrived in town and took over."

"He's running for a national office now," I said with a sigh. "I'm sure he's heard of my family's political connections. I hate to think that he's trying to use me. But . . ."

"He might be coming around because he was impressed with the way you handled yourself when you solved Skinny McGee's murder. Perhaps he came here today as a way to ask for your help in finding out who murdered his friend. Or perhaps he just likes you." She nodded toward the front door. "Speaking of someone who likes you."

Harley Dalton had entered the shop. He was dressed in his regular business attire: a mid-price suit. The jacket was slung over his arm. He looked serious, like a man on a mission. And the way his broad shoulders filled out his white oxford shirt also made him devastatingly handsome.

My heart did a little tap dance when his searching gaze landed on me. I told that silly organ to cut it out.

Harley crossed the room toward us.

"Hey, Harley," Althea said, her voice all light and flirty.

"You're looking good today, Thea," he said, with an ease I'd seen him show only around her and her mother. He leaned his elbow on the display counter. "That color suits you. You're helping out your mom today? I hope it's not because things are slow at your shop."

Althea and Harley had a history that dated back to when Althea had been in high school and Harley had been attending the

College of Charleston. While their romantic relationship hadn't survived the long term, the two of them had developed a strong bond of friendship. Althea was even godmother to Harley's son.

As the two of them talked about the crystal shop, I eased out from behind the counter. I needed to find Bubba. Hopefully he could help me figure out how to rescue the town's music festival from complete collapse.

"So, Harley, what brings you to the chocolate shop in the middle of the day?" Althea asked before I got too close to the door. Her brows started waggling again. She let her gaze bounce from me to Harley and back to me again as she added, "Not that I need to ask."

He straightened and a bit of pink crept into his cheeks. "I'm here to talk to Penn. Legal business." He turned toward me. "Do you have a moment?"

"Actually, I don't." I hitched the strap of my purse higher on my shoulder. "The music festival is falling apart. And I need to see what I can do to—"

"It'll just be a moment," he said. "If it wasn't important, you know I wouldn't be here."

As in, he wouldn't be talking with me unless business forced him to? Ouch. That stung. But, to be fair, he had talked with me that morning when he'd noticed I was upset. That had been decent of him.

"You can talk while I walk to Bubba's house. He's still not answering his phone."

"Bye, Thea," Harley called as he hurried after me. "I'll talk with you later."

"You're not planning on running around the island investigating Stan's murder, are you?" Harley asked as soon as he caught up to me.

I picked up my pace. "Why would you think I'd do that when we both know the police are in hot pursuit of the killer?"

"Because I was there when you almost lost your life investigating the last murder that happened in Camellia Beach."

I pumped my arms to get my body to move even faster. "Stan wasn't my friend."

"But Bubba is," he countered. "And I've heard he's the only suspect at the moment."

"Is that why you came to find me? To give me a lecture?"

"No, I got a call from Edward's office," he said.

"Oh, don't tell me. I don't want to hear it. I can't handle any more problems in my life right now."

"Hiding from your relatives won't make them go away."

It wouldn't. And Harley knew me too well. Running and hiding was my knee-jerk response to trouble. Ever since arriving in Camellia Beach, I'd worked like the devil to change my ways. But old habits had a way of sneaking back up on me.

"Very well," I said with a sigh. "What are Mabel's children—"

"Your aunts and uncle," Harley corrected.

"Yes, them. What are they accusing me of doing this time?"

"Nothing they haven't already accused you of. They've responded to your request for a DNA test. It's been denied."

I walked even faster, pumping my arms even harder as I hurried down the middle of the street. Was I trying to run away? Probably.

"I don't understand it. They're the ones who didn't believe the DNA results Skinny had done for me. They're the ones who keep telling me I have no proof I'm related to them."

"As long as the question of your parentage stays alive, it keeps the contested will in the courts," he pointed out. "So it doesn't benefit them to prove you're related."

"I have a right to know which one of Mabel's daughters is my mother. Don't they understand that?"

Harley jogged beside me. "Can we discuss this while not running?"

I came to an abrupt stop and propped my fists on my hips. "I told you I was in a hurry."

"That you did, Penn." He pulled a linen handkerchief from his pocket and blotted his shiny brow. "But it's too hot out here. I can't go running across the island in a suit. I don't know how you're doing it in those shoes."

Bubba lived at the far end of the island, down by the county park. Dressed in a suit, Harley would be nothing but a puddle of sweat if he had to chase after me the entire way. The humidity hung hot and heavy in the air. My silk blouse was already starting to feel sticky. And my feet were starting to throb in the ankle-wrapped pink pumps despite the fact that they'd been touted to be the epitome of comfort.

"Just listen to me, Penn," Harley pleaded. "And then I'll leave you alone. I promise."

"I'm listening."

He tilted his head and frowned at me. "Penn," he said, his voice softening. "I know this is a sore subject with you. Even though your mother abandoned you, we don't have the legal means to force her into revealing her identity."

"What about Carolina?" I asked. Mabel's oldest daughter had run away years ago. No one had heard from her since. She was the one I suspected was my mother.

She *had* to be my mother, didn't she?

I'd been hoping Florence and Peach, Mabel's two other daughters, would agree to take a DNA test in order to rule them out as parental contenders. But given that Mabel's children had spent the past several months pretending I didn't exist, I wasn't all that surprised they'd turned down my DNA request.

Shortly after learning Mabel was my maternal grandmother, I'd directed Harley to hire a private investigator to quietly search for the missing Carolina Maybank. It was an expense the trustees of my trust fund had agreed to finance. I'd hoped for some news by now.

Harley shook his head. "We still haven't been able to find where she went or even if she's still alive. I'm sorry."

"So this is where it ends, then." I resumed my mad trek down the island. "Thank you for—"

"Penn, wait."

"I have pressing matters that desperately need my attention."

"Penn, there is something else."

With a sigh, I stopped.

"Edward's office has sent a request for you."

"A request? For me?" I held back a laugh. "That's rich. What do they want? The shop? They can't have it."

"No, that's not what the request is about. Florence wants to meet with you. In person. In private."

Florence Corners, Mabel's middle daughter, had never even tried to hide her dislike of me. Before anyone knew I was Mabel's granddaughter, Florence had accused me of conning their mother out of her fortune every time our paths crossed. After the DNA results came out proving my relationship to Mabel, Florence had gone silent. If we happened to be in the same room, she'd look through me as if I didn't exist. And I had a feeling she was the one who was pushing the hardest to keep the contested will tied up in the courts so I couldn't access the money Mabel had set aside for the shop's upkeep.

She wanted to meet with me?

"Tell her no freaking way." My arms pumped with renewed anger as I hurried away from Harley. Yes, I was running. If Mabel's family didn't want anything to do with me, I didn't want anything to do with them. It wasn't as if rejection was new to me. My father's family had been bemoaning my existence from the day my mother abandoned me on their doorstep.

Even so, I swiped at a stray tear that stung my eye and wondered what Florence wanted to say to me and why she needed to say it in private.

Chapter 10

Bubba lived on the southern tip of the island. Except for the vacation homes lining the beach, development on this part of the island was sparse. The land was low and swampy. Ancient scrubby oaks, twisted into strange shapes from years of unrelenting wind, were tangled with thorny vines. They created a thick, arching canopy over the road that seemed to swallow the summer sunlight. Narrow dirt driveways met the main road here and there.

By the time I reached the deeply rutted drive that led to Bubba's place, I was out of breath and thinking Harley had been right—these pumps were impossible for a trek across the island. When I'd bought them, I'd fallen in love with the pink leather bows and sleek shape of their heels and had only half-believed their claim of comfort. I hadn't thought about how impractical they'd be in my new shop-owner lifestyle. I hadn't figured they'd need to weather a stumble through the pluff mud this morning or fill in for hiking boots as I marched clear across the island in search of the music festival's co-chair. Even Bertie's cheap sneakers would have served much better for such a hike.

The fact that I hadn't taken my car only proved how flustered I was that morning. But I hadn't, so I trudged down the dirt road that led to Bubba's cottage.

His small house sat atop tall wooden stilts, giving it the look of an enclosed boathouse in search of a river. Blue paint peeled off here and there, revealing a bright yellow hue from an earlier time. Behind the house, a long wooden dock snaked through the marsh and all the way to the salty river beyond it.

After kicking my pumps off my throbbing feet, I climbed the narrow staircase to Bubba's whitewashed front door.

I knocked.

The door, which hadn't been latched, swung open.

"Bubba?" I called into the cottage's dark interior.

Nothing.

"Bubba?" I called again.

A fat orange cat came out the door and rubbed against my legs.

"Hello, there. Do you know where I can find Bubba?" I asked as I bent down and scratched the kitty behind its ear. It meowed an answer. Unfortunately, I didn't speak cat.

My imagination began to work overtime, conjuring up all sorts of fantastical and horrible reasons why Bubba wasn't answering his phone and why his front door might be sitting open. Steeling myself, I stepped inside his cottage.

What I discovered shocked me.

The cottage's interior, unlike its unkempt exterior, was neat as a pin. Much neater than the apartment Bertie and I kept—and we kept a clean house.

Bubba's cat followed as I moved through the living room—filled with matching wicker furniture and a few knickknacks and photographs—to the kitchen (every surface gleaming), poked my head into a small bathroom (also gleaming), and then stepped into his bedroom.

The double bed that sat next to an open window had been so tightly made that there wasn't even the slightest crease in the brown bedspread. Sheer white curtains fluttered in the summer breeze coming in the window. Even so, the air felt wet and warm in the cottage.

As I stood in the middle of Bubba's bedroom, I couldn't help but wonder how anyone in the South could survive without an air conditioner and, even more important, where in the world he was. It was so quiet in the house I imagined I might start hearing one of Althea's wandering ghosts whispering in my ear.

"Finding you here"—a reedy voice sounded behind me— "now, that is interesting."

I nearly jumped out of my skin. With my hands clutched to my chest, I whirled around. "Police Chief Byrd, aren't you supposed to knock or announce yourself or something?" I demanded breathlessly.

"Don't rightly need to when the door is standing wide open and I'm holding a search warrant for Bubba's house." He held up a paper. He then tilted his head to one side. "What are you doing here? Planting evidence?"

I ignored his insinuation that I had anything to do with Camellia Beach's latest murder. He knew well enough the trouble Stan Frasier's demise had caused for both me and the music festival. I planted my hands on my hips. "You and I both know the door wasn't open. I closed it behind me to keep Bubba's cat from running off."

The police chief shrugged. His massive belly wobbled up and down with the movement. I imagined he played a perfect Santa during the Christmas holidays. "You still haven't answered my question, Penn. What are you doing here?"

"I'm here the same as you. I'm looking for Bubba. He's not answering his phone."

"Nope, he's not," Byrd agreed.

"He always answers his phone."

"Yep, he does."

"He's not here," I pointed out. "The door wasn't latched.

And his cat"—I pointed to the orange purring machine circling my legs—"came out to greet me. So I brought him back inside."

Byrd frowned at the cat and then at me.

Since there wasn't anything else I had say to the police chief, I started to leave. Byrd moved to block the doorway. "I'm going to be keeping my eyes on you," he warned.

"Just find Bubba," I said. "I need to talk to him."

* * *

"He wasn't there, was he?" Bertie asked as her car pulled to a slow crawl alongside me. I was limping down the main road, heading back to the shop. My "comfortable" pumps had rubbed a raw blister on the back of my left heel.

Bertie was behind the wheel of a boat-sized bronze-colored Pontiac. Well, I thought its color had once been bronze. The car's body was so coated in red rust that the metal had given way in several spots, leaving gaping holes in the hood and in the roof. But the car's engine had a smooth purr that rivaled Troubadour's. Troubadour was the hairless cat Bertie had inherited from Mabel.

"Hop in," she said. The breaks squealed the car to a stop. "I'll drive."

I wrestled the rusty door open and slid onto the cracked but immaculately clean vinyl bench seat. Since the car predated automobile air conditioning, all the windows were rolled down. A damp ocean breeze, heated by the bright summer sun, blew against my face. I felt as if I were sitting in front of a space heater.

Bertie pushed on the gas. The engine revved just a bit before the car rolled forward. I could have walked just about as fast as Bertie was driving, but with the blister burning my heel, I was glad for the ride.

"Do you have any idea where Bubba might have gone?" I asked.

Bertie shook her head. She gripped the steering wheel as if she were strangling it.

"Police Chief Byrd was at Bubba's house," I said. "He had a search warrant."

Her jaw tightened as if she were keeping whatever she wanted to say locked behind her teeth.

"Tell me the truth, Bertie. You can trust me. Why is this business with Bubba upsetting you so? You barely know him."

She glanced in my direction for the briefest moment before fixing her gaze back on the road. A car filled with teenagers zoomed around us. I didn't blame them. Bertie was driving slower than a slug on a hot day.

"Bubba's not a killer," she said as her large car rolled to a stop in front of one of the newer, monstrously grand beachfront homes. She pulled onto the grassy easement that served as free public parking up and down the beach and turned off the car's engine.

"He threatened to kill Stan," I reminded her.

"And Althea told me she heard Stan threatening to kill Bubba yesterday. They're words. Bitter words. But only words. Bubba's got passion. That's why he loves his music so much. It's an outlet for all that passion burning up in his veins."

She swung her car door open.

"Where are you going?" I asked. "Why are we here and not back at the shop?"

"Bubba's band rented this place so they could hang out and practice."

"And you think Bubba might be here?" I pulled on the handle and pushed at the passenger side door in an effort to get it open. It wouldn't budge.

"No, but wouldn't that make things easy?" she said over her

shoulder. She didn't wait for me but started up the long run of steps of the elevated beach house.

"Then why are we here?" I called out as I kicked the rusted car door until it opened.

"We're here because your friend Bixby is here, and someone just tried to kill him."

Chapter 11

"It was an accident," was the first thing out of Bixby's mouth when I found him pacing the back porch. His thick black eyebrows were singed. Soot was smeared across one side of his face. It looked as if he'd tried to clean it off but hadn't taken the time to use a mirror.

I dug around in my purse and handed him one of my cosmetic mirrors and a tissue.

He took one look at himself and shuddered.

"What happened?" I asked. Bertie had stayed inside to talk with Bubba's band members. As I'd rushed through the house in search of Bixby, I'd overheard her asking where Bubba might have gone and if any of them had heard from him since last night.

At that moment I couldn't care less about Bubba's whereabouts—or Stan's murder, for that matter. Bixby was the one I needed to protect. He was here as a favor to Tina, and Tina was the only sibling who seemed to like me. I wasn't going to let some overzealous, lovesick fan hurt him—not when he was in my town.

My town?

Just thinking that this town could be mine—as in *my* home—took me aback. But the words felt right. Despite the police chief's objections, this was my town now. It was my home.

And I wasn't going to let some wacko who thought Bixby should love her destroy the peace I enjoyed in my town. Concern for his safety growing, I asked again, "What happened?"

He looked up from cleaning his face. He'd managed to wipe away most of the soot. There was no helping his eyebrows. They'd been burned cleanly off in some parts. "As I've told everyone, it was just a freak accident."

A short man with pitch-black hair stepped out onto the porch. He took one look at me before agreeing with Bixby, "Must have been a faulty gas tank on the grill. We were fixing to cook up some hotdogs when Bixby fired up the pilot light and—*boom!*" He threw his arms in the air as if to demonstrate. "Done tossed our boy here back at least fifteen feet. The railing stopped him from going halfway to Spain. Done called the rental agency and gave them hell. If any of us had been standing directly in front of the grill, we'd been toast. Dead toast."

"Where were you standing?" I asked Bixby.

He gave me one of those sheepish grins the magazines liked to feature on their covers since they made young girls swoon. Despite singed eyebrows, he was still nearly swoon-worthy. "There was a mini fridge next to the grill." He pointed to a blackened spot next to the melted and twisted metal frame that had once been a gas grill. "I was bending down to pull out a beer when Alvin here yelled out, asking me to fire up the grill."

"He done flipped the switch and then—*boom!*" the dark-haired man shouted, reenacting the explosion with the same enthusiasm he had shown the first time, complete with arms flapping in the air.

"Did anyone call the police?" I asked.

"Heavens, gurly, no." Alvin had such a thick, rocks-in-the-mouth Southern accent I had to watch his lips to interpret the garbled sounds coming out of his mouth. "Gurl, weren't you paying attention? Done called the rental agency. They're the ones who should have known it's a hazard to leave a gas grill out on a beachfront deck. Things rust to nothing out here."

"The name's Penn, not girl," I said. I hated being called "girl" nearly as much as I hated being called by my first name, Charity. My paternal grandmother, Cristobel Penn, had named me Charity because she wanted to remind everyone how much of a charity it was that she'd taken me—the bastard child—into her home to raise. "Why would Bertie tell me the explosion was a murder attempt against Bixby? She's not one to jump to conclusions." Unless, apparently, they involved Bubba.

"Got to be nerves. She's an old lady. Everyone knows the older a woman gets, the quicker she gets hysterical over the simplest things. Heck, done left my wife because all she could do was scream anymore."

"Marella left you because you stayed out drinking every night for the last two years of your marriage and you know it, Alvin," Bertie scolded as she came out onto the deck.

"And why did I feel the need to stay out of the house if not because of her constant hysterics?" he countered.

"I don't know. Perhaps it was because every day you peered into your bathroom mirror, you could see a clearer and clearer vision of the grim reaper smiling back at you. I bet that's why you dyed your hair that ridiculous shoe polish black and started carousing all hours of the night in hopes of recapturing a piece of your misspent youth."

He opened his mouth and then closed it again before mumbling, "Couldn't stand her screeching at me about it."

Bertie just shook her head and then turned to me. "Bixby got another letter. A rock came sailing through his bedroom window at the beach house you'd rented for him this morning. Set off the security alarm. The security company called the rental agency, which in turn called the shop shortly after you left. Althea called me."

My voice sounded a little bit shrill as I demanded, "Another letter?" I turned to Bixby.

He shrugged as if it were nothing.

"It was another threat," Bertie said as she crossed her arms over her chest. "It told him to keep away from fires. The rental agency called the shop and read it to Althea."

"Did they call the police?" I asked, my voice growing shriller and shriller still. I glanced at Alvin, who was eyeing me with a knowing look. I felt like telling him I was not becoming hysterical, but saying that would probably sound exactly like the kind of hysteria he expected from women.

"I told the nice lady from the rental agency I'd cover the cost of damages," Bixby said and gave me his innocent boy look. "Once she heard that, she agreed the police didn't need to be brought in."

"I'm sure you just about charmed the pants off her," I grumbled. I didn't know why I'd thought the kisses and hugs he'd given me had been anything special, but I had. And my ego certainly shouldn't have started feeling bruised just because he flirted with anything in a skirt, but it did.

Bixby gave another one of his innocent shrugs.

Despite my knowing he used that smoldering brown-eyed gaze on everyone, butterflies swirled in my stomach as if they were dancing the shag when he looked in my direction.

I put my hand on my belly. "This wasn't a freak accident. You must know that, Bixby," I said as I pulled out my phone. I was about to dial Detective Gibbons when a tall man came out on the deck. He had striking bright red hair streaked with silver locks. If he'd been a woman, I would have said he had a willowy frame. He kind of looked like a long-legged elf, especially since he was wearing green jeans and a faded green T-shirt.

He had a guitar in one hand and a beer in another.

"Yo, Bix, I couldn't find the score sheets you were asking

for," the man in green announced before taking a long sip of his beer. "Bubba must have taken them with him."

"Score sheets?" I asked.

The tall redhead looked me up and down in the same way his smaller bandmate, Alvin, had before answering. "Bix wanted to see the full scores for several songs, including 'Camellia Nights.' I couldn't find them." A sly smile curved his lips, making him look all the more elfish. "I'm Fox, by the way. Fox Caldwell. And you must be the new chocolate shop owner everyone has been talking about. Penn, is it?"

"That's right," I said, and before I knew it, I'd gotten caught up in several minutes of meaningless small talk with Fox and Bertie.

Alvin left to go search for a beer. Bixby leaned against the railing and alternated between gazing out at the waves crashing against the shore and into the compact mirror I'd handed him to frown at his seared eyebrows.

I frowned, too. Someone had tried to kill one of the country's top pop stars while another had killed a singer who had aspired—but failed—to make it to the heights of fame Bixby enjoyed.

Were there two murderers in Camellia Beach?

Two murderers in one tiny town?

While I'd never believed Police Chief Byrd whenever he'd claimed crime didn't exist on this tiny strip of sand, I found it equally unbelievable that an island this size would have two killers on the loose at the same time. And if there weren't two murderers, that would mean that—

"What did you just say?" I rounded so suddenly on Fox that he threw up his hands and jumped back.

"I don't know," he cried with alarm.

"You were talking about Stan and what he was wearing last night. What did you say?"

"Oh, that. I was saying how silly it was that Stan had dressed in the same leather pants and black T-shirt Bixby wears at the end of all his concerts. It was like he was trying to *be* Bixby."

I closed my eyes and tried to remember everything I'd seen at that terrible bonfire. There'd been the congressman's bag of bonbons. There'd also been the two legs jutting out from the piled-up firewood.

I screwed my eyes tighter as I remembered how the leather pants along with the bag of chocolate had made me think I had found Bixby's body in the fire.

What if the killer had thought the same thing? What if Stan, dressed as Bixby, was the victim of an unfortunate case of mistaken identity? What if once the killer had learned of his or her mistake, he or she rushed out to try again?

"I will see you burn," that first threat had read.

Had Bixby's overzealous fan tried—not once, but twice now—to make him burn? The more I thought about it, the more I believed it. For one thing, that second rock hadn't smashed through Bixby's bedroom window until after word had gotten out that it was Stan who had perished in the fire.

And if the first murder was a case of mistaken identity, I needed to make sure Bixby's crazy fan didn't manage to get close to him again, which meant I needed to call Detective Gibbons and alert him to the killer's mistake. And I also needed to tell him how the killer had tried to burn Bixby again.

It wasn't a call I wanted to make. Gibbons was going to scold me for not calling the police right away to report the threatening letters Bixby had been getting. But I could take it.

Besides, Gibbons would have to be grateful I was coming to him now. The threatening letters would explain everything about Stan's murder.

Everything . . . except for Bubba's disappearance.

Chapter 12

"I don't know," Detective Gibbons frowned at the charred remains of the gas grill. He poked at it with the end of the pen he carried everywhere with him. "There are signs of rust. It could have been an accident. I'll have to get an expert down here."

"It was an accident," Bixby called from inside the beach house. "None of my fans would do this. Sometimes they threaten, but none of them would ever go through with it. My fans love me." He'd been pacing in front of a pair of open sliding glass doors. A cell phone was pressed against his ear. I'd thought he hadn't been listening to what was happening on the deck. Apparently, I was wrong.

Despite Bixby's objections, I'd called the detective and reported the explosion as an attempted murder. Since Gibbons was already on the island questioning witnesses from the previous night's murder, it hadn't taken long for him to arrive at the beach house in his white Crown Victoria. He'd come straight out to the deck to have a look.

Two of the three surviving members of The Embers—Bubba was still missing—had crowded around the detective while he crouched down and examined the grill.

Bixby had distanced himself from the investigation. Instead of staying out on the deck to answer questions, he'd moved to the beach house's expansive living room as soon as the detective had arrived. While pacing like a caged animal in front of the open sliding doors, he called his agent and his makeup team to discuss not the murder attempt, but his damaged eyebrows.

Bertie and I kept to the shade of the deck's pergola, where we found two comfortable Adirondack chairs. From our vantage point, we could easily watch both what the detective was doing with the grill and what Bixby was doing inside.

The sun was reaching its zenith. Even with the ocean breeze picking up speed, the summer day was turning into a scorcher. Thanks to the open sliding glass doors, though, we could enjoy the cool air pouring out of the house. Clearly, the band didn't see anything wrong with leaving the air conditioner running full blast while having the doors and windows thrown open. After all, they weren't the ones paying the utility bill.

It didn't take long for the band members to get bored with the investigation and seek the coolness of the indoors. I could hear plates clattering in the kitchen as the men fixed themselves lunch.

Detective Gibbons dabbed his forehead with his handkerchief before joining Bertie and me in the shade. He sat on a chair next to mine.

"Congressman Ezell had given Bixby the bag of chocolate bonbons I found at the bonfire," I reminded Gibbons. "Any fan watching from the crowd could have seen Ezell hand it to him."

He nodded.

"There's a fan out there who wants to hurt Bixby," I said, then began telling him the details of the fiery threats tied to rocks that kept coming at Bixby through plate glass windows.

Gibbons wrote in his little notebook. After I finished, he remained silent for several minutes. His brows furrowed. "I need to see the letters. I assume Byrd has them?"

I looked over at Bixby, who'd put away his cell phone. He was now leaning against the doorjamb, watching me.

"The incidents at the shop and at the rental house haven't been reported." I winced as I said it.

"Penn," Gibbons bit off my name as he leaned forward in his chair. He sounded awfully like a stern father. "I've told you more than once that you are not the police and that you have no business—"

"I tossed them," Bixby said, as if that was what anyone would have done. "It's not as if I haven't had fans throw things at me before. I prefer it to be bras they toss, but some of my fans get carried away and throw harder items."

"Like rocks with threatening notes attached to them?" the detective asked.

"It's happened before. My fans can be . . ." He paused. I wondered if he was searching for a kinder way of saying dangerous. "Passionate," was the word he finally picked.

"You called them crazies yesterday," I reminded him. "You changed your flight plans to get ahead of them."

"That's the cost of fame. You get used to it."

"I don't know how you can get used to people throwing rocks through your windows," Bertie said. "That's not normal behavior."

"There's nothing normal about the music business," Bixby said before going back to frowning at his scorched eyebrows in the compact mirror I'd given him. He honestly didn't seem fazed by the rocks, the threats, or the possibility that someone might have tried to kill him.

If that was what the music business was about, I couldn't understand why anyone would want anything to do with it.

"Stan was wearing leather pants and a black T-shirt last night," I told Gibbons, although I was pretty sure he already knew that from the coroner's report. But sometimes things needed to be said aloud to get the conversation moving in the right direction. "Bixby was also wearing leather pants and a black tee last night."

"The two men don't look anything alike," Gibbons pointed out.

"Thank you," Bixby said without looking up from the mirror. "I hope you think I'm the better looking of the two."

"Apparently my granddaughters do," the detective grumbled. "They've been texting me questions to ask you all morning."

"It was dark last night," I reminded them. "No moon. Bixby and Stan are about the same height. They were wearing similar clothes. And Stan had somehow gotten his hands on the chocolates the congressman had given Bixby."

"He must have dug it out of the trash bin," Bixby wrinkled his nose as he said it. "Disgusting."

"There's nothing disgusting about Penn's chocolates," Bertie spoke up to defend me. Or perhaps she was defending herself. She was the one who had whipped up the successful batch of sweet and savory bonbons, not me. "You can't find chocolate like hers anywhere else in the world."

That last bit was definitely true. The beans the shop used were an extremely rare variety that, when combined with the tough growing conditions in the Brazilian rainforest, produced a symphony of flavors unmatched by any other chocolate.

"I didn't mean to disparage your work, Penn. I love chocolate. It's one of my favorite sweets to eat. I simply don't eat food given to me by a stranger." Bixby lowered his hand. He'd been patting his damaged eyebrows as if that could fix them. He looked up from the compact mirror. "What I meant was that it's disgusting that someone would take food out of the trash. That's gross."

"It's desperation, son," Bertie said. "That man desperately wanted to be you."

Bixby smiled and shook his head. "Who doesn't?"

Detective Gibbons, who'd been sitting back and listening, sat forward again. His entire body seemed to spring to life as he questioned Bixby about his security. Much to my surprise, Bixby admitted that he did have a security team protecting him. He nodded toward the beach to a pair of gentlemen walking past. They were dressed in Bermuda shorts and white button-up shirts, with wide-brimmed straw hats pulled down low on their heads. Large cameras hung like albatrosses around their necks. They looked like typical middle-aged tourists.

Although they didn't appear to be watching the house or Bixby in any way—they were chatting with each other as they strolled—both men had instantly noticed Bixby's nod in their direction and nodded back at him. One of the men raised his hand in a brief wave.

"What do those two say about the explosion?" I asked just as Gibbons said, "I'll need to talk with your team."

"I can have my assistant set that up," Bixby answered Gibbons first. He then turned toward me before saying, "They both told me they thought it was a freak accident. You're worrying about me for nothing. I'm fine, Penn. You have to believe me. I've been dealing with the crazies for enough years now to know when I need to be concerned."

"I'd feel better if I knew who's been throwing rocks at you."

"It's just one of my crazies," he said.

"Who knew that you'd changed your flight?" Bertie asked.

"That's right," I said. "If you changed your flight to an earlier one to keep one step ahead of your rabid fans, how did the stone thrower find out your updated schedule and manage to arrive at the shop minutes after you?"

Bixby shrugged. "I don't know. If my fans know where I'm heading, they'll often arrive several days in advance and watch for me."

Although Detective Gibbons didn't seem at all convinced by my theory that the killer had intended to kill Bixby, not Stan, he did start scratching notes in his casebook when the conversation shifted to the trouble Bixby had experienced with his fans. Before then, he'd just been using his little notebook to fan himself.

"Son, you really need to report these kinds of incidences to the police," Gibbons said in his slow, deceptively lazy drawl. "We can't help you if we don't know there's a problem."

"No offense to your investigative force, but I have my security team to help me keep the worst of my fans at bay. They're the best of the best."

"But certainly the police can—" I tried to interject.

Bixby wasn't listening. "Sure, a few things, like rocks, may occasionally break through security. But I've learned the hard way that reporting every little thing to the police only creates news reports, and in the end it's a PR disaster. Rarely does it result in an arrest or stop the harassment. Often it encourages others to do something similar. So really, it's best for everyone if I keep my mouth shut."

"If you change your mind or something else happens, call." Gibbons handed Bixby his card as he rose from the Adirondack chair. It was the same card Gibbons had given me several months earlier. Only, when Gibbons had handed me that card, he'd lectured me on the dangers of not calling the police and insisted I call him instead of investigating any odd activities on my own. Of course, unlike Bixby I didn't have a security team watching out for me twenty-four/seven.

Security team or not, I couldn't stop feeling nervous about the nameless, faceless fan who seemed obsessed with setting Bixby on fire.

"But you are going to look into the grill's explosion?" I pressed as Gibbons made his way toward the sliding glass door and the coolness of the beach house on his way back toward the street where he'd parked his unmarked cruiser. "Someone might have rigged it to explode."

"Yeah, I'll send a tech to—" Gibbons's seemingly lazy gaze suddenly snapped into eagle-sharp focus. He stared passed me toward the steps that led down from the elevated beach house to the sandy beach below.

A commotion had erupted at the base of the stairs. Gibbons's hand instinctively moved toward his belt, where he'd holstered a gun, as he moved closer to the stairs. The rest of us followed.

Down on the beach, a woman dressed in jeans and bikini top and carrying a large duffle bag had charged toward the vacation house's wooden stairs. She sported a short pixie cut, similar to mine, but with black hair instead of blonde. Even from this distance, I could make out the fiery determination in her gaze as she tried to push past Bixby's security team.

"That's Jody," I said.

"Don't you know who I am?" I could hear her saying to the two men who'd, by this time, grabbed each of her arms.

"What's *she* doing here?" Bertie said with a snarl. Jody, who was Harley Dalton's ex-wife, had tried to bully my maternal grandmother into selling the Chocolate Box's building. In doing so, she'd made a lifetime enemy of Bertie. "Neither she nor that high-priced development company she works for lifted a finger to help out with the music festival."

"I bet she's here about the grill. Looks like she's got tools with her," I said.

At that moment, Jody swung the heavy bag she was carrying and managed to hit the man on her right in the chest with it. With a loud "oaf," he fell backward into the sand.

"She's from the management—" I yelled down, but not before his partner flipped Jody to the ground and pinned her there. He kept her pinned face-first in the sand with her arm twisted behind her until Bixby nodded, wordlessly indicating she had his permission to come up to the house.

The burly security guard said something to Jody and offered his hand to help her back on her feet. She batted it away. Once she was standing, she brushed off the sand that clung to her clothes and skin like cornmeal. She then plucked the duffle bag from the ground as if it weighed nothing. The tools inside it clanked loudly.

"I heard there was a complaint about a grill," she called to us as she marched up the stairs and onto the deck as if she hadn't just been tackled. Heck, she came up the stairs as if she owned the place. Well, she had the right to do that since her employer owned many of the new beach rentals in town, apparently including this one.

"Are you okay?" I rushed over to offer assistance, comfort, whatever she might need. She'd just been knocked over by a burly guy. That had to leave bruises.

"Of course I'm okay," she answered as she dropped the duffle bag with a loud clatter. "And what are *you* doing here? Don't you have your precious shop to run?"

Bertie harrumphed.

"Oh . . . both of you are here," Jody said with a sarcastic edge to her already pinched voice. "*Goodie.*"

"We're here because the house's grill exploded," I explained. "It injured my friend, Bixby Lewis. It could have seriously hurt him."

She looked over at the superstar, who flashed one of his signature melt-a-woman-into-a-pile-of-goo smiles. Her jaw dropped.

It was wrong of me, but I have to admit it felt kind of good to be able to knock Jody speechless. When we first met, she'd acted as if we were going to become best buddies. She'd even said she thought of me like a sister. Despite my inclination to distrust everyone, her whispered confidences and the fact that she, too, was an outsider in this close-knit town had softened the barriers I'd erected around me. I'd trusted her.

Yet her kindness had proved false. She didn't want friendship. Her confidences had nothing to do with our shared outsider status. She'd cozied up to me for one reason and one reason only. The development company she worked for had plans to create a high-density commercial complex with nearly a hundred residential apartments in the upper stories.

The proposed development, which was her pet project, would be centered on the marshfront property where the Chocolate Box sat. Jody had pursued my friendship because she'd desperately wanted to purchase that land. And she'd hoped to win me over in order to convince me to sell it to her.

When I refused, I instantly became her enemy.

To be fair, she also disliked me because I hadn't joined her in trashing her ex. She'd told me many times that Harley was some kind of murderous devil. My decision not to take her word for it had put a strain on our budding friendship even before I'd told her that I'd planned to keep the Chocolate Box. Still, my decision to keep the shop had made her spitting mad. She could barely look in my direction without snarling and making some kind of snide comment.

Bertie kept saying I never needed that kind of friendship in the first place. "That girl is meaner than a skillet full of rattlesnakes."

Even though I agreed with Bertie—dealing with Jody did feel awfully similar to getting involved with dangerous snakes; you never knew when she'd strike—I still felt bad about how things had ended between us. Although most of the town had objected to such a drastic change on the island, Jody seemed to truly believe that the mega-development her company had planned was exactly what the town needed to get the economy out of the gutter.

Jody finally tore her gaze away from Bixby's dazzlingly seductive eyes and glanced at me. She snapped her gaping mouth closed. "*Liar. You're not his friend,*" she said, loud enough for my ears only.

I shrugged.

She hurried across the deck with her hand extended toward Bixby. "On behalf of Sunset Development, let me apologize for what happened. I'm Jody Dalton, senior project manager." She sucked in a shaky breath when Bixby lifted her hand to his lips.

"I'm impressed they sent someone so high up in the company to take care of the problem," he said with a seductive rumble in his voice. "And someone so beautiful."

"Oh, oh, oh. I don't usually do hands-on repairs. We have a handyman who handles these things. But he's on vacation. So I'm filling in."

At that moment, Alvin came out onto the deck with a beer in one hand and a plate piled with food in the other. His grin took a dive when he saw Jody.

"Jody," he said, his grip tightening on his plate. "I done told the office to just bring by a new grill. You didn't need to come."

"I'm not signing off on a new grill when we can fix the old one. I don't know why you didn't fix it yourself," she said, then pointed to the beer in his hand. "Too busy drinking?"

"There ain't no fixin' it," he grumbled as he continued to take his plate over to a large wooden table on the deck.

Jody shook her head. "Alvin took the week off to 'practice' with the band. So I'm stuck covering for him. Just finished replacing a window AC down the block. And after I'm done with this, some jerk in the rental on the other side of the island broke out a window. Instead of eating lunch, I have to go sit and wait for the glaziers to show up."

"Er . . . sorry about the window," Bixby said, but he didn't sound sorry. "I'll pay for the repairs. And I can arrange for someone to handle overseeing its replacement. I don't want to put you out."

"The house with the broken bedroom window? That's the house you're renting?" Jody asked with breathless excitement.

"It's the one Penn got for me. Let me give my people a call. I'll have someone over there right away to make sure the window gets fixed."

"No, no, no. No need. No need. I don't mind giving *you* personal service. Now let me get this grill up and working." She glared at Alvin. "We try to keep everything in perfect condition, but the renters are so careless with the furniture and appliances. What was practically new on move-in day is smashed to bits a few days later. I'm sure that's what happened here." She tilted her head and smiled at Bixby. "I'm glad you weren't injured too badly when the grill failed. Let me see if I can't get it working again."

"The grill exploded," Bertie pointed out. "Not even a root doctor could bring it back from the dead."

Jody's smile tightened. "Well, let me look at it anyhow."

Her smile froze when she saw the grill's charred remains. "What in the world did you do to it?" she shouted over to Alvin.

"Dang thing blew up," he shouted back. "Scared me witless."

Jody poked around at it much like Gibbons had earlier. "Looks as if it was some kind of gas leak. I'll send the cleaners in to get this taken care of and order a new one sent over."

"That's what I thought," Gibbons said as he hitched up his pants. "Gas line leak. Not an elaborate murder plot. Now if you'll excuse me, Penn, I have a murder to investigate."

"Wait. Wait." I chased after him as he hurried through the house. "I thought you were going to have someone come and look at the grill. Jody's not an expert. Someone might have tampered with it."

Gibbons stopped to listen to me. Or perhaps he stopped to

enjoy the blasting AC that made the house feel like the inside of a refrigerator. He looked at me in his fatherly way, then sighed. "I'll send someone over."

"Don't you need to leave an officer here to make sure no one tampers with it? Jody is going to have a cleaning crew dispose of the grill." And I knew darn well that Jody wouldn't cancel the cleaning crew from coming and hauling the grill away just because I asked her to.

His mouth twisted into a funny grimace. "Will my agreeing to do this keep you from investigating on your own?"

"I can't imagine why I'd have to poke around and ask the same questions the police are asking, do you?"

He eyed me curiously before retrieving his cell phone from his suit pocket. While he dialed, he marched back to the deck and barked, "Don't touch the grill. It's a crime scene. I'll have an officer here in a minute to secure the area."

Chapter 13

When we returned to the shop, I saw something that had me unbuckling my seatbelt even before Bertie parked. The Chocolate Box was crowded. A line, a *freaking* line, snaked out the door. I checked my watch. One o'clock. Not one of our usual busy times.

Heck, even during our busiest times of day, lines never got even close to the door.

As Bertie eased her car the size of a boat into a narrow parking space reserved for residents of the building, I kicked the rusty passenger door until it flew open.

I looked at Bertie. She looked at me.

We both looked horrified.

For one thing, we were going to run out of inventory. For another, I'd left Althea working the counter with no backup. Not to mention that when I'd left, the phone had been ringing off the hook from unhappy ticket-holders demanding refunds.

A knot of dread twisted in my stomach. "These aren't customers. They're here about the festival. I bet they want their money back. But we spent the ticket money to pay the bands. Where is Bubba? I need his help figuring out what to do."

"Penn, I wish I knew where that man went." Bertie put her

91

hand on my shoulder. "But remember you're not alone in this. I'll stand by you. Althea will too."

I took a deep breath and walked into the shop. Many of the people in the line grumbled at us, insisting we get to the back of the line.

"We work here," Bertie declared. That quieted the complainers quickly enough.

Inside, we found Althea working the counter, filling bags, taking money. Her hair had fallen from its clips. Beads of sweat had made her brow glow. She looked up, saw us, and nearly fell over with relief.

"Where have you been?" she demanded.

"Why didn't you call?" I demanded at about the same time.

"When would I have gotten the chance?" I noticed then that she'd taken the phone off the hook. The display cases were nearly empty.

That's when it hit me. These weren't unhappy ticket-holders. These were bona fide customers.

"You help out in the front," Bertie said as she slipped on an apron and headed toward the back rooms to search for more truffles, bonbons, and chocolate bars.

"What's going on?" I asked Althea as I hurried around the counter to take her place.

"It's the price of fame," she said as she handed a white bag to the smiling woman on the other side of the counter. The woman then leaned across the counter and snapped a cell phone picture of herself and Althea. "About an hour ago Bixby posted a picture of a box of your truffles on Instagram."

"I did put a pretty red box of assorted truffles from the shop in his beach rental as a welcome gift," I said. "He must have taken a picture of it."

I looked at the people standing in line again and then at the crowd loitering in the shop. Phones were out. Everyone seemed to be taking either pictures or videos of themselves and the shop.

Nearly everyone crowding into the shop was female. While the crowd was young—most looked to be in their teens or twenties—I was surprised at how many women in the crowd sported silver hair. Nearly all the women from the Pink Pelican Inn had come.

These were Bixby's fans?

Could one of them be the rock-throwing super-fan who wanted to set Bixby on fire? Did one of these women standing patiently in the line kill Stan because she thought he was Bixby?

"Could you stop gaping at your success and help?" Althea nudged me with her shoulder.

The two of us diligently worked the front while Bertie shuttled out every bit of chocolate she could find in the back. About an hour into the chaos, Bertie emerged empty-handed.

"That's everything," she said as she wiped her hands on a towel. She then stepped around the counter and said in a booming voice, "Sorry folks, you've snapped up even the smallest of crumbs today. Come back tomorrow and I promise we'll have a new batch of delicious treats for you to taste. You'll have to forgive us for closing early, but we have quite a bit of work to do in the kitchens."

Despite the grumbles from the customers who hadn't gotten to buy anything, Bertie—using her Southern charm mixed with a heavy dose of stern schoolmarm demeanor—easily ushered everyone out the door and locked it behind her.

"Wow," Althea said as she collapsed into the closest chair.

"Wow," I said, sinking into the chair next to hers.

"A picture on social media did this?" Bertie asked, shaking her head.

Althea started to explain to her mother what social media was. Bertie held up her hand. "Child of mine, you don't need to preach to me. I may be old, but I'm not stupid. I have an Instagram account."

Althea looked taken aback. "You do?"

"Don't you?" Bertie asked. She then tossed each of us an apron. "If we hope to have any inventory to sell tomorrow, we'd better get to work."

Bertie headed to the back.

"My mom is on Instagram?" Althea said as she tied her apron strings. "What do you think she's posting?"

I didn't answer. Not because I didn't have an answer to that question (although I didn't). All of my attention was focused on a woman lingering in front of the locked shop. She had a large camera hanging around her neck. Wasn't she the same woman who'd bought a small bag of chocolates from the shop just this morning? The one who'd been asking questions about the murder? Why would she come back?

"Penn?" Althea tugged on the apron still dangling from my fingers. "If we don't show up in the kitchen soon, Mama is going to come looking for us. And she won't be happy about it."

"I'll be there in a minute." I pushed the apron into Althea's arms and rushed to unlock the door. Ignoring the detective's earlier admonition to stay out of the investigation, I stepped outside to talk with the woman.

Calling Gibbons would be pointless. For one thing, he clearly didn't believe my theory that the killer had only accidentally killed Stan. Instead of questioning Bixby's fans, the entire homicide department seemed focused on Bubba's disappearance—as if disappearing at the wrong moment proved guilt.

Another reason calling Gibbons would get me nowhere was simply that I didn't know the woman's name or anything about her. All I knew was that she'd come to the shop twice and was hanging around now when all the other customers had left. By the time the detective could get here, she'd be gone. And even if she was still hanging out in front of the shop, what would he say to her? Would he walk up to her and say, "Excuse me, but the shop owner has issued a complaint that you've shopped in her store too often today?" That would be ridiculous.

No, this was something I needed to do. I wasn't investigating per se. I only planned to ask a few questions . . . just to set my own mind at ease.

I stepped outside. A pair of twisting scrubby oak trees that had to be as old as the Chocolate Box's hundred-year-old building provided shade and cool relief from the summer sun.

"Hello," I said. I then pointed to the bag of chocolates the woman grasped in her hand. "Is there something wrong with them?"

She jumped. "Oh! I didn't see you there."

She was a pretty girl. Perhaps in her early twenties. Her long hair, the color of honey, had been styled in an elaborate twisting updo. Her large blue eyes blinked at me. She hugged the bag of chocolates to her chest like it was a shield, surely squishing the truffles and bonbons that Bertie and I had painstakingly made. I winced.

"Is there something wrong with the chocolates?" I asked again.

She looked at the bag as if she'd just noticed she'd been holding it. "These? No. No. They're fine. Well, I'm sure they are. I haven't actually eaten any." She looked me up and down. "I need to watch my weight, you know?"

My hips had grown considerably wider since I'd taken over the shop, but I tried not to take her comment personally. "Well, I just wanted to make sure everything was okay. I'm Penn, the owner of the Chocolate Box."

"Hiya, I'm Candy." We shook hands. Hers was slender and baby-soft.

"Candy." No last name? I supposed I couldn't complain since

I went by only one name myself. "You must really love chocolate. Isn't this your second trip to buy chocolates today?"

"Oh, these aren't for me." She looked down the road as if expecting someone to appear. A few cars rolled by. A family pulling a wagon filled with towels and beach toys rambled passed. She frowned as she watched them. "They're for a friend. I don't know where he is. He should have been here by now."

"Do you need to borrow my phone?" I offered.

She produced a cell phone from the back pocket of her cutoff jeans. "Thanks. Got my own."

She didn't have the long, slow drawl that marked most residents as island residents. Her clipped way of talking sounded more Western. Could she be from California? That's where Bixby was living these days.

"Are you on vacation here? Or have you come specifically for the concerts?" I asked.

"Oh, I'm here to listen to Bixby sing. His voice is divine. Don't you think so? It's deee-vine."

So it was just as I'd suspected. She was a fan girl. Had she followed Bixby to Camellia Beach? Was she one of his "crazies"? Was she someone who liked to throw rocks?

I didn't have enough information to either think she was a suspect or rule out any wrongdoing on her part. I doubted she'd tell me the truth if I asked outright. And since I wasn't a professional investigator (I wondered if there was a class for that), I wasn't sure what probing question to ask next. In hindsight, the question I ended up lobbing at her created more problems for me in the long run.

"You're waiting for him right now, aren't you?" I tried to sound kind.

Her lips moved slowly as they formed a sly smile. "He told me he likes coming here."

"He told you . . . ? Oh, you mean the picture he posted on social media this afternoon?"

"He has to be careful, you know?" She whispered the next part. "I shouldn't tell you this. But he can't just call me. People wouldn't understand our relationship. His fans expect him to be single . . . available, you know? He can't let them know that he's in love . . . with me."

I nodded.

"I bet he came and saw the crowds and left," she said, still crushing the bag of chocolates to her chest. "Your place is always too crowded. He's going to have to pick a better location for us to meet."

I nodded again.

"You don't believe me." Her loud voice startled a flock of pigeons that had landed in the oak beside the door.

I held up my hands. "I have no reason to question anything you're saying."

Other than the fact that he kissed me yesterday, a bitter voice in my head added.

He also kissed and flirted with Jody, my vicious mind countered.

Her large doe eyes narrowed. "Don't patronize me. I know you think he's attracted to you. He kisses everyone, you know?" she said, eerily echoing my own thoughts. "He has to. It's part of his act. He has to pretend to be someone he's not. He has to pretend he's not in love with me."

"That's got to be hard," I said. "Why do you put up with it?"

She huffed as if I'd just asked the stupidest question ever. "Because I love him and this is the only way we can be together." She looked down the road again. "The crowds scared him off. And I really needed to see him. I have something I need to tell him."

"I could give him your message," I suggested. Another mistake.

"If you know what's good for you, you'll keep away from my man," she growled, then sidled down the road like a petulant raccoon.

As I watched her go, I wished I had heeded Detective Gibbons's advice to keep my nose out of police business. Talking with Candy had been a mistake. I prayed it wouldn't turn out to be a fatal one.

Chapter 14

While I took Stella out for a quick walk, I called Detective
Gibbons to report my run-in with Candy and her obsession with Bixby. Luckily, I got his voicemail, which meant I
could tell him what happened with Candy without having to
listen to his scolding. At least not right away.

I then called Granny Mae. When I was a child, she'd worked
as Grandmother Cristobel's personal assistant and often served
as a surrogate mother. As an adult, I'd lived with her in Madison, Wisconsin, for several years, moving out only after I'd
inherited this shop. She was the smartest woman I knew, which
was why I was calling her. The call went to her voicemail.

She was teaching summer session at the university as well as
taking several classes just for the joy of it. I still hadn't memorized her schedule. The message I left for her was short, just
asking her to return my call. I didn't want her to worry.

Stella tugged on the end of the leash and barked, signaling
that she wanted to get back to the air-conditioned apartment.
While my little dog loved romping around in the cold and
snow, she seemed to hate the heat. The warmer the temperature
grew, the shorter her walks became.

Today, I didn't insist on a longer walk. I had work to do. She
led the way back to the apartment. As soon as I unsnapped her

leash, she growled at Troubadour, Bertie's cat, and then bounded off into my bedroom, where I kept the ridiculously frilly dog bed I'd bought her because—oh, heck, I'd bought it because I'd lost my mind when it came to my little dog. I was constantly buying her over-the-top presents.

When I finally got back to the shop, I saw that Althea had left my apron carefully folded on the top of the glass display case next to a stack of messages. Not quite ready to head into the kitchen yet—my confidence still felt shaky after my last bonbon disaster—I started sorting through the messages. They were mainly from unhappy ticket-holders. Althea had noted on the top of almost all the pink message papers that she'd already taken care of the issue. One message, however, jumped out at me. I read it through, twice.

Florence Corners had called the shop looking for me. The message was similar to the one her brother's law office had sent to Harley. She wanted to talk with me.

My knee-jerk response was to toss the pink slip of paper. Why should I agree to talk with any of them? Florence, Edward, and Peach communicated with me only through terse legal briefs sent to Harley. But what if this was the olive branch I'd been hoping for?

All I wanted was to find my mother. All they wanted was this building. They denied that the first DNA test had any validity. They denied that I was a relation. They denied requests for face-to-face interaction.

As much as I wanted to punish them for the way they'd treated me, I needed them. They were my family. And I needed their DNA to prove it.

So I picked up the phone and dialed, not the number Florence had left for me but another number altogether.

"Harley." I took a deep breath. He patiently waited on the other end of the line. "Tell Florence I'll meet with her."

*   *   *

Bertie, Althea, and I worked in the kitchen, mainly making truffles. Bertie was an artist when it came to decorating them. She guided my hand as I painted gold dust across the tops of the shop's special, sinfully dark chocolate truffles. On the gas stove, Althea started to melt a batch of the shop's exclusive Amar chocolate. The chocolate's intense scent filled the kitchen with its dizzying dark aroma. Its dramatic flavor was suddenly muted when Althea added a less pungent chocolate variety to the pot.

Bertie, certain I could finish up with the decorations on the truffles, moved over to another area on the large counter and started to pull ingredients together to make her famous sea salt chocolate caramels. People drove in from all over the state to buy them.

"We need to open an online store," I said, surprised I hadn't thought of it sooner.

"That's a marvelous idea, Penn," Bertie said as she pulled a large metal mixing bowl down from one of the many open shelves. "But perhaps we should finish making the chocolates for tomorrow first."

I hadn't told either Bertie or Althea about my encounter with Candy outside the shop. I considered telling them about it now as we each worked on separate projects. But just thinking about Candy made me lose my focus. I spilled half the bottle of gold dust on one truffle and had to stop my work to clean up the mess.

By the time I returned to my work of decorating the over-sized tray of dark chocolate truffles that were so sinfully good they deserved their gold varnish (hey, that would make good advertising copy), my encounter with Candy no longer seemed important.

The three of us worked in silence for nearly an hour, broken only when the shop phone rang.

"I'll get it," Bertie said as she wiped her hands on a dish towel.

I followed her. Although I was sure I'd locked the front door, I wanted to be positive.

While I checked the door—it was locked—Bertie picked up the phone receiver. "The Chocolate Box," she sang.

She waved at me to get back to work in the kitchen as she listened to the person on the other side of the line. I'd started to leave the front of the shop when Bertie sucked in such a quick breath that my feet froze in place. My breath caught in my throat as I watched her with concern.

"Yes. Yes," she said, her voice more clipped than usual. "How? Why?"

"What? What's going on?" I asked, which was silly. She was too focused on the phone call to hear anything I said. I could have yelled, "Fire!" and she wouldn't have flinched.

Whoever had called was doing most of the talking. Bertie's lips tightened more and more as she listened. "What?" I asked again. "Who is it?"

Again, she didn't hear me.

After one of the longest minutes, she hung up the phone.

"Who was it?" I demanded.

"Bubba." She frowned at the phone. "He's . . . safe. He's back in town."

I fisted my hands on my hips. "Now tell me the truth, Bertie. Why in the world would he call you?"

Chapter 15

"He called the shop, not me," Bertie said quickly as we both stood in the front of our closed shop. "I picked up. He could have just as easily been talking to you."

"That's true," I admitted. "But you've been worrying about him like crazy all day. What's your relationship with him?"

By this time Althea had emerged from the kitchen. Bertie looked to her daughter and then to me before saying, "I'd worry about any member of the community that went missing. You should know that."

"Did Bubba tell you if he'd talked with Gibbons yet?" I asked.

"He said he had," she said.

"And? Is he off the hook? Is he going to be able to help get the festival back on track? There's no shortage of work that needs to be done."

"He . . . he didn't say."

"Then what did he say? Why else would he be calling here if not to talk about the festival and tonight's concert?" I demanded.

"Did he call to talk to you, Mama?" Althea asked.

"Now why would he do that?" she answered as she scurried back toward the kitchen. "We've spent enough time chatting. The chocolate won't get made by itself."

Althea moved to follow her mother. I grabbed her arm. "What isn't she telling us?" I asked. "What is her relationship with Bubba?"

"I don't know, Penn. I've never seen her act like this before. But ever since Mabel's death, she hasn't been herself. Perhaps this is her way of grieving?"

"Try to get her to talk to you." I pulled the apron off over my head and dropped it on the counter.

"What are you going to do?" she asked.

"I'm going to go talk to Bubba," I said as I grabbed my purse. "I have a concert scheduled and no band to play tonight. I'm hoping he can help with that."

"Ask him about Mama, too."

"You know I will."

*   *   *

While I drove my blue Fiat toward Bubba's creekside cottage, my thoughts drifted to chocolate. Even before I'd inherited the shop, my thoughts had often drifted to my first love—chocolate. This time, I was thinking about a flavor I'd never eaten before, a fiery bonbon.

I shook my head. Who would want to eat spicy bonbons?

Besides, I needed to focus on the music festival and what we were going to do about tonight instead of wondering how jalapeño peppers would blend with dark chocolate.

I parked next to Detective Gibbons's Crown Vic in Bubba's dirt driveway. Several other cars were parked under the trees in Bubba's yard. If I didn't know better, I would have thought he was hosting a party.

Like this morning, the front door hadn't been pushed all the way closed. The simple act of knocking made it swing open.

"Come in, come in!" one of the members of The Embers called to me. He was the tall one with the fading red hair. What was his name? I seemed to recall he was named after an animal. Raccoon? Skunk?

He tried to hand me one of the half-dozen bottles of beer he was lugging into the living room. I thanked him but refused.

"Is Bubba here?" I asked.

He nodded toward the living room. "Follow me."

The small living room felt cramped. Alvin was there. He cheered when he saw . . . *Gator?* . . . enter with the beers. Bixby was by the fireplace, talking with Congressman Ezell. Ezell's nephew Tom was wandering around the room, studying everything as if in awe. Chief Byrd slouched in a sofa with his gaze fixed on me.

Bubba, his hair wet and plastered to his head and with a shiner the size of a saucer darkening his right eye, reclined in a brown leather lounger. Detective Gibbons crouched beside him. He tilted his head to one side as he listened to Bubba, who used expressive hand movements as he talked.

The detective didn't have his notebook out, which was telling. Were the two men really just having a conversation? Did that mean Bubba was no longer the main suspect in Stan's murder and that Gibbons would now pursue Candy for the crime? Or was the detective treating Bubba with kid gloves because of his mother's political connections?

"Hey Penn," Bixby said. He stepped in my path, blocking my access to Bubba. He put his hand on my arm. Again, I was surprised how his touch didn't bother me. Even knowing how he flirted shamelessly with any woman he met and despite my prickly no-touch tendencies, I truly liked it when his bright spotlight turned toward me. Did that make me shallow? Probably. "Did you make any special chocolate treats for me today?"

My face flushed. "What do you think about jalapeños and chocolate?"

"Oooo," he crooned. "Spicy. I would like that."

I stared stupidly into his sparkling brown eyes.

"Thanks, Fox," Bixby said to the red-haired man with the beers. That jolted me out of my daze.

"Fox!" I exclaimed. "For some reason I'd thought your name was Gator or something."

Fox laughed as he continued making his way around the room handing out frosty brown bottles.

"I met one of your biggest fans today," I said to Bixby. He'd twisted off the beer's cap and was taking a long sip. "Her name is Candy."

Bixby coughed horribly as he started to choke.

"I take it you know her," I said and pounded him on his back.

"You okay over there?" Bubba called from his recliner.

Detective Gibbons rose to his feet. When he spotted me, he pressed his lips together tighter and tighter until they'd nearly disappeared.

"You . . . keep . . . away . . . from . . . her," Bixby managed to sputter as he continued to cough. I pounded on his back again. "She's—"

"Miss Penn, you broke your promise," Gibbons growled as he ambled toward me.

"I called you right away," I said, hoping I sounded sweetly innocent.

"You called after the fact. You shouldn't have been nosing in on my investigation in the first place." He grabbed my arm.

I froze at his touch. My hands curled into fists.

Keen detective that he was, he noticed my discomfort and released me.

"Come with me." He paused before adding, "Please. Please, come with me to the deck, where we can talk in private."

"I'm not here to start trouble or to step on your capable toes," I told him in as friendly a tone as I could manage. "I need to talk to Bubba about what we're going to do about tonight. With the concert. It's supposed to start in a few hours and the band's lead singer is dead."

"And I need to talk to you about Candy Graves," Gibbons said.

"Candy?" Bixby pushed his face into the conversation. My pounding on his back must have done the trick. He'd stopped choking. "What about her?"

"On the deck," the detective said to me. I don't think he intended for Bixby to follow along, but that was exactly what the superstar did. Thankfully, Byrd seemed content to remain on the sofa and let his colleague from the county handle my scolding.

The afternoon sun was baking the riverside deck. I held up my hand to block the bright rays from shining directly in my eyes while I dug around in my purse for a pair of sunglasses.

Both Bixby and the detective had sense enough to slip on dark sunglasses before stepping out into the sun.

"What is this about Candy?" Bixby crossed his arms over his chest and took a fierce don't-mess-with-me-or-my-friends pose.

"You have a restraining order against her," Gibbons said to Bixby. "That you filed in LA."

"That's right," was Bixby's terse answer.

The detective nodded. "Your people contacted our department as well as the local police to warn us about her a few days before your arrival."

"Penn said she talked with her today," Bixby said. "That means she followed me to Camellia Beach."

"Is she the reason you changed your flight plans?" I asked.

"She's one of the reasons I did." Bixby turned to the detective and explained how he'd arranged to be on an earlier flight and had driven himself into town to avoid crowds and publicity both in LA and here at the Charleston airport. "If I don't keep a fluid schedule, I'll get mobbed. My fans are beginning to learn that the only place they can expect me to show up on time is at my concerts. Everywhere else will be a surprise."

What an awful way to live. I'd hate it. By the way Gibbons shuddered, I suspected he was thinking the same thing.

"Ms. Candy Graves seems to be adept at finding you." Gibbons flipped a few pages in his notebook. "She's broken into your house three times, into your backstage dressing room five times, your hotel room nine times, and into your parents' house twice."

Bixby sighed. "She's persistent."

"She told me—in the strictest of confidences, of course—that she's your secret girlfriend. And that you let her know how to find her," I said.

"She's told everyone that," Bixby complained.

Gibbons nodded. "It's in the reports."

"Do you think she might be tired of waiting in the shadows?" I asked. "Do you think she might have tried to do something drastic to punish you for not acknowledging your relationship with her?"

"She's not my lover, secret or otherwise," Bixby insisted a little too loudly. He glanced around as if worried journalists were hiding in the bushes.

"In her mind she is," I pointed out. "I'm just wondering if she's the one throwing rocks and if she's the one who started the deadly bonfire last night."

Gibbons groaned. He might have even grumbled something about my unrelenting persistence under his breath.

"But it was Stan Frasier who was killed last night, not me," Bixby pointed out. His troubled gaze shifted to stare into the thick undergrowth and deep shadows that surrounded Bubba's cottage.

"Stan was dressed in leather pants and a black T-shirt, just like you were. And there was no moon. So it was dark. She might have made a mistake," I said.

"There was no mistake." Gibbons walked over to the deck's railing and frowned as he watched a movement in the same undergrowth that had caught Bixby's attention.

We all held our breaths.

A fat raccoon waddled out into the open with a pair of playful kits following closely behind. The trio made their way to the river where a bed of oysters lay barely submerged near the shore.

Gibbons shook his head and then turned back to me. "While I can't discuss the details, I can tell you this, Penn: Stan was the intended victim last night. So there's no reason to put yourself in harm's way by questioning—"

"It wasn't Bubba," I blurted.

"It wasn't Candy," Gibbons said, neither agreeing nor disagreeing with me about Bubba. He then wagged his stubby finger under my nose. "If you put your foot into my investigation again, I just might arrest you for obstruction of justice. Do you understand me?"

"I understand." I clamped my jaws together.

While I understood what he was saying, I didn't agree with it. No matter how hard I tried, I couldn't shake the nagging feeling that Gibbons was wrong about Stan's murder. Dead wrong. Despite the detective's threats to toss me into jail, I wasn't going to sit on my hands and do nothing while the killer went after Bixby. The police refused to link the broken window, threatening notes, and exploding grill to Stan's murder. They were wrong. I felt it in my bones. The trouble happening on the island was connected. I simply needed to prove it. I *had* to prove it because, despite what anyone else believed, I was not going to let Bixby end up like Stan.

Chapter 16

The lone ceiling fan's motor in Bubba's living room whined with every revolution the blades made and did very little to move the sticky humidity that rolled in from the open windows. Gibbons returned to Bubba's side to hand the president of the business association a card and to warn him not to leave town.

"I'll be in touch with you tomorrow," he said to Bubba before turning back to me. "I expect not to hear from you, Penn, unless it's an invitation to sample more of your chocolates."

Not even a minute had passed after the detective and Chief Byrd's departure before Alvin whooped loudly.

Everyone laughed.

I refused yet another offer for a beer as I made my way to talk with Bubba about tonight's concert.

"What in the world happened to you?" The question came flying out of my mouth in place of any of the important ones. More unimportant questions followed. "Where have you been? Why weren't you answering your phone? And what the heck happened to your eye?"

Bubba touched his puffy eye and smiled sheepishly. "Someone conked me on my head."

"Who?" I asked, still not able to get myself on topic.

"If I knew that, I wouldn't be laying around like a lazy old hound dog, now, would I?"

Actually, I didn't know what he would or wouldn't be doing. "Everyone has been saying you killed Stan and then tried to run away."

"You don't have to tell me that. I've been questioned by every officer of the law who resides within a ten-mile radius. Old Hank, he vouched for me, though," he said, referring to Chief Byrd. "He told all the others that I wouldn't go running anywhere so I didn't need to be brought into custody, seeing how there's no evidence against me other than my foolish mouth saying things it oughtn't be sayin'."

"So where have you been all this time?" I asked again.

"Adrift. Literally. I woke up in the middle of the night laying flat on my back on the deck of a shrimp boat. That dang ship had been cast off the dock. The motor wouldn't start up. And there I was—my head throbbing like a damn drum, no phone, and heading out with the tide into the open ocean."

"My word," I gasped. "What happened?"

"The boat eventually ran aground in front of a mansion out on Kiawah Island. Its abrupt stop jolted me off the boat deck. I went sailing through the air and belly-flopped into the middle of a seaside wedding. The flowers broke my fall."

"Flowers?" I asked.

He nodded. "I've never seen so many dang flowers. The bride and groom and justice of the peace were standing within a ring of flower arrangements that had to have been at least four feet high. I remember thinking right before landing on all those white flowers, 'Now, ain't that the prettiest thing I've ever seen?' That's when I got this." He pointed to his puffy eye.

"That wasn't from whoever stranded you on a shrimp boat?"

"Naw, the bride punched me for ruining her perfect day.

Couldn't say I blame her. I did make a mess of all those nice flowers, now, didn't I?"

"I guess," I said, feeling kind of stunned. "So you were stranded on a boat all night? That's your alibi for the murder?"

"The police don't seem to think so. Can't actually prove when I ended up on the boat. Gibbons said I could have put myself on the boat after lighting the fire."

"But—"

"Bubba, the sheet music ain't in that box you told me to look in," Alvin shouted from across the small living room.

"It should be there," he shouted back. "That's where I stored the original."

"Original for what?" I asked.

Bubba had jumped up from the recliner. He started across the room toward Alvin. "For 'Camellia Nights.' Stan didn't know it, but I kept a copy of the sheet music for our song in that plastic bin. The bin comes with me during hurricane evacuations. Every important piece of paper I own is in there. Alvin, stop being so vain and put on your glasses already. It's in there."

"Wait." I jogged after Bubba. "I need to talk to you about tonight. Stan and Ocean Waves are scheduled to perform. What are we going to do? Do you know of any local bands who could take their place without upsetting too many of the ticket-holders?"

Bubba nudged Alvin out of the way and crouched next to the box. "Already got it covered," he said without looking up.

"You do?" He'd been back in town for less than an hour and had already fixed the problem I hadn't been able to fix after worrying about it all day? Not that I should have been surprised. He had contacts in the music community. I didn't. "Who's going to perform? I'll start advertising the schedule change and making new posters right away."

"Ocean Waves."

"But Stan—"

"He was just the lead singer. His band is talented. Super talented. We talked with them as soon as I got here. They agreed that, as a tribute to Stan, they'd want to perform tonight. Bixby will fill the role as lead singer. And I'll play my bass."

I turned to look at Bixby. "Why would you do that?" Why was he so willing to give away his services and sing with these small-time bands? It didn't make sense.

"I'm here to soak up the culture and to be inspired by the authentic beach music being playing in this area. What better way to do that than to play with the bands?"

I supposed that made sense. "Do either of you even know the songs?" Shouldn't they be practicing instead of downing beers?

"We're meeting with the band to run through the playlist two hours before showtime," he said as he flipped through pages in the plastic box.

"Will that give you enough time to actually learn the songs?" I suddenly pictured lines of unhappy people demanding refunds after the show. "I mean, we can't really risk winging tonight's performance, because we don't have the money on hand to issue more than a few refunds."

He looked up at me and frowned as if surprised I would question him about it. "Don't worry so much. It'll all work out."

Don't worry? He was telling me not to worry? Sometimes that's what I did best—worry. I'd learned from Grandmother Cristobel to expect and plan for the worst. Santa Claus was supposed to bring me a bicycle? Don't count on it. That shiny new bike under the tree would go to Tina or Chrissie or one of my even younger siblings. Even if they didn't ask for one, that's what they'd get. While I got socks.

In Santa's defense, they were warm socks.

113

Bixby touched my arm. "It will be fine," he said softly. "I've done this before. I can step in and cover just about any song with just a bit of practice. And no matter what happens, the crowd will love it."

"Will they?" I asked, still feeling unsure.

"Of course they will. Crowds always love me."

And that was why he was the big star. Despite my efforts to fight it, despite knowing how he flirted with everyone he met, I—like everyone else in the world—was already half in love with him.

The tension in my shoulders eased as I gazed at his handsome face. "You're right. Crowds do love you."

"And the press will be thrilled to cover my 'surprise' appearance at tonight's performance."

"Your surprise performance?" I asked.

"Don't put my name on the updated posters. We'll just spring it on everyone. It'll be fun. Promise me you'll come and watch."

"The surprise would add to the excitement and media coverage of the festival," I admitted, staring down at my hand that was suddenly cradled in his hand. He drew tiny circles on my knuckles with his thumb. I blinked several times but didn't pull away. "It . . ." I cleared my throat when my silly voice warbled. "It might even spur additional ticket sales for some of our smaller bands playing tomorrow night."

Despite the giddy champagne-like bubbles bumping around in my head thanks to him, I had enough brain power to wonder if there was some other reason he didn't want to publicize his appearance at tonight's show. Had the exploding grill along with Candy's appearance in Camellia Beach unnerved him?

Thinking of Candy and her obsession with Bixby reminded me of someone else's obsession.

"Bubba," I said. "What's between you and Bertie? She was beside herself with worry when you went missing."

"Bertie?" Bubba muttered as he continued to flip through the papers in his huge box. "She's a bit like you, I suppose. Her heart is as big as the ocean out there. She worries after all the residents on Camellia Beach."

"I suppose," I said. But something felt off about how she was acting when it came to Bubba. "It's not just that, though. She's also swearing up and down to anyone who'll listen that you'd never hurt a fly, much less kill Stan. She even ran off without telling anyone where she was going after hearing that you were the prime suspect for Stan's murder. I presume she went looking for you."

He smiled at that. "Glad to know at least a few people around here have my back."

I'd started to ask him why he thought Bertie was one of his biggest cheerleaders when Gibbons came back through Bubba's front door with two uniformed officers and Chief Hank Byrd in tow.

The officers, both in crisply pressed black uniforms, looked as if the summer heat hadn't affected them in the least. Chief Hank Byrd, dressed in the same slightly wrinkled putty-colored uniform he'd worn earlier with a new coffee stain on the sleeve, was completely soggy. Gibbons, in the same gray suit he'd had on all day, looked slightly wilted as well. His tired gaze narrowed as he passed me. My first thought was that he'd returned to arrest Bubba for Stan's murder.

Bubba must have thought the same thing. He abandoned his search for the score to "Camellia Nights" and scrambled to his feet.

Gibbons only glanced in Bubba's direction. Instead, he stopped and faced Bixby.

"Mr. Lewis," he said, sounding gravely serious. "We have the results on the grill explosion." He held up a staying hand in front of my face before any words (like "I knew it!") could burst out of my mouth. "Ms. Penn was apparently onto something this morning. The grill at the beach house Bubba and The Embers rented had indeed been rigged to explode."

I knew it!

Chapter 17

Even though I'd promised Bixby I'd be there to watch the crowd gasp with thrilled surprise when he and Bubba emerged from backstage to sing in Stan's place, I didn't make it to the concert that evening.

According to Althea, Ocean Waves band members, while somewhat somber, were thankful to be able to perform one last concert in Stan's honor. They were also excited to play their songs with Bixby Lewis singing lead. The ticket-holders were thrilled with Bixby's performance. Althea gushed about how Bixby had sounded as if he'd been singing the Ocean Waves' beach music his entire life.

She also told me how the police had provided a heavy presence both on and around the pier. While the officers had all been given copies of Candy's latest mug shot, they remained alert for *any* odd activities. Three people were caught in their net and arrested for illegal possession of narcotics. Other than that, the night turned out to be blissfully uneventful.

I wish the same could be said for the night I had.

I had returned to the Chocolate Box a few minutes before five o'clock. I was exhausted from the long, emotional day. Even though I'd known all along that the grill hadn't simply exploded, hearing Gibbons confirm my suspicions had done quite a job on my already frayed nerves.

Bixby could have been *killed*.

Candy was still out there, watching, with murder on her mind.

As I eased out of my car and walked toward the shop, I scanned the surrounding area. A man on the deck of the house next door, surrounded by several boisterous boys, stood wearing nothing but board shorts as he grilled steaks and hot dogs. I fought an urge to shout a warning to the man and his children.

Gas grills can *explode*.

I wondered if I would ever feel comfortable using one again.

The building on the other side of the Chocolate Box was a small real estate office that mainly managed vacation rentals. One of the agents was locking up for the night. She saw me and waved. I gave a stiff wave back.

My attention swiftly returned to the surrounding shadowy wooded area across the street and to the darkness underneath the parked cars. Candy could be out there. Waiting. Plotting.

She'd warned me to stay away from Bixby. Had she followed me to Bubba's house? Had she seen Bixby caressing my hand?

By the time I'd reached the shop's locked front door, my heart was jumping around in my chest as if I'd just run a marathon. My hand shook as I stuck the key into the lock.

"Penn!" a familiar voice shouted.

A pair of arms grabbed me from behind.

I whirled around and swung like a boxer.

My fist hit . . . *nothing*.

The attacker had apparently anticipated my swing and had ducked out of the way. I stared down at the figure crouched on the shop's front porch and smiled.

"Tina!" I shouldn't have been surprised to see my half sister. The last thing she'd said to me that morning was that she was getting on the next plane heading south. "You shouldn't sneak up on me like that. I almost crowned you!"

That last bit wasn't exactly true. She'd taken nearly as many self-defense classes as I had. And, after she dated one of the instructors, her skills at avoidance and escape had become something all the other students envied.

"Is that how you greet your family?" she complained from the porch floorboards.

"Lately it is," I said dryly. I offered my hand to help her get back on her feet. "Just wait until you meet the maternal side of my family. They're a friendly bunch."

"I hope you told them that their nasty behavior only makes you feel at home." Tina had always been Grandmother Cristobel's golden child. According to Cristobel, Tina was everything I was not. She was petite, brunette, and had a talent for mastering any task she attempted.

Cristobel's attempts to put a wedge between me and Tina had backfired, though. Her constant doting on Tina and disparaging of me had only worked to push Tina away from the powerful head of the Penn Empire.

Tina set her suitcase, which had toppled over in the scuffle, back on its wheels. It was a small bag, the kind that could easily fit in the airplane's overhead bin. My sister rarely traveled light, which had to mean she wasn't planning to stay long.

It wasn't that I didn't want to visit with her. I loved spending time with her. I simply didn't want to have to worry about my sister getting hurt by one of Bixby's crazy fans. Tina and Bixby's affair had dominated entertainment news headlines during their brief time together. Most of the headlines had started with something like "America's Most Desirable Bachelor and Top Chicago Fashion Designer . . ." And they usually ended with something silly like "Ate Lunch at Uno Pizzeria." "Were Spotted Strolling Along Lakefront Trail."

To an avid fan like Candy who had delusions that she was dating Bixby, these headlines must have felt like daggers to her heart. I shuddered to think what she might do if she believed Tina was back in Bixby's life.

Tina's royal blue silk skirt swished around her legs as I ushered her inside. Her skirt, which she'd paired with a matching silk tank top and simple opal pendant hanging from a chunky gold cord, reminded me of the clothes Althea liked to wear. She'd pulled her long hair into a simple bun. It was a hairstyle she favored when she worked in her atelier.

As always, she looked perfect.

"Why doesn't anyone call for an airport pickup anymore?" I asked as I quickly locked the door behind us and peered out the window, searching for danger.

"Paranoid as ever, I see," she said.

"Not paranoid. Just careful. There's a crazy woman on the loose who warned me to stay away from Bixby or else. I ignored her and was talking with Bixby just a few minutes ago. She might have seen me."

Tina rolled her eyes. "You don't mean Candy Graves, do you?"

"You've heard of her?" That surprised me.

"Of course I've heard of her. She's been stalking our boy Bixby for years now. Do you remember how I followed him on tour for a few weeks when we first started dating? One night I walked into our hotel room to find Crazy Candy standing over the bed with a carving knife. She'd spread out all my clothes and was in the process of slicing them to shreds."

"That's horrible," I gasped.

She shrugged. "They were off-the-rack outfits. So it was okay." She pulled me into a tight hug. "It's so good to see you. And Bixby isn't dead. That's good news, big sis, isn't it?"

"I should have called to tell you that he was okay." I pulled a cloth and a spray bottle of cleaner out from under the counter. "I'm glad you already heard the news for yourself."

She nodded as she wandered around the shop. "Bixby texted this morning after he'd talked with you. He figured you'd have called me all panicked about having found him in the bonfire."

I squirted the cleaner on the glass display case and wiped off a few fingerprints. "If you knew he was alive, why did you still get on a plane and come?"

"I'm here because I didn't think you could handle it alone." She smirked as she watched me carry my spray bottle to the closest café table.

"Handle what?" I scrubbed the tabletop as if trying to wipe off its varnish. "Keeping Bixby safe? Not my job. Now that they've finally realized someone is trying to kill him, the local police and sheriff's department are both providing him with top-notch protection." Actually, that wasn't exactly the truth. While I hated to lie to my sister, I also didn't want her to know how determined I was to do everything in my power to make sure that Candy (or whoever) was trying to hurt Bixby wouldn't succeed. Stan had already died. No one else would die. Not during my music festival. Not under my watch. "There's nothing you need to help me with, not unless you want to learn how to make bonbons."

"No, silly bean." She grabbed the cloth from my hand before I could move to the next table. "Your love life. I sent Bixby here as a gift to you. Perhaps not a gift. That sounds vulgar. Change that to a nudge. The two of you are perfect for each other."

"No, we're not." I tried to get the cloth back, but she danced away with it. "And I'm not looking for a relationship. It wasn't that long ago that I got rid of the Cheese King, remember?"

She blew a raspberry. "Momentary bad judgment caused by a man's pretty face. We've all been there." She stopped in the middle of the shop and looked around. "Wow, sis. This place is cute. I love the seating area and all the adorable vintage teacups on the shelves. Please tell me you use them."

"Of course we use them," I said with a big grin. Adding mismatched teacups and displaying them on the shelves was something I'd brought to the shop. It was one of the few changes I'd made since inheriting it. "I shop flea markets and garage sales every chance I get to add to the collection. The customer gets to pick out which cup to use."

"What if I wanted a drink to go?" She picked up a delicate teacup with hand-painted cornflowers.

"We have disposable cups as well."

With a nod, she carefully placed the cup back on the shelf and then walked over to the display case. "It's empty. Where's the chocolate?"

"We keep it in the cooler at night. Actually, we completely sold out today. We've been working like crazy to refill our stock. Bertie and Althea might still be in the kitchen. I mean, if you'd like to meet them?"

"Of course I would." She threw an arm over my shoulder. My muscles instantly tensed as if my body expected a blow.

Although she'd always been the friendliest of any of my siblings, it was only recently that she'd completely broken with family ranks and admitted that she loved and worried about me. Her expressions of familial affection felt too new, too dangerous. In the back of my mind, I kept waiting for her to tell me that she'd only been joking, that she agreed with the rest of my family when they told me again and again how I was an embarrassment to the illustrious Penn name.

"Come on, silly bean, show me the way to the kitchen. You know I'm dying to see where the magic happens."

"It's not magic," I said. "There's nothing magical about the chocolate-making process. We're following a process that has been used since the late 1800s."

She snorted. "It's just a figure of speech. I know how you feel about magic."

"Which doesn't exist," I said quickly.

"Of course it doesn't," she agreed.

Unfortunately, the kitchen was quiet and empty. "Bertie and Althea must have left for the night."

I reached for the light switches so I could show Tina the workspace. But when I flipped them on, nothing happened.

"That's strange," I said. "A breaker must have been tripped."

Tina followed me to the office where the fuse box was located. Nothing looked wrong.

"Maybe the power is out in the entire town?" Tina offered.

I chewed the inside of my cheek. "Maybe," I said, but I didn't believe it. Not for a minute. This had to be Candy's doing.

I jogged to the back door. It was still locked, thank goodness. She couldn't get in.

The sun wouldn't set until close to nine o'clock that evening, which meant we weren't sitting in the dark.

I pulled out my phone to call Gibbons. As I dialed, I said to Tina, "You have to taste the chocolates we made today. They're in the cooler in the next room. Come on."

Before the detective's phone had even started to ring, the sound of shattering glass tore through the building.

I jumped.

Tina screamed.

Then there was silence.

We both held our breaths (and each other), listening.

"Hello? Hello?" someone said.

I glanced down at the phone I was clutching with a death grip.

"Hello?" the voice was coming from the phone.

I pressed it to my ear. "Gibbons, someone just broke into the shop," I whispered, surprised at how calm my voice sounded. "I'm in the back hallway with my sister. The front window must have been smashed . . . again."

"*Again?*" Tina whispered in alarm.

"Get out of the building if you can safely manage it," Gibbons told me, sounding equally calm. "Otherwise, lock yourself into the nearest room. I'll send some officers to come get you."

He disconnected the call.

"We need to see what's going on out there," Tina said.

I grabbed her arm before she could put herself in even more danger and dragged her into the office.

"We need to stay here." I pushed the door closed. The knob didn't have a lock, so I tried to wedge a chair underneath it. None of the chairs were tall enough to do the trick.

"We need to get out of here," I whispered. "The back door is just a few steps down the hall. Give me a head start so I can get the door unlocked, okay?"

Tina, her eyes wide with excitement or fear or perhaps a mixture of both, nodded.

I counted to three, tossed open the door, and ran toward the back. It seemed as if my trembling fingers were going to fight with the lock forever. Tina, who hadn't waited but had followed immediately behind me, pressed her hands to my back.

I finally managed to turn the lock and swing the door open.

Both Tina and I ran out onto the back patio. I grabbed her hand and kept running toward the back stairs that led up to the second-story apartment.

"Bertie!" I called as we ran into the apartment.

No answer.

Well, that wasn't exactly true. Stella answered with a high-pitch bark. She charged directly at Tina.

"Oh, this must be your little dog, Stella," she said in a

singsong voice as she reached down to the fluffy puppy, who looked too small and too delicate to harm anything.

Before I could warn Tina, Stella chomped down on her outstretched hand.

"Owwwie! She bit me."

"Don't take it personally. She bites everyone." I locked the door behind us and then tossed Stella several bacon treats. "Is your hand okay?"

Tina flexed her fingers as she looked at the red welts on her knuckles. "I think so."

"Sorry about Stella. I'm still working on getting her to stop doing that." I was making some progress. She hadn't bitten *me* in weeks.

I moved about the apartment, not really accomplishing anything. Nervous energy kept me from standing still. Tina stayed near the door. She eyed Stella, who'd thankfully stopped barking. Instead, my little pup was following me around, occasionally nudging my leg, which was doggie language for "Toss me another bacon treat already."

"If you keep feeding her like that," Tina pointed out, "she's going to end up as round as a fuzzy beach ball."

"It's the only way I know to keep her from barking," I said, just as something crashed below us. "Did you hear that? Do you think it's the police?"

I rushed into Bertie's bedroom, which had windows that overlooked the street. The street was empty.

"Do you smell smoke?" Tina shouted from the other room.

"Smoke? No. No. No. That little fire starter isn't going to ruin my shop. This building is over a hundred years old. I can't stay up here and let her just burn the place down." I unlatched the door and started to charge out of the apartment to get back downstairs.

Tina grabbed me around the waist. "You can't go back in. Not if there's a fire."

"We can't let her destroy the shop. Mabel picked me because she believed I could protect her shop, her heritage. Let go of me."

She tightened her grip.

"Police," a deep voice shouted downstairs.

"Thank goodness," I said.

Stella greeted the officer's announcement with a fanfare of yips.

"Let's get down there." I tugged at Tina. She finally relented and followed me as I hurried down to the shop's back door.

"Officer!" I called to one of the uniformed men searching the building's perimeter. His hand moved toward his gun. "I'm Penn, the owner. This is my sister. We're the ones who called Detective Gibbons."

He gave a sharp nod.

"I smelled smoke," Tina said. "Is there a fire?"

"I don't know ma'am. I haven't been inside."

"Can we go inside?" I eyed the back door as if it were the entrance to Shangri-La. "I need to get in there."

I needed to see what havoc Candy had wrought.

"Not until it's clear." He got on the radio. After some back and forth with the other officers, he hooked his radio back on his belt.

"The intruder has fled the scene," he said. "We have men searching the area."

"Is there a fire?" I demanded.

"There was. It's been contained."

"I need to get in there." My voice turned shrill as I pictured a shop in ruins and all of those chocolates we'd spent hours crafting melting into pools of goo.

After some more back and forth on the radio with his fellow officers, the cop led us inside with the admonishment not to touch anything. The police weren't letting us walk through the crime scene as a favor to us. No, they were professionals after all. They wanted me to tell them what had been moved, broken, or even stolen. After all, I might have simply been a bad business-woman who kept a messy shop.

My mouth dropped open at the sight of the office. It had been wrecked. All of the pieces of paper that had once been in the file drawers or in the desk now lay scattered everywhere. Desk drawers lay in splinters on the floor.

The remnants of a small fire still smoldered in the wire trash can.

If I hadn't been here and if I hadn't called the police right away, I might have lost the shop. Heck, Tina and I had been in the shop when Candy had broken in looking to prove she was the one and only woman for Bixby. If we hadn't escaped when we had, I shuddered to think what she might have done to us.

Chapter 18

The next morning, Bertie and I arrived at the shop before sunrise. The police had finished investigating the crime scene around ten o'clock the previous night and had returned possession of the shop to us. A piece of plywood had been nailed to the large opening where the plate glass window had been. The glaziers had promised to arrive by seven thirty this morning to replace it yet again.

Thankfully, Candy had only had time to spill all the paperwork from the office in order to make her trash-can fire. She hadn't touched the bonbons or truffles we'd made yesterday. Nor had she done any damage to the front of the shop (save for the broken window). The kitchens had also escaped unscathed.

"Don't you think it odd that Candy didn't break the glass display case or smash my teacup collection?" I asked Bertie as I sorted the papers still lying in jumbled heaps on the office floor. I'd brought Stella downstairs with us. She "helped" by pushing her nose under a rather thick pile of papers as if trying to tunnel through them.

"Everything you've said that woman has done seems odd," Bertie said as she dumped ashes from the trash can into a plastic bag. "She's plumb crazy. I'm just thanking heaven and the angels above us that she wasn't able to do more damage."

As I glanced at the papers I was picking up from the floor, I couldn't help but realize I had no idea what many of them were about. Since taking over the shop, I'd spent very little time in Mabel's old office. I'd used the room more as a place for Stella to occasionally hang out during the day than as a place to do paperwork.

I started to sort the papers into piles: those that pertained to the charity work Mabel had done over the years, those that pertained to the village of Cabruca in Brazil where the chocolate beans were grown, receipts for the shop, purchase orders, and tax documents from the past . . . *gracious* . . . forty years.

Stella growled and came up from one of her paper tunnels with a yellowed flyer in her mouth. She started tearing at it. While I doubted the old piece of paper was of any importance, I didn't want to take the chance. I tossed Stella a piece of bacon. While she gobbled the treat, I scooped up the paper.

It was a flyer for the Summer Solstice Beach Music Festival. No, it wasn't for the one that was happening this week, which I had thought was the first concert of its kind in Camellia Beach. This flyer was from 1975. And it stated on the top of the paper that the festival was in its *ninth year*.

Apparently Bubba had simply resurrected a festival from the past, from when he was (I quickly did the math in my head) not much older than twenty years old. Why hadn't he told me about the festival's long history? We could have used the fact that we were reviving a popular event from the past in our advertising.

According to what I was reading, The Embers had been scheduled to play both during the opening concert and at the grand finale. On the bottom, the flyer listed the singers with the band.

Singers. Plural.

From what everyone had told me, I had assumed Stan

Frasier had been the one and only singer with The Embers. After all, his leaving had meant the band's end.

The name of the second singer surprised me even more than the fact that the band had multiple singers. I read the name again, just to be certain my tired mind wasn't playing tricks on me.

Singing for The Embers were Stan Frasier and Bertie Bays.

Bertie Bays.

My Bertie Bays.

I looked up at her. She was dusting off one of the filing cabinets and complaining that we needed to get busy in the kitchen instead of messing around in here like a couple of maids.

She was a singer?

With The Embers?

"You sing?" I asked her.

"Of course I do. You've heard me. It's good for the soul. Now let's get out of here; we have a shop to run. These papers can wait, but those chocolates aren't going to melt themselves."

"No, I mean professionally. You used to sing professionally?"

She wrinkled her nose as if my question had made the room stink.

I held up the yellowed and half-chewed flyer. "You sang with The Embers."

"Don't be silly, Penn. I would sometimes get up and perform with the boys. It wasn't professional, not by any means."

"And that's why you've been so worried about Bubba? Because you sang with his band? Because he was a fellow band member?"

"I'd worry about any member of the community if they went missing or were accused of a crime I knew they couldn't have committed. You know that. We'll be opening soon. So if you want to get anything useful done this morning, we'd better get busy in the kitchen."

When I pressed her to talk more about her musical past,

Bertie cut her dark brown eyes in my direction before saying, "You're welcome to waste your time in here thinking about things that no longer matter. The chocolate is waiting in the kitchen, which is where I intend to be."

A woman of her word, she marched out of the office.

Since Bertie was right—we did have work to do in the kitchen—I made sure Stella had everything she needed (dog bed, water dish, treats). My pup's outrageously large butterfly-wing-shaped ears quivered with excitement when she realized I was letting her stay with the paper tunnels she'd created. As I closed the door, I heard a loud rip. I hoped she hadn't sunk her teeth into anything important.

Although I followed Bertie into the kitchen with the intention of getting to work, I couldn't stop the questions from spilling out of my mouth. I mean, who wouldn't be curious?

And yet, no amount of prodding would get Bertie to talk about her old singing days. She was too focused on the chocolate and on making sure I didn't mess up this current batch of raspberry bonbons to talk about anything else.

*   *   *

An hour before opening time, Bertie and I started the process of making another batch of milk chocolate. Unlike most chocolate shops that purchased their chocolate from wholesalers, we made all of our chocolates directly from the bean. It was an intensive process that took several days. By doing it ourselves, we were able to blend different bean varieties to create a wide range of tones, from something so bitter it crinkled your lips to chocolate with an earthiness that tasted as alive as the rainforest itself to the super-sweet flavors found in children's candies during the holidays.

Despite the disasters I'd encountered when following Mabel's recipes for her amazing truffles and bonbons, the act of making the chocolate came almost as second nature to me. Just by smelling the various nibs, I could imagine how the finished product would turn out. My confidence was so strong that I never followed a recipe. Instead, I listened to my instincts.

Bertie smiled as I picked an Ecuadorian nib that consistently produced a light nutty flavor and paired it with the shop's own Amar bean with its complex and sweetly spicy flavors. It was a pairing I'd used when making dark chocolate but had yet to try in a lighter, sweeter milk chocolate.

I processed the blended nibs in a grinder that worked very much like a household juicer to produce a thick brown paste, which was the chocolate liquor. The flavor at this point reminded me of a horribly strong espresso instead of the basis for what I considered the only kind of dessert worth eating. Why waste calories on anything that wasn't chocolate?

While I poured the chocolate liquor into an electric stone melangeur—two large marble grinding stones that further refined the chocolate, mixing it at the molecular level with the cocoa butter, sugar, and powdered milk—Bertie left to supervise the replacement of the plate glass window out front.

With the lid on, the melangeur whirled away, transforming the mix into what I hoped would be a smooth milky chocolate that both surprised and pleased the taster. I wouldn't know the results for two days. That was the minimum amount of time the mixture needed to be ground. Any less time would produce an unpleasantly gritty chocolate.

Since I had some time before the shop opened up, I pulled out Mabel's recipe book and attempted to make another batch of the raspberry bonbons to add to the ones we'd made that morning. Over the past couple of days, we'd sold more of them than any of the other chocolates combined, probably because the raspberries were in season and nearly bursting with sweet juices.

Even though it was a simple recipe, I left nothing to chance and dutifully followed every step in Mabel's recipe book. As nine o'clock approached, I stared down at what I'd made and wanted to howl with frustration.

The raspberry filling oozed everywhere, while the outside chocolate coating hadn't melted correctly. What I ended up with was an unsightly, lumpy mess that tasted faintly of cough syrup.

"What's wrong?" Bertie rushed into the room. "What happened?"

I must have actually howled my frustration. "Nothing." I tossed to the floor the dish towel that was hanging from my apron string. "Isn't it time to open up?"

"In a minute," Bertie said as she picked up the dish towel. "What's going—?" she'd started to ask, but then spotted the mess on the prep counter. "Oh, are those raspberry bonbons?"

"They were supposed to be. But as you can see . . ." I didn't want to talk about it. "I'm thinking about making a spicy hot pepper chocolate bonbon and calling them bonbon fires. Get it? Bonbon fires, because they'll be hot?" I said as I started gathering up the few mixing bowls I'd used for Mabel's recipe.

Bertie frowned at my raspberry mess. "Bonbon fires? Mabel's never made a recipe for something like that."

"I know." I'd studied my maternal grandmother's recipe book until I'd practically had them all memorized. Too bad all that studying hadn't helped me master any of them. I couldn't figure out what the heck I was doing wrong. "I thought I'd play with some flavors and see how it comes out. What I'm picturing is something that would be extra spicy with an infusion of sweet."

Bertie's frown deepened. She poked her finger into one of the raspberry globs and tasted the jelly that stuck to her finger. "I don't know, Penn," she said with a gagging cough. "It sounds like an interesting idea, but don't you think you should stick to learning Mabel's recipes before trying to do something on your own? I'd hate for you to waste your time and energy on something that will turn out like . . ." She moved to the sink to scrub the remaining jelly off her hand. She splashed a little of the tap water into her mouth while she was at it.

"I suppose you're right," I mumbled.

Of course she was right, dang it. I could barely melt a pot of chocolate without burning it. But that didn't stop the explosion of flavor opposites—hot and cold, spicy and sweet—from playing around in my head, urging me to give it a try.

"Spend some more time this afternoon working on some of Mabel's easier recipes," Bertie suggested as I followed her to the front of the shop. She unlocked the front door while I flipped over the "Open" sign.

I agreed to stick to Mabel's recipe book, but I wasn't in love with the idea. None of the recipes ever worked out for me. No matter how hard I tried to follow the steps, I seemed to always miss something. Or, as in the case of the raspberry bonbons, several things.

I filled a large coffee mug for myself and frowned as I looked at the spools of red, white, and blue ribbons that we'd used to tie Congressman Ezell's bonbon packages. Seeing them got me thinking about Stan's murder again and the bonbons I'd found Thursday night at the deadly bonfire. Because Stan had once aspired to be as famous as Bixby, even to the point of dressing like the superstar, I'd assumed he was the one who'd plucked the bag of bonbons from the trash after Bixby tossed it.

But wouldn't it make more sense that his stalker Candy Graves, who believed she was Bixby's lover, had fished it out of the garbage since the bag was something Bixby had held? I wondered if her house was filled with mementos she'd collected from rooting around in his trash. If that was the case, the cellophane bag of bonbons could prove Candy was at the scene of Stan's murder.

I also wondered if Gibbons had found any fingerprints on the bag. I doubted he'd tell me even if he had. Still, it couldn't hurt to ask. My mentioning it might give him the nudge he needed to move him in the right direction. Gibbons still considered both Candy's stalking and the exploding grill that had singed Bixby's eyebrows unrelated to Stan's murder investigation, which troubled me. Although he'd stopped by the shop last night, he'd done it in an unofficial capacity. He was a homicide detective, he'd bluntly pointed out. He didn't investigate break-ins. Candy might have been up to mischief—criminal mischief—but he didn't consider her a murder suspect.

When I'd told him he was wrong, he'd patted my head and told me to get some sleep. Okay, he hadn't actually patted my head, but he might as well have mussed my short blonde hair by dismissing me and my concerns so thoroughly.

"A break-in and murder are two completely different crimes," he'd told me.

I couldn't stop thinking he was wrong. Worries kept spinning around in my head as I filled the morning orders. Worries that no one was taking the threat Candy posed seriously; worries that she would get away with murder for the simple reason that she'd killed the wrong man. We sold out of our chocolate croissants within the hour, but that wasn't unusual for a sunny Saturday morning.

While I refilled the coffee urn at the coffee and tea station, Bertie answered the shop's phone. She beamed a wide smile when she first answered, but her grin swiftly faded. By the time she'd hung up, which had to be less than a minute into the conversation, her expression had turned fierce.

"I need to run an errand," she called over to me. "I should be back before lunch."

"Is everything okay?" I asked.

Although I was sure she'd heard me, she acted as if I hadn't spoken. With car keys in hand and purse slung over her shoulder, she hurried out the door.

My first instinct was to run after her, but I couldn't leave the shop. Instead, I called Althea and told her about the mysterious phone call that had upset her mother. Althea promised to go looking for her and to make sure everything was okay.

I checked my watch: ten thirty. I still hadn't seen or heard from Tina. This morning she'd grunted at me when I'd told her I was heading to the shop. I'd taken the grunt to mean she'd come down for breakfast as soon as she woke up.

Certainly, she was awake and moving around by now. Concerned, I texted her.

She texted back, "On my way."

A minute later she texted, "What's wrong with your cat?"

"Bertie's cat," I corrected. "Nothing's wrong with Troubadour."

"His fur fell out. That's not normal."

"It's OK," I wrote. "He's hairless."

"Why?"

"Don't know. Born that way."

A few minutes later the door swung open as if pushed by a strong wind. The copper bell above the door tinkled a wild staccato tune. "Hey, Tina," I called without looking up from the order I was filling. It was a large box of classic chocolate-covered cherry bonbons for Arthur Jenkins, the slightly hunched octogenarian from the Pink Pelican Inn. He was buying the bonbons for his (hopefully) soon-to-be fiancée. Orders like these were some of my favorites. "I'll be done with this in a minute."

"No rush," a deep voice answered. Definitely not Tina.

I looked up to see Harley Dalton coming toward me. He was dressed casually in dark green board shorts that showed off his muscular legs and a white rash guard shirt that showed off his buff chest. My heart did its stupid double-pitapat whenever I saw him. And seeing him dressed like a surfing god made my heart beat extra quick. I stopped what I was doing and heaved a slow, deep breath as a way to tell my silly heart to settle down.

"Good morning, counselor," Arthur shook Harley's hand. "I see you're taking the weekend off. Good for you. Good for you."

"I promised Gavin a day on the waves," Harley answered, referring to his son. "But I do have a few pieces of business that need my attention first."

"And here I thought it was my chocolates that lured you here," I teased.

"Son, her chocolates are delicious. Nearly as good as Mabel's, God rest her soul. And she's got such a pretty face too. If I lived upstairs from this shop like you do, Harleston, I'd be too big to fit through that door over there in no time."

"You're too kind, Mr. Jenkins." I tied a shiny gold bow to secure the box and carefully handed it to him. "Give my best to Miss Harris. And you'll have to let me know how things turn out."

"After she eats a few of your chocolate-covered cherries, there's no way she'll say no."

I smiled as Arthur sauntered happily out of the store, but it was a melancholy smile. Everyone gave me credit for the truffles and bonbons we sold when in reality they were Bertie's creations, not mine.

Oh, how I wished they were mine.

"What can I do for you today, counselor?" I asked as I handed Harley a to-go coffee cup.

"Thank you. I heard back from Florence. She wants to meet with you. This afternoon. In your apartment. At three. I told her that you work during the day and that you would require more advance notice. But you know Florence. She doesn't take no for an answer. So here I am, telling you when she wants to meet. Just say the word and I'll tell her you're not available. And if you'd feel more comfortable, I can arrange for the two of you to meet at my office and not at your apartment and at a time and day that works for you."

My initial reaction was to tell Harley that he was right, three o'clock today wasn't a good time. I had the festival and Bixby's safety to worry about. At the same time, I didn't want this meeting dangling over my head like the sword of Damocles, always wondering what spiteful thing Florence had to say to me.

And why did she need to say it in private?

All I wanted to do was find my mother. Why couldn't Mabel's children understand that?

"Tell her I'll meet with her." It actually hurt to get those words out of my mouth. Why was I so worried about meeting with Florence? She couldn't upset me any more than she already had. And perhaps, just perhaps, she might even be able to help me in my quest to find her missing sister Carolina, who had to be my mother.

"Penn, you don't have to do this," Harley said quietly.

I shook my head. "No. Today. At three. Might as well get it over with, right?"

"Are you sure?" he asked.

"I'm sure." Yes, I was sure. I needed to do this.

"If you'd like, I can sit in on the meeting with you. We don't know what she has to say. I hope she's coming to offer an olive branch—"

"But given our past encounters, we all know that's unlikely," I finished for him. "You don't mind coming? Even on your day with Gavin?"

"Not when it's for you." He reached over the counter and put his hand over mine. "Besides, Gavin has plans to meet up with his friend Tom after lunch." He sighed. "That boy of mine is growing up too fast. He doesn't want to hang out with his dad all the time anymore."

"Kids these days," I said with a half smile.

Things had been so awkward between us for months that it felt odd (nice, but definitely odd) to have him hold my hand and talk to me. Really talk to me.

"I don't know why—" I started to say at the same time he said, "I know that we've been—"

Before either of us could voice what had been left unsaid for months, Tina came crashing through the shop's front door with the force of a hurricane. The ends of the colorful red, white, and blue silk scarf she'd skillfully wrapped around her head like a turban fluttered in the breeze she'd kicked up.

"Hey, sis," her voice boomed. Her arm was tossed over Bixby's shoulder. Her perfectly plucked eyebrows bounced up and down as she looked at me, then at Harley, who was still touching my hand, and finally at Bixby. Apparently she was as incorrigible as Althea in her attempts to set me up with a man. "Lookie who I brought with me."

Chapter 19

I wondered, and not for the first time, if people who grew up with a mother in their lives found themselves in this kind of trouble. And when I say trouble, I mean man trouble. I'd always figured mothers taught their daughters some secret tricks—passed down through the generations—on how to talk to and manage the male of the species.

I wished someone had taught me something—*anything*—in that regard, because in that moment, as I bit down hard on my bottom lip, I felt like a fish flopping around in a marsh flat at low tide. I had no clue what I needed to say to Harley, who I was convinced had been about to bear his soul, or to Bixby, who Tina had assured me was my perfect match.

"I see you've been down to the beach already," I said to Tina, deciding to ignore the men who were staring at each other while at the same time pretending they weren't.

"I took a little stroll," she said. She was dressed for a day at the beach in a red bikini top with white polka dots and blue short-shorts with a sporty white stripe outlining the curve of her hips.

She looked stylish, as always. I sometimes wished I had just a thimbleful of her fashion sense. I also wished she'd wipe that goofy grin from her face. "I thought you were sleeping in."

"I never sleep in." She laughed as she said it.

I shook my head and smiled at her absurd lie. Just the day before my not-so-early phone call had woken her up from a deep sleep.

"Anyway," she continued, "my stroll just happened to lead me to Bixby's beach rental. We started catching up." She hugged his arm to her side as she pulled him over to the front counter and crowded Harley out of the way.

"That rude woman pushing at you is my sister, Tina." I swatted her on the shoulder before adding, "Harley Dalton is my . . ." Maybe I wouldn't have stumbled over what I wanted to say in that moment if I'd had a mother to guide me on how to act around men. Since I didn't even know my mother's name (*it had to be Carolina, didn't it?*), I ended up sputtering, ". . . m-my lawyer. He's my lawyer."

This description of what he was to me felt inadequate and not at all fair to Harley. He was more than my lawyer. He was my neighbor, my friend, and someone who made my heart race like a frightened jackrabbit's.

"Lawyer?" Tina scoffed. "You look more like a surfer than a professional anything. From what I've heard, my sister has some complicated legal matters, including a lawsuit for this place. Are you sure you're up to the task?"

"He is a surfer. But that doesn't mean he's brainless. Harley knows this island and the law. So I'll thank you not to question his abilities. I'm happy with his services and that should be enough for you."

Tina smiled sheepishly and held up her hands. "Of course, silly bean."

Did I detect a mischievous twinkle in her eyes?

"Thank you for your vote of confidence, Penn," Harley said as he headed toward the door with barely a nod in Tina's or Bixby's direction. "I'll see you at three."

141

"What's at three?" Tina asked.

Instead of answering, I pulled a plate from one of the shelves behind the counter. "You didn't get a chance to taste any of the chocolates last night. Do you have time to sit down and have a snack?"

I started to fix a plate of chocolates, making sure there'd be enough for everyone to have at least three pieces.

Bixby's entire face brightened at the sight of them. "I always have time for chocolate." His voice deepened as he added, "Especially *your* chocolate."

"You are such a shameless flirt," I said as I carried the tray to a nearby table.

It was past the morning rush. The only customers we had at the moment were the red-haired Fox and unnaturally black-haired Alvin. The two band members were sitting on the café sofa while downing coffees with their heads pressed together in serious conversation. They'd been that way for more than an hour.

Since they didn't need me to wait on them, I sat down with Bixby and Tina and indulged in a creamy white chocolate raspberry rosewater bonbon.

"Did you enjoy my concert last night?" Bixby asked after he gobbled a sunflower buttercup (shaped like the flower and filled with sunflower butter instead of peanut butter). He then tossed one of Bertie's sea salt caramels into his mouth.

"I wasn't able to come. Police were here and all," I said, surprised he'd forgotten about last night's arson attempt. Tina had called and warned him about it after the police had released us and the building from their investigation.

"Oh . . . right . . . sorry about that." His cheeks turned slightly red as he realized his blunder. I quickly forgave him. He was a big star, after all, and had more important things worrying his mind than an arson attempt at some unimportant chocolate shop.

"I heard it was a good concert," I said, handing him a dark chocolate ginger bonbon. I'd made these—with Bertie guiding every step of the way—from a recipe I'd found tucked away in the back of Mabel's master cookbook. Although the ginger had a bite to it, it didn't satisfy my vision of creating "Bonbon Fires" for the shop.

He nodded as he chewed. "Wow, this is delicious. You're really good at this chocolate-making thing."

"Bertie's the expert. I'm still learning," I said. Neither Bixby nor Tina seemed to hear me. They were both too busy enjoying their chocolates.

"Whoa!" Tina grabbed the edge of the table and heaved a deep breath. "This doesn't taste like anything I've ever had before."

I'd made sure she'd gotten one of the Chocolate Box's special reserve 100% Amar chocolate truffles. To say they were amazing would be an understatement. The pleasure they gave the palate bordered on the obscene.

"It's pretty good, isn't it?" I said. I went on to explain the history of the rare Amar bean and how my mother's family had formed a partnership about a century ago with the tiny Brazilian village that grew it.

Tina's eyes widened. "You need to move this shop and expand your operations. You could make millions of dollars—hundreds of millions—selling this chocolate."

I shook my head. "That's not what Mabel wanted. The bean is rare not just because no one other than the villagers grow it, but also because the harsh conditions where it's grown are key to the flavor. Grow it anywhere else and you'll lose its complex taste. We barely have enough of the bean to satisfy what we sell in the shop. Most of the chocolates we make have only a small percentage of the Amar bean mixed in to enhance the flavor."

"Then charge hundreds of dollars for each truffle and sell them only to the rich," Tina said, as if it were that easy.

Bixby had reached over and taken the second special reserve 100% Amar chocolate truffle from the plate. After tasting it, he started nodding in agreement with Tina. "You'd be famous."

"I'm already famous." Well, my family was. "Has it made me happy? No."

"But this is crazy good," he pressed. "You need to transform this shop into an exclusive but national brand."

"You should," Tina agreed. "Father could help you launch—"

"I'm happy with this little shop as it is," I said sharply before she could finish that thought. The last thing I wanted was for my father's side of the family to get involved with what I was doing here. This was my shop, not theirs. "Why don't you let me run the business how my grandmother wanted me to run it? If that doesn't work out, I'll take your advice and change the business plan." I tried not to sound offended by their well-meaning advice. It wasn't as if I hadn't already had the same idea: charge a hundred or two hundred dollars for each chocolate bar we made and wholesale them only to high-end boutique bakeries. But that would involve constant travel to hand-sell the brand as well as national (but targeted) advertising. It would involve leaving Camellia Beach.

Although my absence would make Police Chief Byrd a happy man, I'd miss this place.

"You like this life?" Bixby asked.

"Love it," I said.

He looked around at the mismatched cups and saucers crowding the shelves on the walls and gave me a sad little smile. "I see."

Neither of them said much else. I'm sure it was because they were both too polite to tell me I was crazy. I decided to change the subject. Since Bixby seemed to like the spotlight so much, I doubted he'd mind my shining the light back on him.

"You know, Bixby, we really shouldn't have stayed quiet about that first rock Candy tossed through the shop's window. It might have saved us and your eyebrows if we'd reported it to the police right away," I said. "I can't believe I thought—"

"I'm sorry about what happened last night." Bixby shrugged as he said it. "I'll pay for the damage."

"You can't just throw money at this problem. Not and expect it to go away."

Tina nudged him. "This is why she's perfect for you. She won't hold back. She'll always tell you what's on her mind."

"Of course I won't hold back. He could have been killed when the grill exploded." I shook my head. "Well, mister, that's not going to happen. Not on my watch."

Stan had already died. Had Candy killed him?

Bixby stroked his eyebrows. They were no longer singed and missing in some places. They were thick and perfect. How had he managed to get them to grow back like that overnight? "No, I don't think the issue we had with the grill could have seriously hurt me. The explosion wasn't that big," he said. "Candy wants attention. And the more attention we give her, the more she'll do stupid things and make your place look like this." He gestured toward the shop's interior, which caused me to frown and look around.

Bertie and I had worked hard to make sure everything was returned to normal before the shop opened. The interior was cute and kitschy with a touch of midcentury modern. Did he think the blending of styles made it look as if a crazy stalker had wrecked it?

Oh, it didn't matter. I squinted as I looked at his perfect

eyebrows again. "How in the world did you get those to grow back so quickly?"

"His eyebrows? They're prosthetics," Tina answered for him.

"Prosthetics?" Who knew such a thing existed?

"Always have to give my best to the fans, even if it means getting falsies." He stroked his eyebrows as if they were fluffy pets. "I have to say that my surprising everyone by singing last night was a brilliant idea." (It had been his idea.) "I can't remember when I had so much fun."

I glared at Tina. How could she think Bixby and I would make a good match? Sure, his good looks made me want to weep with joy, but he clearly cared more about himself than about anything or anyone else.

"We sang all these oldies songs," he was saying. "The crowd sang along."

Since I doubted he would say anything that would help me figure out how to stop Candy from doing any more harm, I continued to glare at Tina.

"You should have heard the fans. They went nuts at the first few chords of many of the Ocean Waves songs. Did you know your partner, Bertie, used to sing with The Embers?"

I broke eye contact with Tina and whirled back toward Bixby with dizzying speed. "Wait. What?"

"Did you know your—" he repeated, speaking much more slowly and enunciating every word.

"Yes. Yes. I heard what you said. Who told you about Bertie's singing past? And why was anyone talking about her anyway? It wasn't as if she went to the concert last night."

"No, she was there. The entire town—except for you and Tina—came to hear me sing," Bixby said, forgetting that he'd kept his decision to sing last night a surprise. "I was singing with Bubba and looked down and spotted her. She was up front, crowded against the stage with all my other diehard fans. They call themselves the Bixettes." He looked around and lowered his voice before adding, "You might want to have a talk with her. She's got a huge crush on me."

"How do you know?" Tina asked, sounding surprised he'd even suggest such a thing.

He turned to Tina with raised eyebrows and a frown that seemed to say, "Do you really have to ask?"

"How do you know?" I repeated Tina's question because, yes, we really did have to ask.

"When you've performed in as many concerts as I have, you know the look."

He clasped his hands and pressed them to his neck as he tilted his head to one side. He widened his eyes and let his jaw go slack as if he'd just spotted one of Camellia Beach's insanely beautiful sunsets.

"You know, like that," he said with a grin.

"And Bubba was onstage with you when this happened?" I asked, thinking it was Bubba, not Bixby, that Bertie had been ogling. Why wouldn't Bertie just go ahead and admit she had feelings for Bubba?

"Yeah, he rocked on his bass guitar while filling in some of the harmony. We were worried that some of the band members would get choked up without Stan there, you know?" He looked around. "Do you have any more of those dark chocolate truffles?"

Tina looked at me and smiled encouragingly, which only convinced me that she'd lost her mind. Why in the world would she think I'd want to date this guy? She must have—

I jumped to my feet. *"Get him out of here,"* I hissed.

Whether he was shallow or not, I'd made a promise to myself to protect him while he stayed on the island.

"What's going on?" Tina said as she followed my lead and rose from her chair.

"Take him out through the back door," I said. Because at that moment the grinning woman about to waltz through the front door was none other than the rock-throwing, grill-exploding, shop-wrecking Candy Graves.

Chapter 20

"I don't know why you're making such a fuss." Candy blinked her big doe eyes and tilted her head to one side just as Bixby had done a few minutes earlier when aping how women who loved him gaze in his direction.

She'd draped herself in innocence: a white sundress, white sandals—even her long honey-colored hair had been styled to resemble an angelic halo. I didn't know who she was trying to fool with that. I certainly wasn't buying it.

I crossed my arms over my chest and kept my body well out of her arm's reach. "As I've already told you, Candy, you aren't welcome here. I've already called the police."

"Why did you do that? I haven't done anything to you." She threw up her arms.

"You broke that window." I pointed to the large plate glass window that had cost a ridiculous amount of money to replace before business hours and on a weekend.

"An act of passion, and it was only a window," she said as she crossed her arms in a way that elevated her breasts.

"You broke it twice," I said. "And you tried to burn down the shop."

"You're crazy."

"You're calling me crazy?" Was she serious?

"Are you hard of hearing, old lady? Where's Bixby?"

I glanced over at Fox and Alvin. They were still sitting on the sofa in the corner. But they'd stopped their conversation. Both men were frowning as they watched us.

Fox nodded in my direction. He inched forward as if getting ready to put those long, willowy legs of his into action. They'd heard about Candy the day before when Gibbons had informed us that the grill had been rigged to explode. The detective had also shown everyone, including Fox and Alvin, her most recent mug shot. The two men had obviously recognized her.

Candy didn't seem to notice them. She kept glancing over her shoulder, watching the road. Was she watching for the police?

I squinted toward the road as well.

Come on.

Come on.

The police should be here already. It was a small island.

And where was Bixby's security team? If they'd been watching over our superstar, why would they let Candy waltz into the shop in the first place?

"Bixby texted me," she said. Her voice warbled as she glanced out toward the street again. She held up her phone, as if showing me her phone's blank screen would be proof enough that Bixby had actually contacted her. "He told me to meet him here. He said he needed to talk to me."

"Even if he did text you, I'm telling you to leave. I don't have the money to fix anything else you might break in my shop."

Fox and Alvin both stood and took a step toward us in a show of support.

Candy didn't seem to notice them. "I'm here to talk to my boyfriend, not hurt anyone."

"Bixby's not your boyfriend," I said, as gently as I could to someone who'd tried to burn down my shop. In retrospect, my words probably sounded more like a slap than a gentle reminder to a woman with some serious delusions.

Her lips twisted. "That's an ugly thing to say. What do you know?"

"I know you set a fire in here last night."

"That's not true!" she shouted, just as a siren blared in the distance. Candy looked left and right as if frantically searching for an exit. She tossed an ugly curse in my direction and then shouted, "You can't have him!"

She ran like a fleeing coyote out of the shop and across the street to a stretch of vacant land, where she disappeared into a thick stand of oak trees and scrubby underbrush.

"She's certifiable," Fox said as he and Alvin joined me just outside the shop door. The siren grew louder.

Alvin nodded and then said in his thick accent, "Screechin' harpy. Done remind me of my Marella."

The back of my neck prickled as I scanned the woods where Candy had fled. Something about her coming into the shop as if she'd been invited felt . . . wrong. Why would she come here? After what she'd done last night, she had to know she wouldn't be welcome. She had to know I'd call the police.

The whole situation felt like a weird setup.

Like she was being set up?

No, no. Not her. Me. It felt like *I* was being set up.

"Crap. Get down." I grabbed Alvin's arm, since he was the one standing next to me. I pulled him down to the porch's wooden deck in front of the store as I dropped to my knees.

Fox followed, dropping into an ungainly crouch just as a loud pop-pop-pop-pop, like firecrackers going off, shattered the air. No, not the air. That loud popping shattered the plate glass window behind us.

"No! Not again!" I wailed as tempered glass cubes from my brand-new window rained down on our heads.

*   *   *

"I've been running all over hell's half acre this morning thanks to what happened here last night, Penn. What trouble are you kicking up now?" Chief Byrd complained as he stepped out of his cruiser. He yanked up his ill-fitting putty-colored pants and sauntered toward the three of us. Fox, Alvin, and I were huddled together, shattered glass hanging like snowflakes in our hair and on our shoulders.

"Some chick with less than a dozen eggs in her henhouse done been shootin' at us!" Alvin cried.

"It was Candy Graves," I said as I shook the glass from my hair. "She was here."

Byrd cursed.

"That's right," Fox said. "The gal was having a dying duck fit when she left. Took off that way when she heard your siren."

"I don't know what he's saying," I said, hooking my thumb in Fox's direction, "but Candy threatened me, ran off in that direction, and then the bullets starting flying."

"That's what I said," Fox cried.

"It is? I really need to learn this Southern lingo."

The skin around Fox's eyes crinkled as he smiled and said, "That you do, girl."

"She went in there?" Byrd gazed into the woods for about a solid minute before getting on his radio to call for backup.

The officers who arrived first were from the county sheriff's department. These were the professionals. They'd dealt with live gunfire many times before and knew how to secure the area and conduct a thorough search for evidence.

The officers also ushered Alvin, Fox, and me back into the shop. I started brewing fresh coffee to offer to the investigators. While I stood on a stool and poured a jug of spring water into the commercial coffee maker's large tank, Chief Byrd moved to stand behind me.

"How can I help you?" I asked as he continued to stand there with his arms over his wide chest, watching me work and not saying anything.

"You could leave town and take your killers with you," he grumbled.

"They aren't my killers," I pointed out. "The coffee will be ready in a few minutes. You're welcome to a cup."

After peering into the glass display case at Bertie's sea salt chocolate caramels, he said, "Didn't have crime in Camellia Beach until you arrived."

"So you've told me." I forced the words through my teeth. There were so many other things dancing on my tongue. Things like, "Why aren't you doing your job and keeping us safe instead of blaming your shortcomings on me?" Too bad letting those words fly really wouldn't be productive to my long-term life in Camellia Beach.

I kept my hands busy as I waited for the police to finish their business, waited for word to come that they'd caught Candy, waited for someone to tell me I could reopen my shop. The longer I waited, the more my nerves prickled. I felt as if I was grabbing onto a cactus over and over, getting more and more stinging needles stuck in my hands while accomplishing nothing.

Finally, about an hour after the shooting, Detective Gibbons arrived. He climbed out of his ancient Crown Victoria looking composed and in command. His suit's creases were neatly pressed. His shirt was so white that it nearly glowed in the bright sunlight.

While I waited anxiously at the shop's door, my heart pounding with nervous energy, he walked down the road to talk with the county officer who appeared to be in charge of the crime scene.

"Penn?" Alvin called to me from the sofa where he and Fox had settled while we waited to be told we could leave.

"Yeah?" I had to force myself to turn my back to the detective and answer Alvin. Actually, it took all my willpower not to run across the street, grab the detective's arm, and start babbling about what had happened. Chief Byrd had ordered us to stay put until someone told us otherwise. "Do you need something?"

"We're starving like all get out over here. Will you sell us something to eat?" When I didn't answer right away, Alvin whined, "Pleeease?"

I checked my watch. It was close to eleven thirty. "Oh, of course. Let me fix you a plate."

Although all the croissants had sold out, a few chocolate chip sticky buns and a chocolate cinnamon roll remained from this morning's shipment from the Charleston bakery that provided all of our baked goods. I placed the pastries on two plates and carried them over to the hungry musicians. "It's on the house," I told them. It wasn't their fault they were trapped in the shop with me. "Would you like some more coffee?"

They did. As I refilled their mugs, we chatted about the festival. "If being famous means contending with crazy women like that Candy Graves, I'm glad we never left the island," Fox said after biting into his sticky bun.

"It's not like we ever had to worry about being discovered. Everyone with any real talent on the island done be dead now." Crumbs from Alvin's chocolate cinnamon roll sprayed in the air with his words.

"Says you," Fox countered as he chewed. "I could have made it big. Just didn't want the hassle."

"You didn't want to practice, more like," Alvin said.

"Didn't see you practicing that much either."

"I had my woman to keep happy."

"That's just mean," Fox said, taking another big bite of his bun.

"What was it like, playing with The Embers?" I asked.

"Oh, it was a rocking good time," Fox said. "Stan was the real talent in the group. No one sang like him. We just went along for the ride. Though I was surprised Bubba didn't strike it out on his own as well after Stan left. His musical scores were what brought Stan's soggy lyrics to life."

"What about 'Camellia Nights'?" I asked. "Bixby fell in love with the song after reading only a small part of the lyrics."

Both Alvin and Fox shrugged. "Never did play that one. Don't know much about it."

"I done read through the lyrics when Bubba was working on the score," Alvin added. "Didn't much care for it, if you ask me."

"But Bixby read it and seems to be beside himself wanting to buy it and make it into his next big hit," I pointed out.

Alvin grimaced. "That Bixby boy could sing the phonebook and make it into a hit song. Don't mean a thing." He scratched his head. "Bixby wants something, but I can't imagine it's the song he wants. It's just something Stan done scribbled down one morning after stayin' up late drinkin' all night."

"And it's missing," Fox added.

"Still?" That surprised me.

"Even the handwritten notes Bixby found in the songbook have grown legs and walked off," Fox said while Alvin nodded.

I frowned at that, but I had another question to ask them. "Bertie Bays," I said, "she used to sing with the band?"

Both men nodded—Fox enthusiastically and Alvin with an unhappy shrug. "That Bertie had a sharp voice," Fox said.

"More like a sharp tongue," Alvin said.

"Was she a regular?" I asked.

"As regular as her man would allow. He wasn't too thrilled she was singing in bars at all hours of the night with a bunch of rowdy white boys." Fox shook his head at the memory. "No siree, he didn't like that one bit."

I pulled out the old concert flyer I'd stuffed into my pocket and handed it to them. "But he let her sing with you at this concert? How did that go?"

"No, no, no. She didn't sing. Not after—" Fox looked at Alvin, who shook his head.

"Terrible goings on. Some said it didn't really happen, but . . ." Alvin said, still giving that head of his a hard shake.

"What happened?" I needed to know.

"She never sang with us again," Fox said.

"Wouldn't have expected her to," Alvin agreed.

"Didn't matter, though. Stan left not too long after that," Fox said.

"Why? What happened?" I felt ready to pull my hair out. What had happened that was so terrible they wouldn't give me a straight answer?

"Penn? Can I have a word?" Detective Gibbons called from the doorway.

"I'll be right with you." As much as I wanted to speak with the detective, I also wanted to stay and shake those two men until they started talking.

"Go talk to the man," Fox said. "He looks real anxious to get moving on his policing."

"Fine. But we're not done here, not by a long shot," I said, then quickly added, "Let me know if you need anything else to eat. I don't ever want anyone around here saying I starved them."

They nodded and pushed me toward the man I really needed to talk to. Fox and Alvin were discussing ancient history. I needed Detective Gibbons to give me answers to why someone here and now and today had shot at us. And I also needed him to reassure me that the police would be able to keep Tina and Bixby safe.

"So tell me," he said as he pulled out his notebook and pen, "what exactly happened this morning?"

The way he looked at me with his calm steady gaze, his face showing nothing but concern for me and my safety, caused a long-repressed ache deep inside my chest to push its way to the surface. This was how I'd always imagined a father would treat a beloved child who'd suddenly found herself in trouble. It was a look I'd never seen on my own father's face.

I glanced over at my busted window and then at the bullet holes that marred the far wall. The police techs had doubled the size of the holes in the plaster when they'd dug out the bullets. Vintage teacups lay smashed on the floor from a shelf that had fallen from the impact of a bullet. "Candy shot at me. Her bullets did this"— I pointed to the window —"and this" —I pointed to the broken teacups.

He nodded and motioned for me to sit down at the nearest café table. He pulled out a chair for me and one for himself. Like a true Southern gentleman, he remained standing since I was staring dumbly at the chair as if I'd forgotten how to bend my legs and sit.

"Please," he said, with a pointed look at the chair he'd pulled out for me. "Let's talk about what happened."

"My storefront window is shattered." Tears sprang to my eyes. I didn't know if they were from frustration or fear or if I was upset over having to pay the glaziers to come back out and install yet another window. "You told me Candy wasn't dangerous." Although I tried to stay in control, my voice grew louder and louder. "You told me she wasn't a killer. Look what she did. She was aiming at me, but she could have just as easily killed Fox or Alvin."

"Simmer down, Penn." Gibbons held up his hands. "I'm here. I'm listening to you."

"Simmer down? She shot at us!" The words burst out of my mouth.

His brows furrowed as he frowned. He did look sincerely concerned that Candy had shot at us. "We have every available man searching for her."

I drew a shuddering breath and tried again to sound calm. "With a gun. She shot at us with a gun."

"We're searching every car leaving the island. She won't get far," he said.

"She wanted to kill me." Even as those words left my mouth, the beginnings of doubt set in. "She wanted to kill me?"

Was that right?

Like Chief Byrd had done earlier, I squinted toward the stand of trees. If Candy had wanted to kill me, why hadn't she simply pulled the trigger when she was standing not more than a few feet away? Why run a long distance and then start firing? That didn't make sense.

She's crazy, my inner voice reminded me. *Nothing a crazy woman does has to make sense.*

She had told me that Bixby had texted her. She had told me that he wanted to meet her at the Chocolate Box. Why would he want to meet with her? And where was Bixby's security team? Why hadn't they stopped her?

Was she being set up?

But by whom? By Bixby? Why would he want someone to shoot at me?

"Please, Penn," Gibbons said, his voice even quieter and calmer than it had been before, "let's sit down. Talk to me. I'm here to help."

I looked at the chair and then at his kind face again. With a murmured "thank you," I sat down and told him everything. As I spoke, his expression turned harder, darker. His jaw tightened.

He wrote everything down and spoke only when he felt he needed clarification on a point I'd made.

When I'd finished, he closed his notebook and looked up at me. "It seems we've badly underestimated the threat Candy poses to Bixby Lewis and to the community here in Camellia Beach." He shook his head as if not able to believe the words that were leaving his mouth. "I've read all of her arrest reports. It's true that she's done some outrageous things—destroying property, breaking and entering, sending letters—but she never crossed the line. She never got violent."

"Don't all stalkers escalate into violence?" I asked.

"Some do, but from the accounts I've read of Candy, she's been a groupie, following Bixby Lewis around the country for years now. In all this time, she's followed nearly the exact same pattern. She writes letters. She breaks into his hotel whenever she can. And she'll make a mess of any piece of property she can get her hands on that belongs to Bixby's current . . . er . . . love interest." His face turned a bit pink as he said that last bit.

"I'm not his love interest," I protested.

"Candy seems to think otherwise," he said kindly.

"He flirts with everyone," I insisted. I then leaned forward and said quietly so no one could overhear us, "He's so in love with himself, I'm beginning to wonder if there's room in his heart for anyone other than the reflection he sees when he passes a mirror."

He chuckled at that, but his hard eyes and tight jaw remained serious. "We will catch Candy. As the evidence builds, I'm beginning to think you've been right all along, Penn. That girl is a threat. She may even have gone after Bixby and accidentally killed Stan. She might very well be our murderer."

"No, that's not right," I protested. "You told me yesterday that the evidence you found at the bonfire proved Stan was the intended victim. What's changed?"

He sighed. "I must have been reading the evidence wrong."

"I can't believe that. You don't make those kinds of mistakes."

"Yesterday you were convinced that was exactly the kind of mistake I was making."

"Obviously I was wrong. Can you tell me about the evidence? What did you find that persuaded you that the killer had specifically targeted Stan?"

"You already know I can't discuss specific details of the case with you." His shoulders slumped. "But I can tell you that after what Candy did here today, I'm going to go back and review everything we know. And don't worry, Penn, we have teams of officers searching for Candy. We will stop her before she can try to hurt anyone again."

What was wrong with me? He was saying exactly what I'd wanted him to say. Candy was the danger everyone needed to watch out for. So why was I suddenly doubting it? Why did I now think that poor delusional Candy couldn't be guilty of anything more than breaking a few windows?

"I hope you're right." I truly meant it. I hoped with all my heart he was right and I was wrong. After all, catching a crazy woman on the run on an island with only one bridge should be child's play for the police. And once they caught her, all of this would be over. Bixby would be safe. The Summer Solstice Beach Music Festival could continue without a lingering cloud of danger hanging over it. But I didn't believe it. I didn't believe it even as the words formed in my mouth.

Something in the back of my mind kept tugging at me, telling me I knew something, something that would explain why Stan was murdered and why Bixby's life was in danger. The evidence was all there, that nagging voice in my head insisted. Was the evidence there? If it was, I had no clue as to how to fit the pieces together.

Was Candy a killer? My gut said no. But if it wasn't her, who had killed Stan? And why would that person want to kill both Bixby and me? That was the question I needed to answer before Bixby—or anyone else involved with the festival—got hurt.

Chapter 21

Detective Gibbons left the Chocolate Box with a small box of truffles I'd packed for him tucked under his arm and the swagger of a man on the verge of success.

I frowned as I watched him make his way into the heavily wooded area across the street from the shop where Candy had fled and where the bullets had originated. He was heading down the wrong path. Not literally down the wrong path. While this morning's shooting had convinced him of what I'd been thinking all along—that Candy was a crazy killer—it had done the opposite for me. She might be crazy, but I no longer believed it was a killing kind of crazy.

If it were, I'd already be dead.

Gibbons is a professional, I reminded myself. *He won't let himself go too far afield with the investigation.*

Still, I worried about the safety of those closest to me. I also worried about why someone would want to shoot me. Did I know something about Stan's murder that made me a threat to the killer? Had I seen something at the bonfire that would point me to his killer?

I hadn't seen anything that everyone else hadn't also seen. Other than the chocolate bonbons I'd found near Stan's body, I couldn't think of anything of importance that I might know about the murder. And I'd told the police about the bonbons. But there had to be something I was missing, something that had made me a threat to the killer.

Before the day of Stan's murder, I'd never even heard of him. Dealing with the musical talent was Bubba's job, not mine. My role in the festival was advertising, ticket sales, and coordinating with the festival sponsors.

As I swept up the broken teacups, my thoughts spun round and round, always coming up with the same non-answers. I desperately needed to talk things over with someone who could give me a fresh perspective. But I couldn't leave the shop, not with that gaping hole where a window should have been.

I tried to get in touch with Bertie to see if she could come back and watch the shop. I got her voicemail. I then tried Althea's number.

"I'm driving around everywhere, searching for Mama," Althea said, her voice thick with worry. "Where could she have gone? What's happened that's making her act so strangely? She's not answering her phone."

"I don't know," I said. "I couldn't reach her, either. Do let me know if I can do anything, okay?"

I didn't have the heart to say anything about the shooting, not while she was so worried about her mother. I hung up and tried to call Granny Mae in Wisconsin. After ringing several times, her phone also switched over to voicemail.

By this time, I felt so frustrated that I nearly stamped my foot and howled like a madwoman. Not wanting to scare the customers, even though the only two people in the shop were still just Fox and Alvin, I muttered angrily below my breath before calling the window repair shop to order yet another window replacement. Since the glaziers already had the measurements on file, they promised to make it out to the Chocolate Box with the new window around six that evening.

Until then, I'd have to board up the window . . . again.

My gaze traveled back to where Fox and Alvin were still hanging out on the café sofa. Both Chief Byrd and Detective Gibbons had told us we could leave. Or, if I wanted, I could open the shop back up for business. Fox and Alvin didn't look as if they were in any hurry to get back to their practice session. Or perhaps they were waiting for me to go back and interrogate them about why Bertie had stopped singing with The Embers.

Yeah, right. I doubted they were waiting for me. They clearly seemed hesitant to talk about Bertie and whatever had happened that had led her to stop singing with them. Perhaps, if I tried to charm them, they'd slip me a crumb or two of information. With that in mind, I enlisted their help in nailing up boards over the broken window. They held the boards while I swung the hammer.

"Don't go trying to bat your eyes and preen with us, gurl," Alvin drawled with a hacking laugh several minutes into our work on the window. Clearly, my attempts to sweeten them up so they'd loosen their tongues hadn't worked. Not that my failure surprised me. I'd always been better at brusque than charming. "Done seen all those games before. If'n you want to know what Bertie don't want you to know, you'll have to hear it from her own lips."

It took me a solid minute to detangle what Alvin was saying to me. "I'm not digging for gossip. Can't you just tell me about the incident that led to her quitting the band?"

Fox smiled kindly and patted my shoulder. "Bertie would flay us alive if she thought we were telling people stories that were hers alone to tell."

"That's right, gurl. And she'd use that sharp tongue of hers to peel the skin clear off our bodies," Alvin agreed.

"Talk to Bertie. Ask her about it. She might surprise you

and . . ." Fox shrugged as if he didn't believe for a minute I'd get the information I wanted, at least not from Bertie.

"I'm going to close up," I told them after hammering in the last nail. "After getting shot at, I'm too nervous to stay in one place. I need to go for a walk."

"Of course you do, darling," Fox purred. His elfish lips curled into a charming smile. He then offered me a nip of something that smelled like gasoline he kept in a small flask in his back pocket. I thanked him and said I might take him up on the offer another day.

I left yet another message with Bertie, who still wasn't answering her phone, fetched Stella from the office, and locked up the shop.

Upstairs, Troubadour greeted me with meows and looked as if he might even try to rub against my leg in greeting. Stella clearly wasn't going to allow that to happen. My pup surged forward, barking her pretty head off. Her giant tan-and-black ears fluttered like a butterfly in search of a flower. Troubadour, angry that Stella had blocked his path to me, hissed at my pup and then, in true catlike fashion, lifted his nose in the air and wandered back into Bertie's bedroom as if to say he hadn't wanted to greet me anyhow.

Stella looked pleased with herself as she followed me into my bedroom, where I changed out of my business attire and into a lightweight pink sundress. After grabbing a large straw sunhat from a peg by the door, I hooked Stella's leash to her pretty pink collar. As usual, she tried to nip my hand, but I was learning her naughty tricks. I moved too quickly for my silky little hellion to get her teeth anywhere near me. With her excitedly leading the way, I headed down Main Street toward the beach. Stella barked happily as she tugged at the leash, urging me to pick up my pace.

The day was turning into another hot one. The noonday sun blazed down from a bright blue, cloudless sky. A line of cars stuffed with colorful blowup floats and with surfboards tied to their roofs clogged Main Street as day-trippers waited to turn onto the road that led to the beachfront park on the west end of the island.

Halfway down Main Street, I was surprised to see Congressman Trey Ezell coming out of Althea's shop. I would never have guessed the serious congressman was interested in crystals.

"Congressman," I called out to him.

He looked startled to see me but quickly regained his composure. He was dressed in an old-fashioned seersucker suit, the kind of suit many of the long-term residents at the Pink Pelican Inn liked to wear.

"Please," he said, holding out his hands to me in greeting, "call me Trey."

I let him take my hands in his. He held on a tad longer than I would have liked—but then again, some people did that. "Are you okay?" he asked. "I heard what happened. A shooting? At your shop?" He shook his head. "I can't imagine anything like that happening in our quiet town. That Bixby Lewis fellow has certainly attracted some unsavory people."

The congressman sounded suspiciously like the police chief, blaming outsiders for bringing the wrong type of people into town with them. "I don't think blaming the musicians is fair. You have to admit that Bixby has encouraged many families to come and pay top dollar to rent beach houses, have dinners out, and buy hundreds of dollars' worth of souvenirs."

"Yes, yes," he said. "But I heard a woman with a gun follows him everywhere."

"I don't know who pulled the trigger this morning or why." Stella tugged at the leash, anxious to get moving again. I made her sit before tossing her another treat. "It could have been someone local."

"What do you mean? You don't know the shooter's

identity?" he asked, sounding incredulous. "I heard it had to be that young woman who followed Bixby to Camellia Beach."

"Word sure gets around quickly." Not that I was surprised. In a town this size, news tended to spread like a frenzied wildfire kicked up by the summer breeze. Still, I shook my head. "I don't think Candy shot at me."

"Candy?" he asked.

"Bixby's stalker. She was at the shop, but she'd been lured there. By whom? That's the question that needs answering."

"Aha! Are you investigating on your own like you did after the murder this past winter?"

"I wouldn't say I'm Investigating." Of course I was investigating. I simply didn't want to say it. "That would be foolish, wouldn't it?" My investigation of Stan's murder was my way of working to protect Bixby and the festival. It made good business sense, but I doubted anyone else would see it that way. "I'm simply a business owner trying to protect my own interests. And I've been sharing my ideas with the police." At least that last part was true.

"You've come up with some ideas about the murder?" He tilted his head to one side. "Such as?"

"I haven't worked it all out in my mind yet, but . . ." I wasn't sure why I stopped myself from finishing the thought. Probably because some of the ideas in my head were half-baked and not ready to be shared. I shrugged. "Detective Gibbons is a capable investigator. I have faith he'll get to the bottom of what's going on. Is Althea in there?" I asked, hoping the congressman would let me change the subject. I also hoped Althea had been able to find her mother.

"No, no, she's not here," he said, much to my disappointment. He hooked his arm with mine and started to walk with me. I flinched at his touch. Stella growled. "She set aside a geode for me. I stopped by to pick it up."

"I didn't realize you were into crystals." I'd pictured him to be as levelheaded as they come. Perhaps I was wrong. Perhaps he was as nutty as my best friend.

"No, they all just look like overpriced rocks to me. It's my nephew, Tom, who's a rock fan. Or at least that's what he keeps telling me. I was picking him up a present as a thank you for working so diligently with me these last couple of days. With my guidance, his work performance is finally starting to live up to our hardworking family name. You know I come from a long line of politicians? My father ran for governor three times and served in the state senate for more than thirty years."

"Is that so?" I said.

"Tom's going to take up the political mantle after me," he said proudly.

Stella's growls grew louder. I used my big-eared pup's bad behavior as an excuse to get my arm back. I tossed her a treat.

"She's still as feisty as ever, I see," the congressman said with a chuckle. "Little dogs are like that."

"She seems to be," I agreed with an honest smile. I was glad that he didn't insult Stella or try to dominate her, which would only send her into crazy, berserk mode. So many people when they met Stella thought they could instantly stamp out her naughty behavior by looming over the five-pound fluff ball in a big, frightening manner while shouting commands. Let me tell you, that kind of training didn't work with this dog. Frankly, I couldn't imagine that it would work with any dog. But I digress.

"I suppose the police turned your shop into a crime scene. Is that why you're not working?" he asked.

"They've completed their work and turned it back over to me. I just decided to close up for a little while and take a walk."

"You closed up? Where's Bertie? Is she okay?"

"She went on an errand," I said, wondering what my partner was doing that had made her feel the need for such secrecy.

Ezell nodded. "Well, I'm glad you're taking some time away from the shop. I don't want our island's star entrepreneur burning out."

"I don't think there's any danger of that. Trying to figure out how to make a bonbon without ruining it is a challenge I don't think I'll master anytime soon."

"Glad to hear it," he said distractedly as he glanced at his watch. "Listen, I'd love to stay and talk, but I have a meeting with a donor in half an hour. Maybe we can talk later? Perhaps over dinner? You can tell me more about those ideas you have about who shot at you today."

"I'll probably be too busy to eat tonight with everything that's going on with the festival, but maybe another night," I said. I couldn't help but think it was odd and perhaps even a little suspicious that he'd offer a dinner invitation out of the blue like that. It wasn't as if we were friends.

"Well, soon, then," he said with a determined gleam in his eyes. "I would sure like to help you sort through what you know about the troubles going on lately. I especially would like to talk through what you know about Stan's murder. As I've already told you, he was my friend. I'm desperate to see justice served. Maybe if we put our heads together we can come up with some good ideas to share with the sheriff's office."

I'd forgotten that Stan and the congressman had been close, which, of course, explained his persistence in getting together with me. He, like me, wanted to do everything in his power to see justice prevail.

"I'm sure I can use all the help I can get," I said kindly. "Good luck with your meeting. And I'll let you know right away if I hear anything new about the investigation."

"Thank you." He gave my hand a squeeze. "I'll give you a call so we can plan something. I might be able to see something important in the facts you know about Stan's murder that you've been overlooking. After all, I've lived in this town my entire life. Until later."

Stella took the opportunity to bark like a maniac as the congressman hurried away. It was as if she was saying to him, "That's right, buster, run. Come near me again and I'll bite you."

Since I needed all the help I could get in figuring out why someone thought I needed to be silenced, I told Stella to stop trying to scare off a willing helper, especially someone as powerful and well connected and motivated as Trey Ezell. He might be the key to figuring out what had been going on in my favorite island town.

Chapter 22

As soon as I reached the end of Main Street, I kicked off my shoes and buried my toes in the warm sand. My gaze traveled over the vastness of the Atlantic Ocean. Beside me, the pier and pavilion reached toward the horizon. All around, people laughed, tossed beach balls, and read books as they lounged in the summer warmth. Just beyond the breakers, surfers floated on the water like a flock of shorebirds, bobbing up and down as the swells passed underneath their boards. In the distance, the old red-and-white brick lighthouse stood watch over it all.

No one on the beach appeared worried that an armed madwoman might be loose on the island. I doubted many of them knew. I stood there wishing I could be one of them, relaxed and happy. But that wasn't my world, so I called Tina on my cell phone.

Stella, with several happy yips, started burrowing through the sand in much the same way she had through the scattered papers in the Chocolate Box's office. Her white silky tail waved double-time as she used her nose like a little black bulldozer.

Even though Stella was a handful and I would never have thought I wanted a dog in my life, I had to admit having her beside me made me almost as happy as those beachgoers I'd been envying. I smiled as I watched her.

"Penn!" Tina shouted into the phone. "What's going on? Why haven't you been answering my calls?"

"I'd have answered them if you'd been calling me," I said. "No one has called me today."

"I have been calling you," she protested.

"No, you—" I started to say. I pulled the phone away from my ear to see if I'd missed any calls. I'd missed three calls from Tina and one from Granny Mae. How could that be?

My ringer, that's how. It had been turned off. I didn't remember turning it off the previous night, but I sometimes did that on nights when I needed to get a good night's sleep.

"Sorry, Tina. I must have forgotten to turn my ringer back on this morning."

"Don't do that! You had me freaking out that something bad had happened."

"Something bad did happen," I said.

"What! What happened? I knew I should have gone back to the shop. But Bixby insisted we'd only be in the way. He sent a member of his security team to check things out. But the only thing the guard could tell us was that there were tons of police and that no one was able to get close to the front door. Talk to me, Penn. Don't leave me wondering. Are you okay? What happened?"

"If you'd shut up for a minute I'd tell you," I said with a chuckle. "Actually, where are you? I don't want to discuss this over the phone."

After hanging up, I strolled a short way down the beach to where several oversized beachfront mansions elevated on wooden pilings had recently been built on undersized lots. One of the houses was the one we'd rented for Bixby. Tina waved to me from a lounge chair on the deck. Bixby was pacing the deck with a cell phone pressed to his ear.

Down on the beach, a crowd of fans had gathered. They

created a ring around the steps leading up to the house, alternating between gawking and taking pictures with their phones.

"It's okay," he called to the security team guarding the steps. "We invited the girl with the dog. Let her come up."

The same two burly men who'd accosted Jody yesterday gave me a friendly nod as I passed.

By the time I got to the deck, Bixby had stuffed his phone into his back pocket.

Stella, excited at the sight of Tina's and Bixby's bare toes—toes ripe for biting—barked and tugged at the leash for several embarrassing minutes before giving up. With a huff, she started sniffing for crumbs that had fallen on the deck.

I settled into a lounge chair beside Tina and told her what had happened.

"Crazy Candy shot at you?" Tina jolted upright, clearly upset. Stella joined in on the excitement and started barking again. "Everyone knows that girl needs some serious help, but I would never have guessed she'd try to shoot you. Bixby, honey, fetch Penn a drink. I'm sure she could use one."

"Did her bullets hit anyone?" Bixby asked offhandedly.

I frowned as I watched him walk over to the outside bar. How could he stay so calm about what Candy might have done? Was it because this was what superstars had to deal with on a daily basis?

"My front window and several vintage teacups were the only casualty this time," I told him. "The police are searching for her."

"She'll deny doing anything wrong when they find her." Bixby poured three vodka and tonics from the bar. "She always does," he said after taking a long sip of his drink. He then carried the other two over to us.

"I shudder to think what might have happened if you and Tina hadn't taken the back way out. Where was your security

173

team, Bixby?" I demanded as I accepted the cool glass. "Why didn't they intercept her before she got close to the shop?"

"That's a good question." Tina jumped up from the lounge chair and fisted her hands on her hips. "Bixby, where was your security team this morning?"

He flashed one of his devastating smiles as he tried to hand Tina her glass. "You know how I hate having them follow me everywhere. If I'm going somewhere, you know, unexpected, I'll tell them to take some time off."

"But coming to the shop wasn't unexpected," I pointed out. "Candy told me you'd texted her. She said you wanted to meet with her there."

"Preposterous. Why would I do that?"

"Why would you?" I asked.

"I wouldn't. I didn't," he protested.

"Someone texted her, which must mean someone knew where you were going," I pressed, "or someone was following you."

"Unless she made up the part about getting a text," Tina said. "Did you actually see it, Penn?"

"No, I didn't see it." She'd showed me a blank screen, but she'd sounded so hopeful, so certain.

"She didn't get a text. She never does. I'm not even sure her phone is connected to a service." Bixby abandoned his attempts to hand my nervous sister her drink. He placed the glass on a side table and got back on his phone. Whoever he was calling didn't pick up. "Call me as soon as you can," he snapped. "It's important."

"Is everything okay?" I asked.

"No." He ran a hand through his hair. "Your friend Bubba is avoiding me. I think he's doing it on purpose."

"That doesn't sound like him." Bubba was one of the most gregarious men I knew. "The man would talk to a pile of rocks if no one was around to listen to him."

"Perhaps I need to dress like some rocks, then. I've been try-ing to get in touch with him all morning. He's not answering his cell phone."

"That's odd." And I still couldn't get in touch with Bertie. "Have you tried calling any of the other band members? Perhaps one of them knows where you can find him."

"That's the first thing I did. They were supposed to have a practice session all morning, but Bubba canceled it and went running off on some mysterious errand. No one knows where he went."

Just like Bertie.

"He's been gone all morning," Bixby said. He sounded truly vexed. Apparently, someone not returning his phone calls made him more upset than a stalker with a gun.

If I stopped to think about it, his reaction made sense. Bixby was the kind of guy who craved attention. Candy gave him that attention and then some. I was beginning to suspect that one of the reasons he resisted reporting her antics to the police was that they might actually stop her from following him around the country with her unbreakable devotion.

Still, the Bubba I'd known before Thursday would have given Bixby the same kind of attention. Heck, before Thursday, anyone you'd have asked would have told you that Bubba wouldn't leave town without telling at least ten people where he was going. I'd never known him to take longer than a few min-utes to return a phone call.

What was going on with him? Had someone hit him over the head and stranded him on a boat again?

And Bertie? What was she up to? And why did she continue to deny that she and Bubba had some kind of relationship when they clearly did?

And then there was the question of why Bixby had dis-missed his security team before coming to the Chocolate Box that morning. I didn't believe for a minute that he'd done it because he liked to get away from the people who protected him. He wouldn't do that, not while both a stalker and a killer prowled the island. He had to have had another reason for not wanting to be protected. Perhaps it was because he *had* texted Candy and had told her to come meet him. After all, she'd be the perfect person to use as a scapegoat for someone else taking potshots from the woods.

I hadn't thought anything of it at the time, but that first time I'd talked with Bixby, he'd told me how eager he was to get his hands on some fresh beach music. He'd said he wanted to get back to his beach music roots, but the way he kept calling Bubba so he could talk about purchasing the rights to the music, I wondered if something else was going on. How badly did he need that next big top-of-the-chart hit? And what made him think he'd find that hit here?

I really needed to talk things over with someone.

"I think you should leave," I said abruptly.

"What?" Bixby snapped. "Until next Tuesday, this is my place."

"Not you." I held my hands up as if to hold him off. "Although if you wanted to cancel singing with The Embers to get away from Candy's threat, I'd fully support your decision. I don't want to see anyone get hurt."

"You can't get rid of me." He crossed his arms over his chest. "I'm not going anywhere until I finish what I came to do."

"And what exactly did you come here to do? Buy music from unknown musicians or sing?" I demanded.

Tina gasped. "Penn, are you accusing him of something?"

Bixby grimaced. "I'm here as a favor to you, in case you've forgotten. I'm here to sing."

"Good," I said, my voice still crisp. "And I wasn't telling you to leave. I was actually talking to Tina." My sister was my main concern at the moment. If there was some nut out there shooting at me and whoever happened to be standing near me, I needed to get Tina out of the line of fire. Not only would my family murder me if I let something happen to their precious Tina, but I would never forgive myself. I loved the fashion maven fiercely.

"You want me to leave? Now?" Tina cried. "When things are just starting to get interesting? Not on your life."

"It's not my life I'm worried about," I told her.

"I'll be fine."

I wasn't so sure. "Someone shot at me today," I reminded her. "With real, live bullets."

She folded her arms over her chest just as Bixby had. "Then that's more reason for me to stay. You need me here." Her gaze flicked over to Bixby and then back to me again. "Seriously, you need my help."

I didn't need her help, not if she was still looking to fix me up with her ex. "I'd never forgive myself if anything happened to you."

"You're not responsible for me."

"Tell that to Grandmother Cristobel," I muttered before I could stop myself.

Unfortunately, Tina had heard me. "Grandmamma knows better. I'm an adult. If she blames you for any decision I make, she'll hear about it from me. I'm not going to put up with the way she treats you, not anymore. This nonsense has gone on for too long. Someone in our family needs to start standing up for you."

"Thank you," I whispered. I was touched, truly touched. Very few people in my life had ever had the courage to stand up to my formidable grandmother.

Tina pulled me into a tight hug. I tried to relax as I forced my arms to hug her back.

"You're too hard on yourself and everyone around you, silly

bean," Tina said after she let me go. "And I'm going to keep hugging you until you stop making your spine feel like a prickly pineapple."

"Got it." I gulped. A few blinks washed away all evidence that a few stupid tears loomed. "Still, I'd feel better if you took the next flight back to Chicago."

"No way, big sis. You're stuck with me until the end of the festival."

Clearly I wasn't going to win this battle right now, so I chose to retreat. "I need to get back to the shop. I closed it to come here."

"You did? Where's Bertie?" Tina asked.

"I don't know. She's been gone all morning."

"How about your friend Althea? Did you ask her for help?"

I hadn't. "She's trying to find her mother. Bertie has been acting strangely these past couple of days, disappearing without telling anyone where she's going and snapping at anyone who so much as looks at her funny."

"Really?" Tina looked troubled by that revelation. Her perfectly groomed brows crinkled. "You don't think . . ."

"I need to get back to the shop," I said forcefully.

Yes, Bertie's secretive behavior bothered me. I worried about what she'd gotten herself involved with. Was Bubba the reason she was running off again and again without telling anyone where she was headed?

Certainly, she hadn't run off to shoot at me. Although she had been gone when the bullets started to fly, I knew she couldn't have been the one holding the gun.

And Bubba, even though he was missing too, wouldn't want to shoot me. After all, I was helping him make the music festival a success. And even if he had gotten some weird notion in his head that would make him send bullets flying in my direction, he wouldn't have done it with his bandmates standing right next to me. He wouldn't risk harming one of them.

So who had pulled the trigger?

Could Crazy Candy have done it?

Tina hooked her arm with mine and started herding me toward the deck's stairs. "I'm coming with you to the shop, since that's why I'm here. I'm here to help you."

"You're leaving?" Bixby said without looking in our direction. He'd been fiddling with his phone again. Was he sending texts? Or was he playing a game? "If you see Bubba, you'll let him know I'm still trying to get in touch with him?"

Tina didn't wait for me to answer before dragging me down the wooden steps. I felt a little sick to my stomach as I looked in his direction one last time.

There was one scenario I hadn't considered. Bixby wanted to buy the song "Camellia Night." And he seemed desperate to get in touch with Bubba so they could work out a deal. Bubba had acted eager to sell while Stan had balked at the idea. And now Stan was dead and Bubba was avoiding Bixby's calls.

I looked back at the beach house. Bixby had put away his phone. He stood at the deck's railing and was watching us. Despite the day's stifling heat, the grimace hardening his expression chilled me to the bone.

Chapter 23

Three o'clock came too quickly. My hands shook—heck, my entire body was shaking—by the time I met Harley outside my apartment door. You'd think I'd be used to this: indifference and scorn from members of my family. Meeting with Florence should be business as usual, sort of like having Sunday dinner at my father's house.

It wasn't as if I expected her to suddenly welcome me into the Maybank family with open arms. Given my past experience with her, I doubted Florence had anything nice to say to me.

Still, the part of me that would always be that lonely child craving love and attention hoped Florence had set up this meeting today out of kindness. A foolish hope, and yet, because that hope kept whispering cloying "what-ifs" in my ear, my nerves were as jumpy as Stella at dinnertime.

"Are you sure you're ready for this?" Harley asked. He steadied my hand as I fumbled with the key in the lock.

"Are you sure you want to be here instead of spending the day with Gavin?" I asked instead of answering a question I didn't know the answer to.

"Gavin and his friend Tom are running around the island like a pair of lost boys. They've been gone since right after gobbling down an early lunch." Harley smiled as he said it. "It's not been easy for him to find friends in town. There aren't that many families living out here anymore. I'm glad he's teamed up with Ezell's nephew."

"Friendships during difficult times are priceless," I said. "I'm lucky I can consider you a friend."

The sun hung like a big yellow beach ball in the sky. I could hear faint laughter and squeals of joy from tourists enjoying a day at the beach a few blocks away. Tina was downstairs helping out in the shop. Althea, who had searched all morning and into the afternoon for her mother, had also come by to help in the shop. Bertie and Bubba were both still missing.

I'd wanted to talk to Althea more about what she knew about her mother's past, but three o'clock arrived before that conversation happened, and I had this meeting.

"We can still move things to my office. Neutral territory might make you feel better," Harley suggested.

What I wanted was to be relaxing on the beach, pretending I didn't have a care in the world. There was something oddly soothing about the constant sound of the surf battering the shore. Listening to it while soaking in the sun's warmth had the power to wash away life's worries.

This far away from the beach, I couldn't hear the surf. Standing under the cover of the back porch, I couldn't feel the sun's healing warmth. And my worries were as sharp and clear as ever.

Was Bixby a killer or a victim?

What was bothering Bertie?

And why in the world would Florence ask to meet with me—the one person on the planet she seemed to hate most?

Harley frowned as we stood in front of my apartment door. I bit down on my lip but made no move to go inside.

"I think I'd like to . . ." I wasn't sure what I was going to say. At that moment, I had no idea what I wanted beyond the impossible: that Stan hadn't been murdered, that Candy didn't keep breaking my storefront window, that the members of my family loved and cherished me.

Thankfully, I didn't have to walk down that path of impossibilities for too long. Florence, dressed in a 1950s vintage pink-and-peach floral half-sleeve swing dress, came up the stairs with the grace of a famous diva. Not one hair of her spiraling updo moved in the summer breeze. Large sunglasses covered half her face. She wore dainty white gloves. White pearls hung like dewdrops around her neck.

"Harleston," she said with a genuine smile as she reached the top step. She extended both hands to him as she approached. As soon as his hands were in her clutches, she drew him in for a kiss on both cheeks. "What a surprise to see you here today." Her accent, while unmistakably Southern, was so refined it bordered on sounding British. "Oh! I keep forgetting you've rented Mother's tiny spare apartment."

"As a matter of fact," Harley said as he gracefully extracted himself from my aunt's clutches, "I've come at Penn's behest to sit in on the meeting you've requested of my client."

His steady green gaze turned toward me. He gave me an encouraging nod as if to say, "Don't let her spook you."

"Charity"—I cringed at her use of my first name—"you really are always too quiet. I didn't notice you standing there." Florence didn't reach out her arms to me. Nor did she plant dainty kisses on my cheeks.

"Mrs. Corners," I said with a nod as I opened the apartment door with a little too much emotion. The door swung in so quickly it crashed into a console table.

A startled Troubadour hissed at me and ran straight to Harley. Bertie's cat had a weird affinity for my surfing lawyer. He rubbed shamelessly against Harley's pants, doing that strange figure eight cats do with the people they adore.

"Please, Charity, call me—" I didn't get to hear what Florence wanted me to call her. Stella, letting out that ear-piercing high-pitched yip she gets whenever she's nervous, charged the door with her teeth ready to sink into the closest victim. Harley knew enough to step well out of my little dog's way. Florence seemed to take offense at Stella's aggressive behavior and actually lurched forward as if to fight my determined pup.

I scooped up the little beast before she could chomp into one of Florence's pretty pink leather pumps. Stella clamped down on my hand in frustration. It hurt like the dickens, but at least she couldn't bark when she was biting. I gritted my teeth and carried her into my bedroom. I tossed her a handful of treats before closing her inside. She barked and scraped at the door for about five minutes before settling down, which for her was unusual. She generally settled down faster than that.

"Sorry," I said while we waited for my naughty little dog to stop barking. "She gets nervous when new people come by."

"She's a bit of a menace." Even though Harley smiled as he said it, his criticism stung. While I freely complained about Stella's antics, it bristled to hear someone else doing it.

"She didn't chomp into your pants," I pointed out to him. I glanced at his tan khakis and noticed Troubadour still making circles around his legs. "You have to agree that her behavior is improving."

"She's just a little dog." He looked at me with furrowed brows and shrugged as if asking what he'd done wrong. After a moment of tense silence, he added, "Shall we sit down?"

We all found seats in the tidy living room. I didn't offer refreshments. Florence sat on the sofa and crossed her legs at the ankles. Again, I noticed her pink pumps. They were identical to the ones I'd worn the previous day. Also, her vintage dress gave her a fun retro style I sometimes looked for when shopping for outfits. Seeing the clothes on her made me wonder if I needed to undergo a complete fashion makeover.

I sat in the armchair across from Florence. Harley took a seat in my armchair's twin.

"I see you haven't changed anything in here," Florence said with a sour-lemon expression as she looked around.

I shrugged. "No one has picked up the furniture they've inherited."

"That's because no one wants this . . ." She seemed to struggle to find the right word, perhaps a kind word? With a sigh, she concluded, "No one wants this junk."

"I think the words you were searching for were your mother's—and my grandmother's—'favorite things.'" Whether this woman sitting across from me was my aunt or not, I wasn't about to let her sit in Mabel's home and disparage how she'd furnished it.

"I didn't mean to insult you. While I can't speak for the others, Mother's taste in furniture doesn't match my décor. Not even a little bit."

"Your mother wanted you to have something to remember her by. I'd take anything my mother wanted to give me. I'd lap it up like a starving pup in search of crumbs."

Florence held up her hands in surrender. "I am sorry, Charity. I didn't ask to talk with you today to argue or insult you."

I crossed my arms over my chest. "I answer to Penn, not Charity." She knew that. I was certain of it. It wasn't a secret that I recoiled whenever someone called me "Charity." I suspected she was using my given name as a means of tormenting me. "So why are you here?"

She sat back. Her lips thinned into such a tight line that the color of her bright red lipstick completely disappeared. Her sharp gaze latched onto my face as if willing me to break. "I came to . . ." She drew a long breath. "I don't know how to start."

I decided to help her out. "How about we call a truce? You can start by agreeing to take a DNA test to prove you're my aunt."

"I . . . I can't do that." Her voice shook just a bit.

"Can't?" Un-freaking-believable. Then what was she doing sitting in my house? I stood and headed toward the door. If she wasn't willing to help me, I was more than willing to show her how she could get out of my home.

"You have to understand something—" she started to say.

But I was tired and cranky and, quite honestly, I didn't want to understand anything that might come out of this hateful woman's mouth. So I didn't let her finish. "No, you have to understand that I'm desperate to find my mother. I've been searching for my mother, your sister Carolina, to no avail. And your brother went and filed a petition to the court, claiming the DNA test proving I'm Mabel's granddaughter is invalid and asking the court to rule that I'm not a blood relative."

"We didn't authorize the DNA test, and you must understand there's no way we can know that your friend actually got a DNA sample from Mother," Florence countered.

"I know it's true." I touched my chest. "I know it here in my heart. Mabel is my grandmother. And she loved me like a grandmother should love her grandchild. I wish every day I could have had more time with her."

There must have been a sliver of a heart in Florence's chest, for her expression softened just a bit as she nodded.

"What you need to understand, Florence, is that I've lived my entire life not knowing anything about my mother beyond the story of her dropping me off at my father's doorstep. And now that I've discovered this connection to Mabel and a chance that I might finally find out more about the woman who gave birth to me, I'm not going to let it go. You don't know what it's like having that information dangling in front of your face just inches out of reach. Prove you are my aunt, and help me find your missing sister Carolina."

"I—" she started to say something, but I refused to listen. I refused to let her deny me before I could plead my case. Any decent human being would want to help me.

"You see, whether you believe it or not, the DNA results were real. And that means Carolina has to be my mother. She just has to be. What's that? What did you say?"

"I said," she spoke slowly and confidently, "I'm not your aunt." The spiteful woman just wouldn't quit with her denials.

I swung open the door. "Leave."

Harley got to his feet. "I think you'd better go." He reached for Florence's arm. She snatched it away from him and remained planted on the sofa. Her eyes flashed fire.

"You selfish, ungrateful child," she spit the words at me. "You don't understand what your coming to Camellia Beach means to anyone else. You don't understand the pain and upheaval you're causing."

"Leave," I repeated, louder this time.

"Please," Harley said as he extended his arm to Florence, his steely voice making the request sound like a command, "let me walk you out."

"I'm not leaving until she hears what I came to say."

"You have ten seconds to spit it out," I said, my hand still on the door.

And spit it out she did. All in one quick burst, she declared, "I'm not your aunt. I'm your mother."

Chapter 24

A buzzing filled my ears, growing louder and louder until it felt as if my eardrums might burst.

"If you're lying, I'll . . ." I could barely hear Harley's angry voice over the buzzing. Like pictures, his words seemed to come in and out of focus.

Harley had crossed the room without my noticing. He grabbed my arm and held it tightly.

"Wh-what did she say?" I whispered like one of those wimpy heroines who swooned at every surprising revelation.

"She said she is your mother," Harley answered, speaking to me as if I were a child who had just learned the truth about Santa Claus.

"What about Carolina? Carolina is my mother. Isn't she? Isn't she my mother? She has to be my mother. We need to find her. She'll tell us the truth." I couldn't tell you why I wasn't directing these questions to Florence, who remained seated stoically on the sofa as if her revelation shouldn't have made me feel as if someone had just punched me in the face half a dozen times.

"Carolina? You think she'd help you? She couldn't stand Mother's chocolate shop. She ran away from the shop back in the summer of 1975, never to call or visit again. Mother turned mean after that," Florence said, more to the floor than to anyone particular. "My sister might be a coward, but she's not your mother."

I'd imagined this moment in my life happening quite a bit differently. Recently, I'd imagined finding and reconnecting with a mythical, regretful Carolina—not Florence with her angry eyes and sharp words. I'd imagined all sorts of scenarios, such as Carolina confessing that she hadn't been able to keep me because she was dying of an incurable disease and had only a few days to live. Of course, in that scenario, she wouldn't actually be alive to be telling me any of that.

I looked over at Florence again. Instead of paying attention to me, her beloved lost daughter, she was straightening out a wrinkle on her skirt.

That woman was *my mother*?

Troubadour jumped up on the back of the sofa and waltzed blithely over to the perfectly coiffed Florence. He glanced in my direction and then sank his razor-sharp teeth into Florence's shoulder. With a shriek that got Stella barking again, the woman leaped into the air as if her butt were on fire. "That . . . that mangy rat bit me!" She furiously thrust her neatly manicured finger in the cat's direction. Troubadour, in typical catlike fashion, seemed unimpressed by her display. He sat himself down on the back of the sofa and calmly licked his paw. "I'm going to need to get shots for rabies and cat-scratch fever and who knows what else."

I had never particularly liked Troubadour. Ever since moving in with Bertie, I had lived in constant fear that he'd jump onto the sofa and bite me in the exact same manner he'd just bitten Florence.

But in the stress of the moment, I burst out laughing at the sight of Florence flapping around the room like a wounded pelican. I laughed so hard, tears sprang to my eyes. And even though I had trouble catching my breath, I kept laughing.

"It's not funny," Florence wailed. "I need medical attention."

"Calm down there, Mrs. Corners," Harley said. He tried to sound serious, but a chuckle added a few bumps to his smooth Southern drawl. "You don't need a doctor. You need a seamstress. It's your dress that's torn, not your skin."

She stopped flailing her arms long enough to peek down at her shoulder. Sure enough, there was no sign of blood or puffy skin. The only evidence of Troubadour's bite were twin rips, each about an inch long, marring her otherwise perfect vintage silk dress.

"I never expected this kind of reception." She blinked her pale blue eyes. Were they eyes that looked like mine? "I thought you'd be grateful that I'd confess my deepest secret to you."

"Grateful?" I cried. "You thought I'd be grateful?"

I don't exactly know what I'd been expecting when I finally found my mother, but this wasn't it. It wasn't as if I'd spent my entire life dreaming of this moment. I hadn't. I'd spent most of my life feeling angry at the woman who had carelessly left me with a family who refused to love me. What kind of coldhearted monster could do that to her own daughter?

I looked over at Florence, who was still fussing with her ripped dress. She didn't care about my feelings, which I supposed made her exactly the kind of monster—I mean, mother—who could abandon her own child.

Still, her abrupt revelation left me empty. A few tears, a word or two of regret, or even a tight I-wish-I'd-never-left-you hug—were those too much to ask for? Apparently, with Florence, they were.

She'd left because she hadn't cared about me. She still didn't care about me. And no amount of wishing would get me my tearful Hallmark moment.

Harley seemed intent on ushering Florence out the door. But

I wasn't ready to let her go so easily. Questions rolled around in my head, questions that demanded to be answered.

"Let's all sit down," I said. "If anyone needs sweet tea, Bertie left a pitcher in the fridge."

"You don't mean Bertie's so-dang-sweet-that-your-teeth-will-hurt-just-from-drinking-it sweet tea, do you?" Harley asked, licking his lips.

"That's the tea." I moved to pour him a glass. Florence seemed less than impressed by my offering.

"I didn't come here to have a tea party. And I'm not going to sit down as long as that dangerous beast is still in the room."

Troubadour hadn't left his perch on the back of the sofa. He looked pretty darned pleased with himself as he licked his paw and used it like a little hand to wash the backs of his ears.

Harley walked over, picked up Troubadour, carried him into Bertie's bedroom, and closed the door. "He won't bother you anymore," he said. "Let's sit down."

We all took the same places we'd had and stared at each other in awkward silence. It was as if we were enemies behind battle lines waiting for the other to fire the first shot.

"With this new piece of information you've handed us," Harley said to Florence with a sigh, "are you now willing to take the DNA test we've been requesting?"

The question seemed to take Florence by surprise. "What? No. Why do you need a DNA test? I've told you everything you wanted to know. And I've not handed you anything. You have to understand." She looked at me for the first time since revealing that she was my mother. "Charity, you have to understand that no one knows about this. I have a husband. I have my charity work. I cannot risk upsetting the life I've worked so hard to build over a mistake that happened more than thirty years ago."

"Thirty-six." I took several deep breaths. My jaw had tensed up so tightly, it hurt to speak. "Your mistake was born thirty-six years ago. It'll be thirty-seven years in July."

"You have to understand," she said again. "I was a college student. It was my first time away from home. It was fall break. My friends were all going to Chicago. It seemed so cool. We felt so grown up. We went to the clubs. We met guys." She looked away. "But I wasn't grown up. I was young and foolish. And I didn't know what to do."

"You could have talked with your mother," I said. "She would have helped you."

"I wasn't ready for a child," she answered, as if it was as easy as that.

"So you handed me over to my father, who was equally unprepared? You handed me over to his glacier-cold mother?" My voice took on that shrill tone that made me feel ashamed.

"I gave you to a well-connected Chicago family. They had the means to care for you," she said. "You have to understand."

She wasn't listening to me. She wasn't trying to understand the childhood I'd had. By running away from me, she'd denied me my grandmother's love. Mabel would have loved me. Although I'd known her less than a week, Mabel *had* loved me.

I closed my eyes and pinched the bridge of my nose. I needed to remain calm, but all I wanted to do at that moment was scream.

Harley reached over and squeezed my hand. "Without your statement or DNA, Penn has no way to prove she's Mabel's grandmother. Your brother's lawsuit argues that because Penn isn't a blood relative, she shouldn't have inherited the shop. The petition argues that Penn somehow coerced Mabel into creating her most recent will. To protect my client, I have to go public with the information you're telling us now."

I opened my eyes in time to watch panic tighten Florence's

expression. "No, you can't do that. You have to understand. No one can know about this."

Harley, bless him, squeezed my hand a little tighter. "If that's the case, Mrs. Corners, why are you here today? What did you think this confession of yours would accomplish?"

Florence rose from the sofa. "I wanted to give Charity the information she was seeking, that's why I'm here. I wanted to make it so she understood . . ." She hitched her purse—a pricy bright blue leather Prada bag—over her shoulder. "I suppose you don't see it that way."

"The lawsuit," Harley pressed. He released my hand and rose from his chair in an effort to block her path to the door. "I cannot sit on this information and let the business's assets remain tied up in court. Don't forget, your brother had the court put a freeze on the Chocolate Box's bank account and the money your mother set aside for the upkeep of the building. Because of that, Penn has already had to take out a loan just to cover the day-to-day costs necessary to keep your mother's shop open."

Florence's nervous gaze jumped from the door beyond Harley's shoulder and back to me several times before she heaved a deep sigh. "Very well. If I talk to Edward and get him to withdraw his objections to Mother's will, will that be enough for you to honor my wish to keep my secret?"

Was it?

Did I want to pursue a relationship with Florence? Did I want another indifferent parent in my life?

"I cannot recommend to my client that she agree to such a deception. You need to—" Harley started to say.

"Do you have any children?" I asked, surprised I didn't already know the answer.

"No," Florence answered right away. She then paled as she realized her mistake. She quickly licked her lips. "Other than you, that is," she said. "My husband was never interested in raising children."

I nodded, glad to know there'd be no awkward meetings with siblings where I'd have to pretend we weren't related.

"What do you expect from me in exchange for convincing Edward to drop the lawsuit contesting my grandmother's will?" I asked. "Do you expect me to lie about being related to any of you?"

"That would be preferable." She adjusted how her purse hung from her shoulder. "You have to understand that secrets are best kept secret."

Chapter 25

"I'm not going to lie and tell people that Mabel isn't my grandmother," I told Harley after Florence had left. I freed Troubadour from Bertie's bedroom. He hissed at me as if I was the cause of his banishment and made a beeline for Harley's inviting ankles. "I'm Mabel's granddaughter. Whether her ungrateful children believe it or not, it's the truth. I'm not going to let their hatred take away my heritage."

"You're preaching to the choir here." Harley bent down and scratched behind the kitty's bald ears.

"Do you think she'll convince Edward to drop the lawsuit?" I grabbed a piece of dark chocolate from the candy dish on the end table en route to letting Stella out of my bedroom. "Holding a clear title to the building and having access to the business's bank account would make my life easier."

Stella poked her nose out the bedroom door and sniffed. She then bounded out into the living room with a Papillon's burst of energy. Barking, she ran a circle around Harley and Troubadour several times before finding her favorite toy, a yellow rubber ducky, under the armchair. She squeaked it, tossed it in the air, pounced on it, and then, with the rubber duck in her mouth, pranced around the room while squeak-squeaking the toy.

"I don't see any reason why Edward would back down,"

Harley said. "I've never known Florence to have that kind of sway over his decisions. Does your dog ever stop moving?"

"Not when she's excited." As I passed the candy dish again, I grabbed a handful of chocolates, no longer pretending I was going to eat just a few. I knew, and I suspected Harley knew, that in a few minutes the dish would be empty. "She's like a tiny Border Collie with her endless energy."

Stella barked and ran around with her rubber ducky when she was nervous. I ate chocolate.

"Let's go to my office." He grabbed one of the chocolates out of my hand and popped it into his mouth before I could protest. "We need to document what took place during this meeting and get Miss Bunny to notarize it."

"But it's still our word against hers," I pointed out as we left.

"True. But it takes two people to make a child. Now that you know which of Mabel's daughters gave birth to you, you can take that information to your father. Provide him with photographs of Florence from around thirty-six years ago and let him identify her as your mother."

Go to my father? Several months ago, shortly after learning Mabel was my grandmother, I had asked him about my mother. He'd dismissed me. He'd said it had happened so long ago that he really didn't remember much about their short time together. She was nothing more than an iterant fortune teller, he'd said, repeating the story I'd heard my entire life.

If I sent him a photo, would he give me more information? Would he recognize Florence? "I don't want to hear him tell me again how unimportant my mother was in his life. Who knows if he'd even look at the photo?"

Harley nodded. "Florence told us she was a student away from home for the first time and that she'd traveled to Chicago with her friends. She didn't say anything about pretending to be a fortune teller."

"So?" The tale had been such a large part of the fabric of my life, shaping every important decision, that I couldn't even begin to imagine what Harley could be suggesting. The tale had been told to me so many times as if it were gospel truth that it had to be true. How could it not be true?

He gave me a kind look. "Penn, I think it's worth a conversation with your father. It might be a waste of your time, or it might give you some important answers."

"Because Florence isn't going to tell me anything?"

"As long as I've known her, she's always put her needs first," he said. "I don't think she'll change her ways now. But don't you agree that it's past time you learned the truth about your mother?"

Chapter 26

"I don't know if I'd recognize the truth even if it were a crabby alligator that lurched out of the marsh and bit me on the—"

"Althea!" I choked on the iced ginger tea she'd brewed for me. "What are you talking about?" The question sounded more like a strangled wheeze than a question, since I was still coughing and choking on the tea that had gone down the wrong way.

My friend got up from the kitchen counter stool and came around the small peninsula to give me a few sharp pounds on my back. "Is that better?"

I coughed a few more times before nodding.

Although Florence's words had been swirling around in my head along with my own denials—*that woman couldn't be my mother*—Florence's shocking revelation wasn't why I'd rushed away from the shop to visit my friend at her house.

I'd been forced to run because, quite frankly, her mother was twice as stubborn as a hungry badger and had continued to refuse to talk to me. And I needed to talk with someone about Stan's murder and the subsequent attempts against Bixby and me.

When I'd returned to the Chocolate Box around four o'clock, I'd found Bertie working alongside Tina. Althea, I was told, had gone home.

Eager to find out what Bertie had been up to most of the day and if her activities had involved Bubba, I may have bombarded her with questions.

With a big grin plastered on her face, she told me not to worry so much about her. "Penn, I'm an old woman. I've got experience enough to know how to take care of myself. I don't need you fussing around me like a mother hen."

"You do look rather henlike right now," Tina, who was stealing a sea salt chocolate caramel from our inventory, said with a laugh. "Leave the poor woman alone."

"Aren't you a sweet dear?" Bertie said, patting Tina's cheek. That tight grin was still plastered on Bertie's face.

I was an expert on those kinds of grins. I'd once used them as a lifeline. The tightness hid the expression that threatened to contort your face into another direction and shout to the world the hurt and sorrow threatening to consume you.

Weren't we a pair? I was wearing that same grin to hide the shock that currently had me reeling.

"You worry about everyone around you." Bertie pointed her timeworn finger at me. "What you need to do is start worrying about yourself. Those bullets were aimed at you, not me."

I edged my way to the door. "There's someone I need to talk to about all this weird stuff that's been going on at the concerts. You guys don't mind closing up the shop, do you?"

"Where are you going?" Tina demanded. She started to remove the white apron she'd donned sometime during the day. "I'm coming with you."

"No, please stay and help Bertie. It's not fair to leave her with all the work it takes to close up the shop." That wasn't at all true. Bertie and I often traded off the task of both opening and closing the shop in order to allow the other to attend an event, or go shopping, or simply have a life.

Bertie, who could read me better than almost anyone, nodded

gravely. She then said with a fake old-lady warble in her voice, "I would appreciate your help, Tina. If you don't mind?"

At least Bertie was still willing to play along when I needed to get away and poke my nose into places it didn't belong. Though I was sure she wouldn't have been so accommodating if she'd known I was also poking my nose into *her* business.

Tina eyed me as if I were the last piece of chocolate in a candy dish. "I suppose, if you need my help," she said to Bertie, sounding not at all enthusiastic, "I can stay."

"Thank you, Tina." I ran over to her and planted a huge kiss on her cheek, which shocked both of us. "I've got to run."

That's when I rushed straight to Althea's house.

Althea lived in a small cottage in the middle of the island. It was one of a dozen one- and two-bedroom cottages built in the 1950s. Her grandfather had built the cottages to give the black community, who during the height of segregation hadn't been welcome in many of the beachfront inns up and down the Southern coastline, a vacation spot where they could relax and enjoy the cooling ocean breezes. The place had served as a blessed break from the summer's humid and unrelenting heat.

Years after desegregation, the demand for the vacation cottages dropped off. What had once been a bustling business gradually became a largely empty resort that barely covered the bills. Althea's grandmother went to work as a maid in one of the beachfront inns to keep her children fed. And her grandfather started to sell off the cottages.

The whitewashed clapboard homes with rusty tin roofs predated the building requirement that homes on the island be elevated to protect against flood damage. So, unlike many of the beachfront houses on the island with long runs of stairs leading up to the front door, only two low wooden steps led up to the small front porch. Ancient oaks, twisted from years of being battered and shaped by constant wind, formed a thick canopy over the collection of small cottages.

Althea's grandfather had kept one of the cottages for his family's use. Eventually Bertie had moved there with her husband and raised Althea in the small two-bedroom home. And now it was Althea's home. She'd planted a wide variety of herbs, wildflowers, mushrooms, and pineapples, making the approach to her home feel as if I were entering some secret fairy realm.

Not that I believed in such things. I didn't.

Upon my knock, Althea took one look at me and ushered me inside.

The inside of her house smelled earthy-sweet from the various diffused oils she said she used to keep the spirit world sated. The furniture in the tiny living room was eclectic and painted a rainbow of bright colors.

She'd once told me how she'd remodeled the interior, knocking down the wall between the living room and the kitchen to add room for an island that included a breakfast bar. She'd then painted each wall a different color: a deep purple, a bright peach, a sunset red, and a robin's-egg blue. They should have clashed. The varied pieces of furniture should have clashed with the walls and with each other. But, and I have no idea why, the room worked. The explosion of colors created a fun, welcoming space.

"What's happened, Penn?" she demanded after closing the door behind me. "You look as if you've seen a ghost. You didn't, did you? See a ghost, I mean? The spirits have been unusually restless lately."

"You know I don't believe in ghosts. It's been windy. That's what's been restless. The wind," I said as I paced back and forth the small distance between the front door—through the living room—and the kitchen.

"Then tell me what has you looking like . . . like . . . like you *didn't* see a ghost?"

"It's your mother that has me looking like this." Oh, that wasn't exactly true. Of course I was worried to death about Bertie's behavior. But it was Florence's words that had me feeling as if I couldn't breathe.

"My mother? What happened?" Her dark skin turned ashen. "Where is she? Don't tell me she's gone again."

"No, don't panic." I put a reassuring hand on her shoulder. "I didn't mean to alarm you. Nothing's happened to her. She's fine. Really. It's not just her running off that has me worried. It's the fact that when she disappears, Bubba does too. And as much as I want to believe Bubba is innocent in Stan's death, his uncharacteristic behavior ever since that horrible night is terribly suspicious."

"Wait. Bubba has been disappearing, too? At the same time that Mama is running off? It has to be a coincidence."

"It might be a coincidence, but I'm afraid that it's not. This morning your mother got a phone call that upset her, and she went running out the door. Next thing I knew, Alvin and Fox started hanging out in the shop because Bubba had canceled their scheduled practice. I was hoping that if we put our heads together, perhaps we can figure out what's going on. Perhaps we can get a better handle on who killed Stan and who shot at me this morning."

She gasped. "You don't think—?"

"Of course I don't think your mother was involved in either event." I prayed she wasn't. "But she's involved in something. And that something didn't start until after Stan's murder."

"Ohhh, I don't know much of anything. I wish I did. I dearly do." She moved over to her bright yellow sofa and began digging around in the red-and-white striped beach bag she used as a purse during the summer months. "I tried to find where she went today and saw her only after she'd returned to the shop. Now where is it?"

"Where's what?"

"The note I found in Mama's purse."

"You went snooping in your own mother's purse?" I asked.

She stopped searching and looked up at me. "Do you think I'm a terrible daughter?"

"No, I'm wondering why I didn't think of it. What did you find?"

She started digging around in her beach bag again. "It's not here. I'm sure I put it in here."

"Could that be it?" I pointed to her kitchen counter, where a small square of yellow paper was being used as a coaster for an oversized teacup.

Althea let out a cry of frustration and then grabbed the paper, using her silky green shirt to wipe at the water ring that had formed. "I don't know where my head has been lately. I keep doing stuff like that. I hope it's not early dementia. You don't think it might be dementia?"

"I'm sure it's not dementia, Althea. What's on the paper you lifted from your mother's purse?"

"This." She handed me the paper. "It doesn't make much sense."

The handwriting on the paper was perfectly upright but looked as if it had been written by someone with a shaky hand. It wasn't at all like Bertie's clean, tight-looped, sloping letters.

"Secrets are deadly. Look at what happened to Stan."

Frowning, I looked up at Althea. "What does this mean?"

"I wish I knew. It's not Mama's handwriting."

"Definitely not," I agreed. Was it Candy's? It looked different from that first threatening note she'd sent sailing through the shop window, but nerves could have made her handwriting shaky. "Is it a warning or a threat? It sounds like a threat. Is

202

someone threatening to hurt your mother? But why? Did this note come from the same person who killed Stan? Does she know something that could lead us to the killer?"

"I don't know," Althea wailed. "She won't talk to me about *anything*. No one needed to send her this note. She clearly has no intention of sharing her secrets with anyone."

My mind went back to what Florence had said about keeping secrets. She didn't want anyone to know she was my mother. Ugh. Just thinking about it made me throw up in my mouth a little bit.

"Are you okay? You're not getting sick, are you?" Althea asked with alarm.

"I . . ." I couldn't say it aloud. I simply couldn't. "Sorry. My stomach is feeling queasy."

"Ginger tea should help with that." She sounded relieved that my queasy stomach would give her something to do, a purpose. She moved with ease through the kitchen, filling a kettle with water and putting several bags of ginger tea into a teapot.

"Do you have any idea what secret this note is referring to? Do you know of anything your mother may have done in her past that she (or someone else) might want to keep secret? Something that involved Stan?"

"Secrets? Mama?" Althea snorted at the thought. "Goodness, no. She's as straightlaced as anyone could be."

"Did you know she used to sing with The Embers?" I asked.

"Get out of town!" In her excitement, she spun toward me with such speed that she spilled the kettle of water she'd been carrying to the stove. "Mama sang with those good old boys? No, that can't be right."

"It's true." I pulled out the flyer Stella had unearthed in the office and handed it to her.

Her deep brown eyes widened as she read it through. "Mama? Why wouldn't she tell me she sang in a band?"

"She sang with *Stan* in that band." I mopped the water off

the floor with a rag while Althea refilled the kettle. "I asked Alvin and Fox about your mother and that flyer. They said that even though she was supposed to sing with them at the festival, she didn't. They mentioned that something had happened, but neither of them would tell me what it was. But whatever happened, it caused her not to sing with the band ever again."

"And this was in 1975?" Althea asked.

I nodded.

Althea didn't say anything else after that. She just quietly continued making the ginger tea. Her lips moved as she started to squeeze the juice of a lemon into the steeping pot. It appeared as if she was engaging in a silent argument with herself, so I kept my mouth shut.

Our friendship was like that. We could sit together, sipping tea and often something stronger, and not say a word. I liked that about Althea. Despite her crazy ideas about the supernatural, she was easy to be around.

She pressed her lips tightly together as she poured the fragrant tea over ice and then handed me a large glass before pouring one for herself.

We'd been sipping our iced tea while silently contemplating the puzzle about Bertie's mysterious connection with Bubba, The Embers, and Stan's murder for several minutes when Althea blurted out her statement about alligators and truth. Once I'd finished coughing up the tea that had gone down the wrong way, I asked her again what she was talking about.

"Mama," she said, clearly distressed. "That's what this is about. I thought I knew her. I thought we were close, that she was not just my mother but also a friend. But she won't talk to me about any of this. She won't tell me why she's been acting so oddly lately. She won't tell me what kind of trouble she's gotten herself into." Her hand started shaking so violently, she had to put down her glass before she spilled it. She then leaned toward me. With her voice trembling as strongly as her hand, she whispered, "Is Mama somehow involved with Stan's murder?"

"We need to find out. If your mother won't talk with us and the band members won't either, we need to find someone who will. Do you know someone who was around back then? Someone who would be willing to talk to you?"

She closed her eyes and thought about that for a while. "You won't like it," she warned with her eyes still closed.

"I won't like it? You aren't suggesting you want me to talk to a ghost, are you? Come on, Althea, you and I both know that would be a waste of everyone's time and it wouldn't get us any answers."

She opened her eyes. They had a funny glow in them. "Of course it would be a waste of time," she quickly agreed. "Spirits are notoriously unreliable. Now, don't get me wrong; if a ghost comes to you with a tidbit of information, listen to it. It might save your life. But if you go asking the spirit world for specific answers, forget it. What you'll get is—"

"Stop. Please, stop." Her talk of the spirit world was making me itchy all over. I hated magic because of who my mother was—a fortune teller. But Florence hadn't said anything about being a fortune teller. She'd said she was a student. Had a lifetime of fear and hatred of magic and fortune tellers been based on a lie? Oh, it didn't matter. Magic wasn't real. And my friendship with Althea worked as long as we didn't talk nonsense. "Let's just say we agree and change the subject. Who do you think might talk to us about the past?"

"Uncle Kamba. He's a root doctor."

"A what?" I asked.

"A root doctor. Kamba lives on a nearby hummock island that's only accessible by boat."

"Root doctor? So that means he works with trees?" I asked.

She shook her head. "No, not trees. He practices what popular media likes to call voodoo. But it's not voodoo, it's—"

"No. No. No. There has to be someone else." I wasn't going to visit a fortune-telling conman in search of the truth. "Perhaps someone at the Pink Pelican Inn will talk to us." I slid down from the kitchen counter stool. "And in the meantime, if you remember hearing anything about your family from that time, tell me, okay?"

Althea followed me to the door. "Kamba is a nice guy. I spent a couple of summers with him during college, learning from him. He won't tell you anything that isn't true."

I snorted at that. It was rude of me, I knew. But I had trouble controlling my knee-jerk reactions to the unbelievable. When I heard crazy statements like that, I snorted.

"Has anything else happened today?" Althea asked me as she opened her front door for me. "You seem more tense than usual. I mean, even for you."

"Someone shot at me," I reminded her.

"I suppose that would be enough to frazzle anyone's nerves," she said slowly. Her big calico cat brushed my leg as it darted inside with a mouse in its mouth. "That's her rubber mouse, not a real one," Althea said with a laugh. I didn't know why she was laughing. It wasn't as if I'd shrieked at the sight of the mouse dangling from the cat's mouth. Well, not too loudly.

I wasn't sure why I didn't tell Althea about Florence's shocking revelation that afternoon. It wasn't as if my friend would go blabbing about it to anyone in town. Like pretty much everyone else in this town, she knew how to keep her mouth shut about secrets that didn't belong to her. An annoying trait when I needed to get information, but comforting when there was a secret to be held.

I probably didn't say anything simply because I couldn't make the words come out. Saying them aloud would make them true. Even thinking the words "Florence was my mother" made my chest ache.

Anyhow, I thanked Althea. Just before I left, she grabbed me and pulled me into a tight hug. "When you're ready, you know you can tell me what happened to upset you this afternoon," she whispered in my ear. "We're friends. Friends depend on each other, no matter what. Friends protect and help each other."

That's what had me so worried. Had Althea's mother gotten herself in over her head with whatever was going on in this odd town? How far would the protective members of this community go to shield one of their own? Would they conspire to commit murder in order to protect Bertie and her secret?

Chapter 27

The band scheduled to play that evening was a local group that played beach music hits from the late 1940s and early 1950s. Many of the songs were R&B hits of their time.

Bubba had told me the group was popular with many of the area's shag clubs. As usual, he'd been right. Ticket sales had been robust for a band that very few outside the Carolina shag world would recognize. Everything seemed to be going along smoothly enough.

Since it was a few hours before the concert, I decided to spend some time working in the Chocolate Box's kitchen. Tina and Bertie had finished closing up the shop for the day. I hurried through the silent interior to the kitchen in the back of the building.

Since I didn't have the heart to ruin another of Mabel's recipes, I decided to play with the idea that had been bouncing around in my head about crafting a spicy bonbon. I wouldn't follow a recipe; instead, I'd follow my taste buds and see where they led.

The outside world and its problems seemed to fade away as I chopped red hot chili peppers into tiny pieces and mixed them in with peanut butter and paprika. I then rolled the mixture into a dozen equally sized balls. Next, the spicy peanut butter balls were dunked into melted chocolate that was so dark it nearly tasted like finely crafted bourbon. I was in the middle of the dipping process when my cell phone rang.

With melted chocolate simmering in the double boiler, it wasn't a good time to take a call. But with so much going on in my life, I couldn't afford to ignore it.

I glanced at the screen. It was Granny Mae finally returning my call.

"Granny Mae!" I tucked the small phone between my ear and my shoulder—somewhat of a tricky maneuver with my credit-card-thin smartphone. I lowered the heat on the double boiler and wiped my hands on a towel.

By the time I'd finished, the phone had nearly slipped from its perched position on my shoulder at least three times. I gripped it in my hand and pressed it too tightly to my ear.

"How is the chocolate making going?" Granny Mae asked.

Because I loved talking cooking with her, despite the fact that neither of us had much of a clue about what we were doing in the kitchen, I briefly told her about my current attempt to design my own recipe, the chocolate bonbon fires.

"Oh!" she crooned. "That sounds delicious! You're going to have to mail me a box."

"I'm still working on the recipe," I warned as I poked one of the still melty and very experimental bonbon fires with the tip of my finger. "These might taste awful. I haven't really had much time to work on it. The shop's been really busy. And then some nut tried to burn the place down last night. And today someone, probably the same nut, shot at me."

Granny Mae went silent on the other end.

"I didn't mean to blurt all of that out like that," I said as I leaned against the marble counter.

"You're having troubles again?" she asked.

"It all started with the band member I found in the bonfire, or did it start with the rock someone threw through the shop window? I can't keep it all straight."

"Oh, Penn, no." She sighed. "Please tell me you're being careful and keeping yourself safe."

"I'm safe, but—"

"But you're investigating, aren't you? And you need my help sorting through the details?"

"No, that's not what I need to talk with you about." While I could use her help sorting through the details surrounding Stan's murder and how it seemed as if someone was setting up Candy to take the blame, I needed Granny Mae not for her amazing mind but for her generous heart.

"I found my mother," I said with a trembling sob.

"Oh, honey," she whispered. "Tell me all about it."

It took several slow, even breaths before I reined in the anger and upset that had made me feel as if I was losing control. Once my voice felt steady again, I told Granny Mae all about the meeting with Florence and how it hadn't been the Hallmark tearjerker reunion I'd hoped such a moment would be for me.

"She's lying," she said once I'd finished.

Two words. Simply stated.

They were the exact two words I'd needed to hear.

"What makes you say that?" I asked. It suddenly felt as if I was no longer adrift in a sea of emotions.

"If this woman was your mother, she would have hugged you." Granny Mae had tossed me a lifeline. "I know you don't believe me when I tell you this, Penn, but you are huggable."

Those stupid tears swam in my eyes. "She dropped me off at my father's dorm room and never even tried to contact me. I don't think she's the hugging type."

"I know it's hard to be rational about these things. It's too personal for you. So let my rational brain do the heavy lifting for you. If Florence was telling the truth, she'd agree to take the DNA test."

"But she doesn't want anyone else to know," I pointed out. "She's ashamed that I exist. She wouldn't want a DNA test out there that I could potentially use against her."

Granny Mae went quiet for a minute. "That may be true. Still, there's something about what you've told me that's nagging at me. Something's not right about any of this. You need to talk with your father, see if he can corroborate her story."

"Harley told me the same thing."

"Good. I always thought he was a smart man."

"I've talked with my father about this before. He tells me that he doesn't remember anything about her beyond the fact that she was a fortune teller."

"Aha! That's what has been bothering me about her story. Florence told you she was a college student visiting Chicago with her friends during a break. Her story doesn't mesh with your father's. She's lying."

Oh, how I wished that were true.

"So you still think Carolina is my mother?" I asked.

"She might be. Do you still have a detective searching for her?"

"I do, but he's not had much luck."

Her earrings clanked against the phone, which meant she was nodding. "Have that detective poke around in Florence's background for a while. Ask him to find out what she was doing around the time of your birth."

"But what will that accomplish?" I didn't want to stop looking for Carolina. I'd developed all sorts of fantastic reasons why she might be so hard to find. She could have become an undercover agent, living on the edge of danger while breaking open spy rings. And she'd been forced to give me up for my own safety. Or she could have testified against a dangerous crime organization and been required to go into the witness protection program. The new identity assigned to her was an itinerant fortune teller. She always had to be on the run from the bad guys. In both those scenarios, giving me up would have been a selfless and loving choice.

So I guess, in reality, it hadn't bothered me too much that the detective agency searching for her hadn't been able to find her. I wasn't ready for those fantasies to be burst.

"It will help you prove that Florence is lying to you," Granny Mae said. "Also, start thinking about why Florence would lie about this. What does it accomplish?"

"I . . . I don't know." I was surprised I hadn't wondered about that myself. Florence had always come across as selfish and cold. And yet she'd told me today that she had revealed her secret because she thought I needed to know. A selfless act? How very unlike Florence.

In frustration, I picked up one of the melty bonbons and tossed it into my mouth. I chewed the peanut buttery center, expecting the chili peppers to bite me back. They didn't. I didn't feel any heat in my mouth until I'd swallowed the bonbon. Not the result I'd wanted. The heat needed to be on the palate immediately.

"How long has it been since any of Carolina's family has seen or heard from her?" Granny Mae asked.

I pulled my focus away from the chocolates and had to think for a moment before saying, "She ran away in 1975."

That was the same year as the last Summer Solstice Beach Music Festival and the same year something happened to make Bertie quit singing with The Embers. Clearly, whatever had happened to her back in the seventies had caused Bertie to start acting strangely ever since the start of the concert's revival.

"Oh my goodness, I bet it's connected," I said.

"What is, dear?" Granny Mae asked.

"Carolina's disappearance, Stan's murder, the exploding grill, and this morning's shooting. I think they are all connected to the same event that made Bertie quit singing with the band."

Chapter 28

"Taste this," I said to Tina the next morning. I'd spent the early morning hours alone in the kitchen. It was just me and the chocolate and a jalapeño pepper.

It took two tries, but I managed to make a tray of bonbons that contained their pepper ganache filling and held their shape. I'd decorated them with a deep sunset red sugar to illustrate the flame they held inside. After cooling them in the refrigerator for about an hour, it was now time to see if the flavor combinations worked as well as the visual presentation.

Tina, who'd come down from the upstairs apartment in search of breakfast, looked amazing. Her brown hair was pulled up in a ponytail that made her look as if she was still in her twenties. She was wearing the cutest tank-top summer dress cut from a fabric that featured big-eyed panda bears peeking out from behind rosy petals. Her tan strappy sandals looked both comfortable and adorable.

I handed her one of my bonbon fires and held my breath as she took a bite.

"Well?" I asked when she didn't say anything. That's when I noticed her cheeks had started turning a deeper and deeper shade of red. "Do I need to back off on the pepper?"

"*Water*," she rasped and then fanned her mouth with her hand. "*Water*."

There weren't any drinking cups in the kitchen. I grabbed a five-cup measuring beaker and started to fill it with tap water. She snatched it out of my hands before I'd finished and swallowed the water in one loud gulp.

"More." She thrust the cup at me.

I filled. She snatched and drank.

This cycle repeated itself for several minutes before she held up her hand and nodded. "What did you put in that thing, liquid heat?"

I sighed and dumped the tray of bonbons into the trash. "I was trying to make sure you tasted the heat of the pepper right away."

"The heat of the thing hit me like a frying pan."

"Too much pepper." First, too little. And now, too much. It was disappointing.

"Keep working at it. It's a good idea." She slumped against the counter and waved her hand over her opened mouth as if still trying to cool it as I carried several dirty bowls to the sink. "Now let me ask you what I came down to ask before you set fire to my taste buds."

"Set fire to your taste buds? That would be a good slogan for my bonbon fires." I started to fill the sink with hot, soapy water.

"If you plan on selling those, you'll have to have your customers sign a waiver."

"No, I'll tone it down. I'm sure I can work out a recipe that tastes right." Actually I wasn't sure of that at all, but I didn't want Tina to know it. If she thought I was struggling, she'd call in reinforcements—like my father—to come and "help."

"I know you can," she said. "Now let's talk about what happened yesterday. Do you need me to—?"

"Yesterday? The police will handle all that. I'm more

interested in talking about your upcoming fall fashions. What colors will the designers be using? Is there a texture or fabric I should start shopping for that will be the next big thing?"

"Green will be all the rage this fall. The softest mossy green you've ever seen. I'm pairing it with light tans and . . . Wait a blasted minute. You're deflecting, silly bean," Tina said. She'd joined me at the sink and had taken control of the scrub brush. "You have a knack for changing the subject when you don't want to open up about something."

She stood back and looked at me. Water from the soapy brush she held dripped all over the floor.

"I don't know what you're talking about. I wasn't deflecting." I grabbed the brush from her. I didn't need a large puddle to mop up in addition to the pile of dirty kitchen equipment sitting in the sink. I put some muscle into scrubbing dried chocolate from the double boiler.

"Don't play stupid with me. You know exactly what I mean. I'm just wondering what you're trying to hide from me."

I loved Tina. If not for the dangerous situation here in Camellia Beach, I would have enjoyed sitting down with her and unloading all of my troubles. But there was a killer loose on the island, and I didn't want to see her get hurt.

Undeterred by my silence, she pressed on. "Could it be that you don't want to talk about how Bixby and that surfing lawyer of yours are both sweet on you? I still can't believe that lawyer of yours brought over that delicious mole poblano sauce on a whim last night."

"He said he made too much, and he knows I like anything with chocolate in it," I said, trying to suppress a smile. I was sure he'd brought over that flavorful sauce because he knew I'd still be upset over what Florence had revealed to me and he knew I liked to drown my worries in food. It was a decent thing for him to do.

"Riiiiight. He made too much. Don't get me wrong. I'm glad he brought it. It was luscious drizzled over the fish and rice you and Bertie cooked. Oh . . . you're distracting me from the point I'm trying to make again. Where was I? Oh, yes, you don't want to talk about your love life—or rather lack of love life. Or perhaps you don't want to talk about yesterday's shooting. Or maybe you don't want to talk about that mysterious meeting you had up in your apartment yesterday." She looked at me with a smirk. "I know you, silly bean. You don't want to talk about any of it. But what, I wonder, scares you most?"

My cheeks burned. When had Tina gotten to know me this well? Could the rest of my family read me this easily? Was that why they were so adept at getting under my skin?

"I don't have time for these games." I dropped the scrub brush into the sink with such a splash that soapsuds splattered on my face. I wiped them off with my sleeve. "I have to help Bertie open up the shop."

Tina trailed behind me. "Something happened yesterday that spooked you. And, curiously, it wasn't that someone shot at you. I'm here because you need me. Lean on me, Penn. For once in your life, don't shut everyone out."

I stopped in the middle of the hallway. "Give me time. I'll . . ." I had no idea what I would do if given the time to think about it, so I didn't finish that thought. I simply needed time to figure it all out.

With a sharp nod, she let the matter drop.

We found Bertie in the front, sliding a tray of chocolates into the display case. Because I'd closed myself into the kitchen super early that morning to work on my experimental bonbon fires and Bertie always attended early-morning church services on Sundays, this was the first I'd seen her since the previous night. It looked as if she hadn't slept well. Her eyes were bloodshot. She emptied her coffee mug in just a few sips before going back for another.

She kept shooting glances in my direction as if worried I might hound her for information.

That was a fair worry. After we'd enjoyed our delicious fish dinner with its dark chocolate tones last night, I had pressed her to tell us where she'd gone the day before. I had pressed her to tell me about the threatening note Althea had shown me. And when she'd stayed stubbornly tight-lipped about both of those things, I had pressed her to tell us what had happened to make her quit singing with The Embers. It was important that she talked with us. I wanted to help. It could save her life and Bixby's.

Unfortunately, I'd hounded her to the point of aggravation. Soon after supper, she had bid Tina and me good-night and closed herself and Troubadour into her bedroom. A moment later the TV in her room was turned on. The muffled sound of canned laughter from old sitcoms carried through the walls. It continued as background noise in the rest of the apartment all night.

I'd lain in bed listening to the bursts of laughter from her TV while thinking there was nothing funny about this situation.

As we moved around the shop this morning, Bertie kept her distance. She took another sip from her newly freshened cup of coffee and went back to getting the shop ready for customers. She seemed determined to ignore me.

I raised my brows at that and shot a glance in Tina's direction. "You wanted to know what upset me the most yesterday? You're right that it wasn't Crazy Candy shooting at me. It was my three o'clock meeting," I said to Tina. "The meeting was about the Maybank family, specifically about my mother."

"Really?" Tina nearly pounced on me from across the room. She held onto my arm as she waited for me to tell her more. "Have you learned anything new?"

218

This tidbit of information had also gained Bertie's interest. She put down the tray of freshly baked croissants that had just come off the delivery truck and wiped her hands on her apron as she turned toward me. A look of compassion softened her hard expression.

Bertie had dearly loved Mabel. They'd supported each other both with this shop and also emotionally. Losing her had left a gaping hole in Bertie's life. These past several months, she'd floundered as if unsure how to move forward. Thankfully, my own floundering in the shop's kitchen had kept her mostly busy. Her love for Mabel had clearly spilled over onto me. I loved her too. And I was grateful for everything she did for me. It was time I did something for her.

I glanced down at my hands. They shook just a bit while I decided exactly how to proceed. I didn't want to say anything that would hurt Bertie. But if I wanted to help her, I needed to do this. "I have learned a few things about my mother. But there are still several questions I need answered."

"Questions about Carolina?" Tina asked.

I smiled and nodded. "Yes, about Carolina."

Bertie wouldn't talk to me about her past? She wouldn't talk to me about what had been going on between her and Bubba this past week? She wouldn't tell me why she was carrying a threatening note around in her purse? Things were at an impasse. But Granny Mae, with that clever mind of hers, had inadvertently given me the key to get Bertie back on my side with this investigation.

My mother.

"I know Carolina ran away from home. But what I don't understand is why. Learning the answer to that might be crucial to finding out what happened to her and where she went."

"Shouldn't the private investigator you've hired be able to answer that question for you?" Tina asked.

I shrugged. "He's more focused on finding where she lives

now, and not with much luck." I turned to Bertie. "Did Mabel ever tell you why Carolina ran away? Was it really because she didn't want to run the Chocolate Box? You were living here at the time, weren't you? Do you know what happened?"

Bertie closed her eyes. "Lots of things were happening on Camellia Beach around that time."

"When did she run away from home?" Tina, bless her, asked.

Bertie, her eyes still closed, furrowed her brows with distress. "It was the summer of 1975."

I held my breath, hoping she'd tell me something that would help me connect the dots between Stan's murder and the mysterious occurrence that had happened in the days leading up to the last Summer Solstice Beach Music Festival that had apparently affected so many lives.

When Bertie opened her eyes, she looked at me as if her heart was breaking for me. "Mabel didn't like to talk about it," she said softly, "but she believed Carolina was involved with a man who didn't treat her right."

"How old would she have been at the time?" Tina asked.

Bertie thought for a moment. "She had to have been in her mid-twenties. She'd graduated from the College of Charleston a few years earlier and had been working with Mabel in the shop. Everything seemed to be going smoothly. But there was talk on the island that Carolina wasn't happy."

"Because of her man trouble?" I asked. "Do you know who she was dating?"

"I remember it like it was yesterday," Bertie said. Her lips twisted into a tight frown.

"Who?" Tina pressed.

"Who?" I begged.

She kept her silence for so long that I started to doubt she'd answer.

"Bubba," she said finally.

Chapter 29

I knew it! It *was* all connected. Stan's leaving the band and my mother's . . . er . . . *Carolina's* disappearance. They had both happened around the time of the Summer Solstice Beach Music Festival. Carolina had disappeared shortly after the festival. Stan had quit the band. His leaving had caused The Embers to break up. This had also happened shortly after the festival.

And Bertie had quit the band a few days *before* The Embers were scheduled to play at the festival.

"Did something happen between Bubba and Carolina? Is that why she left?" I asked Bertie.

"Some say he was the reason. Others say Carolina was unhappy working for her mother," was all she'd tell us.

Several hours later, Tina came along as I walked toward the pier. "Did you hear how Bertie answered your question this morning?" she asked. She'd added a straw sunhat and a pair of oversized sunglasses to her flowers-and-panda bear ensemble. I owned a similar pair of sunglasses. On her, they looked perfectly normal. On me, they looked ridiculous. "Obviously, she knows what happened. What do you think she meant when she said Bubba didn't treat Carolina right? Was he abusive? Did he cheat on her? Did he use her for her money?"

"I don't know," I said.

The street was unusually crowded with beachgoers and beach music fans. I had to step into the road to get around a family window shopping at Althea's crystal shop.

"Bertie knows why Carolina left," Tina whispered as she stuck close to me. "She has to. So why won't she tell you?"

"Probably because it involves her," I said with a sigh. In Althea's window display was a geode. The purple crystals encased in stone sparkled in the bright sunlight. "I think that's why she's acting so . . . oddly. And I suspect whatever happened all those years ago between her and Bubba and Carolina is also why she stopped singing with the band."

"But why would it matter now? And why would Bubba's idea to bring the band back together get Stan killed?" she asked.

"I don't know." I stared at the geode in the window, thinking how kind it was for Ezell to buy his nephew a thank-you gift for his help this weekend. The fact that Ezell had even known that Tom liked rocks spoke volumes about his temperament. He'd make a good senator. I hoped I would be able to help him find his friend's killer. "Maybe if they sang, someone might remember the past and the killer didn't want that to happen?"

"Stan didn't even want to sing with The Embers. You'd already convinced Bixby to take his place."

"And Bixby was excited to do it. He loved the songs, especially 'Camellia Nights,' which was the last song Stan wrote before leaving to make a name for himself on the national stage."

"Bixby told me about that song. He sang a bit of the refrain, 'Three times three, he took her out to sea . . . under a Carolina moon on a Camellia night.' It's catchy."

"But now the sheet music for the song is missing." Just like Carolina went missing forty years ago. "Stan left the band before they could sing 'Camellia Nights.' Is that important?"

"I hate to say it, Penn. But everything you've told me so far makes your friend Bubba look guilty. He's the one with the grudge against Stan. He's the one whose bad behavior might have chased Carolina Maybank from the island." She grabbed my arm. "We need to find out what Bubba did to Bertie to chase her away from singing with the band."

"I don't think he did anything. Bertie has been defending his innocence," I reminded her. "She told us herself that she wouldn't stand by and let an innocent man be accused of something he didn't do."

"She does seem very passionate about him," Tina agreed, just as her cell phone chimed. She looked at the readout, smiled, and then sent the call to voicemail.

"Who was that?" I asked.

"Oh, that? One of the editors from *Vogue*. The magazine wants to do an interview. I'm supposed to set up something for this coming week at my studio."

"What an opportunity. And you're getting calls from the editor on a Sunday? They must really want to talk with you. You should have taken the call." This was the perfect reason for Tina to pack up and go back to Chicago where the streets weren't crowded with killers. Well, it was Chicago. But you get my meaning.

"You're not getting rid of me that easily. We have a mystery to solve and a murderer to catch. So what do we do next?" Her smile grew by mammoth proportions.

"We don't do anything." I certainly wasn't going to do anything with her following along like a baby duckling. "I promised Detective Gibbons I wouldn't investigate."

"But he's chasing after Candy while the real perpetrator is walking around with no one the wiser," Tina said.

"Perpetrator? Are you trying to sound like a dime-store detective?" I asked with a chuckle.

"One of us needs to start acting like an investigator." She gave her hips a sassy swish. "They haven't caught Candy yet, have they?"

"I don't know." I dialed Detective Gibbons's number.

He picked up almost immediately. "Please tell me you've been keeping yourself out of trouble."

"I've been trying to. Do you have Candy in custody yet? Or do I still need to keep the glass replacement company on speed dial?" I spotted Congressman Trey Ezell walking down the street. He was dressed in khaki shorts and a white lawn cotton button-up shirt. I'd never seen him look so casual. It was a good look for him. When he saw me watching him, he raised an arm and waved.

"Candy has so far eluded us," the detective grumbled after a lengthy pause.

"How can that be? This is a small island," I demanded.

"It is," he agreed. "And my team has scoured every inch searching for her. They've done it multiple times now. She must have taken a boat to the mainland."

"Penn!" The congressman started hurrying toward us.

"And have you reviewed the evidence? Do you now think she's the one who killed Stan?" I asked the detective, hoping he'd say no.

"She's a likely contender," he said, as if he was leaving several important details out of that answer.

"I don't think she shot at me."

The congressman had reached us. He raised a brow when he heard me say that.

"I think someone set her up to make her look guilty," I said, which made the congressman's jaw drop.

"You promised you wouldn't get involved," Gibbons said.

"I'm not getting involved! I've just been doing a little thinking. And while nothing is really clear in my head, I can't come up with a reason why Candy would kill Stan."

"You told me you thought Candy killed Stan by accident and that Bixby was her intended victim," Gibbons reminded me.

"Yes, but why would she want to kill the man she's been following around the country for years? Is she looking to retire? No, she still loves him. And what's her motive to shoot at me from a distance after standing not more than a few feet from me? She's a stalker, not a killer."

Gibbons huffed. "Why are you parroting back to me everything I've been telling you?"

"Because you've been right all along," I had no trouble admitting.

He huffed again. "We still need to find Candy."

"That's true. Please let me know when you do. And detective?"

"Yes, Penn?" he growled my name as if he wanted to reach through the phone and shake me.

"While I promise not to investigate, I will be keeping an eye out for anyone who wants to shoot me, because someone *did* shoot at me yesterday, and I have no idea why. Plus, I have a festival to run. And I'm going to do everything in my power to make sure everyone stays safe."

"We have an ongoing investigation. You must know by now, I'm not at liberty to tell you everything we know. But I can tell you that we're doing our best to keep you and everyone else in Camellia Beach safe," he said brusquely. "So please, keep your wandering eye from wandering to places where it ends up putting you in any further danger."

By the time I disconnected the call, Congressman Ezell's mouth was hanging open. He quickly snapped it closed.

"You haven't seen Tom around, have you?" he asked once his jaw was back in working order.

"No, why?" I hoped nothing was wrong.

"He was supposed to meet with me on the pier half an hour ago to prepare for a photo shoot the newspaper scheduled for this afternoon, and he's not shown up."

"Have you tried calling him?" Tina asked.

"I have, with no luck." He looked at her and smiled. I quickly introduced the two. He turned on his polished politician charm as he shook her hand while boldly declaring himself to be South Carolina's next U.S. senator.

"That's impressive," she said.

"It would be even more impressive if I knew where my nephew went."

"I heard he's been hanging out with Harley's son Gavin," I said. "You might want to try calling over there."

He thanked us and started to walk away. But then he suddenly stopped and doubled back. "Not to intrude, Penn, but I couldn't help but listen in on your phone conversation. Were you talking with Chief Byrd or Detective Gibbons?"

"Gibbons," I said.

"You shouldn't give him such a hard time. He's a good man. I have total faith that he'll be able to do the job," Ezell said.

"I do, too," I agreed. "I just wish he'd catch whoever has been terrorizing our town a little quicker."

"Yesterday couldn't be soon enough for me," he agreed. "I feel as if we're all standing around holding our breath while waiting for the next attack. You and I really should put our heads together. I might be able to help you put your thoughts in order. We could sit down somewhere right now and work through what we know."

"As a matter of fact, we were about to get some lunch and talk about how we can try to fill in the gaps of what we know," Tina said. "We'd love for you to join us."

I glared at Tina. That wasn't what we were doing. We were heading to the pier to check in on the festival. And why would she invite someone neither of us really knew that well to be part of something I wasn't planning on doing in the first place?

She smiled sheepishly. "We do need to eat."

Ezell readily agreed to join us for lunch. "I think if we talk things through, we might be able to come up with something to tell the detective. He's not a local, so he doesn't know the history as well as a native, such as I, would."

Since the Dog-Eared Café was one of my favorite lunch spots on the island, that's where we headed. The café was located in a newly renovated one-story building in the middle of the island about a half-block off Main Street. The bright blue concrete-block structure with equally bright green trim had once served as the island's Laundromat. A small sign beside the door featured a silhouette of a howling dog.

After we all perused the menu, I ordered my usual, a Thai shrimp wrap. Tina ordered Bertie's favorite, the crab cake sandwich. And Ezell ordered a coffee. "I don't have time to stay too long," he explained. "I still need to find Tom before the photo shoot."

"We understand," Tina said with a kind smile. "We'll take whatever time you can spare."

"First off, I want to hear your thoughts on what's going on, Penn. Did I hear you tell Gibbons that she didn't think Candy was behind yesterday's shooting? Everyone else on the island believes otherwise. I heard she was in the shop threatening you and then ran into the same vacant lot where the shots came from. Sounds like she's the one to me."

"That's what the real shooter wants everyone to think," Tina declared. She leaned forward and whispered, "Penn is certain Candy was set up."

"Really? Why?" Ezell's eyes lit up. His voice matched Tina's level of excitement. They both sounded eager to go chasing after a deadly killer with no regard for their own safety.

"It all goes back to something that happened more than forty years ago," Tina said. "At the last Summer Solstice Beach Music Festival, in fact."

Ezell's brows rose. "Really?"

"The congressman was good friends with Stan Frasier," I warned Tina. I didn't want her to inadvertently say something insensitive. "They'd been friends since childhood."

It was her turn to say "Really?" She latched onto the congressman's arm. "Then you are exactly who we need to be talking to. You must know what happened back then."

The waitress interrupted whatever Ezell was about to tell us when she arrived with our drinks. She stayed to chat a bit about the warm weather and to talk about how great the festival had been for business.

Tina, who looked as if she was about to burst from anticipation, took a sip of her sweet tea and then insisted the waitress go and brew her a fresh cup of unsweetened tea, providing specific instructions on how the freshly brewed tea should be poured into a pre-iced glass before adding ice.

"That should keep her occupied for a while," Tina declared after making the poor waitress promise to do every step in the process with great care.

"You had better give her a huge tip," I said. "That was cruel."

"No, it was necessary. We need privacy," Tina countered. "And you already know I'm a generous tipper."

Ezell shook his head. "If you hadn't already told me the two of you were sisters, I would know it now."

"Sorry about that." I pressed my hands to my heated cheeks, but inside I was smiling. This was the first time in my life I truly felt as if I had a sister. Not a half sister who was raised to compete with the other half siblings for the scarce attentions our father afforded all his children, but a full-blooded, love-her-no-matter-how-crazy-she-makes-me sister. It felt good. Really good.

Tina didn't notice me hugging myself or the goofy smile I was now wearing as I watched her. She pressed on with questioning Ezell as if the waitress had never interrupted her.

"Congressman, what can you tell us about Bubba's relationship with Carolina Maybank?"

"Please, when I'm on the island, I'm just Trey," he said as he sat back in his chair. His eyes softened as he looked past the both of us. It appeared as if his intense gaze had transported him back in time. "Carolina Maybank. I haven't thought about her in ages. She was a spirited girl who loved this island. She loved everything it had to offer—swimming in the ocean, fishing off the pier, walking along the sandy beach in the moonlight, boating through the marshes. She painted. Did you know that? Her landscapes were the best. Even all these years after she ran away, I still have one of her paintings hanging in my office. It depicts the marsh at sunset. A shrimp boat is making its way up the river to its home dock as bold streaks of red, bright yellow, and dark purple color everything in the scene. Whenever I look at it, I'm home."

The goofy smile plastered on my lips grew larger as I listened. This was my mother he was talking about. And she was talented and sporty and—I sighed—someone I would have loved to have in my life.

She wasn't a con artist who professed to be magical.

She wasn't a parasite who had taken advantage of a naïve college boy.

And she wasn't my mother.

Florence had stepped up and claimed that honor.

That last thought sobered the smile right off my face. Ah, well. Whether Carolina was my mother or not didn't matter. I needed to find out more about her and if her disappearance had anything to do with Stan's murder. "Do you know why she left the island?" I asked.

"Sadly, no," Ezell said. "If I remember correctly, it seems she just packed up and left one day. Maybe your family can help you answer that question. Maybe one of them even knows where she went."

"I have asked. Her siblings all say they haven't heard from her since the day she left town." I tapped my fingers on the table. "I heard she left because the man she was dating at the time treated her poorly. Do you know anything about that?"

He chuckled. "Is that old rumor still going around? It was all a lie, you know. Vicious, really." He looked around before lowering his voice. "I hate to speak ill of the dead, especially when the dead man was my friend, but it was Stan who started that rumor. He told everyone that Bubba was stepping out on Carolina, which was ridiculous. Bubba had bought a diamond ring for her and was on the verge of proposing. I have firsthand knowledge of it since I'm the one who drove him into the City of Charleston to the most respected jewelry store on King Street."

"What happened?" Tina leaned forward and asked.

Ezell shook his head. "Carolina left. But don't you believe for a minute that was the outcome Stan wanted. He'd started the lie because he hoped Carolina would fall into his outstretched arms. He wanted to console her and . . . more."

"Why? Why would he sabotage a close friend's relationship for a woman who hadn't expressed any romantic interest in him?" Tina asked.

Ezell checked his watch and told us that he needed to run. He hoped we could get together again soon to finish our brainstorming. As he stood, he dropped a few dollars on the table to cover the cost of his coffee. I thought he was going to leave without answering us.

But I was wrong. Before walking away, Ezell lowered his voice and said, "Bubba and Stan may have played in the same band, but they were never friends."

Chapter 30

"Again, I have to say it. It looks like Bubba is guilty of murder," Tina leaned across the café table and whispered.

I'd been pushing my coleslaw around my plate while thinking about how Stan had sabotaged Carolina and Bubba's relationship. Could a bad breakup really be the reason Carolina had disappeared without a trace for over forty years? "I can't imagine Bubba holding onto a grudge for that long. It all seems unbelievable."

"Did he ever marry?" she asked.

"Who? Stan? I don't know." I gave a piece of mayonnaise-drenched cabbage another push with my fork. Because of Stan's meddling, Carolina had moved away and changed her identity? That didn't make sense.

"Are you paying attention to me? I'm asking about Bubba. Has he ever been married?"

I had to stop and think about that. "I don't know. We'll have to ask Bertie."

"I know he's your friend and all, but you need to consider the possibility that he's responsible for the murder and mayhem happening on this island. If he never married, perhaps it's a sign he's been pining for Carolina all this time."

"But if the motive for murder is revenge for breaking up a relationship, why wait forty years?"

Tina shrugged. "Isn't this the first time Stan has returned to Camellia Beach?"

"That would make Bubba an awfully lazy murderer. He waited forty years for the man he wanted to kill to come back to the island? That doesn't make sense. Why wouldn't he simply travel to where Stan was singing and kill him there?"

"Don't forget how Stan vowed to stop The Embers from selling their songs to Bixby. That last argument might have caused Bubba to snap and commit what they call a crime of passion." Her voice dipped into a lower, more dramatic register as she said "crime of passion."

"You really need to lay off watching all of those crime dramas on TV." I poked at a raisin with a fork tine. The café added them to the coleslaw to make it taste extra sweet.

"Think about it, Penn. Even if you like the guy, you have to agree that his alibi for the night of the murder is weak. Does he really expect us to believe that someone hit him on the head and set him adrift on a boat?"

I set my fork down on my plate. "He didn't do it."

"What makes you say that?"

"Bertie." I wasn't going to finish my lunch, which was a mini-tragedy in itself. The food here was always amazing. I waved for the waitress.

"Bertie? Are you serious?"

"I am. She trusts Bubba. And I trust her."

I worried about Bertie. I worried about what she was doing and where she was going. But deep in my heart, I trusted her.

Tina shook her head but didn't say anything because the waitress had just arrived with the bill. After chatting with us for a while about the food, the server carried off our plates.

"You're crazy," Tina whispered as soon as we were alone again.

"Crazy? Because I believe Bertie? Perhaps you're right. I do have a bad track record when it comes to trusting the wrong people."

"Oh, Penn, I didn't mean it that way," she said gently. She placed a more than generous tip on the table. "There's nothing wrong with trusting the people in your life. I know that's been hard for you. And I'm so happy that you've finally started to feel confident enough to let people who love you get close to you. You're finally letting me get close to you. But you also need to realize that some of the people you love might be wrong."

Some of them might even have been dead wrong.

*   *   *

On the pier, many of the concert vendors had decided to keep their booths open during the day, which was a smart move. Tourists flocked to the pop-up shops, voraciously buying everything from concert T-shirts to beach music CDs to silly hats. As Tina and I passed a booth selling Beach Boys bobbleheads, a tourist started feeding popcorn to the seagulls. Dozens of the large white birds gathered and, shouting at each other, began fighting for prime positions, which appeared to be directly above Tina's and my heads.

The seagulls seemed to echo the frustration of the angry voice in my head. "If the killer isn't Candy," I asked, "why would someone want to shoot me? What threat would I pose to anyone on this island? No matter what you think, Bubba wouldn't shoot at me, especially not with his bandmates standing right next to me in hitting range."

"Does that mean you've changed your mind? Do you think Candy is responsible for the shooting?" Tina put a hand over her sunhat and hurried me away from the growing flock of noisy birds.

Had I changed my mind? "You have to admit it would simplify things, wouldn't it? If we believe Candy is guilty, all the pieces kind of fall into place. She killed Stan by accident, thinking she was killing her unrequited love. She then rigged the grill to explode, damaging Bixby's perfect brows. Finally, she shoots at me. And in the middle of all this, she breaks into my shop and tries to set it on fire. Every piece of the puzzle gets wrapped up quite nicely in a pretty bow—Candy's *demented* pretty bow, but a bow nonetheless."

"But she didn't do it." Tina turned around abruptly, just as a gust of wind blew her sunhat from her head. Long strands of her brown hair pulled loose from their bobby pins and whipped in the wind like Medusa's snakes. She grabbed at her unruly hair and tried to tuck it back into place with no luck. The wind was too strong.

"Here." I handed her the sunhat I'd managed to catch before it sailed over the pier's railing and into the sea.

Congressman Ezell's booth was a few yards away. I spotted the congressman right away. He was talking with a woman holding an expensive-looking camera. Several of the residents from the Pink Pelican Inn were gathered around him like he was a rock star. A man with a walker reached out and started to vigorously shake his hand.

Young Tom, dressed as if he should be heading to church instead of sitting in the heat hours before a beach music concert, wandered past us. He dragged his feet with every step.

"I'm glad to see your uncle found you. He was worried," I said to Tom.

"Oh, hi, Miss Penn," he said. "There are so many people out today, I didn't see you. Uncle Trey wanted me to take some pictures for some newspaper, and I'd spilled ketchup on my suit. I had to go home and change. Have you talked with Bixby Lewis lately?"

I hadn't, which worried me. Candy was still on the loose. And, despite my doubts about her guilt in Stan's murder, she could be dangerous. I raised my brows in Tina's direction. She shrugged and said, "After yesterday, I can understand why he'd want to keep his distance from the shop. He texted this morning to say he was planning to spend the day practicing with The Embers."

"They're playing tonight?" Tom asked.

I nodded. "It's the last night of the festival. Bubba had said he wanted the festival to go out with a splash from the past with the Embers reunion."

"And Bixby will be playing with them?" Tom asked with the first bit of excitement creeping into his preteen ennui.

"He is." I pressed a finger to my lips. "But it's a secret, okay?"

"Are you a big fan, Tom?" Tina asked.

The boy nodded. "Oh, yes. Bixby is the greatest. Don't you think so?"

"He's pretty great," she agreed. "Be sure to come to the VIP area so you can get a good view tonight."

"If Uncle Trey lets me, I'll be there. Thank you." With a little more bounce in his step, he started to walk away. "Don't forget to vote Ezell in next week's primary," he called to us as if reciting a line in an amateur play. "Every vote counts."

"I'm sure your uncle will do a great job," I called back. As Tina and I continued down the pier, my cell phone buzzed.

I checked my phone's screen. "It's Althea," I said as I answered the phone.

Without much of a greeting, Althea told me she had some new information about her mother. I agreed to meet with her at her house right away.

After I disconnected the call, Tina glared at me. "I'm not going to let you ditch me."

"I wasn't going to—"

She didn't let me finish. "Whether you want me to or not, I'm coming with you to hear what Althea has to say. End of story. Okay?"

"Okay." I noticed the congressman had left his booth. Bags of bonbons sat out in the hot sun on his display table. If he didn't put them away soon, they'd melt.

"No, you can't talk me out of it," Tina argued. "Wait . . . did you say okay?"

"Afterward, if there's time, I want to try my hand at making bonbon fires again. I could use a taste tester." I smiled.

"Ohhhh . . . you're not going to get me to do that again." She trotted alongside me as I hurried down the steps of the pier.

I was anxious to hear what Althea had learned.

Thankfully, Althea's house was only a few blocks away.

"I'm sure this next batch won't be nearly as hot," I said, pumping my arms and stretching my long legs as we made our way down one of the streets that ran parallel to Main Street.

"I'm not going to risk it," Tina said. "You need to be your own taste tester."

"But where's the fun in that?" I laughed.

"It wasn't fun the first time."

"It was for me. Okay. Okay." I held up my hands in surrender. "You win. I'll taste them first. But when I'm in the kitchen, it would be a huge help to me if you could run by Bunky's Corner Store. With everything that's been happening as well as the work we've been doing with the festival, neither Bertie nor I have made it to the grocery store in ages. The fridge is empty. And then afterward could you work the front of the shop for me?"

"Why does it feel like you're trying to ditch me?" Tina asked, sounding suspicious.

"I do want to work in the kitchen. And if we don't want to eat chocolate for every meal, we need to put some food in the fridge. And if you could lend a hand in the shop, it would be a big help to me." None of that was a lie. But I also wanted to do one other thing, something I didn't want to discuss with anyone. Something that just thinking about doing made me feel as antsy as Stella after she'd spotted a squirrel in a tree.

As we rounded the corner to Althea's cottage, I noticed Tina was trying to study my face as if searching for the deeper truth in what I'd told her.

"If it's too much of a bother, forget I asked," I said. "I just thought—"

"Oh, shut up and just give me a shopping list already." She thrust out her hand. "I'll pick up whatever you need."

"Thank you, Tina," I said. "I do appreciate it."

"Yeah, yeah. Just promise that someday you'll tell me what you're really planning on doing this afternoon."

"I'm going to work in the kitchen. Cross my heart."

She shook her head in disbelief. I'm sure she would have badgered me further if we hadn't just arrived at Althea's house. Althea was working like a berserker as she weeded the front garden.

When she spotted us, she jumped up and wiped at the muddy knees of her jeans before peeling off her equally muddy gloves. "Come on in," she said as she carefully placed the gloves in a bucket that held an array of gardening tools. "The iced tea is waiting."

She served the tea and fussed in the kitchen before I told her to go ahead and spill it already.

"I visited Uncle Kamba this afternoon." She held up her hands. "Now don't give me that look. He was living in Camellia Beach throughout the seventies, and he was willing to talk to me.

What he does for a living and the things he believes in shouldn't matter to you."

I tried to wipe the look of revulsion off my face. Althea was right. I shouldn't judge someone, especially someone I'd never met, based on their supposed belief in the supernatural.

Tina nudged me. "If you keep pursing your lips while squinting like that, your face is going to get stuck looking like that painting of the *American Gothic* chick."

Althea chuckled. "Watching the two of you together makes me wish I wasn't an only child."

"You don't have to be an only child." Tina tossed her arm over Althea's shoulder. "You can be our honorary sibling."

Something happy squeezed in my chest. It felt as if Tina were hugging me too. Despite the danger of a killer on the loose, I no longer wanted to stuff Tina onto a plane and send her away. I wanted her to be here with me and the rest of my makeshift family.

I was so wrapped up in all this familial happiness I'd forgotten the reason why Althea had called this morning visit. It was Tina who put us back on track.

"What did you learn from your uncle?" she asked.

Althea gave me a cautious look before answering. "He told me something interesting about Mama. He said she'd quit singing with the band because there was talk, vicious talk about her having an affair with Bubba."

Ezell had just told us how Stan had lied about Bubba's supposed affair, but he'd left out the part about Bertie. "None of that talk was true, though," I told her. "Your mother wasn't having an affair with Bubba."

"I know that," Althea said sharply. "Of course the talk was wrong. But Uncle Kamba said, true or not, the rumors caused all sorts of trouble between Mama and Daddy. It may have been the reason why Mama had me so late in life. Did you know she was thirty six when she had me? That was old for back in the seventies.

"She'd been focused on her career at the naval base and had been busy singing with The Embers. She hadn't really wanted a child. But soon after quitting The Embers, she got pregnant with me, and then she quit her job at the naval base too. Her life completely changed. Turned on its head." Althea frowned. "Kind of makes me sad. She had me in order to smooth things over with Daddy?"

Both Tina and I pulled Althea into our arms. "You know your mother thinks the world of you," Tina said.

"No woman ever loved her daughter more," I said. "She's happy."

"But her past clearly troubles her," Althea said. "If it didn't, she wouldn't be so secretive about it now. She wouldn't be running off without telling anyone where's she's going. Why is she doing that?"

"Maybe she's trying to protect you," I said. "She doesn't want you to find out about the rumors and the trouble it caused between her and your father. She doesn't ever want you to think you weren't wanted."

Althea looked up, and after swallowing hard, she nodded.

"Thanks, I needed to hear that." She dabbed at her eyes with a tissue. "I know you're right. But I can't help but feel sad about the terrible time Mama must have gone through. It must have felt like the end of the world for her."

Chapter 31

"George Penn," came my father's crisp voice through my cell phone's speaker.

I shivered. He'd answered the phone as if he was taking a business call even though it was close to four o'clock on a Sunday afternoon. I didn't know who he thought he was fooling. I knew his secretary would have told him it was his eldest daughter on the line.

Keep your cool, I told myself as I stirred the ingredients for my latest attempt at making the perfect sweet-and-spicy bonbon fire while Tina worked out front.

"Good afternoon, Father," I said, hoping I didn't sound petulant. I felt petulant.

"Good afternoon," he said, still sounding as if he was talking with a business associate. "What do you need?"

I took a quick breath and plunged in as if I were diving blindly off a cliff while hoping I'd land in a teacup of water. "As you might recall, I've been searching for my mother. I think I might have . . . um . . . found her. I was wondering if I sent you a picture of the woman who claims to be her that you'd take a look at it and tell me if she looks at all familiar."

He didn't answer right away. And when he did, his voice sounded even chillier than before. "Charity, I've already told you that I don't remember much about her. It was such a long time ago. Have this woman take a DNA test. It'll be more conclusive. And for God's sake, Charity, don't give the woman any money or let her give any interviews."

I closed my eyes. He should have known by now that I was smarter than that. Thanks to the countless lies and betrayals I'd endured over the years, I'd erected such ironclad barriers that I barely trusted even close friends like Althea and Bertie.

Instead of telling him any of that, I simply said, "Yes, Father."

"Once you get the DNA results, I expect you'll send me a copy," he said. I could tell he was ready to get off the phone.

"She won't agree to take a test," it pained me to tell him.

"Charity!" he barked. "You should know better than to believe this woman. If she's not willing to prove she's your mother, she's clearly not your mother. If this faker goes to the press, it'll only upset your grandmother."

"But if I could send you some pictures of her and her sisters, perhaps you——"

"You should be glad to have the family you have and not worry about finding a woman who couldn't be bothered with offering even part-time care," he said right over me.

"But I found my maternal grandmother. I sent you a copy of the DNA report, remember?"

"And I'll tell you again what I said to you then. I cannot remember anything about your mother. It happened a long time ago, and I didn't have a relationship with her. It was a mistake. She conned me into believing things I shouldn't have believed. That's what fortune tellers do, though. They con people. Like a nesting parasite, she took advantage of a young well-to-do college boy and then left him to take responsibility of her offspring. Now, you'll have to excuse me. I have a tee time that starts in a few minutes."

He disconnected the call.

Well, that had gone about as well as I'd expected. I sprinkled finely chopped jalapeño peppers into a mixing bowl.

At least he'd told me something I'd wanted to hear, I mused before deciding I needed some fresh air. He'd told me that Florence wasn't my mother.

Sure, he had no way of knowing if it was true, but I enjoyed hearing him say it. As I clutched that thought tightly to my chest, I headed out the shop's back door.

I'd barely made it more than a few steps onto the patio when Harley came around the corner.

I was surprised to see him without his surfboard. I'd never seen him dressed in a suit and tie on a Sunday. No matter the weather, he would find his way to the waves. I always figured surfing was his religion.

"Are you coming from church?" I asked him.

He looked down at his suit and shook his head. "No, not church. I spent the afternoon in Edward's office."

Any happiness I was feeling at the thought (wrong or not) that Florence wasn't my mother dropped into the pit of my stomach like a ten-pound sack of flour. "Edward? As in my uncle who is suing me Edward? What could he possibly want to talk to you about? And on a Sunday?"

"He says he wants to make a deal."

"Do you think this is Florence's doing?" I still couldn't bring myself to think of her as my mother. "She said she'd get him to drop the lawsuit."

"I don't know, Penn. He didn't mention her. It could be that he knows his case can't possibly stand up in court and he's trying to get what he can out of you by pretending to be the good guy."

"You sound nearly as suspicious as I usually do," I said.

"I'm a lawyer. I get paid to be suspicious."

"I hope you're not charging me triple-time for working on a Sunday. My family might be rolling in dough, but I'm not.

My grandmother keeps my trust fund locked up behind so many trustees and red tape, it's nearly impossible to get access to any of it."

He held up his hands. "I'm not charging you. Not for today. Not for battling the Maybanks for what is rightfully yours. This, I'm doing for you as a friend. You should know that."

"Should I?" I quickly waved the words away as if erasing a chalkboard, because those two words opened a door to a conversation that felt more vulnerable than I was ready for right now.

"Penn, you should know that I—"

I blurted, "I called my father."

He raised a brow. "You did?"

"He won't provide any help," I said.

He didn't act surprised.

"He said I should tell Florence to take a DNA test or else forget that she ever talked to me."

"She'd like it if you forgot what she told you," he said.

"I know."

"So why did she tell you?"

"I don't know. Carolina might be dead." I'm not sure why I told him that. It was really just a queasy feeling that had started sloshing around in my chest since I'd spoken with Ezell about why Carolina left. Nothing, not even that conversation with my father, could vanquish the queasiness.

He chewed on that thought for a while. "That would explain why she's never contacted any of her family members in the past forty-odd years." He frowned. "Are you okay?"

"I will be," was the best I could answer.

"Are you going up?" He nodded toward the stairs leading to our apartments. "I have a roast in the slow cooker. I'd be happy to share."

"My sister is in town," I reminded him.

"She's welcome to come too. And Bertie. And"—he sighed—"Stella."

"What about Gavin? I thought this was your weekend with him."

"It is. But he's hanging out with his friend Tom. They have some big hush-hush project they're working on. He said he'd be back in time to go with me to tonight's concert."

"When you have such little time with him, it must be difficult to let him go."

"Harder than you might imagine. But, at the same time, I want him to be able to have a regular childhood and spend time with his friends." His lips pulled into a wistful grin. "I do get him for the entire month of July and a couple of weeks in August. So that's something."

"You're a good father," I said.

"Keep telling me that. Perhaps one day I'll believe it."

I would have done just that, but a late-model red sedan came careening down the road as if it was completely out of control. The two of us ran around to the front of the Chocolate Box. We both watched in horror as the car made a sharp turn and bounced over the shop's low front porch. Wheels spinning wildly, the car crashed through the front of the shop.

The plate glass window shattered into millions of pieces.

"Not again!" I cried.

Forget the building, I told myself. *Someone might be hurt.* I ran straight to the red sedan. Steam poured out from the hood of what looked an awful lot like Bubba's car.

"I'll call the authorities," Harley said. His phone was already in his hand.

The sedan driver's side door had been flung open. I poked my head into its interior, expecting to find a medical emergency.

It was empty.

Maybe the driver had been ejected from the car.

I held my breath and visually scanned the building's badly damaged porch, troubled by what I might find.

Nothing.

"Stars and garters! What in a rotten melon rind is happening in this town?" Alvin shouted as he ran out of the gaping hole that used to be the front of my shop. "Done gone and started thinkin' the ceiling is going to collapse on our heads after that chrome grill came flying through the window."

"Is everyone okay?" I asked. "Did you see who did this? Where's the driver?"

"Didn't see nothing but that dang car careenin' toward us. The car done come right at us. Can't say I stood around watching. Bertie came running at us like a scalded haint and pushed Fox and me clear out of the way."

"A scalded *what*?"

"Haint! Haint!" he shouted. When he saw the blank look on my face, he added, "Gurl, that's an angry ghost. Fox and I done come by to get some more of your chocolates while Bubba and Bixby each attended to some business. What a time to be here. We'd just stepped into the shop when it happened. But what can I say?" He patted his belly. "We done needed fuel for our practice session."

"But everyone is okay?" I asked again, just as someone inside groaned.

Alvin and I exchanged worried looks before I hurried through the smashed storefront to get inside. Harley followed a few steps behind us.

Much to my horror, I found Bertie lying flat on her back, her leg twisted at an odd angle. Fox knelt by her side. Neither of them looked well. Bertie's skin had turned frighteningly ashen. Fox's cheeks looked alarmingly green.

I dropped to Bertie's side. "Has anyone called EMS?" I demanded.

Fox swallowed hard. "I did," he croaked.

"The fire department is on their way too," Harley said. "They'll be able to help."

Bertie turned her head toward me. "Gather at the river," she groaned. "My leg hurts."

"Oh, Bertie. Bertie. Bertie," I babbled, because that's what I did when I was nervous. "Your hair looks good." Yep, that was me, the girl who babbled *and* said stupid things.

Though I wanted to do . . . *anything* . . . to help ease her pain, I knew keeping her still was the best thing for her until medical help could arrive. I hugged her hand to my chest as if it were the most precious thing in the world. "Hang in there, Bertie," I whispered. "EMS is on their way. They'll be able to help you."

I prayed it was true.

It had to be true. If not for Bertie's talented hands, I wouldn't be able to keep the shop open. I needed her. I needed her like a child needed her mother.

"Hang in there," I whispered again.

"Don't look at me like I'm already dead. I'm not going anywhere. I just need to get my leg fixed up." That was my Bertie. Always so brave.

I swallowed. Hard. "Did . . . did you see what happened?"

"A car busted through the window over there," she managed to answer, even though she was clearly in great pain.

"Yes, yes, but did you see the driver?"

She shook her head and then groaned. "All I saw was the car. It knocked me flat on my back."

I leaned in closer. "Who would do this?"

"If I knew the answer to that question, I wouldn't be lying here like this, now, would I?" she said, then hissed in pain.

I winced.

Thankfully, the police, fire department, and a team of EMTs

all arrived at the same time. Glass crunched under their boots while sirens wailed loudly outside.

I kissed Bertie's knuckle and started to get up to give the EMTs room to work. Bertie grabbed my hand and pulled my ear close to her face. "The lighthouse," she rasped. "I'm awfully worried about"—she swallowed hard—"the lighthouse. Look at what happened to Stan."

"The old lighthouse?" I asked. I glanced over my shoulder at Harley, who shrugged.

"She's talking gibberish," Alvin said. "Happens when a woman is out of her head with pain."

"Has anyone called her daughter?" Fox asked the room at large.

"Oh, no, she'll be worried to death. I need to call her." Because I was flustered, it took longer than usual to work through the menu screens to get to the smartphone's actual phone function. "What hospital are you taking her to?" I asked the EMTs while selecting Althea's number from my favorites list.

Everyone in the shop fell silent as the EMTs wheeled Bertie away. I said another little prayer that she would be okay. Not just because she was vital to the shop but also because I loved this woman with her no-nonsense ways more than I'd ever loved anyone in this world.

I vowed I would personally make sure that whoever did this to my Bertie would pay.

Chapter 32

"What in the world happened here?" Tina demanded. Actually, she used several stronger words when she stepped into the shop through the opening that was once a window, squeezing around the smashed-up sedan.

She carried a paper grocery bag in each arm. She'd come in through the window because the police were blocking the door.

A younger uniformed officer from the town spotted her and trotted over. "Ma'am, you can't come in here." He held up his hands as if he were directing traffic. "This is a crime scene."

"And Penn is my sister." She gestured with her elbow since her hands were full. "I'm coming in."

The officer looked at Tina, who'd been taught by our father how to hold her own in the toughest of situations, then over at Chief Byrd. Byrd was busy questioning Alvin, who waved his arms wildly as he explained quite loudly what had happened. Seeing that he wasn't going to get help from a higher source, the young officer held up his hands again. "You'll need to leave."

"You'll probably want to question her," I told him. "She might have seen something. She can sit with me while I wait my turn to give our statements."

He frowned at me and then at Tina and finally shot a pleading glance toward Chief Byrd, who was still busy with Alvin.

"She can sit right there." He righted an overturned café chair. "But she cannot move from that spot or touch anything."

I nodded.

"You made the right decision, officer," Tina said, then handed him her groceries. "Be a dear and carry those to the upstairs apartment. There are several items in the bags that need to be refrigerated."

"He can't do that," I told her, shocked she'd act so brazenly around an officer of the law.

"Oh, you're right, Penn. I don't know what I was thinking. Give the man a key."

The officer, his hands now filled with the shopping bags, sputtered unintelligibly.

I found the key in my purse. Tina took it from me and slid the key ring over the officer's pinky finger. "It's the first apartment up the back stairs," she told him. "You can't miss it."

He sputtered a bit more before realizing no one was going to come to his rescue. Standing up to a determined Tina was rather hopeless. With a grunt, he headed back out the way Tina had come in.

I had to give him credit. Most men put up more of a fight before giving in to her demands.

Tina didn't sit where the officer had told her to sit. She didn't sit at all. Instead, she stood with her hands on her hips and glowered at me.

"You told me you were going to work in the kitchen," she said.

"I did."

"No, you were lying to me. I could tell by the way your nose twitched when you were talking that you were lying."

"You're making that up. My nose doesn't twitch when I talk."

"Am not."

"Are too." I held up my hands. "This car accident didn't

happen because of anything I did. I wasn't even near the front of the shop. I was out back talking with Harley when the car came careening around the corner, tires squealing."

"Really?" Tina squinted at my nose as if trying to see if it was twitching.

"My nose doesn't twitch." Even so, I slapped my hand over it to keep her from seeing whether it was twitching or not. "I was out back talking with Harley about the court case concerning this shop."

I looked around at the crumbling walls, the broken window, the long, jagged crack that had opened up in the ceiling, and the smashed tables and chairs in the seating area. The display cases and most of the items on the shelves had survived unscathed, which was a blessing. But I worried about the structural integrity of the building. Fixing the damage would involve much more than a call to the glaziers. I was going to have to close the shop during the height of tourist season, which could mean a loss of thousands of dollars of dearly needed income.

I dropped into the chair that the officer had set up for Tina. The adrenaline from the accident and from seeing Bertie rushed to the hospital was starting to wear off, leaving my legs feeling like wet noodles.

"Bertie was hurt," I said. "Her leg looked pretty bad."

Tina gasped. "Is she okay?"

I shrugged. "They took her to the hospital. I haven't heard anything since they left."

"Who did this? Candy?" Tina asked.

I shook my head. "The police can't find the driver. And no one inside saw who was driving. Heck, both Harley and I witnessed the accident, and we didn't see the driver run away from the car." I gazed at the chrome grill of the red sedan sitting silently like a beached whale in the middle of my shop. "It's Bubba's car."

"I knew it!" Tina slapped her leg. "Didn't I tell you? He's behind all of this."

I shook my head. "He's not a stupid man. And why would he want to crash into the shop? Look who's here. His bandmates Alvin and Fox. Alvin told me that the two of them had just entered the shop when the car came crashing through the window. If Bertie hadn't pushed them out of the way, they might have been . . ."

Oh my goodness. Why hadn't I thought of it before? I pressed my hands to my mouth. It was so obvious.

"What?" Tina demanded. "What are you thinking? Talk to me, Penn."

"I just realized I've been wrong about everything. And I mean everything. Will you please stop hovering over me like that? Try to find a chair that's not broken and sit down next to me."

It took her three tries to find a chair with four sturdy legs. She set it up so it was facing the chair I was using and then perched at the edge of the seat, her body leaning eagerly toward me. "Spill it."

"Stan, a former member of The Embers, was killed in the bonfire," I said as I held up one finger. I held up another. "The exploding grill was at the beach house The Embers had rented, not Bixby's rental house." I lifted a third finger. "Fox and Alvin were standing right next to me when someone shot at us. No, someone didn't shoot at us. Someone shot at them. I'd assumed I was the target because Candy had been there confronting me and because this is my shop and perhaps because I'm totally egotistical and make everything about me." Was that why Tina thought Bixby and I would make a good match? "But this isn't about me." I lifted a fourth finger. "Someone tried to run down Alvin and Fox with Bubba's car. Someone is trying to kill off the members of The Embers. And I suspect that person is trying to do it before tonight's concert."

"Tonight's concert?" Tina gasped. "That means the killer is getting desperate."

"Which would explain why someone would drive a car through the front of my shop," I agreed. "Sounds like an act of desperation to me."

"It could still be Bubba who's trying to knock off his bandmates. After all, the killer hasn't tried to kill him."

She had a point. But then I remembered the incident on the shrimp boat. "The killer hit him over the head and set him adrift in the ocean. That's a murder attempt."

"Which he could have faked," Tina was quick to counter.

I would have continued the argument, but Harley, who'd been on the phone with the hospital, came over. His expression was grim. He still held his phone in his hand.

"What's going on? How's Bertie?" I asked, terrified of the answer. Broken legs could be serious. They could be deadly if the leg broke at the wrong point.

Harley shook his head. "She's in surgery. We won't know the extent of the damage until she gets out. It's a wait-and-see situation right now. If you'd like, I could drive you to the hospital when we're done here. Althea is there all by herself. She's a mess."

"No," I said. I felt guilty saying it, but as Tina had pointed out, the killer was getting desperate. The concert was tonight. If the goal was to kill off the band members in order to keep them from playing, things were about to get very deadly in the next couple of hours. "There's something else I need to do. Can you go and sit with her and tell her that I wish I could be there too?"

"Please tell me you're not going to the old lighthouse." Harley said.

"I'm not going to the old lighthouse," I said.

He leaned down with his hands on his knees and gave me a hard look. "Are you telling me the truth?"

"What's at the lighthouse?" Tina asked.

"I'm not looking to put my life in danger. I just need to stay here to make sure there's enough security at the pier tonight. I need to make sure no one else gets hurt."

"What's at the lighthouse?" Tina asked again.

"I don't know," I said. "Bertie told me I needed to go to the lighthouse because she's worried about something that's happening there."

"Is that where Bertie has been going? The old lighthouse?" Tina wondered.

"I wish I knew," I said. I then implored Harley to go comfort Althea at the hospital and send constant updates on Bertie's condition. I also begged him to put Stella and Troubadour in his apartment, since there was a chance that my apartment, which was directly above the Chocolate Box, could end up falling into the shop.

"So where are you going?" Harley asked after he'd reluctantly agreed to do both. "What are you planning to do besides arrange for additional security on the pier, which you could do by phone?"

"After talking to Gibbons, you mean?" I nodded toward the detective who'd just trudged through the door. He stopped to talk with Chief Byrd. "I think I need to have a talk with Fox and Alvin. Hopefully, they'll have some idea why someone is trying to kill them."

Chapter 33

"It done must be my ex," Alvin exclaimed after I suggested the killer was trying to go after the band members. "She's always said she'd be the death of me."

"It ain't your ex. She's always said *you'd* be the death of *her*," Fox corrected.

"Well, the way she done nagged at me, you'd think she was gunning for my death."

We were all standing outside in the heat of the afternoon—Detective Gibbons, Tina, Alvin, Fox, and I—while I waited for the engineer I'd called to come and take a look at the building. I needed her to tell me if the ceiling would collapse if we moved the car. The police had completed their job, except for towing Bubba's car off to the impound lot. Gibbons had sent a few of his men out to pick up Bubba for questioning, even though he seemed about as convinced as I was that if Bubba had wanted to kill his fellow bandmates, he wouldn't be stupid enough to use his own car.

Gibbons, after hearing Alvin accuse his ex of murder, held up his hands. "I find it hard to believe that Marella would steal Bubba's car and drive it through the shop in order to kill you, Alvin."

"And what do you know of her?" Alvin demanded.

"As it so happens, I know her well. She sings in the church choir with my wife and me," Gibbons said. "She's been singing in that choir with us for the past twenty years. You'd know that if you'd ever attended service."

"Never been one for churchin'," Alvin said, then snapped his mouth closed.

"What?" I asked. "What did you just realize just now?"

"Done realized that if someone doesn't want the band to play tonight, we might get slaughtered on that stage." He paled and then leaned against a display case as if his legs could no longer hold him. "I ain't playing."

"Do you feel the same way, Fox?" Gibbons asked.

The lanky man scratched his ruddy whiskers. "Don't rightly know."

Even though Gibbons had questioned everyone extensively already, he flipped open his notebook again. "Chief Byrd and I have already made plans to beef up security, but no one will be upset if you decide not to perform tonight."

Speak for yourself, a heartless voice in my head snipped. *You don't have to pay the refunds on the unused tickets.* Luckily, I had my lips pressed together tightly enough that those words didn't escape.

"Have you had any luck locating Candy Graves?" I asked. Although I didn't suspect her of this crime—why would she want to hurt The Embers' band members?—her involvement couldn't be ruled out altogether.

Gibbons shook his head. "I think she must have somehow gotten herself off the island. But we've not been able to trace her. It's as if she's just vanished."

Just like Carolina Maybank had vanished? That sinking feeling returned to the pit of my stomach.

"Do you have any idea why someone wouldn't want the band to come back together and play?" Tina asked Fox and Alvin.

I was as interested in the answer to that question as anyone else, but I didn't get to hear it.

255

Tom Ezell came running up to the shop. "Miss Penn! Miss Penn! I need to have a word with you."

He'd shed his suit coat and tie and had rolled his white, sweat-stained shirt up to his elbows.

I stepped away from the others. "What is it, Tom?"

He skidded to a halt and stared wide-eyed at the car sitting halfway in the shop. "What happened here?"

"Someone thought we offered drive-through service," I said. "What can I do for you?"

"I didn't put the bags of chocolates into the cooler, and they all melted. My uncle is furious. Is there anything you can do? Can you make some more?"

The poor sweaty boy looked miserable. I had a feeling his uncle, who'd said more than once that he was grooming his nephew to follow him into politics, had given Tom a hard time. That was something I could relate to.

I patted his shoulder. "I wish I could whip you up a couple dozen more bags of our pretzel bonbons, but"—I gestured back toward the shop—"as you can see, we're not open for business."

Tears filled his eyes. "Uncle Trey is going to murder me."

"Would it help if I spoke to him on your behalf?" With Bertie in surgery, a killer looking to strike tonight, and the intrigue that Bertie seemed to think happened at the old lighthouse, I really didn't have time to go play peacemaker for a family squabble. But I also didn't have the heart to send young Tom away. All I could do was hope he wouldn't take me up on my offer.

"You'd do that?" he asked hopefully.

"Of course I will." Granny Mae, who'd once worked as Grandmother Cristobel's personal assistant, had occasionally stepped in for me when things got tense between me and either my father or Grandmother Cristobel. When she did, it had felt as if she'd saved my life. How could I not do that for Tom? "Let me wrap up here, and then I'll follow you down to the pier. I'm sure we can come up with a plan for tonight. That is, if the concert isn't canceled."

"Canceled?" he asked.

"Sadly so," I said. "It looks as if someone is trying to kill the band members. It might be too dangerous to go forward with the concert."

He followed me like a lost puppy over to where Gibbons and Tina were still talking with Fox and Alvin.

"I'd put my money on whoever stole that song Stan wrote," I heard Fox say as we got closer. "Stan never did let us play the song. Doesn't that seem strange? If nothing else, he should have insisted that we let Ocean Waves sing it in order to give his band a second hit and a shot at winning a second Grammy. I reckon if you find the song, you'll find the killer."

"Bah," Alvin scoffed. "You done never heard it. It wasn't all that great."

"What about Carolina Maybank?" Tina asked. "Do you know why she left town? Do you know where she might have gone?"

Alvin shook his head. "Bad happenings, that."

"She and Bubba had a falling out," Fox said.

"Over Bertie," I said.

The two men looked surprised. "Bertie told you about it, then?" Fox asked.

"No, she didn't," I confessed. "But I've been asking questions around town."

It was the detective's turn to look surprised. "Penn! You promised you were going to leave the police work to the police."

"I have been." I raised my hand like a Girl Scout making a pledge. "I've only been asking around about Carolina Maybank because I think she's my mother, and I've been trying to find her. It's nothing new. I've been trying to find her for the past several months."

That sinking feeling in the pit of my stomach dropped

several notches deeper. Besides all of those fantastic reasons (such as her being in witness protection or a spy) that I'd dreamed up to explain why the private investigator couldn't find even a trace of Carolina, there was one other (and perhaps even more plausible) reason why her whereabouts couldn't be traced. It was because she'd never left the island.

No, she couldn't be dead. Because if she were, that would mean that Florence really was my mother. And that would simply be awful.

"Carolina has to be my mother, and I have a right to know what happened to her. I have every right to try to find her," I protested a little too loudly.

Alvin raised his brows at my outburst. I was sure it had only further proved to him that all women were prone to hysterics.

Tina put her arm around my waist. "Yes, you can't tell my sister what to do."

"Let the poor girl find her mother," Fox implored.

Gibbons sighed. "I'm not trying to stop you from looking for your mother. I am concerned about your safety, though. Someone tried to burn down your shop while you were in it. Someone shot at you."

"Shot at Alvin and Fox," I corrected.

"We have no way of knowing that for sure. You were in the line of fire too," he was quick to say. "And now this happened. And Tina has been telling me about how Carolina Maybank left town shortly after The Embers broke up, and that you think what's happening in town today could be related to the reason she left." He paused just long enough to suck in a breath. "Something is going on, Penn, something that is terribly dangerous. You can't go running around asking questions that might make you vulnerable."

"Point taken," I said. "But the concert is tonight. And then, whether The Embers sing or not, the festival is over. The danger should be over too, right?"

"I don't know." The detective's brows dipped. "If someone wanted to stop a concert, there are simpler ways to accomplish it than attempting to commit multiple murders."

"Then what is the purpose for all this?" Fox asked as he pointed to the rear end of the car behind us. "Why shoot at us and then try to run us down?"

"That cursed song." Alvin looked as if he'd suddenly found religion. "Stan didn't want us to sing his song, so his haint done come back to sabotage our reunion concert."

"Alvin, I don't think this is the work of a ghost or your ex-wife. But I do aim to find out what's going on," Gibbons said. He then looked directly at me. "And I don't need your help doing it. Go to the hospital and take care of Bertie."

Chapter 34

"Though I want to, I can't leave and go to the hospital," I told Tina after Gibbons, Alvin, and Fox had left. "Not now. Not with everything that's going on."

I picked up a broom and started sweeping the broken glass into manageable piles on the porch's broken floorboards. I didn't know why I felt compelled to do that. The messes both outside and inside were too big to clean up with a push broom.

Both Harley and Althea had recently sent texts to let us know that Bertie was out of surgery and doing as well as could be expected for someone who'd just been hit by a car.

"Of course you can't go to the hospital. You have to wait for the engineer. And then we need to figure out what to do about this gaping hole," Tina said.

"Um . . ." Yes, there was that. And I hadn't forgotten that I'd promised to help young Tom Ezell smooth things over with his uncle.

"Penn," Tina demanded, "what are you planning to do?"

"I need to go to the pier." I explained to her about Tom's situation and the promise I'd made.

She looked around. "Where did he go?" she asked.

The last I'd seen him, he'd wandered away from the group

to stand under the large oak tree that provided quite a bit of shade to the front of the building. But he wasn't there now.

"Perhaps he was worried about staying away too long and rushed back to face his uncle?" I knelt down and swept glass shards into a dustpan. "I need to get over to the pier to make sure security is being tightened and that everything Althea was supposed to be handling tonight is getting done. I also need to find out if we're going to have a headliner band for tonight's performance. Have you heard from Bixby lately?"

"I sent him a few texts. He said he was looking for Bubba . . . again. What about Bubba?" Tina asked. "What is he doing? Have you heard from him?"

"I haven't." Which was troubling, seeing as it was his car that was sitting in the middle of the Chocolate Box. "If you could stick around here to meet with the engineer and watch over the shop, I could run over to the pier and check that everything is ready for tonight as well as talk with Ezell about Tom. And I'll also try to get in touch with Bubba. I need to make sure he's not been arrested, because if he has been, there definitely won't be a concert tonight."

"No way," Tina said. "I'm not letting you run off on your own."

"But I can't just leave the shop open like this." I pointed to the gaping hole.

She, in turn, pointed to the police officers, who were standing around while we waited to get word that the car could be moved without causing the second floor to collapse. The car was, after all, evidence. "They can watch the shop, and the engineer doesn't need you or me hovering around while she works."

Tina was right. Hanging around the Chocolate Box wasn't going to protect anyone at the festival or help us find the vile person responsible for putting Bertie in the hospital.

"Very well," I said. "Let's go."

We'd made it as far as Main Street when I grabbed Tina's arm. I then glanced at my phone just long enough to check the time. "Bertie was worried about something over at the lighthouse. Although I told Gibbons what she said, he didn't write it down in his notebook. He's not going to do anything."

"But what about tonight's concert?" Tina asked. "Shouldn't we make sure everything is okay at the pier?"

She was right, of course. But I didn't make a move toward the pier. We stood at the corner of East Europe and Main, dumbly staring at each other.

"Let's go take a quick look," we both said at the same time.

Ten minutes later, I was parking my car where East Africa came to a dead end on the north end of the island. The drive had led us to where a footpath led out to the abandoned red-and-white-striped lighthouse.

At one time, there'd been a house connected to the lighthouse. The two-story clapboard structure had crumbled into the encroaching sea decades ago. Black-and-white photos of the old keeper's house with the lighthouse rising up behind it were popular items at the tourist shops. I'd purchased a hand-colorized print and had it framed and mounted on the wall behind the cash register in the shop.

"Are you sure you want to do this?" I asked Tina, who sat in the passenger seat with her seatbelt still wrapped across her slim middle.

"Of course I do." She unsnapped the seatbelt. "Don't you?"

"I'm having second thoughts," I said. "It could be dangerous."

Just then a large family came down the sandy path. The father was pulling a wagon piled with beach chairs, a cooler, and a volleyball net. The mother chased after two young boys, who were spraying the rest of the family members with oversized water guns.

"Yeah, it looks like it's really dangerous down there," Tina said as a second family—also pulling a packed wagon—came into view. A third family parked their SUV next to my Fiat and started to get ready to follow the trail to the lighthouse, which was apparently a popular family picnic spot.

We kicked off our shoes, got out of the car, and headed down the well-used path.

The lighthouse sat at the edge of the water. At high tide, the ocean completely cut the lighthouse—and the small surrounding strip of land, protected by a tall red brick seawall—off from the rest of the island. Fundraising efforts were under way to slow the lighthouse's slow slide into the sea.

By the time we reached the shoreline, it was slack tide. Soon the water would start to rise again. But for now, getting to the lighthouse was as easy as crossing the wet sand and climbing the brick seawall.

We followed a family over the seawall and stood on the elevated weedy ground surrounding the lighthouse. I didn't see anything out of place. There wasn't any evidence of digging beyond shallow holes made by children.

The opening for the lighthouse itself had been boarded up long ago due to safety issues. Again, there wasn't any evidence that the boards had been tampered with. The heads of the nails holding them up were coated with thick ruddy rust.

"Nothing," I said as I looked up the lighthouse's brick exterior.

"Why did Bertie want you to come here?" Tina asked as she turned a full circle.

"I don't know. We'll have to ask her."

"This is a beautiful spot." She picked up a conch shell and held it to her ear. "I can hear the ocean."

"So can I," I said, laughing. "It's right there."

Tina handed the shell to a young girl who was running around with a bucket filled with "treasures." The girl squealed with delight and ran off to show her mother. Tina and I climbed down from the lighthouse and trudged back across the damp sand.

Since it was such a beautiful evening—and, yes, because I did want to show off to my sister just a bit—I led her down a side trail that cut through the heavily treed maritime forest. The trail led us to a hidden cove at the back of the island. While we could hear conversations of beachgoers in the distance, this part of the island felt as if it were separated from the rest of the world.

Dolphins frolicked in the cove. Birds flew overhead. And to our left, a large animal—a deer perhaps—crunched through the trees and thick underbrush.

Tina tossed her arm over my shoulder. "I can see why you like it here. It's quite magical, isn't it?"

"Not magic, but it is beautiful."

Tina poked me in the side and laughed. I laughed too. And for a glorious moment, I forgot about all about my ruined shop, Stan's murder, and the search for my mother. But moments like these were as ephemeral as the tide.

The large animal that had been rustling in the nearby trees suddenly charged at us like a raging bull. Tina yelped. I screamed.

We were on the verge of diving into the water for safety when the figure barreling toward us stopped abruptly and raised her hands.

"Candy?" I said, because it wasn't an animal at all, but a woman. Scratches crisscrossed her face, arms, and legs. A gash on her chin oozed blood. I was glad to see her. Glad to know my worries that she'd met a bad end had been unfounded.

Her breaths came in sharp huffs as she turned her head left and right before focusing on us. Her shoulders hunched as if she planned to charge again.

I held up my hands. "We're not your enemy."

Worried about what she might do, I kept a keen eye out for any sign that she might have a gun. Sure, I thought someone had set her up to take the blame for the shooting yesterday, but that didn't make me cocky to the point of stupidity. She might easily have gotten that gash on her head when she crashed Bubba's car through my shop's front window.

"I'm not dating Bixby. I'm not even interested in him," I said, my hands still in the air as if I was surrendering. I tried to push Tina behind me.

Candy huffed several more times before straightening. She propped a hand on her hip. "You're not his type. He likes"— she looked me up and down—"fashionable women." Her gaze moved to Tina. "Like her," she added.

I knew I shouldn't have taken offense, but I did.

"What's wrong with what I'm wearing?" I'd paired a pale pink pleated skirt with a white silk blouse. It was an outfit I'd worn to my former job as director of marketing for the Cheese King. Nothing about the outfit was shabby.

Candy, dressed in the same white dress she'd had on yesterday—it was now tattered and stained—waved a hand at me. "It's all too plain. Boring. You look like a secretary who hasn't an ounce of imagination. Nothing you wear has any personality."

"Oh." I bit my lip. She might be delusional, but she also might have a point. "Wait. What I'm wearing and whether it appeals to Bixby doesn't matter." What mattered was that a killer—*probably not Candy*—was still on the loose.

Candy's chin was still bleeding, which worried me. "Are you okay?" I asked. I started digging around in my purse in search of a tissue or a bandage.

"What?" She seemed confused by my concern.

"What are you doing?" Tina asked.

"She's bleeding." I pointed to Candy's chin and then held up a pack of tissues. "Do you need help?"

Candy backed up. I supposed she didn't want to risk the

possibility that I would try to get within arm's reach. "I . . . I just ran into a little trouble. I'm okay."

She'd been on the run from the police all night. I had no idea where she might have been hiding herself. But I did know that the vegetation on the island included tough plants sporting thorns, thick leaves, or stinging hairs. They had to be tough to survive the harsh conditions they faced on a narrow spit of sand at the edge of the ocean. If she'd been keeping to the island's wild areas, she was probably lucky to look as good as she did.

"I know someone set you up yesterday," I said, hoping I might gain her trust. If she had seen someone in those woods, I wanted to know. "I know that whoever lured you to my shop wanted you to be blamed for shooting at me."

Her hunched, ready-to-run stance loosened just a bit. I took that as a positive sign.

"I also know that you didn't kill Stan." I didn't know that as a fact, but I was hoping to make her believe I thought it was true.

Her brows furrowed. "Who's Stan?"

"The man who died in the bonfire," Tina said.

"Oh!" Her eyes widened. "That guy. Yeah, why would I hurt him?"

"Why would you?" I agreed. "What I'm wondering is why anyone would want you to take the blame for his death and for shooting at me yesterday?"

She shook her head. "There are lots of nuts in this world. I don't even begin to try and understand them."

"*That's rich, coming from a nutter like her,*" Tina whispered in my ear.

"*Of course she doesn't think what she's doing is nuts,*" I whispered back.

"What? What are you saying over there?" Candy demanded.

"Nothing," I said. "When you ran from the shop yesterday,

did you happen to see anyone in the woods with you? Someone with—I don't know—a gun?"

She shook her head.

I decided to try another line of questioning. "Who do you think sent you that text telling you to come to the Chocolate Box?" I asked.

"Bixby sent the text, of course. He wanted to see me."

"Are you sure?" Tina asked. "Did it come from his number?"

"Oh, yes." She plucked her phone from her back pocket and held it up for me to see. As it had been the day before, the screen was blank. I didn't know what she thought our seeing her phone would prove. "He texts me all the time."

"He does?" Was that the truth or another one of her delusions?

I hated to think of Bixby as a suspect, but I'd be negligent if I ignored his strange behavior. That he was obsessed with buying Bubba and Stan's song and that Stan's death had cleared one hurdle to his purchasing the song made his actions look suspicious.

Heck, he could have rigged the grill to explode in his own face just to make it look as if his life was in danger as well.

I knew Candy would shut down if I suggested the man she loved might be capable of murder, so I asked her about his motive instead.

"Why do you think Bixby is so interested in buying Bubba and Stan's song, 'Camellia Nights'?" I asked.

"He needs it," she said, as if it were as simple as that. "Just like he needs me."

"Needs it? I don't understand," Tina said.

Candy's shoulders slumped. "I provide Bixby with supplies for his . . . *you know* . . . habit. And Bixby also needs new material in order to keep the hits coming. Didn't you know? He hasn't written a new song since he's dated you," she said, wagging her finger at Tina. "Why do you think he travels around the country, visiting these obscure music festivals every couple of years?"

"Because he's looking for inspiration?" Tina asked.

"That's what he wants everyone to think. He's looking to buy prewritten songs, songs that he can make into hits."

"Lots of singers don't write their own work," I pointed out. "Why doesn't he simply hire songwriters to do the work for him?" And why was I having this conversation with a crazy woman?

She huffed. "This is Bixby Lewis we're talking about. Haven't you read his Wiki page? He's considered the preeminent song-writer of this generation. Song*writer*, not singer."

"And what supplies do *you* give him?" I asked.

She smiled coyly. "Hits of another kind."

"Drugs?" Tina sounded shocked.

"My boy doesn't do drugs. But I'm his Candy shop," she giggled as she said it. "He loves me for it."

Had Chief Byrd been right all along? Was the motive for Stan's murder and everything else that had been happening on the island drugs? Ohhh . . . rock stars and drugs. How had I been so naïve?

Drugs would explain why Bixby had been acting so cagey around the police. It would also explain why he'd never wanted to press charges against Candy and why he'd sometimes ditch his security team.

"I don't believe you," Tina said.

"You don't have to." Candy pulled a Ziploc bag filled with white pills from her pocket and tossed it at Tina. "With the crazy crowds around here, I haven't been able to get close to him, and I can't get past his security to get into his bedroom. Give that to him for me. My poor boy needs it."

"If you do this for him, why did you throw a threatening letter tied to a rock through my shop window and then through his bedroom window? And why did you try to burn my shop down?"

"I keep telling you, I didn't set fire to your silly chocolate shop."

"And the rocks?" Tina asked. "Did you throw those?"

"Sometimes Bixby needs to be reminded who really loves him. He needs to know I'm here for him. Always here for him. I'll make him burn."

"You're crazy," Tina said.

I think I was a bit crazy too, because I believed her.

The leaves behind her started rustling again. Candy jerked her head in the direction of the sound.

I grabbed her arm before she could run off. "Let me help you."

She shook her head violently. "He's coming."

"Who?" I tightened my grip on her arm. "Bixby?"

"No, why would I run from him? It's the man who's trying to kill me."

"Who?" I asked again.

"Some old guy. He must want what's in that bag I gave you." Like a slippery fish, she twisted her arm out of my grasp and took off running past the cove into the marsh's tall grasses. "You'd better run too. He'll kill you!"

Both Tina and I tried to chase after her, but she'd disappeared from view within the maze of tall grasses, and Tina refused to step foot in a place where snakes and alligators might live. So we doubled back to the cove to confront the "old guy" who'd so thoroughly frightened Candy.

It was Bubba who came out of the woods. He stood huffing and puffing in the clearing with his hands on his hips. "There you are, Penn," he said when he spotted us. "I've been looking everywhere for you."

"You have?" I asked. "Why didn't you call my cell phone?"

"Someone stole my cell phone and my car too."

"I know where your car is. It's in my shop," I said. "And I mean that literally. It's in the middle of my shop."

"Someone used your car as a weapon and crashed it into Penn's shop," Tina added as she discreetly picked up the bag Candy had tossed at us. I took it from her and stuffed it into my purse. "Do you know anything about that?"

"Yeah, I heard," he said as he rubbed the back of his neck. "Gibbons's men picked me up and questioned me about my missing car and told me where it had been found. But they wouldn't give me anything other than a few scant details about the crash. Was anyone hurt?"

"Your car ran Bertie down," I said. "She just got out of surgery on her leg."

Bubba cursed. The force of his words made him lose his balance. He staggered back several steps. "She's going to be okay, though, isn't she?"

"I hope so. In the shop, she told me she was worried about the lighthouse. Do you know what that could have been about?" I asked.

"Not a clue. I wish I did. I wish I understood what was going on here."

"How did you manage to find us? And where in the world have you been?" I asked, still feeling suspicious. Were Tina and I standing next to a killer? Had he been chasing poor Candy through the maritime forest with hopes of silencing her before she could talk to the authorities and tell them she wasn't the one with the gun yesterday and wasn't the one who'd been driving Bubba's car?

"You want to know what I've been doing today? I've been . . . I've been . . . Oh heck, I was out searching for the lost sheet music for 'Camellia Nights.' Bixby has been helping me, because he still wants to buy it. And we still are hoping we can sing the song at tonight's concert." He dragged a hand through his thinning gray hair. "I don't know what's going on in my town. Even at its worst, things have never been as bad as this."

"Really?" I said. "I think it's time you started telling me about the last Summer Solstice Beach Music Festival and what happened back then that is causing all this trouble today."

Chapter 35

Bubba kicked up a fuss, swearing up and down that Stan's murder couldn't have had anything to do with a concert that had happened forty-some years ago. "It simply couldn't," he insisted. His shoulders slumped after his fiery protests fizzled. His voice softened. "If bringing back the Summer Solstice Festival caused Stan's death, that would mean I'm complicit. That would mean all of this is my fault."

I patted his shoulder. "You can't blame yourself."

Tina rolled her eyes. She started to say something. But before she could get the words out, several worried-looking men burst through the trees and ran into the hidden cove.

Apparently our screams had attracted the attention of quite a few families. No less than half a dozen men and women had found their way to the hidden cove to make sure we were okay. Tina and I thanked them profusely and asked them to keep an eye out for Candy, who clearly needed medical as well as psychiatric help. With that done, we all headed back toward where I'd parked my car.

On the way, I called Chief Byrd to report Candy's location. I knew I should have called Gibbons, but I didn't want to listen to him scold me for poking around at the old abandoned lighthouse. Instead, I asked Chief Byrd to share that information with the county detective. He promised he would.

I felt as if a huge weight had been lifted off my shoulders. The police would pick up Candy, and she'd get the help she desperately needed. And my shop would certainly be safer with her in custody.

While I was on the phone, Tina texted Bixby. He immediately texted back that he'd join us at the pier in about ten minutes.

Bubba climbed into an old truck he'd borrowed from a friend and followed as we drove back to the shop.

"How did Bubba find us?" Tina asked as we drove toward the small downtown. "We didn't tell anyone where we were going. We didn't even know we were going to take that side trip to the cove."

"We'll have to have to ask him," I said as I steered my car into the first available parking space near the shop.

"Is that safe?" she demanded. "Think about it, Penn. Candy was frightened. She said someone was chasing her. And the only other person in the woods besides us was Bubba."

"Number one, we don't know that Bubba was the only person in the forest." I opened the car door. "Number two, we still have two police officers standing guard over the shop right now. Only an idiot would try anything with them around."

The area around the Chocolate Box was more crowded than I'd expected. Bubba's car sitting in the middle of my wrecked shop had turned into a popular photo spot.

The police had their hands full keeping the gawkers at bay.

I called out to them as we approached. "Your engineer just left," the officer Tina had charmed into putting away her groceries rushed over to tell us. "She said the building's bones look fine."

"That's a relief." The impact of that tiny piece of good news on my mood surprised me.

"A wrecker is on its way to haul off the car." He pointed to

Bubba's red sedan. "As soon as the car is gone, you'll be able to go back into the shop."

"Good. Good." I suddenly felt as if I could tackle anything else that might come my way. "I still have the boards for the windows. Tina, how are you with a hammer?"

"Never needed to use one," she admitted. She then batted her gorgeous large eyes in the police officer's direction. Before I knew it, he'd volunteered himself and the rest of the officers to put up the boards for us.

"There you are," Bubba said as he caught up to us. He was breathing hard. His gigantic body swayed with each step. His tree-trunk-sized arms swung at his sides. I couldn't help but think that if he wanted to kill a man, he could easily do it bare-handed. But Tina was wrong. He wasn't a killer.

"I'm awfully sorry for this, Penn." He shook his head like a sorrowful hound dog. "Awfully, awfully sorry."

"Were you the one driving the car?" I asked. Tina crossed her arms and took a warrior's stance next to me.

"No, of course I wouldn't have driven my car into your shop. I loved that car." His brows furrowed. "But I should have been more careful with my car keys and phone. I'd left them out on the kitchen counter at the beach rental. Anyone could have wandered in from the street and taken them."

"If that's true, how did you find us at the hidden cove?" Tina demanded.

"Dumb luck. Yes, I wanted to find your sister, but as I already told you, I was searching for the missing sheet music. Arthur Jenkins told me that when he and his fiancée were picnicking over near the cove this afternoon, they heard some boys singing beach music. He said it was a catchy tune and sang the 'three times three' refrain from 'Camellia Nights.' After hearing that, I ran straight over there to see if I could find the boys."

"Boys? How did some boys get their hands on the stolen

song?" I asked. "And what were they doing with it over near the lighthouse?"

Bertie had been worried about the lighthouse? Had Mr. Jenkins told her about hearing the boys singing out there as well? Was that why she'd wanted me to go there? I wished she had trusted us to help her with whatever investigation she'd been conducting.

"I don't know what those boys were doing, or even if they had my song," Bubba said. "Why would anyone want to steal it in the first place?"

"Candy would, because it was something Bixby wanted," I said, though I didn't really believe it.

"If that's so, why is she trying to hurt the remaining band members? Why is she only targeting The Embers? After all, Bixby also sang with the Ocean Waves," Tina asked as I started leading everyone toward the pier.

"Someone wants to hurt the band members?" Bubba gasped. "Nah, that doesn't sound right."

"Unfortunately, it does when you look at everything that has happened so far." I started listing the events that had brought us here: Stan's murder, Bubba's getting set adrift at sea, the missing song, the exploding grill, the shooting, and Bubba's car careening through the front of my shop.

By the time I'd finished, we'd reached the base of the pier. It was getting close to seven o'clock, but since today happened to be the longest day of the year, sunset wouldn't take place until closer to ten o'clock. The concert was scheduled to start at eight. There were two opening acts before The Embers, so Bubba's band wouldn't have to be onstage until a little after dark.

Even though we had plenty of time, I still needed to make sure we were going to have a headlining act.

Bubba continued to shake his head in disbelief that anyone would want to hurt him. "I make it a point to never disagree with a beautiful lady, but I'm having a devil of a time believing what you're telling me. It has to be something else."

"Drugs, perhaps?" I said, desperately hoping we could let the police wrap up Stan's murder and everything else in Candy's crazy little bow. "Candy told us just now that she is a small-time drug dealer."

"She didn't actually say that," Tina corrected. Though she was technically right, the bag of pills in my purse suggested otherwise.

"A drug deal gone wrong sounds more plausible than some plot to kill off members of a long-forgotten singing group," Bubba said. "No one gives two licks about The Embers. Sure, the older locals are excited to relive a piece of their youth by hearing us sing. Other than that, I can't imagine why anyone would get their panties in a wad over our reunion."

"Stan didn't want you to sing," Tina reminded him. "I heard that the two of you almost came to blows over it."

"Stan's dead," Bubba was quick to point out. The way he said it, as if the man's death were a personal victory, made me uncomfortable. But then Bubba flashed that toothy smile of his. "Come on, Penn. Don't look so glum. You know the police will sort it all out. In the end, you'll see, things are never as complicated as they seem. We'll find the misplaced song and the police will catch that crazy Candy girl. I agree with you. Her erratic behavior has drugs written all over it."

"Does that mean you're willing to sing tonight?" I asked.

"Heck, yeah. You'd have to tie me up with a rope to stop me." Which meant I had at least one performer for our grand finale—as long as the police didn't change their minds and arrest him first. "Now I just need to get confirmation from Fox, Alvin, and Bixby that they're willing to sing as well."

"Can't speak for Bixby," he said. "But Fox and Alvin will do it. They always come through for me."

As the three of us climbed the steps of the pier, Tina texted Bixby to find out where we could meet up with him.

The entire area buzzed with excited activity. Workers were preparing the bandstand. Tourists crowded around vendors' booths, buying concert memorabilia. Security officers and police officers prowled the pier like swarms of army ants, alert for any sign of trouble.

Residents from the Pink Pelican Inn had made the foot of the pier their living room for the weekend, setting out chairs and tables and game boards. Many of them congratulated me on how well it'd been going. They all seemed to be enjoying themselves immensely. Upon seeing that, despite tonight's uncertain success, I smiled.

"How did the proposal go?" I asked Arthur Jenkins when I spotted him seated in an armchair that belonged in the inn's lobby.

"She said yes!" he crowed, his entire face beaming. "I think it was your delectable chocolate-covered cherries that did the trick."

I tossed my arms around his neck and gave him an impromptu hug that surprised even me. "Where is the happy lady? I want to congratulate her."

"Taking surfing lessons." He nodded toward the water. Several silver-haired ladies were gathered around a buff, darkly tanned surfer who had his hand on a stack of beginner foam surfboards.

"Where do I sign up?" Tina asked as she leaned precariously over the railing to get a closer look at the instructor.

"That's what all the women say," Arthur complained.

Bubba stayed to talk with Arthur while I hooked my arm with Tina's. "Come on. We don't have time to ogle the locals."

"Speak for yourself." She batted my hands away. "You already have a surfer."

"A surfer who is my lawyer and friend. Look, there's Ezell. You can stay here. I need to talk to him about Tom."

Tina stayed at the railing only a few moments longer. I supposed she stayed to prove that no one could pull her away from a good-looking man, not even her sister.

She caught up to me as I approached Ezell's booth. The cellophane bags of melted chocolate lumps wrapped in pretty patriotic ribbons were still on the table.

"I'm just about fit to be tied thanks to that boy," Ezell blurted when I tried to stick up for young Tom. "He let all your chocolates melt and then went off to who knows where. He was supposed to be back at the booth to help me more than half an hour ago. Let me tell you, he can't pull stunts like this with members of the legislature. He'll lose all standing."

"He's only eleven," I tried to gently remind him.

"He turned twelve last month," he snapped. "It's high time that boy got his act together. He has his future to think about. Last fall he failed to win class president at his school because he didn't put enough effort into his campaign. He didn't shake enough hands. He didn't make enough friends."

I was glad Tom wasn't around. Clearly, Ezell needed to stop projecting his own worries about the senate race onto his young nephew.

I put my hand on his sleeve. "I'm sure that after watching how you run your campaign this summer, he'll do much better next time. After all, how many boys his age get to help our next senator run for office?"

My faith that he would win seemed to appease him. He patted my hand. "You're right, Penn. I do wish he had put those chocolates in the cooler, though. He knew better. I'd told him and told him to—"

"Penn! Bubba told me that you confronted Candy," Bixby interrupted. I barely recognized the superstar. He was dressed like a slob again. A hat was pulled low on his head. A few feet away from him stood four men, dressed casually enough, but their stiff-legged stances and roaming gazes pegged them as members of his security force. "Did she say anything about taking that song Stan wrote?"

Ezell didn't seem to mind that Bixby had butted into the conversation. He plastered his sleek politician's grin onto his face and stepped forward to shake Bixby's hand. Bixby and Ezell exchanged brief pleasantries before Bixby turned back to Tina and me. "Well?" he pressed. "Did she mention the song?"

"I didn't think to ask her about it," I said.

Bixby's face turned slightly pink. "You didn't think to ask her? She breaks into any place I'm staying with a mind to wreak havoc for me. And you hadn't considered her responsible for taking the one thing around here that really matters? What's wrong with you?"

"Lay off her." Tina pushed herself between Bixby and me. "I was there too, and I didn't think to ask her about your silly song, either."

His face turned a shade pinker, but his voice wasn't so sharp when he spoke. "I wish you had thought about it."

"If Crazy Candy took the song, wouldn't she have destroyed it by now?" Tina asked. "It's not like she left my dresses intact that time she broke into your hotel room."

"The song doesn't belong to my—" He waved his hand in the air. "Never mind. You didn't ask."

"If she has a copy, the police will find it when they pick her up," I said. "She can't elude them for much longer. They'll find her."

"I wouldn't bet on that," Bixby grumbled. He then drew in a quick breath as if trying to steady himself. Was he agitated because he really needed that song for his next big hit? Or was he agitated because he hadn't gotten a "hit" from Candy in several days?

"Bubba told us that he thought some boys had the song," Tina said.

"He did?" Bixby perked up at that news. "Why didn't he tell me? Where are the boys?"

"We don't know." I looked around for where Bubba might have gone. "Bubba didn't know who those boys were. All he knew was that a few people heard them singing the song this morning. They were at the old lighthouse."

"Is that so?" Bixby's eyes narrowed as he glanced over to where Bubba was chatting with another resident of the Pink Pelican Inn. The way he worked the crowd, you'd think he was running for senate. "I wonder why Bubba didn't tell me about that."

"Maybe he didn't tell you," Ezell answered, "because he found someone who'd pay him even more money for that song. That's what Stan would have done."

Chapter 36

We left Ezell, who seemed anxious to get back to greeting potential voters and talking up his message. Bixby kept saying that he needed to talk to Bubba, so we found a partially secluded table at the pier's waterfront restaurant where we could all sit down and discuss . . . everything.

A basket of deep-fried clams arrived at the table almost immediately. A few minutes later a second basket of conch fritters and deep-fried sea bass arrived, compliments of the music-loving chef.

While the seafood was mouth-wateringly good, the tension at the table was palpable.

"I didn't tell you what Arthur told me because I didn't know if it was true or not," Bubba tried to explain to the petulant rock star.

Bixby churlishly folded his arms over his chest and turned away from Bubba. "It's not like I need to buy that song. Don't get me wrong, it's great and all, but I was trying to do you and the town a favor. I don't need it. I write my own songs."

Tina and I exchanged glances.

"I don't know what Ezell is talking about. I don't have another buyer." Bubba flapped his hands. "Why would I do such an underhanded thing?"

"Money," Bixby said out the side of his mouth.

"Stan was the one who was always angling for a way to sneak a few bucks out of someone's wallet, not me. If I cared about money, I would have left this town when Stan did. There was nothing holding me here."

"Because Carolina left you?" Tina asked.

Bubba looked surprised.

"We know what happened," I said. "We know about the rumor connecting you and Bertie."

"It wasn't just a rumor. I loved Bertie, you know." He dipped a conch fritter into a cup of spicy cocktail sauce. "I was ready to marry Carolina, but I loved Bertie. How crazy is that? I would never do anything to hurt either woman. Not in a million years."

I glanced over at Tina, who looked just as troubled by his surprising revelation as I was.

"Why are you telling us this?" I demanded, shocked he'd admit (unprompted) to such a thing. What angle was he trying to play? Was he even telling us the truth?

He finished chewing his fritter. "Because this guy thinks I'm a money-grubbing swindler and because of the way your sister is looking at me. She already thinks I'm guilty of murdering Stan. I suspect you agree with her. You think I killed Stan and then ran my car into your shop."

"Don't forget how we found you chasing Candy through the woods just now. She said an old man was chasing her, trying to kill her, and then you appeared," Tina added.

"Old man? You think I'm an old man?" He sighed deeply. "I suppose you would think I'm old. Still, it hurts." I looked me directly in the eye. "I wasn't chasing Candy. Although, if I'd known that sick young'n was running through the woods just ahead of me, I might have. For her own good, she needs to be caught."

"You loved Bertie?" I asked, getting back to his first

revelation. My hand shook as I took a sip of my sweet tea, causing the ice to clang around in the glass. Was this the secret Bertie had been desperately trying to hide? Was this the secret Bertie had been threatened over? I hated to ask the question, but I had to. "Does that mean the rumors were true? Was she cheating on her husband with you?"

"No! A million times no," he protested. "She was classy. But the feelings—as wrong as they were—they were real. At least they were for me."

"We found a note in Bertie's purse that said, 'Secrets are deadly. Look at what happened to Stan.' Did you send that to her? Were you warning her to be careful?" I asked.

He dipped a clam in cocktail sauce. "She showed that to me. She had no idea what it meant or why she found it tucked under the windshield wiper of her car. I don't either."

"She showed it to you?" *And not me?* I was hurt.

He nodded. "She's been helping me track down the missing sheet music. She's got a good heart, that one. She wants to help the town just as much as I do."

"But you have no idea why her looking for the music made someone—Candy perhaps—nervous enough to threaten her?" I asked.

"No idea at all." He bit into the clam.

"Do you know where Carolina went?" Tina asked.

"I wish I did. I've always wanted a chance to talk to her, to explain things. It breaks my heart to know that she cut ties with everyone in Camellia Beach, including her own family, because of me."

"Breaking a woman's heart like that is a hard burden to bear, man," Bixby stopped pouting long enough to say. "I know it only too well."

Those two sure had inflated opinions of their effect on the women in their lives. I found it hard to believe that Carolina would run away and join a band of traveling fortune tellers just because she thought Bubba had been cheating on her. Something else must have happened to her. I feared her tale had ended more than forty years ago.

"So let me get this straight." I grabbed one of the conch fritters before Bubba ate them all. "Stan wanted Carolina. He started the rumor that you were cheating on her. When she didn't fall into his waiting arms, he packed things up, wrote a song that was even better than 'Camellia Nights,' and left Camellia Beach. Is that what happened?"

"Why was Stan so set against having anyone sing 'Camellia Nights?'" Tina asked before Bubba could answer me. "If it was so good, you'd think he would have wanted Ocean Waves to sing it."

Bubba shook his head. "I can't figure any of it out. Even though it happened back in the seventies, I remember it as if it were yesterday. We were fixing to practice the song when he grabbed the sheet music from everyone's stands and ran out the door. When he returned about an hour later, he told us he was quitting the band."

"Is that when he told you he thought the rest of you were too small-town for him?" I tasted the fritter. It was chewy and salty and delicious.

"No, that didn't come until later. The next day I confronted him. He came into town driving a shiny new car as if he'd already hit the big time. I demanded right away that he tell me what was going on. That's when he told me he was going out to California to find his fortune. Strange thing about it is that he didn't show anyone in town the song that was going to become his big hit, 'Love on the Waves.' It was such a campy hit. Why didn't he show off that song before he left? I never even had a clue he'd written a second song. Not that it mattered. It was his song. But still, he always liked to show off. He liked to prove he was better than the rest of us."

"He didn't write it," Bixby said. He uncrossed his arms.

"What?" I asked. "I thought he won a Grammy for writing it."

"I talked with a friend of mine who works for the record company that initially signed Stan. My friend asked around about Stan with some of the old-timers and found out that the company only signed him as a favor to some bigwig politician. The company provided the song."

"That doesn't make sense." Bubba chewed on the last conch fritter. "Why would everyone say he wrote 'Love on the Waves'?"

Bixby shrugged. "Happens all the time."

Was that what Bixby did . . . all the time? Had Candy been right about him traveling to small-town music festivals to buy the song rights and then claim them as his own?

Bixby had told Tom that all a singer needed was one good song. But that wasn't right, was it? One big hit didn't make Stan's career. His band fell into obscurity soon after "Love on the Waves" faded from popularity.

"If he had his big hit, why didn't the record company keep providing him with more good songs?" I asked.

"I don't know." Bixby picked one of the fried clams and sniffed it. "If I were to guess, the industry execs didn't like that they'd been pressured to sign a singer they hadn't discovered. After fulfilling what the politician wanted them to do, they probably stopped putting any effort into producing any future records for Ocean Waves."

"That stinks." I kind of felt sorry for Stan. "You didn't happen to get the name of the politician, did you?"

Bixby tapped his chin. "It was something like Kramer or Farmer or Framer?"

Not Ezell.

"How did he get some politician to do that for him?" Bubba wondered aloud. "It wasn't as if any of us came from anything. His parents were teachers at the public school."

But that wasn't quite true. Bubba's mother had been an influential politician. But their family name was Crowley, which didn't sound anything like Framer or Farmer.

"Perhaps Trey Ezell's daddy pulled some strings with one of his political colleagues to help Stan get started," Tina said.

"What? Ezell?" Bubba shook his head violently. "Why would Ezell lift a finger to help Stan? They weren't friends. Ezell would come and drink and listen to us play. He'd sometimes drive us into the city if he happened to be going in that direction anyhow. But he went to private school. His friends all went to private school. He'd never do anything to help a gang of poor hellbenders like us get ahead."

I looked at Tina and wondered if she was thinking the same thing. Ezell had claimed to be Stan's friend. He'd also told us that Bubba and Stan weren't friends. And now Bubba was telling us the complete opposite.

One of them had to be lying.

Tina raised her brows and nodded toward Bubba. Of course she'd think he was the one who was lying. She believed he was the one who was guilty of murder.

"Maybe Stan had something on Ezell that convinced him to ask his daddy for help," I said and then looked directly at Bixby. "Candy mentioned drugs. Maybe Ezell had sold Stan drugs. Don't all musicians use drugs?"

Bixby jumped up from his chair. "If we're going to perform tonight, I'd better get going." He dropped some cash on the table and then, with a nod to his security team, hurried away.

Chapter 37

I followed Bixby as he fled without answering my question. He was moving quickly. I caught up to him just outside the entrance of the makeshift backstage area on the pavilion's second floor. I flashed my badge to get close enough to talk to him. "I need a moment in private."

He glanced around and then pointed to a curtained-off area. Inside the curtains we found musical instruments in their black cases, neatly stacked by band name.

"Candy gave us this to give you." I held out the bag of white pills for him.

He crossed his arms over his chest. "I don't know what that is."

"She said she's your supplier."

His ears turned red. "She also tells people she's my lover."

"Well, if it isn't yours," I said and started to stuff the bag back into my purse.

With a growl, he grabbed it. "You going to turn me in?"

"Not for this. No, I'm going to tell you to give the poor girl a break and leave her alone. You give her attention. You let her bring you—what is it?—some kind of opioid? And she gets nothing in return. No wonder she throws rocks at you."

"It's not opium." He stuffed the pills into his baggy jeans

pocket. "It's vitamins. Anti-aging vitamins if you must know. They're illegal in this country. Such stupid laws. But Candy knows a source who buys these for her in South Korea. They work. They keep my face looking like this." He struck a pose. "And they keep my hair looking like this." He posed again. "My voice, my face, and my hair are my life. I'm king of the mountain in the rock world. I need these pills or else a younger singer will come along and knock me off this peak I'm standing on right now. I can't let that happen."

"It's only a matter of time before the police pick her up," I warned.

"Not likely."

I narrowed my gaze at him. "What do you mean? What have you done to her?"

"I haven't—" He tossed his hands in the air. "I don't have to explain myself to you. I don't have to explain myself to anyone. Get out of my way."

He pushed me aside and nearly tore the curtain from its rod in his haste to escape. Tina was standing just outside the room. The look on her face was harsh. Was she upset with me for confronting him?

She followed me through the backstage area. She didn't say a word until we had emerged into the sunlight. "I didn't know," she said. "I swear."

"Of course you didn't. You wouldn't have put up with anyone who was taking advantage of a mentally ill woman like that."

"Do you think he killed Stan?" she asked.

"You mean, do I think Stan found out about the illegal vitamins and tried to add Bixby to his money-making scheme? Bubba said Stan was always looking for ways to make more money. It's possible that's what got him killed. But that wouldn't explain the attempts against the rest of the band. If those attempts were actually targeting the band, that is."

"So we don't think Bixby is guilty," Tina said.

"I didn't say that."

*   *   *

Just as the first opening act started playing, the state police arrived to help out with security. I spotted Gibbons giving orders in the VIP area, which he'd commandeered and turned into a makeshift police headquarters.

Things would have been so easy if Gibbons had gone ahead and caught Candy already and found some evidence on her that proved she killed Stan. Given how things were right now, after confronting Bixby, I didn't know what to believe anymore.

The sun, lower on the horizon, was still a bright yellow ball in the sky. The clouds, which had been white and fluffy most of the day, were gradually taking on a more ominous shade of dark gray. I wasn't surprised. Afternoon thunderstorms were the norm at the beach whenever the weather turned hot. But I was concerned.

Tina hooked her arm through mine to keep us from getting separated in the crowd. I didn't mind. Someone in this crowd was a killer.

"We're running out of time," she told me. "The Embers go onstage in less than two hours."

"And we need to find the killer?" I started to turn around to head over to the VIP area to talk to Gibbons.

"No, silly bean, we need to find the sheet music." She gave my arm a tug. "Listen to me," she shouted in my ear over the music that was growing louder and louder, "the police are searching for the killer. They don't care about a missing song. We do."

"You're right." Drat it. "The Embers need to sing 'Camellia Nights' before Bixby buys it. That way they can get credit for writing it."

"Plus, Bixby can't buy what he doesn't have."

"Let's go find it." This time, I was the one who tugged at her arm.

"Where do we begin?"

"Haven't you been paying attention?" I urged her to pick up the pace. She stumbled a bit over her feet as she followed me through the dense crowd of people.

We wove our way down the length of the pier until we reached the "Ezell for Senate" booth. The melted chocolates had been swept from the table and the booth was empty.

"He must be shaking hands with potential voters again," Tina said, not even slowing her step. We were women on a mission.

The residents from the Pink Pelican Inn were still set up in their do-it-yourself living room at the shore side of the pier. I steered us toward them.

"You," I said, pointing to Arthur Jenkins.

"What?" He cupped his hand to his ear.

"We need to have a word with you," Tina said.

"What?" he repeated.

I crouched down beside his armchair and shouted, "Did you recognize the boys who were singing the beach music this morning?"

"The boys?" he shouted back. "No. Didn't see them. Just heard them shouting the words. Terrible singers, them boys. Catchy tune, though." He started to hum.

"You didn't recognize their voices?" Tina had crouched beside me. She cupped her hands around her mouth and shouted toward Arthur, "They had to be locals."

Arthur shook his head. "Children keep away from us as if afraid they'll catch our old."

"Thank you," Tina shouted as she jumped back up to her feet. She grabbed my arm again. This time I stumbled as I struggled to keep up. "You really need to dress more appropriately for

island life," she scolded. "Those shoes are completely impractical. You're getting a makeover before I leave. Ah, there he is."

"Who?"

She pointed to the bottom of the pier's steps. Bubba stood
there with his arms crossed. He spotted us and waved.

"I texted him and asked him to meet us here."

She did? "You did? I thought we weren't chasing the killer."

"We aren't. And there's more police in this small area than
at a policeman's ball. Come on."

I still had no idea what she hoped to accomplish by meeting with Bubba. But since I felt fairly certain he hadn't killed
anyone—this was Bubba we were talking about—I went along
with her.

We got the obligatory greetings out of the way, which were
shortened by the fact that Bubba needed to get ready for his turn
onstage. The first band had plunged into the driving beat of
their last song.

"Tell us everything you know about those boys singing your
song," Tina said.

But I had another idea. "Bubba, do you remember Stan's
lyrics?"

He looked at me and then at Tina before saying, "The score
for the song was in my hurricane box. I don't know what in the
world happened to it."

"I'm betting Candy took it and dumped it. And some boys
found it," Tina said. "We need to find out more about those
boys."

"No, that's not the right question," I argued. "Bubba, you
must remember some of the lyrics, don't you?" I dug around in
my purse. "Can you write down what you do remember?"

"Don't know how that would do us any good," Bubba complained. "Bixby won't buy a partial song."

"Please"—I held out a small notebook I found in my purse—"humor me."

With a sigh, he took the paper. I quickly found a pen and pushed it into his hand. He clicked the pen open and closed several times. Its nib had barely touched the paper's surface when he looked up at me. "I don't remember the entire thing."

"That's okay. I don't want to sing it," I said, while Tina sputtered something about how this line of thinking wasn't helping us find the song. "I just want to understand what the song is about."

"Oh, that's easy. It's about Camellia Beach." He started to hand the notebook back to me.

I refused to take it. "It's about more than that."

With a nod, he started writing. He wrote several lines, hummed for a while, and then wrote a few lines more. By the time he'd finished, about half the page was covered.

He handed me the notebook. "There is another verse, but I can't tell you hide nor hair about it."

"That's fine." At this point, I was happy to get anything. That is, I was happy until I read the words he'd written. My heart dropped.

The first verse was about a man taking a woman for a ride on a boat on a channel that cut through the tangle of marsh grasses behind the island and stopped for a while at the old red-and-white brick lighthouse. The man then came back alone "under the starry sky in the middle of a steamy Carolina night."

"Yeah, it's a sad song," Bubba said after I gasped. "Stan was writing from a dark place. His girlfriend had recently broken up with him. He'd taken it pretty hard."

I gave Bubba a hard look. "Really? His girlfriend left him at the same time you lost your girlfriend? Don't you think that's a little convenient? I heard Stan was the one who started the rumor about you and Bertie."

He rubbed his stubbly chin. "I heard that, too. But Stan swore he hadn't."

"He loved Carolina," Tina said.

"Half the men on the island did. You should have seen them go after her like hound dogs chasing a bone. It was ugly. But this song is about Stan's girlfriend."

"Who was Stan dating?" Tina asked.

"Some groupie from Charleston. Oh, what was her name? Sandy? Lisa? Something like that."

"And Stan took her out on a boat and returned without her?" I was surprised how calm I sounded. My heart was hammering in my chest harder than the band's racing drums. "Didn't that raise an eyebrow or two?"

"Metaphorically, Penn. He was upset as all get out. He wrote a song about losing a woman, not a song about killing one."

"Are you sure?" I sure wasn't.

I needed to think.

Still clutching the lyrics of the song in my hand, I stumbled away from Bubba and Tina. None of this made sense. If Stan had killed someone, why would he write a song about it? And, more important, why would someone kill *him* over that song more than forty years later?

And then I remembered what Bubba had said about Stan always angling for ways to make money. Had he been blackmailing someone because of this song, someone with political connections? Bubba might not have had money, but his family—like Ezell's—had been politically active and well connected at the time.

But if Bubba had killed Carolina, why would he willingly hand over these lyrics to anyone?

Chapter 38

"Three times three, that's all there was left on the sea on that steamy Carolina night," Bubba noted that the ending chorus line repeated over and over at the end of the song. Was that a clue?

After Bubba left to get ready for the concert, I dialed Gibbons's number. He answered on the third ring by grumbling, "You promised you wouldn't meddle—"

"I know, I know. My sister is a bad influence. Have you located Candy?"

"She's being transported to the county hospital as we speak. Thanks for the tip. You may well have saved her life."

"So you believe her when she says someone was trying to kill her?"

"One of my officers pulled her out of the water. The girl was trying to swim off the island and got caught up in a deadly undertow. She's lucky to be alive."

"Well, I'm glad she's safe. But I have to ask you," I quickly added before he could disconnect the call, "did she give a description of the man who was chasing her?"

"Why are you asking him that?" Tina poked me sharply on my arm. "Ask him if she mentioned the sheet music."

"You already know I can't discuss the case, Penn." The

detective's voice felt as sharp as my sister's jabs. "You worry about the festival and leave the police work to the police."

"But I—" I started to say. He disconnected the call before I could finish. "What?" I snapped at Tina who was still poking my arm.

"You should have asked him about the sheet music and if they saw any boys in the woods when they were searching."

Tina was right, but not for the reason she was thinking. Yes, we needed to focus on finding the missing sheet music because it was the key to discovering who killed Stan. It was also the key to figuring out what had happened to Carolina Maybank, the woman I still considered my mother.

"Penn! Penn!" I heard someone calling over the swinging sounds of the second opening act.

I turned around and spotted Harley and Althea. With the deep reds of the sunset at their back, their bodies were in silhouette. They were running toward us as if the devil were chasing them.

All the blood started to rush out of my head. "What . . . what's happened? Is Bertie—?"

Althea reached me first. "She's fine," she assured me. "She's sleeping comfortably."

"Then what's wrong?" I asked, because something was definitely wrong. Even in the dim twilight, Harley looked pale.

"It's Gavin," he croaked. "He's missing."

"Oh, no. Have you asked Jody if she's seen him?" I said.

Harley nodded. "That was the first call I made. After she accused me of parental neglect and told me she'd see me back in court, she admitted she hadn't seen him today."

Tina wrapped her arms around Althea, who was starting to cry. "When was the last time you heard from him?" she asked Harley.

"I touched base with him as soon as I got to the hospital to let him know where I was. He said he was with Tom and Tom's uncle. I talked with him again at six. He told me he'd meet me at the apartment at seven. He told me not to worry because he was eating dinner with Tom and Ezell."

"He was lying to you," I said.

"My boy doesn't lie," Harley snapped. He stepped away from us and dragged his hand through his hair several times before coming back. "Why do you say he was lying?"

"I saw the congressman around seven. He was furious that Tom hadn't returned to help out at the booth. He said he hadn't seen the boy all afternoon. I, however, saw Tom right after you left for the hospital. He was upset because he'd let the chocolates Bertie and I had made for the congressman melt. Gavin wasn't with him."

"He wasn't?" Harley punched at his phone's screen. "I'm calling the police."

"While you do that, let's go talk to Ezell," I said. "He might have seen them."

Ezell's booth was still empty, and the congressman wasn't answering his phone. I wasn't surprised. With the music blaring through the oversized speakers, I couldn't imagine how anyone could hear their phone's ringer.

On the first night of the festival, Ezell and Tom had watched the concert from the VIP area. But since the police had taken over use of the VIP area, we knew he wouldn't be there. Althea, Tina, and I did a quick run through the crowd. We didn't see Ezell, Tom, or Gavin. I also didn't see half the people I knew were attending that night. The crowd was that large.

The boys aren't here, a nagging voice in the back of my head kept telling me. I stopped in the middle of the pier so I could think. And then I remembered something important.

Harley had told me earlier in the day that Tom and Gavin had been working on a super-secret project. "You don't suppose

Tom and Gavin are the boys Arthur heard singing near the light-house?" I shouted the question to Tina and Althea as we made our way back to the pier's steps.

"What did you say?" Althea shouted over the music.

"The boys—" I shouted.

"What?" Tina shouted.

I grabbed my sister's arm with one hand and Althea's arm with the other and led the way off the pier.

"Tom was there with his uncle at Bubba's house around the time the sheet music for 'Camellia Nights' went missing," I said. "It's possible that he took it."

"Why would he do that?" Althea asked. "He's a good kid."

"Even good kids do stupid things," Tina pointed out. "They're kids."

"But what would he want with it?" Althea asked.

"I don't know," I said.

Harley came jogging down the pier's steps. "Chief Byrd has his hands full with concert security. They can't send anyone out to search for my boy until the festival is over."

"That won't be for hours," Tina cried.

"We'll help you find him," I said.

"Of course we will," Althea said.

Someone decided that it would be best if we split up into two teams. One team would search the east end of the island while the other team would search the west.

"Are you sure Gavin's not at the concert?" I asked. The pier was wall-to-wall people, as was the beach below.

"I can't be sure of anything," Harley said. "I texted Jody again. She texted back that she has some friends helping her search the crowd down on the beach."

"That's surprising," Althea said.

"You shouldn't be surprised she'd help search for Gavin."

Harley started pacing. "Despite how she acts toward me, she loves her son."

"No, I'm surprised she has any friends," Althea said.

Harley shrugged. "Hank promised he'd have his men on the pier keep an eye out for the boys."

"Okay, since Jody and the police have the festival covered, let's get going." I grabbed hold of my sister's arm.

"I'll take Tina with me." Althea looked determined. "We'll search the east end."

Both Althea and Tina pushed me so hard, I fell face-first into Harley's side. Even during a crisis, those two were incorrigible.

Embarrassed, I apologized to Harley and focused on straightening my skirt. The last thing I wanted to do was see the look on Harley's face. Was he glad they'd pushed me in his direction? Or was he annoyed?

If I were in his shoes, I'd be annoyed. Our focus needed to be on finding his son.

"Let's get going." And then I saw it. Just a flicker. At first I thought it was distant lightning. But then there it was again. Steadier this time. An ethereal white light glowed as if powered by the ghost from a bygone era in the spot where a powerful lamp had once shone out to sea.

I lifted my arm and pointed to the crumbling lighthouse that rose up on the distant horizon. "I think I know where the boys are."

Chapter 39

The boards over the lighthouse entrance had been pulled away. The door itself swung with each gust of wind, its rusty hinges crying out as if the movement caused the building pain.

"Lord, I hope they're not up there," Harley whispered as he directed his flashlight to the waterlogged and rotting wooden steps beyond the door. "The place is on the verge of collapse."

We climbed single file, taking each step gingerly, testing the wood, testing whether the tread would bear the weight of one more person. The wind outside picked up. It howled as it whirled around the curving stairs. Finally, we reached the top where a light had once sat. Most of the windows were missing. A light rain came in on the wind and cooled our faces just as thunder crackled in the distance.

"Daddy!" Gavin cried out in fear and relief. He was wet and at the moment looked much younger than his eleven years. He ran and threw himself into his father's arms.

"What's going on here?" Harley demanded. He wrapped his arms protectively around his son's thin frame and held him close.

I took control of the flashlight and saw right away that we weren't the first ones to find the boys. Congressman Ezell stood in the middle of the room with his hands on his hips, looking as if he wanted to strangle his nephew.

Tom huddled against the far wall. His lips started quivering. "I didn't mean to do any harm."

"While everyone was busy with the concert, the boys thought they'd do a little vandalism," Ezell said.

"We didn't—" Gavin protested.

"Don't sass me!" Ezell barked. "You're already in enough trouble as it is."

Harley didn't say anything, but I noticed his expression had hardened.

Tom straightened his slumping shoulders and cleared his throat. The voice that came out of his mouth sounded nearly identical to his uncle's. "I take full responsibility."

"You're lucky you didn't fall over the edge up here and die," Ezell scolded.

Tom lowered his head. "I stole the sheet music. Gavin didn't—"

"This is your doing?" Ezell reared forward and grabbed his nephew by his shoulders and shook him.

"Mr. Bixby Lewis said all a singer needed was one good song to make it into the big time," Tom sobbed. I could hear Gavin behind me sobbing as well. "And then . . . and then Mr. Lewis kept going on and on about how great 'Camellia Nights' was. So when we were at Mr. Bubba's house, I took it."

Ezell shook his nephew again.

"Go easy on the boy," Harley said, just as Althea, Tina, and I moved to intervene. "Let's get out of here before the floor falls out from beneath us."

Ezell didn't move, but he let his hands fall away from Tom's shoulders.

The boy trembled as he backed away from his uncle. "I don't want to major in political science. I don't want to run for office.

I'm not interested in politics. I keep telling you that I'm a rock fan."

"Yes, yes. You like rocks. That's a hobby, not a career," Ezell roared.

"No, uncle. Not rocks. While I appreciate the gesture, I'm not interested in those geodes you keep buying for me. I like to sing. Why do you refuse to hear me? I don't want the life you have. I want to sing."

"You stole 'Camellia Nights' because you picture yourself becoming some kind of scheming pop star?" A vein on Ezell's reddening temple started dancing. "You stupid, stupid boy. Do you know what you've done?"

I stepped in front of Ezell, blocking his path to his nephew, and held up my hands. "We can talk about what he did and why once we're out of this deathtrap."

Three times three, the song's chorus clamored in my head. *Three times three.*

Stan had been adamant about keeping anyone from ever hearing that song. He'd quit the band and took what he'd thought was the only copy with him when he left the beach. Soon after, things started happening for him. Good things. And when his time in the spotlight had passed, though he struggled and played with his band for very little money, every couple of years he always bought a new flashy car.

Arthur Jenkins had wondered who Stan was blackmailing. How else could he be getting that kind of money?

"Three times three," Stan had written those lines after Carolina disappeared. Was the song a confession? Or had he used the song to accuse someone else of the crime? Someone like—

"Trey," I said and shone the light in his face. "Three times three. That's the catchy refrain in the song your nephew took. You've heard those lines. Stan showed you the song shortly after he wrote it all those years ago, didn't he? And then he threatened to do what? Did he threaten to sing it with The Embers in front of a big crowd?"

The congressman shook his head. "I don't know what you're talking about."

"Let's get out of here," Harley said.

I motioned to Tina to get Tom.

The rain was coming down harder now. I wondered briefly if the concert had been canceled. From the corner of my eye, I saw that Tina had Tom's hand and was leading him to the steps. Harley followed with Gavin.

"Let's go," Althea said. I held my ground. They didn't understand the danger the congressman was to the boys. They didn't understand that the congressman had never intended to let Gavin and Tom leave the lighthouse alive.

I doubted the boys had even come up here alone. After all, Ezell was the only one with a flashlight. I suspected he'd brought them up here to make their deaths look like a terrible accident. I needed to keep Ezell as far away from those boys as possible.

"You tell everyone to call you Trey, but that isn't your real name, is it? It's a nickname. Trey is what people call someone who is the third person in a family with the same name. In your case, you're also the third *politician* in your family with the same name, aren't you? You're actually Thomas Ezell."

"My name isn't a secret. I'm Thomas Ezell the third. It's a good name. A historic name."

" 'Three times three,' Stan's song goes." I gave the small circular room a pass with the light of my flashlight. Harley, Gavin, Tina, and Tom were gone. Althea stood at the steps, waving at me to go with her. I moved to go, but Ezell produced a gun from inside his coat pocket. He pointed it directly toward my chest.

"You're not going anywhere," he said, using the same tone he used when trying to convince voters to cast their ballot with his name on it.

I raised my arms in surrender. "You loved Carolina May-bank. You told me yourself that you have the picture she painted hanging in your office."

"Everyone loved her." The wind had picked up. It was hard to hear Ezell's voice above it and the sound of the waves crashing below. "But I knew she was Bubba's girl."

"You hated that," I said, since he obviously had no plans to let me leave. "You hated that she'd fallen for an impoverished island boy instead of someone like you, someone in her family's economic bracket."

He shrugged. "She was slumming. Men do it too. It didn't mean anything."

"But Bubba had bought a ring. You told me that yourself."

Rain splattered against my face. I could feel rather than see Althea as she came up behind me. She squeezed my hand.

"What did you do to Carolina?" I shouted over the howling wind. "Did you hurt her?"

Ezell looked older, grayer as he stood in the drenching storm. His silver suit molded against his skin. His hand shook as he pointed the gun at me.

I knew if I ran, he'd shoot me in the back. He couldn't let me get away, not now, not after I'd figured out the puzzle in the song, the puzzle that had broken up The Embers and had kept Stan Frasier away from Camellia Beach for decades.

Heck, I suspected he planned to shoot me no matter what. That's why I didn't feel as if my actions were reckless. Instead of playing it safe, I felt duty-bound to press him for the truth.

Someone needed to hear the truth.

"Did you hurt Carolina?" I asked again.

"Shut up!" he shouted.

"She was my mother!" I shouted back. "I have a right to know what happened to her!"

That bit of news seemed to take him by surprise. "She told

me . . ." The dratted wind stole the words that emerged from his lips and tossed them into the turbulent waves.

"What?" I shouted.

He shook his head and yelled, "Impossible!"

"What's impossible?" Although I suspected what he was implying, I needed to hear him say it. Unfortunately, he wasn't willing to confess to murder. At least, not to my mother's.

"You should have listened to the detective—he's a good man. You should have never stuck your nose into Stan's death. It had nothing to do with you," he said instead of admitting to anything.

"You made it my business when you left a bag of my shop's bonbons at Stan's feet. You made it look as if Bixby was the intended victim."

"*Your* bonbons?" He shook his head. "It was *my* campaign literature the police found at the bonfire."

"Did you place it there, or did Stan fish the bonbons out of the trash in some desperate attempt to be more like Bixby?" Althea asked.

He swung the gun toward Althea. I pushed her behind my back.

He huffed. "I put them there. I'm going to be this state's next senator, and I wasn't about to let anyone, especially not a washed-up loser like Stan, stop me. The two of you won't stop me, either."

I held up my hands. "Of course, we aren't going to stop you," I said in a desperate attempt to keep him from shooting us. "You have been so clever. First, you made Bubba look guilty by making sure he didn't have an alibi for Stan's murder."

A sinister smile tugged at Ezell's lips. His gun lowered just a bit. "He had just as much motivation to kill Stan as I did. I was sure he'd think I was doing him a favor. That's why I had to frame him. I didn't want him thinking someone was out there helping him sell that cursed song to Bixby."

If I wanted to stay alive, I suspected I needed to keep him talking. "And then you made Candy look guilty. Did she rig the grill to explode, or was that you?" I tapped my chin. "It must have been you. Candy couldn't pull off something that almost fooled even the experts into thinking the explosion was an accident."

The tension in his expression seemed to ease a bit. "Thank you. That was my handiwork."

"Who were you targeting? Bixby or one of The Embers?" Althea asked, her voice usually subdued.

"Didn't matter, did it? Bixby wanted to buy that stupid song. With him out of the way, it would reduce the urgency to find the missing score for 'Camellia Nights.' But after Bixby expressed interest in buying it, I knew getting rid of him wouldn't stop the band members from wanting to find it and try to sell it to another singer. Killing off one of The Embers would have slowed them in searching for it."

"And you needed to find the score before they did?" I asked.

He nodded slowly. "I'd thought Bertie had taken it. I thought I was going to have to take care of her."

At his mention of Bertie, I could feel Althea behind me starting to get agitated. I felt agitated too. Yet it would be dangerous to let our agitation show. So I said quickly, "How did you convince Candy to come to the Chocolate Box the morning of the shooting? Setting her up to take the blame for that was inspired."

"Inspired, yes. But I needed more time at the shooting range with my handgun. Or perhaps I should have practiced on your fat partner first."

"That's my mother you're talking about!" With a growl, Althea charged Ezell. I grabbed her arm, but, dang, my friend had anger-fueled strength, which seemed to be the same kind of super-strength that allows upset mothers to lift cars off their babies. As I struggled with Althea, I saw out the corner of my eye Ezell shifting his gun's aim from us to the doorway and back to us. I closed my eyes, sure my body was about to feel the sting of a bullet.

"The police are on their way," Harley shouted as he pushed me to stand behind him. I jostled with Harley in an effort to get him out of the line of a fire. He was a father, for goodness' sake. "Drop the gun. It's over. You're not going to be our next senator. Not after this."

Ezell looked at the gun in his hand and then back at us. For a moment I thought he'd toss his weapon to the ground and give up. He couldn't kill all the witnesses. The boys and Tina had already gotten themselves to safety.

Besides, Tom had the song. When the old-timers on Camellia Beach heard it, they'd start to remember. It wouldn't take long before one (or many) of them came to the same conclusion I had—that Ezell had killed Carolina Maybank.

What choice did he have other than to surrender?

But I was wrong. He did have other choices.

He fired his gun.

Chapter 40

"Taste this." I handed Tina one of my latest attempts at making the perfect bonbon fire.

She gingerly held the chocolate treat between her thumb and index finger and sniffed it. "Have *you* eaten one yet?" she asked.

"No. They just came out of the fridge."

She placed the bonbon on the shop's kitchen counter between us and gave it a finger-shove in my direction. "No way. You taste it."

"Mama said I could find you back here," Althea said as she entered the kitchen. "What are you talking about?"

"Chocolate. Penn finished her latest attempt at making a spicy bonbon." Tina picked up the bonbon we'd been pushing around and held it out to Althea. "Would you like to be the first to taste it?"

"Really?" She looked at me. "You wouldn't mind?"

I shook my head.

Tina smirked.

"I'm honored." Althea took the bonbon and held it as if it were her most precious possession.

Guilt overtook me. "Althea, wait."

But it was too late. She'd already taken a bite. A large bite.

I jogged to the sink to fill a measuring cup with water.

"Milk is a better antidote for heat. Water just makes the

burn hotter," Althea said, then put the rest of the bonbon in her mouth.

"Why'd you do that?" I dumped the water back into the sink while Tina grabbed a milk jug from the fridge.

"Because you made it," Althea said. "It's pretty dang hot. The heat hit my palate right away. But the cream cheese filling cools things off nicely. The cheese probably has a similar effect to drinking a glass of milk."

"It didn't set your mouth on fire?" Tina asked.

"Should it have?" Althea raised a brow.

"My last attempt was a disaster. Tina was my taste tester. After I set her mouth on fire, I gave her several measuring cups of water to drink, which I suppose only made matters worse."

"Probably," Althea agreed. "If someone doesn't like spicy food, this would probably be too much for them. But I like spicy food. The hotter the better. It's good."

"Really?" I asked.

Althea beamed as she nodded. "Really. Try one."

With the measuring cup filled nearly to the brim with milk clutched in one hand, I took a tentative bite. Chocolate heat flooded my mouth. Tears were about to spring to my eyes when the cooling power of the cream cheese touched my palate.

It wasn't a candy you'd binge on, eating one after another in quick succession. But it could work as a specialty item.

"A crisp white wine would pair nicely with this," Tina said. She'd braved a taste as well. "It's definitely a chocolate for adults."

"It is," Althea agreed. "What are you calling them?"

"Bonbon fires." I winced as I realized how inappropriate the name might be after everything that had happened over the past few days. "You don't think it's too soon, do you? I mean, after what happened to Stan?"

Althea thought about it for a moment and then shook her

head. "In a week or two, everyone will be talking and thinking about something else."

Tina took another bite of the bonbon she'd lifted from the cooling tray. "This doesn't taste anything like that fireball you had me try. What did you do differently?"

"I rolled the dark chocolate shell in hot pepper powder and not with the filling. That way the first taste is hot and then the cream cheese can counteract the heat," I said. "I'm so excited that it worked. It did work, didn't it? I mean, do you really think I can sell these?"

Both Tina and Althea nodded their approval.

"I suspect they'll be insanely popular," Althea said. "People around here certainly enjoy having their food on the spicy side."

"Really?" I was afraid to believe it.

"What's wrong with you?" Tina punched me in the arm. "Why are you acting as if you accidentally came up with the formula for world peace or something?"

"Because that's what it feels like to me. This is the first time I've managed to make any kind of chocolate without Bertie standing over my shoulder, correcting me as I made mistakes."

It was Tina's turn to ask, "Really?"

"I've been struggling," I admitted.

"So all the chocolates out there for sale," Tina asked, "you didn't make them?"

"Not without someone helping me. Bertie has been doing most of the work. Althea has been helping when she can. And I've been grateful. But this is my shop, and I want to feel as if I can handle the work."

"You've been doing a wonderful job," Althea protested. "And you know Mama loves working here. If she didn't, she wouldn't do it."

"Thanks." I loved having Bertie and Althea's support. But I

was still glad I was finally making progress. I'd made those bon-bons on that tray. And they were edible.

It all felt like a dream, a wonderful too-good-to-believe dream. I'd finally mastered the art of crafting the perfect bon-bon. Clearly, it was the act of following a recipe that had been holding me back.

"Someone pinch me," I said.

Tina obliged.

"Ouch, not so hard." I rubbed my sore arm. I wasn't dream-ing, nor had I died and gone to heaven.

Three days had passed since the confrontation up in the lighthouse. I wasn't dead.

A remorseful Tom Ezell had returned the sheet music to Bubba. Bixby had taken one look at the full score and asked to buy the rights to it.

I placed the bonbon fires on a hand-carved wooden platter and carried it out into the shop. Bertie, who'd been sprung from the hospital just that morning, was holding court from the sofa in the corner. A cast that looked as if it belonged in the space age hugged the leg she'd propped up on the sofa's cushions.

Although we hadn't opened the shop, that hadn't kept the residents from coming by. Despite the boarded-up front win-dow, the cracked plaster ceiling, broken floorboards, and com-plete disarray of the place, the sitting area was full.

Bubba ran up to me and gave me a bear hug that nearly tipped all the bonbons onto the floor. When he pulled away, he took the platter from me and set it on the display case.

"I'm just back from seeing Bixby off at the airport. He's going to put Camellia Beach on the map with our song. Did they tell you? He's going to buy 'Camellia Nights.' I can't thank you enough for the weekend you gave us. Having a big star like him sing with The Embers—it was a dream come true for us."

"I'm glad you didn't get rained out."

"Rain wouldn't have stopped us." He put a hand to his heart. "We were jamming on that stage like the angels were singing with us. I'm sorry you missed it."

"So am I." I tried to pick up my tray.

But he wasn't ready to let me go. He bent down to whisper in my ear, "I saw how Bixby looked at you. Are you tempted? Do you see the two of you becoming an item? Do you fancy yourself living a life on the road with him in the glare of paparazzi flashbulbs?"

"Gracious, no!" The words flew out of my mouth with such force that everyone in the room turned to stare at me. "I mean"— my cheeks flamed—"I'd have been flattered if Bixby had been interested in me, but he wasn't. I'm just glad your concert went off without anyone getting hurt."

"Speak for yourself." Harley came up and took a bonbon from the wooden platter.

"The bullet only grazed your shoulder," I said.

"And you cried over me as if you thought I was a dead man," he reminded me while dramatically hugging his left arm, which was bound in a sling.

"Only after she tackled Ezell," Althea said.

"All in a day's work." I picked up the platter Bubba had set aside.

"You tackled a killer with a gun and pinned him to the ground until the police arrived," Harley said. "You're lucky you didn't get shot too."

"She knows how to take care of herself." Tina came to my defense. "She was one of the best students in the self-defense classes we took together. You don't mess with my sister because she can kick some serious butt."

"Don't I know it," Harley said. His eyes widened with surprise after he took a bite of the bonbon fire he'd taken. "Wow, that's good, Penn. I can't remember Mabel ever making these."

"It's my own recipe." I felt all fluffy with pride.

We were all having fun while eating chocolate and sharing stories when Gibbons came in, tracking mud all over my broken floorboards. The hum of happy conversation came to a sudden stop.

It was as if reality had just crashed into the shop. "Detective," I said and offered him a bonbon fire from the tray.

He frowned at the bonbon sprinkled with red hot pepper powder. "I've heard talk about your attempts to make spicy chocolates. I like hot food like the next Southerner, but I don't think I have the iron stomach required to survive these." He tried to give back the bonbon.

I refused to take it. "Taste it. I think it'll surprise you."

His enjoyment of the chocolate didn't erase the pall his presence had cast over the shop.

"Has Ezell admitted to anything?" Harley asked.

"No, he's only talking with his lawyer, but there's no fighting the evidence or the fact that he shot you." Gibbons took another bonbon from the tray. "He's not going to get out of jail for a very long time."

"So Stan had been blackmailing him for forty years?" Tina asked. "There must be some kind of record of the payments."

Gibbons nodded. "Once we knew to look for them, they were easy to find. He must have given Stan several million dollars over the years. My guess is that with Bixby's interest in buying 'Camellia Nights,' Stan went to Ezell and demanded a large lump sum of money."

"But Ezell wasn't able to pay, was he? His finances had to be carefully documented for the election commission," I said.

Gibbons took yet another bonbon fire from the tray. "That's what we think. So instead of agreeing to pay, Ezell killed him. But then he had to get his hands on the copy of the damning song. He probably would have gotten away with Stan's murder if his nephew hadn't stolen the sheet music before he could."

"And Ezell thought Bertie had stolen the music," I surmised.

"He's the one who kept sending me those nasty notes?" Bertie asked. "I thought it was someone warning me they'd tell Althea about what had happened between me and her daddy unless I gave Bixby the song. That letter had me chasing my tail, trying to find the missing sheet music so I could protect my Althea."

"Mama"—Althea rushed over to her mother's side—"you should have told me. I know you love me. Nothing from your past could change that."

Bertie patted her daughter's hand. "I was so ashamed."

"Because you loved him?" Althea asked. "Because you were tempted to cheat?"

Bertie gasped. "Hush, child. I wasn't saying anything like that. I was ashamed that I let a few ugly words chase me away from doing what I loved to do—sing. My leaving the band wasn't what caused me to have you. I was already pregnant with you before all that unpleasantness happened."

"You were?" I couldn't remember having ever heard Althea sound so pleased.

"Why did you tell me to go to the lighthouse?" I asked while Althea hugged her mother. "Had you heard about the boys singing the song over there?"

She nodded. "I heard the boys singing while I went searching for the music. The one boy sounded like Harley's boy, so I was extra concerned. Tell that detective to leave a few bonbons for me. I haven't tasted them yet." I hurried to Bertie's side and handed her the last one on the tray. She smiled as she bit into it. "Penn, I'm mighty glad you did as I asked and went over there for me. You saved those boys' lives."

Harley nodded. His eyes suddenly looked misty.

Detective Gibbons cleared his throat. "Yes, well. While this is all very . . . touching. Penn, I came here to talk to you."

"You did?" I waited, half expecting to endure yet another sharp dressing down for sticking my nose into his investigation.

"She was there," he said softly, instead. He placed a hand on my shoulder. "She was exactly where the song said he left her. She was buried deep in the sand around the lighthouse. The dental pattern is an exact match." He took a deep breath. "I'm sorry."

"How would Stan know about what Ezell did?" I demanded, refusing to face my disappointment at hearing that the woman I'd thought was my mother had been murdered five years before my birth.

"It's in Stan's lyrics. He was out night fishing, which around here means drinking on a boat. He saw Ezell with Carolina and followed them."

"He saw the murder?" I was shocked. "If Stan loved Carolina as much as he said he did, why didn't he turn Ezell in? How could he be so cold?"

"Greed makes people do ugly things," Gibbons said.

"Have you told Mabel's children?" Bertie asked.

"I have. Edward seems to be taking it the hardest. I am sorry, Penn. I know you thought she could be your mother."

"Yes." Oh, how I'd hoped it was so. "But she died years before I was born."

Gibbons nodded. "I did want to tell you something else." His voice sounded thicker than usual. "While Ezell isn't going to confess to anything, he did make one big mistake."

"What's that?" Tina asked before I could.

"He left his fingerprints on Bubba's car keys. We know he drove the car through your shop. I'm sure he also tried to burn the shop down when he was searching for the sheet music in your office. After all, he was convinced Bertie had taken it. You should be able to sue him for damages," Gibbons said.

314

"It would take years to get any money out of him." Harley moved to stand shoulder to shoulder with me. "Penn can't wait that long to fix up her shop."

"What are you going to do now?" Bertie asked me.

I looked to Harley. He slipped his hand around mine.

"I suppose I need talk to Florence." It hurt to say aloud what I'd tried to deny since Saturday. "She's my mother, not Carolina. That's what she came to talk to me about. That's what I didn't want to tell anyone. I suppose the two of us will need to decide what kind of relationship we're going to have."

"I meant about the Chocolate Box," Bertie said in that gruff voice of hers that I loved. "What are you going to do about that gaping hole where a window should be? We can't open the shop with it looking like this."

"Oh, that? The engineer said there was no serious structural damage, so we're cleared to start making repairs. I'm not sure how I'm going to pay for them, but they'll get done . . . eventually."

"That's what I wanted to hear." Bertie nodded to someone standing behind me.

I turned around and saw that she'd actually nodded to a large group of someones standing behind me. The residents of the Pink Pelican Inn had come armed with power tools. Just beyond the door, I spotted a bright red pickup truck precariously packed with what looked like half the inventory of the local hardware store.

"Here in Camellia Beach," Arthur Jenkins said as he ambled forward, "we make sure we take care of our own."

The sawing and drilling and hammering that followed sounded like sweet music as Althea, Tina, and I headed into the kitchen to make more chocolate. I looked forward to many more uneventful days like this in my peaceful little town of Camellia Beach.

Recipes Snipped From the *Camellia Current*, Camellia Beach's Local Newspaper

Biting into a piece of fine chocolate is like falling in love. But with chocolate, you'll never have to suffer through a bad breakup.

—Tina Penn, *honorary* resident of
Camellia Beach, SC

Harley's Slow Cooker Mole Poblano Shrimp Stew

All of your neighbors will be singing your praises when you serve Harley's special shrimp stew swimming in a rich mole sauce. Use the extra sauce as a dip for tortilla chips and offer it as an appetizer. Serve the stew over white or brown rice.

Ingredients

Coarse salt
Freshly ground black pepper
1 (28-oz) can diced tomatoes
1 medium yellow onion, coarsely chopped
2 dried ancho chilis, stemmed
1 can chipotle chilis in adobo sauce (for a milder sauce, use
    only a few chilis and a tablespoon of the adobo sauce)
¼ cup sliced almonds, toasted
2 tbsp sunflower seeds
2 tbsp sesame seeds
1 tbsp peanut butter
1 tbsp raisins
3 oz 70% or higher fair-trade dark chocolate, finely chopped

6 garlic cloves, smashed and peeled
3 tbsp extra-virgin olive oil
¾ tsp ground cumin
½ tsp ground cinnamon

2 lbs shelled deveined uncooked medium shrimp, tails removed, coarsely chopped

Remove stems and seeds from ancho chilis. Lightly toast in dry pan. Place all ingredients except shrimp in blender. Blend on high for 1–2 minutes or until smooth. Pour sauce in slow cooker. Cook on high 3 hours. Add shrimp. Cook on high an additional 30 minutes.

Mabel's Sweet and Savory Cheddar Cheese and Pretzel Bonbons

Word has gotten around that Penn can't manage this recipe. Well, this editor has tried it without encountering any trouble. The sharp cheddar cheese perfectly complements the rich chocolate shell and salty pretzels. Serve the bonbons after a cheeseburger cookout or with popcorn on movie night. They'll delight your sweet tooth.

Ingredients

2 tbsp butter
2 tbsp cornstarch
1 cup whole milk
2 cups shredded sharp cheddar cheese
1½ cups pretzels
12–24 oz fair-trade semisweet chocolate, chopped (Amount is dependent on the size of the cheese balls. Smaller balls means you'll need more chocolate.)
1 tbsp coarse sea salt

In medium saucepan, heat butter and corn starch over medium low heat. Whisk until bubbly. Add milk. While whisking, bring to a simmer. When white sauce thickens, take off the heat. Gradually stir in shredded cheese until melted. Crush the pretzels. (Put in freezer bag and hammer with a meat tenderizer until you end up with about ¼ inch pieces.) Cool in freezer for 30 minutes. Roll into ¼ to ½ inch balls. Roll the cheese balls in the crushed pretzels. Return to freezer for at least another half hour. Melt semisweet chocolate in double boiler or microwave. (To melt in microwave: In microwave-safe bowl, heat chocolate in small batches on 50% power for 2 minutes. If not melted, continue to heat for 30-second intervals. It won't look completely melted. Stir until smooth.) Dip cheese balls into melted chocolate. Coat completely. Set on cookie sheet lined with parchment paper. Sprinkle lightly with ground Himalayan or sea salt before chocolate sets. Place in refrigerator for at least 1 hour to set. Store in refrigerator in airtight container. Makes 24–36 bonbons depending on size of cheese balls.

Penn's Microwave Bonbon Fire Kindling

Penn told this editor that if our readership wants to taste the original bonbon fires, they'll have to buy them from her at the Chocolate Box. If you like spicy, it's well worth the trip to Camellia Beach to get one. While you're visiting the shop, you can also find out what fresh trouble Penn has found. Although I can't bring you the bonbon fire, Penn did agree after much cajoling to share this quick and easy recipe for spicy Bonbon Fire Kindling, which is like a fiery chocolate bark.

Ingredients

6 oz 70% or higher fair-trade dark chocolate, chopped (or use 6 oz semisweet chocolate chips)

1 tsp cinnamon

½–1 tsp (depending on the amount of heat you want) red pepper flakes

1 tsp paprika

½–1 tsp (depending on the amount of heat you want) ground cayenne pepper

1 tsp salt

In microwave-safe bowl, combine the chocolate with all other ingredients. Melt on 50% power for 2 minutes. Stir. If not melted, continue to heat for 30-second intervals. Stir vigorously until smooth. Spread on cookie sheet lined with parchment paper. Cool in refrigerator until set (about an hour). Cut into "kindling" strips. Store in refrigerator in airtight container.

Mabel's Chocolate-Covered Cherry Bonbons

This recipe is a must-have for anyone collecting chocolate recipes. Chocolate-covered cherry bonbons are what many people think of when someone mentions a bonbon. Mabel Maybank shared this recipe with me shortly before her passing. She taught me its steps so I could in turn teach them to Penn. Despite my patient nature, Penn still hasn't quite mastered the recipe. Working with her is driving me batty while also threatening my already not-so-trim waistline. It's not a hard recipe to learn. To prove it, I'm sharing this recipe with all of you, the readership of this paper. I know you'll make Mabel proud.

Ingredients

3 tbsp butter
3 tbsp light corn syrup
1 pinch salt
2 cups 10x powdered sugar
36 maraschino cherries
12 oz semisweet chocolate chips

Combine butter, corn syrup, and salt. Add sugar and mix until smooth. This makes a fondant. Chill in refrigerator for ½ hour. Drain cherries and let dry on paper towels. Flatten a small amount of fondant in your hand and wrap around a cherry (completely cover the cherry or juice will leak out and make dipping difficult). Repeat with remaining fondant and cherries. Refrigerate fondant-covered cherries and let harden. Melt chocolate in double boiler or microwave. (To melt in microwave: In microwave-safe bowl, heat chocolate in small batches on 50% power for 2 minutes. If not melted, continue to heat for 30-second intervals. It won't look completely melted. Stir until smooth.) Dip fondant-wrapped cherries into melted chocolate. Coat completely. Set on cookie sheet lined with parchment paper. Place in refrigerator for at least 1 hour to set. Store in refrigerator in airtight container. Makes about 36 bonbons.

Acknowledgments

W hom do I acknowledge first? That's easy. Bonbons. They're darn difficult to make. At least they are for me. Writing this book caused hours of frustration in the kitchen and way too many additional inches around my middle. Yeah, thanks for that, bonbons.

The next round of thanks goes out to the two women who rescued me from my bonbon disasters. Holly Herrick, author of the most delectable cookbooks, brainstormed with me and shared knowledge of how to craft a chocolate bonbon that even someone like me could handle. Fabulous mystery author Linda Lovely was kind enough to share with me some of her tried-and-true family bonbon recipes, especially a version of the cherry bonbon recipe that shows up at the end of this book. Thank you!

Also, since we're talking about talent in the kitchen, I need to thank Michael Hoffman, the bean-to-bar chocolate artisan behind Bitte Chocolate in Charleston, SC, for spending an afternoon teaching me all about the delicious chocolate-making process and patiently answering all of my silly questions. If you find yourself in Charleston, buy one of his chocolate bars.

Let me give an extra special shout out to musician Stan Yeager of Yeager Park for answering my questions about beach music, shagging, and band life. He's a great guy and nothing like the Stan in this book.

A big shout-out to my agent, Jill Marsal, for believing in my series, and to my talented editor, Anne Brewer (and to all the folks at Crooked Lane Books). I've said it before and I'll say it again: y'all make publishing a book fun.

I'd also like to thank the incredible authors in the Lowcountry Chapter of Romance Writers of America, Sisters in Crime, and Mystery Writers of America, especially Vicki Wilkerson Gibbins, Cynthia Cooke, Amanda Berry, Nina Bruhns, Dianne Miley, Nicole Seitz, and Judy Watts for patiently listening as I worked through the sometimes bumpy process of writing.

Finally, a million thanks to Jim and Avery. These books are for you and wouldn't happen without you. I love you.

Read an excerpt from

IN COLD CHOCOLATE

the next

SOUTHERN CHOCOLATE SHOP MYSTERY

by DOROTHY ST. JAMES

available September 11, 2018 in hardcover
from Crooked Lane Books

CROOKED
LANE

NEW YORK

Chapter One

I love the taste of the ocean. After an early morning swim, the salty flavor lingers on my lips for hours. And at night, especially after a steamy August day, that same salty flavor floats in the air on tiny droplets of water imprinting the memory of how the moon shined against the backdrop of a twinkling starry sky. Or how I'd ohhed and ahhed over the dinoflagellates, those single-celled, ocean-drifting plankton, caught up in the tide as they glowed fantastic colors with each crashing wave. Or the excitement of finding evidence that a sea turtle had laid her eggs on our humble coast.

Since moving to the small island town of Camellia Beach tucked away in the Lowcountry of South Carolina seven months ago, the taste of salt in my food (especially when paired with dark chocolate), has made me feel at one with the coast and all the teeming sea life that resides just beyond my adopted small town's shoreline.

On what seemed like an uneventful Tuesday night in the back kitchen of my boutique chocolate shop, the Chocolate Box, I set out to develop a sea salt chocolate turtle candy that captured the flavor and wonder of the ocean and its special creatures that live there.

Sometimes, though, *sometimes* that same flavor mimics the salt of tears, serving as a bitter memory of painful losses and heartfelt failures. And fear.

As midnight approached I hung my apron on its peg. The pecans had burned. My turtles oozed out of their molds. And they tasted nothing like the majestic ocean. Hopefully tomorrow I'd have better success.

I exited the shop through the back door, locking it behind me as I stepped onto the building's back patio. A few feet away the land faded into the grassy marsh. The summer wind playing in the tall cordgrass made soft swish-swish sounds. The night hung like a bar of unsweetened chocolate over the river. In a few hours the moon would rise. But, for now, the darkness made the world seem wider, emptier.

Despite the disappointing mess I'd made in the kitchen (I was used to those) and despite the gloom outside, I smiled as I breathed in the salty air that made the island smell almost sugary sweet. This tiny piece of paradise was my home. I still couldn't believe my good luck in finding it.

That silly smile was still plastered on my face as I moved toward the exterior back stairs that led up to the building's two second-story apartments. I didn't see the movement in the shadows until it was too late.

A dark figure jumped out in front of me.

Startled, I swung my fist. The person ducked. I swung again. The shadowy person, who must have been some kind of master ninja, ducked again. Suddenly, fear beat like a drum in my throat. I screamed and clutched my chest as if I'd suffered a fatal heart attack and screamed again. You'd better believe I screamed.

My assailant started laughing. It wasn't a happy sound. But then again her laughs never sounded happy.

"Jody Dalton, what are you doing? You scared me half to death," I managed to say even though my heart was beating faster than a marathon runner's at the end of a race. "If you're here to see Harley, he's not home. He's attending some kind of lawyers' conference in Columbia."

Harley Dalton lived in the apartment next to mine. He also had once served as my grandmother's lawyer and now looked after my legal interests. I considered him a friend and felt rather protective of him, especially when it came to Jody, his ex-wife. She'd come by from time to time to cause him grief.

I fisted my hands on my hips and stood my ground. Jody was a tall woman, taller than most men. I was as well, which meant we glared at each other on an equal plane. She wore her hair in a no-nonsense pixie cut. I did too. Her hair was silky black while mine was blonde and awfully frizzy in all of this humidity. She looked me up and down, lingering on my frizz, before she also put her hands on her hips.

"You were just bursting to tell me that Harley's away, weren't you?" she snapped. Her snippy tone reminded me of my little papillon dog who nipped and snapped at pretty much anything that moved. "Were you hoping I'd be crushed to learn you knew something about that no-good ex of mine that I didn't know? Don't be. I know where he is."

I opened and closed my mouth while I continued to worry about what was going on in my chest. My heart still didn't feel as if it was working quite right. Until tonight, I only knew of one person who could elude my carefully honed self-defense moves. And that was my halfsister Tina. It startled me to realize my skills weren't quite as invincible as I'd once thought.

"If you knew he was away, what are you doing here? And why

in the world are you jumping out at me in the middle of the night like some kind of madwoman?" I demanded.

"I didn't jump—" she started to say. But she abruptly stopped when my business partner and roommate, Bertie Bays, called down the stairs, "Are you okay down there, Penn? I heard screaming."

"Jody's here," I yelled back because I didn't know how else to answer the question. Was I okay?

"Tell her Harley's away at that conference," Bertie called down to me. She'd leaned so far over the porch's railing it looked as if the bright yellow scarf she'd used to tie back her hair might slip over her face.

"I know full well where he is!" Jody shouted. She then said to me, "I'm here because Gavin left his board shorts up there. He's got an early morning surf competition, and he thinks those pants of his lucky." Her voice suddenly sharpened as she bit out, "I don't need to explain myself to the likes of you. Get out of my way."

"Harley lets you go into his home when he's not there?" I moved to block the stairs. Just last month Jody had called the police simply because Harley had parked his car in front of her house while Gavin, their ten-year-old son, had run inside to pick up his laptop computer. She told the police that she'd felt her ex's presence outside her home had constituted a threat. She'd wanted them to arrest him. They didn't.

I knew this, not because Harley had told me. He hadn't told anybody about it. It was their son who'd come into the shop, tears flooding his eyes. Gavin had begged me to tell him why his mother hated his father so much. Unable to explain what even I didn't understand, I'd wound my arms around the skinny boy, hugged him, and told him that both his parents loved him and that was all that mattered.

"Harley has no say in this. My son's belongings are in his apartment. As Gavin's mother, I have every right to go in there and get them."

"That's not true," I said. "Where's Gavin?"

"He's spending the night with a friend. Get out of my way."

I stood my ground. "Call Harley. Get his permission. And then I'll move."

"Oh, I'll call him." She started to move away. But then she turned back to me and smiled viciously. "Be warned, Penn." She took a step toward me. "You think this town actually loves you? You think you can wave your chocolates around and charm Harley? You think you can take over as Gavin's mother?"

Did she really think I wanted to date Harley? He'd made it clear that he considered me his friend and only a friend. Did she think I wanted to take her place in Gavin's life? "I would never try to take your place."

"Watch yourself, Penn. I know you. I've also heard all about the lies you've been telling everyone."

"Lies?" I abhorred lies.

"Don't pretend to be innocent. Not to me. I know all about who you are . . . and more importantly who you *aren't*." With a look of triumph, she crowed loud enough for even Bertie (who was still standing at the top of the stairs in her quilted housecoat) to hear, "Mark my words. As soon as the truth comes out, *Charity* Penn, Sunset Development will own your chocolate shop. And you'll have nothing. You don't belong here. You've never belonged here."

"What are you talking about?" No one could take my shop away from me. My maternal grandmother had left it to me in her will.

Jody didn't answer. Instead, with a sharp laugh, she said as she walked back toward the road, "I'm going to enjoy seeing everything you don't deserve stripped away from you. It's time people around here start realizing the emperor has no clothes." She was halfway down the road. Her voice seemed to echo in the darkness as she called over her shoulder, "In case you're too dense to get it—you're the emperor and those clothes of yours are sorely lacking."

Chapter Two

"Would it kill you to move a little faster?" I asked the painter a little over a week later. He'd been repairing and repainting the Chocolate Box's stained and lumpy ceiling for the past eight days.

I stood next to his ladder, tilted my head back, and squinted as I looked up. His brush moved like a snail sliding across a leaf. However, the ceiling looked perfectly smooth.

"Can't rightly rush if you want me to do what needs to be done," he drawled. His Southern accent, unique to the natives of Camellia Beach, lacked the hard twang most people associated with the South. While the island accent was sometimes difficult to understand, the slow cadence of his words sounded melodious to my Midwestern ears. "The layers of paint up here tell the story of the hacks with a paintbrush who have done this ceiling wrong. Takes precious time to fix it."

I squinted up some more, admiring his work. The Chocolate Box had been selling the world's best chocolates for nearly a hundred years. When I'd inherited the building (which included this shop, the Drop In Surf Shop next door, and two upstairs apartments), the roof leaked, the stairs were rotting, and the water-stained ceiling looked as if it might fall. Johnny Pane's efforts with spackle and paint were impressive. But that didn't keep me from wishing he'd hurry up and finish already.

Since I couldn't afford to close the shop while we waited for him to finish, we had to block off half the shop with a curtain of plastic that surrounded his ladder. In doing so we had to remove the tables and chairs from the area where he was working, which meant we'd lost about a third of the seating area for our customers.

On this particularly sticky Thursday afternoon, the Chocolate Box was packed with residents and beachgoers in search of a cool break from the seemingly endless August heat. I needed that seating area.

Despite the ocean breezes, the beach in August felt like the inside of an oven. The unrelenting heat prickled the nerves of even the incurably happy. But inside the shop, which had survived hurricanes and murders, the newly renovated air conditioner provided a welcomed blast of cold air. Laughter filled the space as Bertie and I each carried trays of gourmet chocolate milkshakes to our eager customers.

I handed a tall, frosty glass to Bubba Crowley, the president of Camellia Beach's business association. I still couldn't believe my good fortune. And I don't mean the kind of fortune that could be spent in a store. That kind of fortune rarely made anyone smile. I meant the kind that came with finding a place where I was surrounded by friends, a place where I felt like I belonged. No matter what Jody had claimed, I wasn't going to let anyone take this place away from me.

"The shop looks fantastic," Bubba said in his jovial booming voice after he took a long sip of the wintry milkshake. Bubba was a big man around town, not just because of his positive influence on the business community. He resembled a small-sized giant. "Adding milkshakes to your menu was a stroke of genius." He took another sip. "Plus, like everything else in here, these are remarkably delicious."

"That's high praise indeed. Thank you." After I'd inherited the shop, Bubba was one of the first and most vocal supporters of my efforts to keep it open. "I'm always drinking chocolate milkshakes in the summer. I figured since I was making it for myself, I might as well start making extras to share with everyone else."

He nodded as he sipped some more. "Makes sense. Good business sense." His gaze traveled around the busy shop. "They certainly are a hit with . . ." His voice trailed off.

His roaming eyes had come to an abrupt halt. His mouth tightened as if suddenly pained. "What is it?" I started to ask with concern. But then I saw what he'd seen: Bertie Bays.

Bertie had been my grandmother's best friend. For decades she lived with Mabel Maybank in one of the upstairs apartments and worked with her in the shop. Despite her seventy-plus years, Bertie had more energy than I did when I was in my twenties. She loved Camellia Beach and this shop nearly as much as Mabel had. After Mabel's death, Bertie had agreed to stay on (temporarily) as my partner. She'd told me more than once that she planned to retire and move to a retirement resort community in Florida after I mastered the recipes.

I *never* wanted her to leave. I'd be lost without her. Luckily, it didn't look as if I'd ever learn Mabel's recipes. I was a disaster in the kitchen.

Dressed in mom jeans and a faded blue "Chocolate Box" T-shirt, Bertie served a trio of milkshakes to a table of giddy teenage girls. Her dark skin glowed with a youthful luster she claimed was from good genes and not an antiaging serum. It had to be true.

I'd searched our apartment more than once for her hidden stash of facial creams and found nothing.

Bubba lowered his voice and asked, "Has she said anything? I mean, about me?"

"Not a word," I whispered back. "Have you said anything to her?"

His head dropped to his chest. "Haven't had the nerve."

"She's not married anymore." Bertie had been a widow for nearly twenty years. A few months ago, Bubba had confessed that when he was young and foolish, he'd fallen for Bertie. She'd been older and married, and he'd been engaged to another woman, so he hadn't acted on his feelings. But now, forty years later, neither of them was married or dating. And he still cared for her.

I nudged his shoulder. "You should sit up. She's looking this way."

His head snapped to attention. His back straightened. An awkward, almost grotesque, grin took over his usually handsome features.

Bertie noticed and laughed before turning her attention back to serving the milkshakes on her tray.

I needed to do the same. "Call her. Ask her out for lunch. As friends, if it's too scary to call it a date," I suggested as I headed toward the next table.

"I'll do that," he said. "Next week. Or perhaps the week after that."

"My gracious, Penn, you've been busy," Ethel Crump, who was sitting with a couple of full-time residents from the Pink Pelican Inn, exclaimed when she looked up from her cross-stitch project and noticed me approaching their table. Her voice sounded hoarse, like the scraping of branches against a window. She cleared her throat. It didn't help. "I was a little girl the last time this place looked this good."

Her friends both agreed with great enthusiasm that the shop had never looked better.

"Thank you." I set down napkins and drinks for Ethel and her friends. I dearly wanted to ask Ethel how many years had passed since she'd been a little girl coming to this shop. In a town where nearly all of its residents qualified for senior discounts and the local hotel, the Pink Pelican Inn, doubled as an informal retirement home, Ethel Crump was considered as ancient as the island's weathered oaks with their twisted and gnarled branches. No one knew her age. And like a proper Southern lady, she wasn't telling.

Ethel set aside her needle and rubbed her knobby and stiff knuckles. The almost translucent skin on her face was loose and hung from her jowls like a pleated silk skirt. "Does the fact that you're fixing up the building mean your grandmother's children are no longer contesting her will?" she asked.

Her question shouldn't have surprised me. This was a small town. Of course everyone would know all about how Mabel's children wanted to get their hands on the building. They didn't want the shop, mind you. None of them seemed to care about keeping their family's legacy alive with the chocolates. They only wanted the land so they could sell it to Sunset Development, the local development company where Jody worked.

Why would Jody accuse me of lying? More than a week had passed since my late-night encounter with her, and I still had no idea why she'd said such a thing to me. Even if I had told a few lies (I hadn't), how could a lie or two make me lose what Mabel had given me? This was my shop.